T0274374

TEARS of
THE NAMELESS

GEORGE MANN

PRESS

LOS ANGELES·NEW YORK

STAR WARS TIMELINE

THE HIGH REPUBLIC

FALL OF THE JEDI

REIGN OF THE EMPIRE

YOUNG JEDI
ADVENTURES

THE ACOLYTE

THE
PHANTOM
MENACE

ATTACK OF
THE CLONES

THE
CLONE WARS

REVENGE OF
THE SITH

THE
BAD BATCH

SOLO:
A STAR
WARS STORY

OBI-WAN
KENOBI

STAR WARS
REBELS

ANDOR

ROGUE ONE:
A STAR
WARS STORY

AGE OF REBELLION

A NEW HOPE

THE EMPIRE
STRIKES BACK

RETURN OF
THE JEDI

THE NEW REPUBLIC

THE
MANDALORIAN

THE BOOK OF
BOBA FETT

AHSOKA

RISE OF THE FIRST ORDER

STAR WARS
RESISTANCE

THE FORCE
AWAKENS

THE LAST JEDI

THE RISE OF
SKYWALKER

For Elliot. Brave and bright.

Printed in the United States of America

First Edition, September 2024

10 9 8 7 6 5 4 3 2 1

FAC-004510-24193

ISBN 978-1-368-09517-4

Library of Congress Control Number on file

Design by Kurt Hartman, Soyoung Kim, Scott Piehl, and Leigh Zieske

Visit the official *Star Wars* website at: www.starwars.com.

SUSTAINABLE FORESTRY INITIATIVE

Certified Sourcing

www.forests.org
SFI-01681

Logo Applies to Text Stock Only

STAR WARS
THE HIGH REPUBLIC
TRIALS OF THE JEDI

Worlds suffer inside the formidable
OCCLUSION ZONE, where Marchion Ro
and his band of Nihil marauders,
untouchable by the Republic, rule with
an iron fist.

Jedi Master Avar Kriss has escaped
from this occupied space and, along
with fellow Jedi Elzar Mann, leads the
Jedi and Republic in a desperate fight
against the Nihil and their Nameless
creatures.

But a new danger now threatens the
galaxy. A mysterious BLIGHT has begun
to spread randomly across worlds,
slowly infecting areas and turning all life
in its path to dust....

PROLOGUE

Vernestra Rwoh gunned the engines of her stolen Nihil ship and willed it to gain altitude.

Instead, the entire fabric of the shoddy, thrown-together vessel groaned and rattled under the stress of her hurried climb, and she feared it might shake itself apart around her at any moment.

Why had she chosen *this* ship, and not one of the two clearly more robust fighters that were currently pursuing her? They were sleek-looking things of a design she'd never seen before, with two extended wings and central torpedo-shaped bodies. Not like Nihil ships at all, in fact. Which led her to conclude they must have been stolen.

She shook her head, cursing under her breath.

She lamented the loss of her Jedi Vector, the wreck of which was currently lying somewhere far below, on the surface of Vixoseph I. It would never fly again. And besides, there was every chance the creep of the blight that had infected the planet would eventually consume it, just as it was slowly consuming the organic matter in its path.

Vernestra twisted the ship, corkscrewing up in a straight line as one of the fighters let loose a burst of cannon fire that raked the flank of the stolen ship, causing one of the ill-fitted ablation plates to ping free. It tumbled away beneath her as she fought to maintain control, arcing to the left and slowly bringing the nose of the ship back down to level off. The gravitational forces involved in pulling off such a maneuver at high speed pushed her back into her seat and set the entire cockpit rattling again.

Her injuries—the bruised ribs and head gash she'd sustained in her fight with Marchion Ro on Vixoseph I—flared in pain.

She eyed the readouts on the decrepit control panel. Both fighters were gaining on her.

There was no way she was going to make it.

Unless . . .

"Are you up to this?" she said, asking the ship as if it were able to respond.

Of course, no response was forthcoming. There weren't even any droids aboard to hear her.

"I'll take your silence as complicity?"

As if in reply, the substructure of the freighter gave another long rending moan.

Too late to complain now.

Vernestra steadied her breathing. She closed her eyes and reached for the Force, then felt it respond, guiding her hand as she yanked back fully on the control lever, causing the nose of the ship to pull up sharply. Around her, everything shook, from the bolts in the walls to the seat she was in. She gunned the engines again, keeping the lever pulled back so the ship was propelled into a tight loop, coming up and around and, as she released the controls, screaming straight into a dive toward the pursuing fighters, who were still locked in their earlier climb.

Vernestra winced as her chest was compressed by the sudden pressure. She felt as if she were being stabbed in her left side. She fought to catch her breath.

Ahead, the pilots of the two Nihil fighters were obviously panicking, trying desperately to drag their vessels out of the way to avoid the impending collision.

Vernestra held her course.

Time seemed to slow.

One of the fighters peeled away. The other spun on its central axis as it climbed, aiming to give her room to pass so the flank of her ship would slide past its underbelly. The pilot was no doubt thinking they could then pull off a similar maneuver—probably with much greater finesse—and come down hot on her tail again.

That wasn't going to happen.

Vernestra yanked the control lever and sent the ship into another tight corkscrew. It caught the fighter as it passed, clipping the other ship's protruding wing and sending it spiraling off into what she hoped was an uncontrollable dive.

She fought the controls, leveling out with a screech of

protesting metal just as the spiraling fighter impacted with the trees below, detonating in a bloom of yellow-and-orange light.

One down.

Better than nothing.

Vernestra checked the readouts. The other Nihil fighter was already circling back around on her tail. She stabbed at the buttons on the console. The ship kicked as the thrusters burned.

And then she was climbing again, riding a spike of super-heated fuel toward the pale sky.

She'd told Bell and Burryaga she'd be right behind them as they'd fled the planet in pursuit of Marchion Ro, but it had taken her longer than she'd hoped to get her hands on a ship. She was anxious to get to Coruscant as quickly as possible to make sure everyone understood the implications of what she'd seen Marchion Ro do on Vixoseph I.

She'd watched him walk through the blight unaffected. Not only that, she'd seen him grab a fistful of infected matter and hurl it at a Drengir, infecting the plantlike creature while simply dusting it off of himself, before setting off for Coruscant to speak to Chancellor Soh.

Vernestra didn't know if any of this was evidence that Ro really could control the blight as he claimed, but it was certainly proof that he wasn't entirely lying.

That said, if he did have the power to control it, he hadn't exercised it to save all his own people. In the camp from which she'd stolen the ship, Vernestra had glimpsed evidence of several Nihil who were in the midst of succumbing to the infection.

So either Marchion Ro wasn't quite as all-powerful as he

claimed, or he didn't give a damn about the fate of his Nihil followers.

Vernestra suspected the truth was somewhere in the middle.

Alarms blared as the remaining fighter closed the gap between them. Cannon fire flickered by as Vernestra swung the ship first left, then right, narrowly avoiding the spray of laser shots.

She was well aware the same looping maneuver wouldn't catch her attacker off guard twice, and regardless, she didn't think the stolen ship could take the strain. But she was alone, and there was no one to operate the twin-mounted blaster cannons in the other chair, or to handle the flight controls if she tried to do it herself.

So—it was down to hope, luck, and faith in the Force.

Great.

Vernestra corkscrewed again, narrowly avoiding another spray of burning shots.

And then she was pushing through the planet's upper atmosphere, the dark crescent of space appearing on the horizon like a reverse dawn.

"Nearly there!" she bellowed, encouraging the machine. "Come on!"

She just had to get beyond the planet's gravity field, and then she could make the jump to hyperspace.

She felt a jolt as one of the fighter's shots glanced off the ship's hull. Her shields were basically gone. She silenced the shrill alarms, gritting her teeth as she rose through the last of the wispy atmosphere and slid out into the void, continuing her dizzying, spiraling climb.

The fighter was still gaining.

She heard the flight computer warn her that the other ship had a full lock on her engines.

She braced herself, holding firm. Any deviation now would be certain death.

Just a moment longer . . .

The console chimed.

Vernestra punched the hyperdrive, watching as the starscape around her shifted and stretched into a tunnel of mesmerizing blue light.

With a satisfied sigh, Vernestra settled back in her seat, clutching her aching ribs.

She wondered what awaited her on Coruscant.

At the very least, she hoped they'd saved her a bed in the medical bay.

PART
ONE

ONE

Jedi Padawan Amadeo Azzazzo had never seen anything quite so desolate as the sea of blight-infected gray ruin that spread out below the rocky promontory on which he stood.

It stretched in every direction, all the way to the horizon, where it met the still vermillion sky of Cethis—kilometers of what had once been lush forest reduced to washed-out ashen husks.

An obliterated landscape doused in gray.

Amadeo scanned the billowing wastes. No movement except the slow stirring of the breeze. No life, not even the twittering of carrion birds or rats. Neither could he catch the cloying scent of vegetation or taste the morning dew that should have hung fresh in the air.

Nothing.

Here and there, peppered erratically, a clump of trees remained, a defiant last stand against the spreading plague, but even these had been leached of all color, all semblance of life.

It was heartbreaking—a forest dying before Amadeo's very eyes. And it wasn't the first. It was just like Vixoseph. In fact, this was the third mission he'd undertaken with his master, Mirro Lox, to evacuate civilians from the sudden appearance of patches of . . . well, he wasn't sure exactly how to describe it. Nor had he any real sense of what had caused it, whether it was a natural phenomenon or something more malign. He knew some Jedi believed there to be a link between the blight and the mysterious creatures known as the Nameless, although so far as Amadeo knew, no clear evidence connected them as yet.

All the Jedi and the Republic knew was that the blight was spreading, although in what pattern, for what rhyme or reason, none of them could be sure. The blight seemed to strike without logic. A patch would appear on one world, slowly growing and consuming the organic matter, but neighboring worlds would be spared. It didn't seem to follow any obvious trajectory and was not spread by travelers passing through hyperspace.

And yet, where it did strike, the results were devastating, leaving nothing but a decaying echo of what had once been.

No matter what stood in its way, the blight consumed it. He only hoped that those working on the problem could figure out how to stop it, and soon.

The breeze ruffled Amadeo's curly brown hair. Chilled, he pulled his robes closer around him.

"Are you all right, Padawan?"

He turned to see his master, Mirro Lox, approaching. Lox's dark eyes were fixed on Amadeo, and he was rubbing a hand over his shorn stubbly hair. The red light of Cethis's sun made his brown skin gleam.

"Do you think we'll find a way to stop it?" asked Amadeo, returning his view to the blight-infested forest below.

Lox nodded. "I do, Amadeo. I believe the Force will guide our hand, and all will be well." He clapped Amadeo on the shoulder. "And in the meantime, we're doing good work out here. The problem *will* be solved. And while we're waiting for that solution, it's just another opportunity to do what we always do."

"Help people who can't help themselves," said Amadeo, repeating his master's often-used phrase, in his best approximation of Lox's voice and accent.

Master Lox erupted in booming laughter. "See! You're learning." He knew that Amadeo didn't mean it disrespectfully. This was a routine they'd been through a hundred times before. "Seriously, though, Padawan—you should take solace in it," continued Master Lox. "Helping people is no small thing. It's a tonic for gloomy thoughts, and it's what we do best."

Amadeo nodded. "Yes, Master."

Master Lox was right. They *were* good at protecting people. And being maudlin didn't suit him. It was just, sometimes, witnessing the blight, seeing what it was doing . . . it could weigh a little heavy.

Amadeo shook it off. There was work to be done, and he was ready to do it. He needed to be more like Master Lox, always searching for the positive angle. He looked up at his master and smiled. "What next?"

Lox beamed, but his next words were lost amid the ear-splitting thunder of transport ships coming in to land nearby. Amadeo turned to see three of the enormous vessels, with Republic Defense Coalition insignia hastily emblazoned on their pristine flanks, descending, landing gear unfurling. High above, their security escorts circled like predatory eagles, watchful over their descent.

Master Lox gestured with his thumb, and Amadeo fell into step as the other man set out toward the landing zone to greet the new arrivals.

Across the top of the plateau, evacuees huddled in a mass of tents, hastily constructed shacks, and the shells of ground vehicles. It was a sorry sight—dispossessed families forced to leave their homes, their belongings, their lives behind, fleeing the spread of the destructive wave. As they walked down the central aisle of the makeshift camp, Amadeo glanced from side to side, his heart going out to the dozens of small children crying in their parents' arms, the wandering adults with lost expressions, the teens, like him, whose lives had just come crashing down around their ears.

As a Jedi, he was used to living a nomadic life, shifting from place to place between missions, but these people had set down roots and were now being uprooted to prevent their settlement being overrun by the blight.

The settlement had, until recently, been a large urban sprawl shaped like a circle, with spurs that radiated from a central hub known as Haven, surrounded by kilometers of vast lush forest. According to their preliminary surveys, most of the forest to the east of the settlement had already succumbed to the blight before they'd arrived. Soon, if left unchecked, the blight would reach the edge of Haven itself. The decision had come to evacuate the population before that happened—and before any of the people became infected.

Amadeo, Lox, and the small contingent of RDC volunteers who'd joined them on their mission had helped guide these evacuees to this central gathering point, high enough above the main sprawl of the settlement that the blight hadn't quite reached it.

Yet.

The RDC team had already established a more permanent settlement on an island to the south, where they'd hastily erected a small town's worth of prefabricated homesteads, a water-filtering plant, and a handful of municipal buildings. This wasn't the first time they'd done such a thing, and their processes were becoming better honed with every new settlement.

The evacuees would be moved there, along with whatever belongings they could carry and most of their vehicles and droids. Amadeo could see them now as the RDC volunteers began to organize people into lines while droids saw to the loading of equipment and belongings onto the three carriers, which had settled in a neat row, rear bays sighing open to reveal their cavernous interiors. Soon each of them would be crammed full. It would take several trips to ferry everyone over, and even longer to get them settled.

Despite the sullen faces he saw around him, Amadeo felt a burst of hope. These people had been saved. They would go on to start new lives. It would be hard, but these were first-generation settlers on Cethis, so they'd known hardship for much of their lives. They could do it again. And maybe one day, when the blight was gone, they could return. That was something worth clinging to. That was what made it all worthwhile.

Every life counts.

"I'll go with the carriers," he said. It was the last thing he wanted to do, which was exactly why he knew he must do it—and with enthusiasm, too. It would mean settling disputes among the locals as they fought over their new homes, or helping families unload their possessions, or showing them how the water pumps worked.

A Jedi does not turn away from their duty. He'd been reminded of that not so long ago, the last time they were on Coruscant. He'd been offered a taste of another life, one beyond duty and meditation and the tenets of the Order, and it had worked to reaffirm his commitment to who he was and who he thought he always would be: a Jedi. As a youngling, he'd dreamed of exploration on the frontier, of exciting adventures deep in Wild Space or on the verges of the Outer Rim, like the Pathfinders of old, making contact with exciting new people and visiting unknown worlds.

When Master Lox had taken him as a Padawan, Amadeo had quickly learned that the life of a Jedi was not always like the stories he craved, full of wild adventure and limitless danger. But what Master Lox had shown him was how to have *fun*, how to find joy in even the mundane chores of a Jedi's life, how to turn every day into an adventure so that even on days like this, facing hardship and dismay, together they could always find a way to laugh and remember how lucky they were.

Amadeo started toward the waiting transports, but Master Lox caught his arm.

"No, Amadeo," he said. "The RDC can take it from here. We should report back to Coruscant. We may be needed elsewhere."

Close by, a young human girl of around twelve was arguing vehemently with a man Amadeo took to be her guardian.

"No, Aaila! It's too late. I'm sorry. We can't go back. I know it's hard but—"

"We left them behind!"

"Aaila . . ." The man sounded exasperated.

"But what about Papa Jo, Elias, Miramo, Iriana . . ." The girl gave a heaving sob.

"We had no choice."

Master Lox had stopped for a moment, listening. He glanced at Amadeo, one eyebrow cocked in a sort of half frown that Amadeo knew only too well.

Amadeo followed him over to where the two arguing refugees were standing on a small reed mat. Their only belongings appeared to be crammed into a small backpack, which was propped against a nearby rock.

"Hello," said Lox. His voice was calm, level—nonconfrontational. "I know you must be scared and confused, but everything is going to be all right."

"I'm sorry," said the man. He ran a hand through his wavy dark hair. He looked tired and was covered in grime.

"No need," said Lox. "Is there anything we can do to help?"

The man shook his head. But the young girl shot him a dark look. "Yes," she said. "Maybe."

Lox dropped to a crouch, bringing himself down to the girl's eye level. "Go on."

"We left them."

"Who?" asked Lox. "Who did you leave?"

"Our friends and neighbors," said Aaila.

Lox lifted his eyes to look at the man.

"We didn't have any choice," he said, a hint of pleading in his voice. "They were too slow, and I had to get Aaila to safety."

Lox inclined his head in understanding. This man had only done what so many others would have done in his position: he'd opted to save his family. Amadeo could hardly blame him for that.

"I don't want to go without them," said Aaila.

"How many?" asked Lox.

"About twenty," said the man.

"Were they infected?"

"Not when we left them."

Lox glanced at Amadeo. "Padawan?"

Amadeo studied Aaila's expression. This wasn't the petulant outburst of a child failing to understand what was going on around her. She knew what the blight would do to her friends if they were left behind in the infected forest. Amadeo's heart went out to her. No one should have to live with something like that—especially a child. "Do we have time to take a look?" he asked.

Aaila looked up at him optimistically.

Lox nodded approvingly. "It'll take several hours to get every-one on the transport ships. If we've missed people, we need to go back." He stood, flexing his broad shoulders and beaming. "Now," he said to the man, "you'd better tell us where to start."

TWO

Close to the base of the rocky plateau, around the westerly side, a surprisingly large pocket of forest remained unblemished by the blight, allowing Amadeo to glean a sense of how beautiful the environment here had once been.

All of this, lost.

He could hardly bear the thought.

The undergrowth was thick and damp, clinging to his boots as he cut his way through large fernlike fronds in pursuit of Master Lox, who'd charged ahead, his blue lightsaber humming as he slashed his way through the dense vegetation.

At first Amadeo had balked at the notion of cutting down living trees and plant life for their own convenience, but then it struck him—the trees would be dead soon anyway. The blight was closing in from all directions and there was nothing to be done. Better that they focus on getting to the stranded people in the hope they still lived. So his own, green-bladed lightsaber sang in his fist as he swept it back and forth, clearing a makeshift passage through the sinewy stalks and branches.

Aaila's father had explained that they'd fled from the farthest extremities of one of Haven's radiating habitation spurs on the outer edges of the settlement.

The main road through the forest—the most direct passage to the spur in question—had been cut off by the encroaching infection, but there was still a chance that some of the remaining inhabitants were trying to make their way to safety through the trees.

Only, the ground cover was so thick and overgrown that it was near impenetrable—at least, without a lightsaber. If they were out there, it was likely they'd miss the transports and be stranded if Amadeo and Lox couldn't find them.

"You okay back there?" called Lox over his shoulder.

Amadeo grinned. Master Lox tended to check in on him—a lot. For the longest time Amadeo had railed against it, found it stifling and constrictive, as if it were somehow indicative of his master's lack of trust in him. Amadeo had proved himself time and again, on dangerous missions or during delicate diplomatic situations, or simply through his adherence and central belief in the Jedi Code. And yet still his master continued to check up on him, often.

Lately, though, Amadeo had come to realize that it wasn't

that his master was showing a lack of faith in him. It was simply that Mirro Lox *cared*. He genuinely wanted to know that Amadeo was okay, and he was seeking reassurance for his own sake, not his Padawan's. It was a measure of the man that he was always thinking of others before himself.

"I'm right behind you, Master," he said, severing another low-hanging branch with a sweep of his lightsaber.

Amadeo sensed movement and glanced sharply to the left, just in time to see a colorful bird burst out of the foliage nearby, taking wing and spiraling up toward the canopy above. Red light fell in thin shafts through the bushy leaves, dappling the forest floor. The whole place was vibrantly alive. Amadeo could sense it through the Force—the scurrying, burrowing creatures; the pulsating rhythms of the trees; the deep fungal network that connected them all beneath the soil. So much life. He could sense, too, the inherent fear, the bubbling undercurrent of urgency, the desire to flee. There was no calm acceptance of coming death among the flora and fauna of Cethis—only the animal instinct to *run*.

"We're lucky to see this," said Lox, once again finding the tiniest sliver of positivity amid the gloom. "All this may be gone soon. We're privileged to witness the forest's last moments."

Amadeo cocked his head, listening—not to the sounds of the forest but to the deep thrumming of the Force, the vibrations of the world around him.

The presence in the trees.

It wasn't just the animals that were scared.

"That way," he said, pointing off to their right. Lox turned, a single eyebrow raised in question. "That's where they are. The beings we're looking for. I can sense their fear."

Lox gave a single nod and then set out in the direction Amadeo had indicated. No hesitation, no doubt.

Amadeo hurried after.

It wasn't long before his instincts were proved correct. Less than a kilometer deeper into the forest, the trees opened into a large natural glade, their gnarled boughs forming an irregular ring around a clearing carpeted in thick moss and fallen branches.

Amadeo heard them before he saw them—a group of about twenty beings crashing through the undergrowth at a pace that seemed inadvisable, given the tangled branches and uneven footing.

"Hey! Over here!" called Lox.

Both of the Jedi powered down their lightsabers.

Lox waved his arms.

Amadeo saw flashes of color amid the dense foliage. Tunics, robes, jackets. A glimpse of a Rodian. A Pau'an. A Quarren.

Their fear rolled over Amadeo like a crashing wave.

"It's not just the blight," he said hurriedly. "They're running from something else."

Lox planted his feet, scanning the tree line.

The villagers burst from the trees, scattering into the clearing.

The Quarren—an elderly male in a tattered blue flight suit—stared at the two Jedi, wild-eyed. "It's coming! It's in the trees! It's coming!"

The other villagers had caught sight of the Jedi, too, and were converging on Amadeo and Lox.

A thunderous rumble sounded deep within the trees where they'd emerged. And then another. And another. Amadeo's mouth was suddenly dry. He saw the uppermost branches of the trees swaying with the movement of whatever gargantuan horror was pursuing them.

"Get behind us!" bellowed Lox. His lightsaber flared back to life in his fist.

Amadeo followed suit, rolling his shoulders and adopting a defensive stance.

A moment's silence.

And then the creature burst from the trees in an eruption of shattered branches, bright plumage, and deadly talons.

It was huge—the size of a small shuttle—an immense feathered lizard with a tall slender body and enormous fleshy wings that it was presently walking on like powerful front legs. Its head was domed, tapering to a long pointed beak filled with an array of jagged teeth. It had a row of three beady black eyes on each side of its head.

And it wasn't happy.

It opened its beak and screeched, so loud that Amadeo felt his entire body vibrate with the shrill sound and cowered at the wash of its fetid hot breath.

The creature twisted its head, swinging its beak back and forth, taking them in with its six glassy eyes. And then it lurched forward, moving at near impossible speed, its beak yawning wide as it came for him.

Amadeo's instincts took over. He threw himself to the right, leaping into the air and tucking his knees close to his chest as he somersaulted out of the creature's way, passing between the two halves of its open beak in the few seconds before it snapped shut.

He landed, twisting and bringing his lightsaber up and around before him. Lox was already there, throwing himself in, using the weight of his body as he slammed the hilt of his lightsaber against the side of the creature's head.

It screeched again, staggering back, and then threw open its massive wings, propelling itself into the air with a series of brisk downward strokes. The backdraft caused Amadeo to stumble, and a quick glance told him most of the civilians had been thrown off their feet.

He craned his neck, watching the creature fly in tight circles above the clearing. Stretched taut, its wings had become almost translucent, revealing a skein of blue veins against the pale red light of Cethis's sun. Its enormity cast the whole grove in deep shadow.

Close by, Lox was telling the villagers to stay down. It wasn't over. Amadeo could sense it, too. The creature was in desperate pain, its thoughts clouded. He tried to reach out to it through the Force, to soothe its agony, but found himself repelled by the sheer ferocity of its pain, its despair. As it described concentric rings through the air above them, Amadeo thought he could see why.

The creature had been infected by the blight.

One of its legs was hanging limp, trailing behind it as it flew, the flesh pale and gray. Fingers of infection had crawled up its lower back, too, spreading across its scaly hide, causing the once-vibrant feathers to fade and crumble.

Amadeo felt a pang of sorrow for the creature. With the

forest nearly entirely depleted, its hunting grounds and all the prey within them had gone. It must have been close to starvation. And now the blight was slowly consuming it, too.

It screeched angrily, circling as it eyed each of them as potential prey.

"Ready, Padawan . . ." said Lox, his voice low.

The creature was coming about for another dive. Amadeo tracked it, brandishing his lightsaber.

"Don't let it touch you," said Lox.

"I wasn't planning to," quipped Amadeo.

"It's infected. One scratch from that hind leg . . ." His voice trailed off, allowing the implication to speak for itself.

You'll be infected, too.

"I know."

The creature shrieked and dived.

Amadeo circled, giving himself space, watching as the giant lizard plummeted like a depth charge, its wings tucked close to its sleek body, its bright feathers rippling with the force of its descent. It was utterly beautiful—and deadly.

And yet . . . something was wrong.

As Amadeo watched, the creature twisted in the air, altering the angle of its dive. It wasn't coming for him, or Lox, despite the fact they'd made themselves clear targets.

It was heading straight for the huddled group of civilians.

Amadeo locked eyes with Lox. And then he ran.

Lox understood immediately, intuitively. He pivoted, dropping to one knee and lowering his left shoulder, the tip of his lightsaber scouring the damp ground.

Amadeo leapt, propelling himself with the Force, one foot briefly landing on his master's lowered shoulder, using it as a stepping stone to throw himself even higher, even farther.

He sailed through the air, his lightsaber reversed in his right hand so the humming blade traced the length of his forearm, extending past his elbow.

Below, the civilians cringed, terror flowing off them in waves.

Amadeo spun, bringing his right arm around in a wide, smooth arc as his trajectory intersected that of the diving lizard.

He felt the blade bite, felt the creature's mind flare momentarily in panic before its anguish and its hunger and its pain all bled away.

Amadeo sailed past, his lightsaber flickering out as he tucked himself into a ball.

The creature's wings, no longer folded tightly against its falling body, flowered open, buffeted and whipped in a bizarre dance, sending the lifeless corpse careening chaotically into the nearby trees. It hammered into a massive trunk, rebounded, and then crashed noisily to the ground, just behind where the villagers lay cowering.

Amadeo landed gently, rolled twice, and then sprang to his feet.

He glanced around, hurriedly checking that everyone was okay. The civilians, unharmed, were staring at him in slack-mouthed awe. Amadeo nodded briefly in acknowledgment, but he wasn't feeling good about what he'd been forced to do. He'd taken a life.

Lox jogged over. "You made the right choice, Amadeo," he

said, instinctively answering a question that Amadeo hadn't even had a chance to vocalize. "And you relieved its suffering. I'm proud of you."

Amadeo looked over to the creature's crumpled, broken body. Closer now, he could see the blight had taken more of a hold than he'd first thought. There were mottled traces of its strange pale touch around the lizard's throat and across the top of one wing. It couldn't have had long left.

The villagers were slowly helping each other to their feet.

"Wait," said Lox, waving his hand to urge them to stay low.

"What is it?" said Amadeo.

Lox was studying the trees again. "There's another one. Watching us. Waiting for the opportunity to strike."

Amadeo reached for his lightsaber.

"Not yet," said Lox.

Amadeo's hand fell from his holster.

Lox shot him a glance. "You ready to try that move we've been practicing?"

Amadeo stared back at him, wide-eyed. He knew exactly what Master Lox was referring to: a flip-and-push maneuver that they'd attempted several times in training, and that usually ended with Master Lox in a bundle of tangled limbs on the floor. "But we've never managed to pull it off!"

Lox winked. "That's because it's never really *mattered* before. We'll get it right this time."

"Why?" said Amadeo, smiling at his master's enthusiasm despite himself.

"Because we have to," said Lox. He reignited his lightsaber. "Get ready. It's coming. . . ."

Amadeo sensed movement among the trees, heard the heavy crash of the creature's footfalls.

Lox flung out his left arm. Amadeo stared at it for a split second before clasping it firmly with his right hand. He felt Lox's fingers tighten around his wrist.

They locked eyes.

Someone close by screamed.

The lizard creature thudded into the clearing.

"You've got this," said Lox as he started to run.

Amadeo clung tight, running, too, so the two Jedi began spinning in fast circles, arms locked together as they wheeled, gathering momentum. . . .

"Now!" bellowed Lox.

Amadeo released his grip, shoving forward with the Force, throwing everything he had into propelling his master high into the air, using the momentum of their spin to aid his launch.

Amadeo tumbled to the ground, head spinning, as he watched Lox soar, his lightsaber extended like the tip of a spear.

The lizard creature—which Amadeo could now see was crusted in pale blight down its left flank—launched itself into the air as it burst through the trees. Unable to alter its trajectory, it tried to twist its head away from the oncoming Jedi, rearing back. But it was too late, and Lox's lightsaber pierced its lower jaw just above the throat, thrusting upward into its skull and killing it instantly.

Lox landed first, heavily, before rolling to a stop on the far side of the clearing.

The dead lizard crashed to the ground with a thud beside him.

A cheer erupted from the villagers, most of whom were still on the ground, staring up at Lox in awe as he got to his feet, dusting himself down. He waved them quiet, wishing to discourage their praise. But when he walked back over to join Amadeo, he couldn't hide his grin.

"Told you we could do it," he said, his voice low.

Amadeo stifled a laugh. "Yeah," he said, glowing with pride. "You were right, Master."

Lox clapped him on the shoulder. "Now, let's see about getting these people back to their friends."

The villagers were watching them nervously.

"Jedi . . ." said the Pau'an. "Why . . . ?"

"Your friend Aaila sent us," said Amadeo, finally catching his breath. "We're going to help you get to safety."

"Aaila! Then she and Mikal made it?"

"They did," said Lox with a broad grin. "They're okay, and they're waiting for you."

"We saw the transport ships," said a human woman in a dirt-smeared brown tunic and pants. She was leaning heavily on the Quarren, evidently unable to put any weight on her left leg. "We thought we were too late."

Amadeo smiled. "Don't worry. We have time. You're safe now."

The Quarren glanced behind them, off into the trees. But Amadeo could tell that he was seeing something far beyond the tangle of moss-covered branches and leaves—all the way to his devastated blight-ridden home. "Safe?" He sounded unconvinced. "There's a part of me wondering if we'll ever be truly safe again."

"I understand," said Amadeo, adopting his best reassuring tone, just like he'd seen Master Lox do a hundred times before. "You've all lost so much. But we can offer food and shelter, away from all of this. At least until we can figure out how to stop it."

The Quarren nodded, still seeming unsure, despite Amadeo's well-meant words. And if Amadeo was truly honest with himself, a part of him felt exactly the same.

The blight is coming, and there's nothing we can do to stop it.

THREE

Affie Hollow was feeling good.

In fact, she was feeling better than good. She was feeling *great*.

Things were going well. The Byne Guild was growing in both size and influence, and although the credits weren't flowing as freely as perhaps they once had, the missions they were undertaking were actually making a difference.

Yes, the galaxy was a mess. Yes, it was still split by the Nihil's appalling Stormwall. Yes, people were suffering everywhere she looked. She didn't believe for one moment that Marchion Ro's grandiose offer to save the galaxy from the blight was genuine. How could it be, after everything he had done? It had to be some sort of trap, or some gesture designed to disarm and confuse the

Republic. And meanwhile, the Nihil continued their raids and their murderous sprees and their persecution of anyone they set their sights on.

The Stormwall disaster had given Affie purpose. It had shown her how she could help. She, Leox, and Geode—they weren't fighters. They couldn't keep up with the Jedi. But they *could* help in the fight against the Nihil. Because there was one thing they *were* experts at—piloting the *Vessel.*

Take now, for instance: they were doing something tangible, something that would help make people's lives better, even if just for a while.

They were transporting two Jedi—along with a cargo hold brimming with fresh supplies—to the planet Oisin on the border of Nihil space.

The Oisinians, like those on many of the other worlds close to the Stormwall, were struggling with dwindling supplies. Their trading partnership with the planet Malorin had been abruptly cut off when the Stormwall expanded, with Malorin trapped on the wrong side—or at least, what Affie and the rest of the Republic would consider the wrong side. The Nihil side—the Occlusion Zone.

The two worlds, Jedi Master Eve Byre had explained, had held a reciprocal trading agreement for centuries, and it was likely that the populations of both worlds were suffering as a result of the Nihil's unilateral actions. They couldn't do much for the Malorins behind the Stormwall, but they *could* do something for the Oisinians.

"How far out are we?" asked Affie, stretching her weary limbs and yawning. She was sitting in the copilot's chair on the flight deck of the *Vessel*, beside Leox Gyasi, who was leaning back in his own seat, both legs up on the edge of the console as the nav computer handled their flight path. His grizzled face was cast in the shimmering blue glow of the hyperspace transit. His hair was tied back in an unkempt ponytail, and his stubble-encrusted chin looked closer to a beard than clean-shaven.

Slowly, he lowered his boots and sat up, casting his eyes over the readouts. "Couple hours yet, Little Bit," he said.

He returned to his previous position, hefting his booted feet back onto the console.

"Okay," said Affie. She pushed herself up out of her chair. "I'll go check on our passengers."

Leox gave an absent nod. "Make sure Geode hasn't fleeced them of all their credits. You know what he's like when he has fresh victims for his games."

Affie laughed. She *did* know. She'd fallen victim to Geode's masterful bluffing too many times herself.

She ducked out of the flight deck and strolled back to the common area, where the two Jedi were both sitting in meditative postures on the deck, their legs folded beneath them, hands resting on their laps, eyes closed.

Affie couldn't suppress a brief laugh. It was perhaps the most Jedi thing she had ever seen. There was no sign of Geode, who was presumably somewhere in the rear of the ship, probably running diagnostic checks. He was a stickler for perfection when it came to the ship's engines.

For a moment, Affie stood there awkwardly watching the two

Jedi, unsure what to do. They both had such serene expressions on their faces.

She was about to turn back to the flight deck when one of them—a tall muscular Zeltron with burnished red skin—opened one of his amber eyes to regard her.

"Greetings," he said.

Affie turned her amusement into a bright smile. "Hi, Zaph."

Affie guessed Jedi Padawan Zaph Mora was around sixteen years old, but it was hard to tell, given his towering physique. He was tall, even sitting down, with broad shoulders and thick muscular limbs. Even his robes seemed a little too small, as if he'd recently grown and hadn't had time to pick out new ones at the Temple. Which wouldn't have surprised Affie, the way all the Jedi seemed to be running from one thing to the next at the moment.

Nevertheless, he seemed to be quiet and considerate, and very respectful of both his master and his duties as a Padawan.

He opened his other eye and stretched. "You good?"

"I'm good," she replied, crossing to the refreshment station and pouring herself a drink. "You want something? I bet you're thirsty after all that . . . meditation."

If Zaph knew she was teasing, he didn't let on. He glanced over at his master, who was stoically maintaining her meditative vigil. Then he looked back at Affie. "Thank you. I'd like a cup of water, please."

Affie poured him one and took it over to him. He was getting to his feet as she approached and received it gratefully. He sipped it gently, nodding in appreciation.

Affie smiled. She'd never seen anyone appreciate a cup of water quite so much as Zaph. Come to think of it, she'd known few people who appreciated *anything* as much as Zaph. Every new environment, every new person, every taste and smell—he seemed to relish it.

"Why do you do that?" she asked, dropping onto a bench that was recessed against the wall.

He came over to join her, still stretching and testing his muscles. "Do what?" He watched her, seeming amused.

"Savor it like that. The water, I mean. Most people would just gulp it down and be done with it."

Not Zaph, though. Not even after a brutal training session. She'd observed as much earlier in the flight, when he and his master, Eve Byre—the human woman still sitting on the deck nearby—had spent over an hour sparring with their lightsabers. Even then, he'd been the same, sipping the water like each drop was more precious than coaxium.

Zaph studied the cup of water in his hand. "I believe in being thankful for every morsel that the galaxy provides. I wish to appreciate the sustenance it offers, the life it enables." He took another small sip. "It is a joy to be alive, is it not? To be here, in this moment. To be aware of all that is happening around us, that we are a part of? I merely seek to honor each moment fully as it passes, and enjoy the pleasures it affords."

Affie nodded. "That's such a wise way of looking at things," she said. "To never let a moment pass unmarked."

Zaph gave a slight shrug. "The Force grants us these fleeting moments of time as individuals before we once again become a part of the whole. We must consider how we spend them."

Affie smiled. As thoughtful and kind as Zaph seemed, he was also *intense*. She liked him, though. And she liked that he seemed to know who he was and how he wanted to be. That sort of confidence and surety wasn't something that had come easy to her. She wondered if it was different for Jedi—if growing up in the Order meant that you always had direction and purpose. A part of Affie thought that would be nice, but mostly she thought that sort of discipline would never have suited her. It just wasn't her style.

One thing certainly resonated with her, though—the thought that it was important to consider how to spend her time, her life. And that was exactly what she'd been doing.

She sensed movement and turned to see Zaph's master, Eve Byre, was stirring from her own meditation.

Eve was a human with pale skin and dark brown hair that she wore tied back in a taut ponytail. She had a strong jaw and startling amber eyes, and an unfamiliar accent that seemed formal and—at times—a little matronly. That said, from the short time Affie had spent with her, Eve's affable nature seemed to belie that surface formality.

Affie watched as the Jedi woman opened her eyes.

"I'm sorry if I disturbed you," said Affie.

Eve waved a dismissive hand as she got to her feet, uncurling from her meditation posture with easy grace.

"I wouldn't worry about that," said Zaph with a chuckle.

"Master Byre has an astounding ability to meditate anywhere at any time. I've never seen anything like it."

Okay, so maybe Zaph wasn't quite as uptight as she'd thought.

Eve shot him a look, but Affie could see the hint of a smile twitching at the corner of her mouth. "Is that right, Padawan?"

"You know it is," said Zaph with evident affection. "And it's a compliment. I only wish I had your focus."

"You don't do too badly," said Eve. She narrowed her eyes. "For an apprentice."

Zaph laughed and took another sip of his water.

Affie grinned at the obvious fondness between the pair. She wondered how long they'd been master and Padawan.

"You have news?" asked Eve, looking over to meet Affie's gaze.

Affie shrugged. "Not so much. We're still a couple hours away from Oisin. Just thought I'd come say hi."

Eve nodded. "You have questions."

Affie was taken aback. That wasn't why she'd come back here, was it? She'd just wanted to check on her passengers. But then, she'd also been thinking about the mission, about the good it would do. She nodded.

"I suppose I do."

Eve smiled graciously. "Then if I can answer them, I will."

"I was just wondering—all the supplies we've got back there for the Oisinians"—she waved her hand in the direction of the hold—"how long will they last?"

"Not long enough," replied Eve. "But there's more than just grain and protein packs in those crates. We've brought seed. A whole harvest's worth. When the Stormwall first went up, in the aftermath of Starlight Beacon's fall, missions like this were all about relief. About helping people to survive in the here and now. Now they're about building a sustainable future. About helping people like the Oisinians find a way to support themselves now the old trade agreements they once relied upon have been broken."

That made sense. Everything had changed. And so everything needed to be rebuilt. Sometimes that meant fixing up cities and reconstructing homes; other times that meant helping societies cope with economic or ecological pressures that hadn't existed before. But surely it was all still temporary, until the Nihil's reign of chaos and terror could be dispelled.

"Aren't you hoping to reestablish all the old trade routes once the Nihil are defeated?" said Affie. She'd heard Chancellor Soh say as much on one of her many broadcasts: that the Republic and the Jedi would look to restore the galaxy to its former state—or at least as close to it as possible—once the Nihil mess was finally put right. Although no one seemed to have any idea exactly when that might be.

"When the Stormwall comes down—and I have no doubt it *will* come down," said Eve, "we can no longer assume the worlds that have been trapped inside the Occlusion Zone are as they once were. The relief effort will be double-fold as we attempt to support them or reintegrate them into the Republic community."

Affie thought about the terrible regime under which the people of those worlds must have found themselves. She hoped Eve would be proved wrong, but none of them could know the long-term effects of being cut off from the rest of the galaxy and subject to the brutality of the Nihil.

Liberation couldn't come soon enough.

It was good that the Jedi and the Republic were at least thinking about the future, though, about a time when the Nihil would be defeated or gone. For too long, they'd been on the back foot, retreating to Coruscant in the face of the Nameless threat.

Affie understood that fear, that danger—she'd seen what those creatures could do to a Jedi—but there had to be a way to fight back. And if there was, she knew people like Reath Silas and Vernestra Rwoh would find it. She knew what they were capable of. And she wasn't letting go of her hope, her faith in them.

The time would come.

And in the meantime, she would do her bit. She would run as many relief missions as needed to help keep the people of the galaxy alive.

"So, what's the plan?" she said. "Deliver this shipment and then head back to Coruscant for another?"

"Oh, no," said Zaph. "We're *part* of the shipment. Master Byre and I are staying on Oisin."

"You are?" Affie knitted her brows. "I signed up for a return trip."

"I'm sorry," said Eve. "A small misunderstanding. We're staying behind for a few weeks to assist the Oisinian government with their fortification plans. There's been talk of Nihil raiders periodically breaching the Stormwall with their Path drives and attacking the outlying settlements."

Affie nodded. "But then you'll need to be picked up again to go back to Coruscant?"

"Once we're done on Oisin, yes," said Eve. "If that's agreeable?"

Affie smiled. "No problem." She got to her feet. "I'll go make sure Leox knows. No doubt we can fit in a handful of other transport runs while we're waiting."

More opportunities to help. That couldn't be a bad thing.

"Thank you, Affie," said Zaph.

Affie shot him a parting smile as she made for the flight deck, still holding her drink.

FOUR

Cohmac Vitus was no longer a Jedi Knight.

He thought about that fact every single day.

It was a realization that still shook him to his core, a statement he had never imagined he would ever make. The very idea of it had been utterly inconceivable until just over a year ago, when the galaxy had seemingly turned on its head and his inevitable departure from the Order had begun.

Some days it felt almost normal, this lonely nomadic life he had adopted since he'd walked away in the aftermath of Starlight Beacon's fall. Other days—most days, if he was honest with himself—it still felt raw and painful, like an open wound that refused to heal. A wound he couldn't stop prodding and one he had inflicted on himself, even if it was for the best of reasons.

Leaving the Order had been the single hardest decision of his life. He'd abandoned everything he knew—his friends, his *family*. He'd left behind everything he had ever believed in.

And he'd done it because he no longer felt that capable of being a Jedi. He'd lost faith—not in the Jedi but in himself, in his beliefs.

In the past, he'd always been sustained by his faith in something greater, a galaxy filled with vibrant life and compassion, by the good that the Jedi could do out there among the stars. But that outlook had been challenged too many times, by the emergence of fairy-tale monsters made real, by the deep loss of so many friends, by the Nihil and the Great Disaster and the Republic Fair and Starlight Beacon.

It was all so much.

Too much.

He could hardly bear it.

What could he—Cohmac—do to make a difference in a galaxy so riven by chaos and uncertainty?

How could he be a figurehead, a teacher, a leader when he couldn't even see the path ahead for himself?

The answer was—he could not.

And now even the Jedi were floundering. Perhaps worse, they were hiding, just when the galaxy needed them most.

The Nameless were an existential threat to the very nature of the Jedi, a terrible danger weaponized by those who would see the Order brought to its knees. But retreating to Coruscant, relying on the Chancellor and the Republic to shield them, bringing a fallen Jedi into their midst—all of it seemed like the first stages of accepting defeat.

And so Cohmac had left, walked away. After all this time, after knowing nothing else, he was no longer a Jedi—even if the thought of it pained him every single day.

The problem was, he might have been clear about what he *wasn't*, but he was very unclear about what he *was*.

What happened to a Jedi once they'd left the Order? What did they become?

Who was he without the tenets that had shaped his entire life?

He had no answers to these questions. It was such a rare occurrence that he wondered if anyone did.

He felt unanchored. Adrift. *Alone.*

And worse than all that, Orla Jareni was gone. The one person who might have helped him understand the choices he had made. His oldest friend.

He'd felt her passing through the Force, felt the shockwave of it like a physical blow. And though he knew that she was now one with the Force, it still *hurt*.

He'd searched for her since—at length. Meditating, reaching out, even returning to some of the places they'd been together. Just to be sure, in case what he'd sensed had been wrong and she was still alive.

But there was nothing—a void where she had once been, both in the Force and in his heart. Consequently, things just felt . . . unfinished. He felt incapable of moving on, as if there was still something that needed to be done, a line that needed to be drawn under Orla's death.

Unable to settle on a new purpose, Cohmac had defaulted to what he knew. He had continued to investigate the origins of the Nameless, to try to understand them and so find a way to counter their terrifying abilities.

Perhaps he was doing it to bring closure to Orla's story—to find a way to honor and respect her now that she was gone. Or perhaps he was trying to find a different way to approach the problem, to show the Jedi Council that there were other options.

The Nameless weren't the real threat. At least, not on their own. He was certain of that. They were merely creatures that were somehow being used and manipulated by the Nihil, weaponized in a way that nature could never have intended.

Many of the Jedi seemed to think they were some kind of monster, emerging from the old myths and cautionary tales to terrorize them, just as their masters had warned them about when they were frightened younglings.

But Cohmac was convinced that wasn't the full story.

That was why he was here on Thall, searching the litter of a long extinct civilization.

There was one other reason, the one he didn't want to think about or give any credence to: the suspicion that, just like the Jedi Council, he was running away from his problems.

It wouldn't be the first time.

But thoughts like that weren't helpful. They weren't going to help him figure out what to do next.

He'd come to Thall following the story of an ancient civilization of people known as the Tolemites—a people who, in several fragmentary legends, had encountered entities that, if Cohmac was reading between the lines correctly, might equate to the Nameless. If he could find any trace of these Tolemites, he figured he might be able to learn from what had happened to them, how they had survived their encounter with the so-called Force Eaters.

His pursuit of the Tolemites had seen him bounce across seven planets in the Outer Rim, picking up slivers of information or the tiniest threads of a new lead amid the archives, ruins, or folklore of the people. And a picture was beginning to slowly emerge.

He'd been forced to move quickly on at least three occasions, when one of the Nihil's latest Jedi hunters—somewhat ironically, given the fact he'd surrendered his position in the Order—had caught his scent.

He'd managed to shake them each time, but he knew they hadn't given up. They never would—not until they were stopped. And with the protective Guardian Protocols still in effect, so far as he knew, most Jedi were keeping close to Coruscant, venturing out only for short sanctioned missions. Meaning anyone living out in the field would remain a prime target.

Which all amounted to the fact that he had to work faster to find the information he was looking for. What he would do when he found it, he still wasn't certain. He knew his former Padawan, Reath Silas, would be on a similar trail, although Reath's preferred methods involved scouring the Jedi Archives rather than getting out in the dirt and the living history. It was one of the reasons they'd worked so well together.

But that was the path to more unhelpful thoughts, and Cohmac didn't have time to wallow in the past, no matter how fresh it still felt. There was work to be done.

He had left his ship, a small light freighter he'd named the *Excavator*, on the outskirts of the city ruins, close to the entrance to a vast warren of catacombs that—according to his preliminary scans—were almost extensive enough to mirror a small settlement in their own right.

He'd then spent the past two days hiking through the ancient decaying architecture, picking his way through the detritus of another time, imagining the lives people had once led here.

It had been a civilization to rival any of its era. Cohmac could tell from the tumbledown wreckage of huge municipal buildings, the great flagstone-paved avenues—now erupting with thick tree roots and carpets of emerald moss—and the sheer volume and extent of the overall sprawl.

The city had been abandoned millennia ago, and while there were small pockets of settlements elsewhere on the planet, they were largely confined to the northern hemisphere.

The current residents of Thall had allowed these ruins to return to nature in favor of erecting more modern towns and communities—and because of the superstitions surrounding the events that led to the fall of the ancient culture. The truth was long since shrouded in time, but it was said that the people who'd lived here had just . . . disappeared one day, as if they'd suddenly up and vanished, leaving no clue or trace of where they had gone.

What was more, the surviving records showed that they had been deeply spiritual, believing in the omnipotence of the Force, its prevalence in all living things—followers of a Force religion now long forgotten.

But given the Tolemites had been spreading those sorts of ideals and beliefs throughout the galaxy at the same time the civilization on Thall was thought to be at its zenith, Cohmac could only hope that there would be some evidence of a connection between the two cultures, and perhaps some sign that would point him toward the location of the Tolemites' missing homeworld.

Cohmac hopped over a low wall, running a hand through his damp hair. It was hot and humid, and a low mist curled from the damp ground. He wore light brown pants and a loose gray-blue tunic beneath a tattered brown robe. He'd allowed his hair to grow a little longer, and his goatee—although still largely trim—was beginning to itch.

He was close to the ruins of what looked like some sort of large hall or meeting place, approached by an arcade of columns that had long since fallen like splayed fingers on the ground.

Low single-story homesteads huddled in neat rows. A wide street, now thick with bright green moss, had once been a main thoroughfare. And in the distance stood the crooked tower of what might have once been a church or similar religious structure. It hung precariously over the lip of a chasm, poised like its foundations could give way at any moment.

"Perfect," said Cohmac, surprised by the booming sound of his own voice. He realized he hadn't spoken aloud for over a week.

He chewed his lower lip thoughtfully and then set off at a brisk pace, making a beeline for the tower.

It was as good a place to start as any.

FIVE

Jedi Knight Reath Silas peered at the strange disarticulated hand suspended in the canister on the workstation and moved to wipe his brow on his sleeve, forgetting for a moment that he was wearing an enclosed protective suit over his robes.

No wonder it was hot in the laboratory.

He lowered his hand, dropping into a crouch so his eyes were level with the canister. The containment field inside it lent the dead flesh an unusual bluish hue. The hand had been leached of all natural color, veined with striations of pale infection. The fourth and fifth fingers had crumbled to ashy flakes, leaving nothing but stubs of corrupted flesh that terminated at the knuckles. Reath could see where the infection had begun to spread through the tissue of the fingers, creeping like growing vines around the flesh of the wrist, hungry, malevolent, and restless, stilled only by its suspension in the canister.

This was the crawling death of the blight, the horror that was somehow spreading through the galaxy. And this was what it did to *people*. If the owner of this hand—Cair San Tekka—had not acted so swiftly and decisively, severing the infected appendage at the wrist, his entire body would have been overcome within a matter of days, weeks at best.

There was no cure for the blight. To touch it was to die. Which was why Reath was wearing a protective suit, despite the fact he was handling the sample through the thick glass of its canister.

He wished he could have talked with the former frontier ranger Jordanna Sparkburn, who had seen the blight firsthand and had sent him the infected hand at Vernestra Rwoh's request. As it was, he had the limb itself, and that would have to suffice—for now.

He had noticed no appreciable change in the appearance of the hand, but he'd been studying it for only a couple of weeks. It would be foolhardy to assume that the blight's corrupting effects were *completely* stilled by the presence of the suspension field, but without it, the canister itself would have been infected almost immediately. The blight seemed to treat both organic and inorganic material equally, in that it corrupted and consumed them all, but its taste for organic matter seemed much more virulent, and the rate at which it consumed flesh and vegetation far outstripped the ponderous way it attacked the inorganic.

So far, nothing they'd found could slow it or prevent its gradual spread.

They needed answers, and fast. And the Jedi were counting on Reath, and others such as Emerick Caphtor, to deliver those answers, all while looking into the threat of the Nameless, too.

No pressure, then.

Reath walked along the line of canisters he'd gathered on the workstation of his laboratory, nestled deep in the heart of the Jedi Temple on Coruscant. He'd taken over an existing analysis laboratory, tweaking its layout to suit his needs. It was spacious, with gleaming white walls, floor, and ceiling, and a series of partitioned workstations and booths. Two buzzing airborne droids were currently engaged in running tests on the other side of a thick glass partition, attempting to measure the decay rate of Nameless flesh, scraped from the corpses of dead creatures by Republic scientists.

Before Reath were samples taken from several Drengir consumed by the blight, along with infected fragments of stone and plant life brought back from two worlds where the blight had appeared—all lined up in matching canisters and held in small suspension fields.

He felt perhaps he was drawing closer to some sort of revelation but wasn't yet sure if it would prove useful or not. It seemed that the blight affected different substances, creatures, and beings at different rates. He was unclear about why this should be.

More important, though, he was still attempting to discern if there was any real connection between the effects of the blight and the Nameless. From his months of research in the Jedi Archives,

Reath was *certain* there was. There were old stories and legends that alluded to ancient plagues and to creatures that seemed to feed on the Force, and in each of these rare occurrences, the two things appeared to go hand in hand. Where one arose, the other would inevitably, eventually, follow. Or so it seemed. The problem with legends was that they were unreliable and full of misinterpretation, exaggeration, or downright fiction. Teasing out the threads of what might be real and trying to corroborate his theories was how he spent most of his days—that and studying the samples in the laboratory and looking for clues in the empirical evidence.

And yet he still hadn't been able to figure out, beyond the obvious superficial similarities, why it was that both the blight and the creatures left their victims in a similar condition. But the blight was affecting *everything*, and the Nameless seemed to affect only people who were steeped in the Force, such as the Jedi.

So what was he missing?

He clicked his tongue against the roof of his mouth as he studied the withered vine of a blighted Drengir, observing the speckling gray pattern that mottled its entire length.

And then he almost leapt out of his skin at the sound of an unexpected voice from the other side of the room.

"Um, hi. Hello. Not disturbing you, am I?"

Reath glanced up from the suspension canister to see Padawan Amadeo Azzazzo standing on the other side of the sealed doorway. Amadeo was wearing a sheepish expression, a kind of lopsided grin that was half-affable, half-embarrassed, and entirely endearing.

Inwardly, Reath sighed. He had work to do, and he'd been hoping for some uninterrupted time to focus. He hadn't made any real progress for weeks. And while he had his theories, he was running out of ideas for how to put them to the test. He just wanted time alone to think through his options, to try to come up with a new approach to the problem, to keep staring down the lens of his microscope in case something new presented itself.

He didn't really know Amadeo, except to greet and nod to on the odd occasion that they passed each other in the corridors of the Jedi Temple, but something about the younger man—and he did *look* young, with his tanned skin, dark hair, and boyish good looks, despite being only a couple of years Reath's junior— suggested he needed to talk.

Reath raised a hand. He crossed to the door and peered at Amadeo through the clear panel. "Amadeo," he said. "Of course not." He gestured to the series of protective suits hanging from a rail close to where the Padawan was standing. "But you'll have to put on a suit if you want to come in. We can't risk anyone being exposed to the blight."

"Oh, of course," said Amadeo, grabbing a suit off the rack and slipping it over his robes. He folded down the clear headpiece—a bubble of transparisteel—and ran his finger along the neck seal to secure it. "Okay, good to go."

Reath opened the door and ushered Amadeo inside, gesturing toward a stool near the workstation he'd been using.

"I mean, I know I *am* disturbing you," said Amadeo, crossing the lab and pulling out the stool. "What I really meant to ask was whether you *mind* being disturbed."

"I don't," said Reath. "The truth is, I'm at an impasse anyway."

"Right, well. That's why I'm here," said Amadeo. He lowered himself onto the stool. Reath could see that he was buzzing with nervous energy.

"I'm sorry?" said Reath. "I'm not sure I follow."

Amadeo rapped his fingertips on the workbench. "I, umm . . . Well, I thought I might volunteer my services. To help."

"Oh." Reath realized when he saw the look on Amadeo's face that the word had sounded less than enthusiastic. "I mean, great. In what way?"

"Well, I know I'm more of an 'out in the field' sort of guy, but I've seen the blight firsthand and I know that time is of the essence. While I wait for my next assignment, I want to do what I can to help. There's so much riding on us figuring this out."

"Don't remind me," said Reath with a wry smile.

Amadeo pursed his lips and drew two pinched fingers across the front of his transparisteel hood, as if to indicate his lips were sealed on the subject of the Council and the need for urgent progress.

"So . . . you want to roll your sleeves up and help in the lab?" said Reath, trying to keep the dubious tone from his voice.

Amadeo shook his head. "No. I mean, I'm happy to help in whatever way I can, but that's not why I came. Like I said, I've been out there, a *lot*. I've seen what the blight is doing to the worlds it's touched. I figured, I don't know, I might have a useful *perspective*."

"You've seen infected worlds," said Reath, nodding. "I've seen samples of the blight here in the lab. And I've read all the reports.

But I haven't seen it close up like you have, out there on the frontier, where it runs wild."

"That's what I thought," said Amadeo.

Reath shrugged. "I've been so busy in the Archives. . . ." He felt a stab of chagrin. His work here was important. The others were relying on him. He was the one who was supposed to be putting all of it together, taking the findings and making sense of them.

But what if he'd just defaulted to his usual comfort zone, burying his head in his research and forgetting to look up? Perhaps he should have been out there, too, alongside those like Mirro and Amadeo, witnessing the impact of the blight in person. Perhaps then he wouldn't be so stuck for answers now.

He glanced at Amadeo's expectant face—and made a decision.

Now wasn't the time for worrying about distractions, for isolating himself even further from his fellow Jedi. Now was the time to take all the help he could get.

"Tell me," said Reath, dragging out a stool and sitting opposite Amadeo.

"What do you want to know?" said Amadeo, clearly delighted to be useful in some way. Reath found himself warming to the other Jedi's friendly manner and upbeat tone.

"Just describe it for me," said Reath. "Whatever you think is relevant. Anything might help. There must be something I haven't considered. It might spark something."

Amadeo nodded. "It's like a plague, I guess," he said. "Transmitted by touch. On Cethis—that's where I saw it last—it had kind of erupted spontaneously, festering amongst the forest there.

All of the plant life had just . . . crumbled into a sea of lifeless gray. As if the essence had been sucked out of the landscape. Everything was friable, turning to ash as soon as something touched it." He looked down at his hands. "There doesn't seem to be any way of stopping it, or anything that can resist it."

"You evacuated some settlers?" asked Reath.

"Yeah. We moved a community to another location, on an island several hundred kilometers from the epicenter of the outbreak," said Amadeo. "It should buy them time. But it's hard, trying to persuade them to leave their lives behind and start again. Especially as we can't even promise them that the blight won't spread to their new home eventually."

Reath could only imagine the toll it must have taken on Amadeo, and Mirro, and all the others—Jedi or otherwise—involved in the evacuation missions. It was a wonder Amadeo was still as upbeat as he was. "They'll understand," said Reath. "With time. And I'm sure they won't have to give up their homes again."

"You really think so?" said Amadeo. He sounded hopeful, as if Reath held all the answers he'd been looking for. Reath knew that he didn't.

Perhaps, though, he could still offer hope.

"We'll find a way to beat it," said Reath. "And soon."

Amadeo nodded. "Master Lox said you think there's a connection between the blight and those creatures the Nihil are using to hunt Jedi."

Reath nodded. "And what do you think?"

"I've been lucky, so far. I haven't come close to any Nameless.

Do you think they're carriers of the blight? Have you looked at correlations between known sightings of the creatures and the spread of the infection?"

"That's interesting," said Reath. "But I think it goes deeper than that, somehow. There doesn't seem to be any connection between the locations where we've encountered the Nameless and the spread of the blight. There was no sign of the blight on Starlight Beacon, for example, and although we believe several of the creatures went down with the station, Eiram has so far remained unaffected."

Amadeo frowned. "So what's the connection, then?"

"That's what I'm trying to figure out," said Reath. "When a Force Eater attacks a Jedi, it seems to do exactly what that name suggests—drain the living Force that flows through the victim, depriving them of not just their life but their very essence. It leaves nothing but a husk of what the person once was. The blight seems to have a similar effect, but it's far less discriminatory, and seems to be transmitted between victims by touch, or else arrives on a planet seemingly by chance."

"I suppose it's a matter of how you look at things," said Amadeo.

"What do you mean?"

"Well, a person's body is made up of various different systems. Nerves, organs, skeleton, and so on. That's true of most life-forms in the galaxy. We're all different, but we're all the same in lots of ways. Our bodies are like miniature ecosystems, with all the different elements working in harmony with each other. That's right, isn't it?"

"Yes," said Reath. "That's a very succinct way of putting it."

"Well, isn't a planet just a bigger ecosystem?" said Amadeo with a shrug.

"So what you're saying is it's a question of scale."

"I think so," said Amadeo. "I'm not really sure."

Reath nodded. "Okay, let's work it through. We're thinking on a macro scale. Consider each world a single living organism, like people in a crowded room. It's been my theory for a while that the Nameless are attracted to hunt the Jedi because of our proximity to the Force. It's the thing that binds us to one another, the one similarity in our incredible diverse Order. The creatures' hunger seems to ignore species or gender or origin. They seek us out, hunt us, for access to the living Force, and then take it from us, draining us of our connection to it. They do that irrespective of who we are or where we come from. Now, if you're right, if we start thinking of planets as organisms rich in the Force . . ."

Amadeo tapped the workbench excitedly with his fingertip. "Then the blight is like a giant Nameless, sucking the Force out of whole worlds."

"Not quite, but the analogy kind of works," Reath replied. "It's like you said. Each world is a macroorganism. And the Force runs through everything, right? Every living thing. So the blight could just be doing what the Nameless do on a larger scale."

"Consuming worlds to drain them of the Force," said Amadeo. He shuddered at the thought.

"Yes," said Reath. "It's possible. It doesn't mean the blight is aware like the Nameless, or alive in any true sense."

"But they might share a common ancestry," said Amadeo. "Or at least be somehow related in the way they work."

Reath peered at Amadeo, impressed by the younger man's insight. "Yes. Exactly. Which, if true, could imply that the Nameless and the blight originated or evolved in the same ecosystem or planet."

Amadeo beamed. "And if we can figure out where, we might be able to use that information to defeat the Nameless *and* stop the blight," he added.

Reath felt a surge of renewed enthusiasm. Talking to Amadeo had been exactly what he needed: a fresh perspective, away from all the test tubes and samples and constant going around in circles. "It's a good theory," he said. "A great theory, in fact. The difficulty now is figuring out potential candidates for that location. All while trying to keep on top of these tests. There might be evidence in the samples that will help us prove the connection, too."

Amadeo got down from his stool. "Well, I'm glad to be of help." He glanced at the door. "I suppose if you're going to start running more tests, I should leave you to it. . . ."

"Unless you want to help find some evidence to back up your theory?" said Reath. "Like you said, there's a lot riding on this. The more help I can get, the better. Assuming you want to?"

Amadeo grinned. "Where do I start?"

SIX

The passageways weren't like the ones at home.

No, no. Not at all. Not in the least. Sicarus remembered them. Very well. He remembered the damp, moldering smell. The soft touch of the clay. The roots and shoots and worms, wriggling and wriggling and wriggling, deep in the soil of Cerosha. Down beneath the trees. Down in the hidden temple, the place where he was born. He didn't remember much else of the time before, but he remembered the tunnels. Always the tunnels. Always hiding.

Here the passageways were different. Harsh. Gray. Built from stone. Part of Father's *cloud fortress.*

And now this place was his home. He was born elsewhere,

but he was *made* here. Created anew. Given unto life with a fresh purpose.

The thought made Sicarus chuckle.

What a purpose it was. What a *joy*.

No, these were not the tunnels of his old life. One thing about them was the same, though. They were dark. Gloom-ridden. *Fuliginous.* He rolled the word around on his tongue, speaking it aloud. It came out as a whisper but was nevertheless picked up and echoed through the empty tunnel, reflecting back at him as he walked.

He giggled again.

Words in the darkness.

Words had power. Words were names and names imparted meaning.

But some things didn't need a name. Some things were more powerful if you couldn't speak of them.

Some things were Nameless.

Another fit of giggles.

But wasn't Nameless a name? Wasn't it just another word, now encoded with so much meaning? With such thoughts of despair? Of pain? And perhaps salvation, too?

Oh, the irony. Delicious and sharp. Like a blade on a tongue.

His fingertips traced the roughly hewn surface of the wall as he walked. Yes, it was dark here. But that was the way he liked it. The darkness was a comfort, a warm embrace. The darkness was his friend, for it was where all the welcoming things lived. Just like the wriggling, burrowing worms. Just like them, and other things.

Sicarus scratched at his arms, his fingers like anxious spiders. He was itching again. On the *inside*. Prickly needles under the skin. The wrong fluids running through his veins. The bad stuff.

Why did his body fight him so? Why did it refuse to accept the gifts it had been given? He couldn't understand. Not when his mind craved them so willingly.

Father makes me better. Father makes me whole.

None of the Brothers back on Cerosha would understand. They couldn't see that *this* was the true path. The only path. They sought salvation through the Ninth Door, but Sicarus had been shown another way. He'd been saved. And now he would be the one to bring clarity to the galaxy. He and the other Children of the Storm.

He scratched again, this time at his throat. The itch was becoming unbearable. He glanced down at his fingernails, saw he'd drawn blood.

The wrong blood.

Too red. Too bright. It was supposed to be purple, like the pallor of his once fair skin.

Frustration fizzed in his brain. He twitched anxiously. One of his eyes seemed to wink without closing its lid. Like the world had momentarily stuttered. When it came back to life it pulsed with a familiar glow. A multicolored hue, a different spectrum.

And then it faded again, returning to the same comforting darkness.

Enough.

Enough lingering.

I must see Father. And soon.

Father could make the itching stop. Father could make everything better. Father was going to change the galaxy.

He hurried on through the labyrinthine passageways, trying to ignore the shuddering spasms in his extremities, the crawling itch under his skin.

The fortress was a warren. But it was a warren with a hidden heart.

At last, he saw light. It scalded his dark-adapted eyes.

Too used to hunting in the gloom. To lurking in the shadows. A predator patiently waiting to inflict sudden, obscene violence on its prey.

The light was slanting through an open door.

"Nine. Nine doors," he muttered, remembering. And then he shook his head, vehement.

Not the Ninth Door, no. That is long forgotten, Sicarus. Long ago. An old life.

This was Father's door. Sicarus hurried through.

And there he was. Larger than life. Scalpel in one hand and bone saw in the other. Dressed in a black leather apron over his old tattered robes. Stooped over a surgical table where he was making *adjustments* to one of the pack. A nip here, a tuck there. A little graft . . .

He turned as Sicarus entered the room. Peered down at him.

His father—not his true father, the one who'd sired him, but an honorary title Sicarus had awarded the Ithorian because of the love he had shown the boy, the attention he had lavished on him—was named Boolan. He was one of Marchion Ro's Ministers, a leader among the Nihil.

In many ways Boolan was typically Ithorian, with his

immense curved neck and hammer-shaped head (a head *so* full of wonders) and solid broad shoulders. In others he could only be described as unique: his insight, his talents. His *vision*.

Boolan gestured for Sicarus to come forward.

Sicarus did as he was bid, scratching unconsciously at his arms. He tried not to show just how uncomfortable he was, but as ever, Father knew. He knew Sicarus better than Sicarus knew himself.

"Is it time for your shots again already?" said Boolan. His voice emanated from a small vocoder attached to his throat, lending his words a harsh electronic edge. He studied Sicarus, blinking.

"I believe so," said Sicarus, projecting his voice above his usual whisper. The whisper that he saved for himself, for his own thoughts.

On the table, the creature was whimpering. It was an ungainly sound, unseemly for such a magnificent beast. A faint metallic tang hung in the air, hinting at exposed innards, spilled blood.

Boolan didn't spare the creature a glance. Sicarus knew that its suffering would soon be over. Yes, yes. It would become so much more than it had been. Another wonder for the hunting pack. He hoped that he might be granted the honor of leading it into the wilds. Watching it work.

Husk, husk, husk.

Father looked at him then, curious.

Had he said that out loud? He stifled another giggle with his hand.

"Soon, Sicarus, my child. I know how you hunger for the

hunt," said Boolan. He patted the mewling beast on the surgical slab. It turned its head, frond-like tentacles curling weakly from its mouth. "You're quite alike, you know. You and this magnificent beast. It's . . . in your blood." Boolan made a harsh grating sound that might have been a laugh.

In the blood. Yes. The *right* blood.

Sicarus nodded, twice. Just to make sure Boolan had seen it. The hunt. Yes. How he hungered for the hunt.

It had been months since Sicarus watched the young Jedi woman crumble in the woods of Parinne as she'd scrabbled back in the dirt and moldering leaves, eyes wide and staring, seeing all the things that weren't there and none of the things that were.

It had been so beautiful to set her free like that.

To let her just . . . fade away. To ease all her pain and suffering. To bring *peace*.

Sicarus had cried afterward, kneeling over her ashen remains. Cried in joy.

It had been his first time. His first success. He'd done it many times since. And soon he would do it all again.

Soon!

Just the thought of watching yet another Jedi crumble like so much dust, of making his father proud, of fulfilling his newfound purpose . . . It was almost too much to bear.

He scratched at his arms again, growling in frustration at the anxious feeling that seemed to want to creep up the back of his neck, prickling, prickling.

There were voices in that anxiety, too. Old voices. Voices from the past, crowding in the forgotten corners of his mind, trying to be heard. Whispers that weren't whispers, urging him to reconsider, to turn back to the Ninth Door, to forget about the singing blood and the pain and the Jedi and the brilliance of the galaxy that his new father had shown him.

He twitched, trying to shake the voices loose. They always got louder when he needed his shots. He hummed tunelessly to drown them out.

"Come. Sit," said Boolan, gesturing to the chair.

Sicarus turned to look at it. The big padded seat with its straps and restraints and the large brace of needles and other glinting tools that hung above it on looping chains.

The chair.

The place where it had all started.

The place from which he'd been reborn.

Sicarus hurried over and lowered himself into the seat, quickly strapping himself into its tight confines, winding cords over his arms, binding himself to the chair's old worn embrace.

Boolan crossed to a workstation on the other side of the laboratory. He withdrew a small metal canister from a refrigerated hold, vapor billowing around him with a hiss.

He held the canister up before him, examining the label with his beady black eyes. Then, with a slow nod, he turned and selected a hypo-syringe from among the equipment laid out on another nearby station. He clipped the canister into the base of the hypo-syringe and crossed to Sicarus's side.

Sicarus presented his wrist. He felt ashamed of the crusted blood and skin beneath his broken fingernails.

His skin, *his* blood. The red stuff.

The sight of it turned his stomach.

All wrong. *Wrong.*

He twisted his head away.

His left eye was non-blinking again. With every flicker the world around him seemed to change, as if the dull gray reality of the before-life, the old times, was trying to push its way through, to conquer his skittish thoughts. The voices were back, urging him to fight, to run. But he didn't want to run.

"Blood," he whispered. "The right blood."

"Yes," said Boolan, leaning closer. "The right blood."

He pressed the hypo-syringe against the flesh of Sicarus's wrist.

A jolt.

And then . . .

The world exploded in a sheet of pain.

Sicarus bit down, tasting gritty blood. Behind his closed eyes, deep inside, he saw swirling colors and lights. Felt the new world imposing itself on the old, blotting it out, waking his senses to something different and fresh, something clear and honest and new.

For a moment he was no longer Sicarus. No longer confined to the itchy shell of his old self. He simply floated, drifting through the dancing lights and pain.

And then he slammed back into his shuddering body.

He trembled, his limbs twitching. His eyes opened but he was still seeing somewhere else, a world of vibrant colors and shapes that couldn't ever exist.

He felt fear.

Yes, *fear.*

More fear than he had ever felt before. Delicious, comforting, welcome fear.

Something trickled from the corner of his left eye, warm and wet.

He breathed. Sharp. Cold. Clear.

Tasted something on the air. Felt his nerves flare.

The voices had gone. Retreated. Lost again.

His gaze narrowed. Everything looked so bright, so colorful.

And there was Father.

So proud.

Sicarus could see it in the sheen of his eyes. The way he was studying Sicarus's face, so close.

"There," purred Boolan. He stepped back, regarding Sicarus silently.

Slowly, Sicarus smiled. "Thank you, Father."

His sensorium was alight with color. Everything was bright and sharp. All the edges were clear, defined. He felt focused. Ready.

Powerful.

And he could taste it. Flowing around everything, around Father, around the pitiful beast on the table, around himself.

It was electric. He could taste the Force, as if it were a scent on the breeze. He could feel its flow and ebb, free and serene. It was all around him.

"Anything to report?" asked Boolan.

Sicarus shook his head.

"Good." The Ithorian gave him one last appraising look and

then began undoing the straps that bound Sicarus to the chair. "I have a task for you."

Good.

Good, good, good.

"What is it?"

"The Jedi." Boolan practically spat the words, even through the digital tones of the vocoder. "I've received reports that they have sent aid to the planet Oisin, on the border of the Occlusion Zone." He finished releasing Sicarus from his bonds.

Sicarus climbed down from the chair, straightening his robes. "I see."

Boolan placed the hypo-syringe back on the workstation. "This is not unexpected. They are ever tenacious. However, it presents an opportunity, does it not?"

"A fresh hunt?" said Sicarus, unable to prevent the tightening in his throat, the sudden flood of anticipation.

"A fresh hunt," echoed Boolan in affirmation. "You may take three of the pack. Seek out the Jedi. Intercept them. Destroy them."

"Husk," said Sicarus with a quiet giggle.

Boolan opened the refrigerated storage unit where he kept the canisters of blood serum, derived from the precious, precious blood of the Nameless. He removed three. "You may take these," he said, holding them out to Sicarus. "And a droid that will help administer them when required."

Sicarus hurried over and took the canisters from Boolan, slipping them into the deep pockets of his robes. "Thank you, Father."

Boolan turned his back on Sicarus, indicating that his audience was over.

Sicarus bowed anyway and then backed toward the door, refusing to take his eyes off Boolan's back.

"And Sicarus?"

"Yes, Father?"

"Do not return until the pack has been fed. Am I understood?"

Sicarus rubbed his hands together in utter delight. "Yes, Father. I understand."

SEVEN

The skies of Oisin were beautiful and clear, tinged with the rich amber glow of late evening, as the *Vessel* slowly arced across the upper atmosphere before dipping low on a steady spiraling descent toward the surface.

Affie rested her hands on the console and peered out the forward viewport as a forest of immense trees came into view, their leafy tops billowing in the breeze. Enormous birds with brilliant plumes of blue and red and yellow took wing, bursting out from the cover of the branches like spilled paint, as the *Vessel*'s engines stirred the silence. "Would you look at this place!"

"One of the prettiest views I've ever seen," said Leox, smiling as he watched Affie beam at the shifting landscape.

"To think that a place like this is so close to the Stormwall.

That the Nihil could strike at any moment . . ." Affie shook her head. "To think that even in a paradise like this, people are suffering."

"People everywhere are suffering because of what the Nihil have done," said someone behind them, and Affie shifted to see the two Jedi—Eve Byre and Zaph Mora—entering the small flight deck.

Affie turned back to the view. They were descending more slowly now, through the boughs of the towering trees. The corners of the ship's viewport were beginning to mist up with condensation caused by the sudden spike in humidity. "But we're going to put that right," she said. "Aren't we?"

"We are," said Zaph, his voice level and assured.

Affie dropped back into the copilot's seat, but Leox had the landing under control and was following the flight path provided by the Oisinian authorities who were coming out to meet them.

She twisted in her seat, looking back at Geode.

He was monitoring the status readouts on the display screens behind her, still silently tracking the irregularities in the performance of the main thrusters. As Affie understood it, they were small unaccounted-for spikes of fuel consumption. Leox thought they were probably nothing, a sign of the *Vessel*'s age, but Geode couldn't seem to let it go. But then he'd always been stubborn when he set his mind on something. She figured he'd sort it out sooner or later. Besides, it didn't hurt to be careful.

She turned back to the viewport just as a proximity alarm wailed, stark and shrill in the confined space of the flight deck.

Affie almost jumped out of her skin. Warning lights lit up bright red on the console before her. "What the . . . ?"

Leox was hurriedly consulting the readouts.

Affie reached forward and silenced the blaring alarm.

"What is it?" asked Eve.

Leox was hauling on the ship's controls, dragging the *Vessel* out of its lazy descent. The ship slewed, then began to climb again, bursting out of the top of the leafy canopy, splintering a whole swath of thin upper branches.

"Another ship, right in our flight path!" exclaimed Leox. "The darn fools! They nearly took us out!"

Affie leaned forward, pushing against her restraints as the *Vessel* began to level off. Leox was reaching for the comm, presumably to contact the Oisinians.

"Wait . . ." Affie narrowed her eyes. She could see the other ship now, below them, moving through the forest toward the landing pads on the edge of the settlement where they'd been told to meet the Oisinian delegation.

It was slightly larger than the *Vessel* but a lot less sleek, with a conglomeration of rusted panels and hatches bolted to its ancient frame. Sprayed in bright blue paint on its flanks and tapered nose was the swirled symbol of a single eye.

Affie's heart was in her mouth.

It was a Nihil ship.

"Raiders," said Zaph, giving voice to what they were all thinking.

"What were you just saying, Little Bit?" said Leox. He

71

thumbed the transmitter on the comm. "This is the Byne Guild ship the *Vessel*. Do you read me, ground control?"

The reply was a crackling, rumbling voice. "Yes, we read you, *Vessel*. Please hold."

Leox looked exasperated. "No, no, no! Don't tell me to hold. Don't you realize there's a Nihil ship coming in hot on our flight path?"

A moment of silence followed, punctuated only by the hiss of static. And then: "A *Nihil* ship? They're not answering our calls. We thought . . ."

Affie leaned over. "Never mind what you *thought*! Raise the alarm!"

"Right. Yes! Alarm . . ."

Leox clicked off the comm.

"Can you get us lower?" said Eve. She was watching the Nihil ship through the viewport.

Leox twisted around in his seat to look at her. "Oh, no. We agreed to a transport mission. We don't have the capabilities to take on a Nihil raiding ship."

"You do," said Eve, her voice level.

"You have us," added Zaph, jutting out his chin.

Affie grinned.

Leox sighed.

Geode maintained a nonjudgmental silence.

"What are you thinking?" said Affie.

"Get us close and we can do the rest," said Eve. It was delivered in such a matter-of-fact tone that Affie couldn't help believing her.

"But we don't know how many Nihil are on board," said Leox. "And we can't back you up if things go wrong."

"They won't," said Zaph. "The Force is with us."

Leox held up both hands. "Okay, okay!" He shook his head in resignation. "What do you need me to do?"

"Can you bring us down directly on top of them?" asked Eve. "About twenty meters overhead. You'll only have to hold us steady for a moment."

"Only!" muttered Leox.

"We can do it," said Affie. She looked at Zaph and then Eve. "You're going to drop down onto their ship . . . while it's moving?"

Eve nodded. "And cut our way in with our lightsabers. They won't be expecting Jedi."

We hope, added Affie silently. *We hope they're not expecting Jedi and haven't brought one of their pet Nameless along for the ride.*

"All right," said Leox. "I'm taking her down." He dipped the nose of the ship.

Eve turned to Zaph and nodded. "Ready, Padawan?"

"Ready, Master."

They ducked out of the flight deck, heading for the boarding ramp.

Affie watched them go.

"Jedi," said Leox under his breath. But the corner of his mouth was curled in a barely concealed smile. "Always ready to walk right into the middle of danger. . . ."

Affie laughed. "I don't know what that says about us."

"It says we're just as much fools as they are." Leox glanced over. His eyes shone. "You ready, Little Bit?"

"Ready."

The *Vessel* swept low among the towering tree trunks, dipping into a broad channel that had obviously been cleared as an approach to the landing zone. Affie watched as they gained on the Nihil ship, willing the raiders not to open fire.

Which, of course, they did, almost as soon as she'd acknowledged the thought.

Laser fire sprayed from twin cannon turrets mounted on the rear of the hodgepodge ship, and Leox jerked the controls, causing the *Vessel* to bank dramatically, first to the port, then to the starboard side.

"Hold her steady!" came a bellowing voice from the rear.

"I'm trying!" countered Leox, rolling his eyes.

Affie heard the shrill scream of rushing air as the boarding ramp began to lower.

"Almost . . . there . . ." said Leox. "Almost . . ."

Affie watched the Nihil vessel on the monitor. It blinked red as the two ships momentarily aligned. "Now!" she yelled.

There was no acknowledgment from the Jedi.

The Nihil ship fired again, and Leox grimaced as he yanked the controls, causing the *Vessel* to jerk suddenly to the left. The shot grazed the underbelly of the ship as it passed, triggering a wail of alarms that Leox hurriedly silenced.

The *Vessel* lifted, pulling back and slowing.

Affie was out of her chair, craning her neck to peer down at the Nihil ship.

She watched as the two Jedi landed gracefully on the back of the raider, lightsabers flickering with brilliant blue and yellow light as they pierced the ship's hull, anchoring them to its metal carapace as it rushed through the looming forest.

Within seconds they'd forced a breach, and she watched as first Eve, then Zaph, disappeared through the ragged circular openings they'd cut in the hull, the edges still glowing bright with molten metal.

Silence permeated the flight deck as Affie, Leox, and Geode all watched through the viewport, anxiously awaiting any sign of what was happening in the Nihil ship below.

The ship stayed on its current trajectory, heading directly for the landing zone and the bristling spires of the settlement beyond, which were beginning to show themselves on the horizon.

They couldn't allow the Nihil to open fire on the civilians.

Affie counted the seconds, holding her breath.

Time was running out. The Nihil would be on top of the Oisinians within moments.

She gripped the edge of the console, unable to tear her eyes away.

The nose of the Nihil ship dipped slightly before coming back up.

And then the whole vessel slewed dramatically to the right.

Affie exhaled.

"Wait for it . . ." Leox warned. He was watching as closely as she was, even as he brought the *Vessel* around in a wide circle to keep them above the listing Nihil ship.

The raider seemed to stutter, and then a pall of smoke erupted from its engines. It dropped slightly, banked again, and took a shrieking nosedive into the ground, churning a long furrow of dirt and mulch as it slid disastrously toward the edge of the landing zone and the array of Oisinian soldiers in the process of lining up on the smooth asphalt with their weapons drawn.

Finally, the ship stuttered to a halt.

Affie felt a burst of hope. Another Nihil incursion defeated! And it would never have happened if they hadn't been there, just at the right moment.

This was why they were taking missions like this: to make sure the Jedi were there when they were most needed. She turned to Leox. "Take us down!"

"Already on it," he replied, chuckling under his breath. He shook his head. "Those Jedi . . ."

Affie beamed, rocking back in her seat. "I know, right?"

Even Geode seemed impressed.

EIGHT

Down in the levels beneath the Jedi Temple, the air seemed musty and cold, as if Reath had somehow left Coruscant behind and was traversing some alternate surreal realm, a place where shadows lingered and nothing was as it seemed.

Reath was certain it was just a trick of his mind, but nevertheless, he drew his robes a little tighter around his shoulders as he walked.

The thing was, he was well aware of what lurked down here in the darkness: a being both pitiful and dangerous, a man imbued with immense power, a living testament to what the Jedi should never become.

Azlin Rell.

A name with which to conjure nightmares.

The fallen one. A Jedi who had embraced the dark side of the Force. Anathema to everything the Jedi were supposed to stand for. A man who had killed hundreds—thousands, even—in his efforts to shape the future, when he caused the destruction of an entire city on Travyx Prime simply to ensure that no one would discover the knowledge that was said to reside there. Knowledge that might have led them to the Nameless.

Azlin's fear of the Nameless had come to define him, to shape his every thought. He had dedicated his unnaturally long life to understanding them so they might be defeated. He claimed to have done it all for the Order that had once been his home.

Master Yoda believed that Azlin could offer them the insight they needed in the fight against the Nameless, and Reath had come to believe it, too. The truth was, if Azlin held information that could help them defeat the Nameless, then Reath had no choice but to follow it up. He would defend these excursions to visit Azlin until his last breath—he sensed the disapproval of several Council members every time the subject came up—but that didn't mean he had to *like* them.

In fact, the truth was quite the opposite. Being in Azlin's presence set Reath on edge and raised questions in the young Jedi that he was unsure exactly how to answer.

It wasn't that Azlin shook his faith in the Force, exactly, or made him question the Jedi Order and its tenets. If anything might have done that, it would have been the fall of Starlight Beacon, the deaths of those he cared about, the desertion of his master, Cohmac.

Cohmac's abandonment of the Order had shaken Reath to his core. The man he had trusted above all else, who'd taught him so much, had just turned and walked away, leaving Reath to fend for himself and the Order without one of its most distinguished assets in its greatest time of need.

Reath was still trying to understand Cohmac's decision, to make sense of why he had felt the need to run, or whether Reath himself could have done anything differently to persuade Cohmac to stay.

Yet, despite all the doubt and the guilt that abandonment had stirred within him, Reath had remained steadfast in his commitment to the Jedi Order. More than that, he was determined to prove Cohmac wrong, to show him that the Jedi were capable of bringing the crisis to an end. If anything, it had spurred Reath on in his research.

Being around Azlin *had* changed Reath, though, as uncomfortable as it was to admit it. Azlin had caused him to think twice about what the dark side of the Force really was, or at least what it represented—to reappraise what he'd taken as fact.

To Reath, the dark side had always seemed taboo, something that was spoken of in hushed whispers but rarely openly discussed. It represented the dangerous path that should never be walked, the turn into darkness that masters were often warning their Padawans about. It was the very opposite of everything the Jedi stood for. If the Jedi represented light and life, then surely those like Azlin, who had embraced their fear and anger, stood for darkness and death.

He'd assumed those who'd given in to the temptations of the

dark side were weak, or greedy for power—lost, at the very least, without true purpose beyond extending their own powers, and their lives, at the expense of others.

Now, though, Reath was beginning to wonder whether that fundamental belief was true. While Azlin was clearly a deeply troubled man—one who had made truly terrible decisions—he wasn't the power-hungry tyrant Reath had once imagined all dark side users to be.

What Azlin had shown him—or rather, what Reath had discerned from his interactions with him—was that, like all things in life, the man's motivations had nuance.

In many ways, Azlin's goals were still aligned with those of the Jedi Order. He could never be a Jedi again, not after the things he had done, but he clearly saw the path he had taken as one born out of necessity. He'd been traumatized by his encounter with a Nameless and had spent the past century and a half trying to overcome that fear.

Reath couldn't agree with his choices, of course—especially when it came to manipulating Master Yoda and unloading an orbital strike on a city full of innocents—but what interested Reath was Azlin's firm conviction that what he was doing was for the good of the Jedi Order and not merely himself.

Where Master Stellan had made the ultimate sacrifice when he had given his life to prevent Starlight Beacon from crashing into Barraza City on Eiram, Azlin claimed to be driven by the same conviction to do what was right, no matter the cost. Clearly, it was a way of justifying his actions, a kind of cognitive dissonance that allowed him to make sense of his trauma and the atrocities he committed out of fear.

Reath knew that, if their positions had been reversed, Azlin would have saved his own life at the expense of the city, finding a way to justify his survival above that of all those who would have died in the nightmare that followed.

Reath hoped that if he ever faced a similar decision, he'd be able to make the right call.

It was a question that kept him awake at night. So far, he had found no answers in his meditations. And so, despite how uncomfortable it made him, he continued to visit Azlin in his cell in the lower levels of the Jedi Temple. He told himself he sought the revelations that Master Yoda had spoken of—and there was truth in that. But had he also decided to give Azlin Rell the benefit of the doubt? He certainly pitied the man for everything he had been through. And wasn't compassion a key quality of the Jedi, after all?

He also had to admit—talking to Azlin made him feel *listened* to, in a way that he could never get from datacrons and lab results and data. While he knew he could never trust the man, they *had* formed a connection—an *understanding*—through their shared goal of solving the Nameless problem.

Reath pushed the uncomfortable thought from his mind. Something to deal with another day. He was almost there.

He slowed as he approached Azlin's quarters. The carpets in the passageway were thin and poorly maintained, or perhaps just old. The living quarters down here rarely saw use. In fact, Reath wondered if they'd been used at all, any time in the past hundred years, with the obvious exception of their current occupant.

He took a deep breath and let it out, found his center.

He turned the corner. As usual, a Temple Guard stood outside Azlin's door, stiff and attentive, his lightsaber pike inactive but clasped before him, his face hidden behind the smooth painted mask adopted by all his rank. Reath didn't know the man's name—those of the Temple Guard had taken a vow of anonymity in their deep dedication to the Jedi Order—but he recognized the way the figure stood, favoring his left side as if carrying an old injury. He'd seen the man many times before during his semifrequent visits to Azlin's cell, and Reath gathered that—just like the other Temple Guard posted at the entrance to this lower level—he'd been assigned to guard Azlin following Azlin's recent actions and the bombing of the city on Travyx Prime.

That was why Azlin had been moved to the lower levels of the Temple. It seemed the Council didn't quite know what else to do with him, and despite everything that had happened, Master Yoda—although more cautious—was still advocating on Azlin's behalf.

Reath approached the door to Azlin's cell and nodded to the Temple Guard in acknowledgment. A minute incline of the Temple Guard's masked head served as permission to proceed.

Reath stood before the door. He knocked twice and then stepped forward, allowing the door to slide open before him.

Silence. Reath could hear the sound of his own breath, the thudding of his heart. He closed his eyes, steadied the quickening beat. Felt it slow.

And then . . .

"Come."

The voice was breathless, dry.

Reath stepped into the small chamber beyond. The darkness was near absolute.

Reath's boots scuffed the floor as he took another step into the gloom. The room was simple, clean, and sparsely furnished—a desk, a chair, a small heating unit, and a cot in a recessed alcove at the rear. The only light emanated from a small lamp on the desk, its emitter turned so low that it cast the room in an eerie twilight. Reath knew that the light came on only when the door to the cell opened to receive a visitor. Azlin's blindness meant he had no need for such things.

The wall immediately behind the desk, which had once been covered in smooth featureless plaster, now bore countless months' worth of bizarre diagrams, symbols, and cyphers scrawled in languages Reath didn't recognize. They were jumbled over the entire wall, some of them overlapping one another. Here a sketch that looked like a star map, there a mathematical equation, and then scrawled over the top of it, a diagram of concentric circles that seemed to be describing the inner workings of a mechanism or puzzle. They were never intended to be read; that much was clear. They were near indecipherable.

It looked like the product of someone struggling to make sense of their own fractured mind, the feverish workings out of a prophet. Which, Reath supposed, would be one way of describing the room's occupant.

Azlin Rell sat on the low cot, his shoulders hunched, his

robes tight around his frail frame. His hood was raised like a cowl, casting his features in stark shadow. His head was turned to the side. He didn't look at Reath when he spoke.

"Something has changed," he said. His voice was a light rasp, air rattling in his ancient lungs. His chest hardly seemed to move, as if the rise and fall of breathing was simply too normal for such a being. "I sense your fear."

"I've told you before. I'm not afraid of you," said Reath.

Slowly, Azlin turned his head to regard Reath. The light caught his desiccated brown flesh. He smiled, slow and toothy. His startling hollow eye sockets regarded Reath as if the blind man could still see him. The flesh in those ancient pits was withered and ragged, like tattered old leather. It was a sight that had haunted Reath's dreams for months. It was said—and Reath had so far been too respectful to ask—that the man had gouged them out himself in a state of uncontrollable terror, to prevent himself from ever having to look upon a Nameless again.

"Indeed," said Azlin. "But if it is not me you fear, then *what*?"

Reath shook his head. "Nothing. You're wrong. I'm not afraid." He wondered if he was protesting too much. What could Azlin sense in him that he could not sense in himself?

"You must acknowledge your fear, my boy. It is the only way you'll survive what is to come."

"And what is to come?"

Azlin's lips curled in a crooked smile. "It is too soon to answer that particular question, my young friend." Azlin made a sound that might have been a laugh, but it was more like a rattle. "Have you learned nothing from our conversations? Tip the scales too early, and everything I've planned for, everything I've foreseen, will come crashing down around us. It is a delicate balance. Do that, and the Path of the Open Hand will win."

The Path of the Open Hand.

The old sect of fanatics that had given rise to Marchion Ro and the Nihil. Azlin remembered them from almost one hundred and fifty years earlier, from a time when the leaders of that once peaceful sect had learned of the Nameless and first turned them against the Jedi. Azlin still called the Nihil by that name. Whether it was an affectation or some sort of deep insight, Reath couldn't be sure.

"And what if you're wrong?" said Reath. "What if all you're trying to do is justify the terrible things you've done, the mistakes you've made?"

"Are you prepared to take that chance?" replied Azlin. There was a sly playfulness to his tone.

"It's not up to me," said Reath.

Azlin smiled indulgently. "Isn't it?" He lifted his chin so the light played across his face, darkening the pits of his eyes. "You understand that I . . . *see* things."

"Perhaps," said Reath. "I understand that you've made difficult choices in the pursuit of your goal. And I believe that you really do care, about the Order, about defeating the Nameless—"

Reath started, his mouth suddenly dry. One moment Azlin had been sitting on his cot, stooped like a crooked finger, speaking in slow, ponderous tones—and the next he was standing before Reath, so close that his breath was warm and stale on Reath's upturned face. He fought the urge to take a step back.

"And about *you*, Reath. I care about you, too. You must see that?"

Reath moistened his lips. He didn't know how to respond. Was it even true? Or was this another of Azlin's games? "Yes," he said after a moment. "I do."

"Good. Good," said Azlin. "It is important that we understand one another, Reath. I know you do not trust me—"

Reath began to object, but Azlin raised a hand to stop him. "And nor should you. I am not the trustworthy type." He leaned closer still, and Reath couldn't help edging away. "But know that I have faith in you, Reath. Know that I believe in you. You can succeed where I have failed. Where everyone has failed. So long as you listen, and learn."

"I'm here, aren't I?" said Reath.

"You are. You are. And you understand. I know that. You see the truth. That everything I have done, *everything*, has been to stop the Nameless." Azlin reached out a hand, gripping the sleeve of Reath's robe. His flesh was papery and liver-spotted, but his grip was like talons. "The rest of them are so shortsighted, Reath. They fear what they do not understand. Even Master Yoda, in his wisdom, cannot quite bring himself to fully trust me. But you? You're different."

Or easier to manipulate. The thought didn't sit well with Reath.

"I'm not like you, Azlin," said Reath. "I never will be."

"Indeed," said Azlin cryptically. "Indeed. And that is your strength." He turned his back on Reath. "Did you bring more tea?"

Reath nodded—a wasted gesture—and withdrew a small pouch of dried leaves from his robes. "Yes, here."

"Then put the kettle on," said Azlin, returning to his perch on the edge of his cot. "You know how it relieves my old chest."

He'd returned to playing the helpless old man. But he wasn't fooling anyone—least of all Reath.

Reath crossed to the desk, turning up the lamp, ignoring Azlin's wincing. He weighed the kettle in his hand—there was enough water, thankfully—and set it on the heating unit to boil. Then he took a cup and tipped in a small amount of the potent leaves.

"Not joining me today, eh?"

"I don't like what this stuff does to my dreams," said Reath. "Every time I come here and drink it, I have a restless night."

"And you think that's the tea?" said Azlin.

Reath didn't reply. He stood in silence for a moment while the water slowly began to bubble in the kettle.

"Why are you here, Reath? What brought you to my door this day?"

Reath hesitated. "I have a theory. That the Nameless and the blight might share a common ancestry. Perhaps they're related. They might even have originated in the same place. I've been talking to a friend, Amadeo, who's seen the blight firsthand. We got to thinking—the two crises appeared around the same time, and the effects they have on organic matter are similar."

"An interesting path of study." Azlin sounded impressed. "And you've come to ask me if I can shed any further light on your theory?"

Reath felt a brief glow of pride at the other man's acknowledgment. He really did understand the joy to be had in such research, in teasing out the details and forming theories. After all, he'd spent more than a century doing it. "Yes. I suppose so," said Reath.

Azlin smiled, revealing yellowed teeth. "Don't you think I would have told you already?"

"I don't know what to think," said Reath with a sigh. He'd hoped the man would be more forthcoming today, more ready to talk. But instead, he seemed to be in the mood for toying with Reath again. "I don't know how much you're withholding from me. You insist on these cryptic games."

Azlin shook his head. He sighed, his smile disappearing. "Cryptic games? No, Reath. No games. If I have withheld anything from you, it is simply because you are not yet ready to hear it."

"That isn't for you to decide. You're not my master, Azlin. You claim to want to help us—"

"I claim to want to defeat the Nameless," said Azlin, cutting him off. "And I shall do it however I think best."

"You're not the only one, you know," said Reath.

"The only *what*?" asked Azlin.

"The only Jedi to face one of the Nameless and survive," said Reath.

Azlin laughed. "Take a look at me, Reath"—he gestured with both hands—"and tell me, does this look like survival?"

Reath didn't answer. He felt a spike of guilt for provoking the old man.

"There are so many times when I wished that I hadn't lived. That the creature had finished me off on Dalna. That I'd found *peace.* Instead, I've had to live, *for a century and a half,* knowing that the Nameless were still out there. Knowing that one day, I'd have to face them again." Azlin reached up and lowered his hood, exposing his thin black hair, which fell in strands about his shoulders. "Do you understand what that's like, Reath? Of course you don't. How could you?"

The kettle had begun to screech.

"I understand more than you think," said Reath. "I understand you chose the dark side out of fear."

"Perhaps you do," replied Azlin, his tone conciliatory. "But let me assure you of one thing, my young friend."

"What?" said Reath.

Azlin offered him a crooked smile. "For a Jedi, there are far more dangerous things in this galaxy than the dark side."

NINE

Thirty Years Earlier

Jedi Padawan Cohmac Vitus faced the canyon and felt his guts churn.

It was a *long* way down—so far down, in fact, that even if he narrowed his eyes, he couldn't quite see the bottom. He knew there was a river down there—a fast-flowing one, too—and a lot of jagged rocks, the sort that would shatter a human body if it were to drop on them from above. *Especially* from a height like this.

The thought churned his guts again.

What was wrong with him today?

It wasn't that he was *scared* of the jump. He was a Jedi. He wasn't ruled by fear and emotions like other beings. It was more that he had an awful presentiment that if he tried to make the leap, he would fail. And failure meant a long tumbling fall to oblivion.

Or at least, the passing of his physical form and the absorption of his spiritual being into the Force.

And why should he take such a risk on a *training* run? It seemed unnecessary.

Yet he'd made dozens—hundreds—of jumps like this before and barely given them a moment's thought. He'd been doing so ever since Master Simmix had first encouraged him to test the limits of his abilities.

So what was different now?

Cohmac stood still, feeling the heat of the sun beating down on the back of his neck.

He'd come out for a run, a training exercise with his friend and fellow Padawan Orla Jareni. He'd been winning, too—or at least, he was beating her in their playful race. She still hadn't caught up to him . . . although it helped that he'd figured out a shortcut.

They'd come to Wadi Raffa with their respective masters, Simmix and Soveral, in response to an apparent sighting of a marauder named Fixian Wrak and their crew, who had been raiding nearby settlements in recent weeks. It was a small-scale operation, but the local forces had been unable to stop the raiders, and so the Jedi had volunteered to serve as a deterrent.

So far, it was working. The Jedi were making their presence known, and the raiders were nowhere to be seen. Although, as Master Simmix often reminded him, there was still time yet. Cohmac would have called the serpentine Fillithar a cynic if he hadn't known better. Master Simmix was merely patient, and he understood much about the way people worked.

Cohmac found himself hoping his master was right and the raiders *would* come back eventually. He wanted to try out the new lightsaber techniques he'd been practicing, and it would be the perfect opportunity. Not that he planned to wield the weapon in anger against the raiders, but he was certain that when they came, they'd do it with guns blazing and he'd be called on to use his lightsaber defensively. And, well, if it helped to deter the pirates, that could only be a bonus.

In the meantime, though, they were stuck here, waiting.

With no proper training facilities available to them, but with the benefit of the craggy wilderness and barren slopes behind the settlement, he and Orla had planned a route for their morning run—something with plenty of hurdles and opportunities to test themselves. And as usual, they'd egged each other on by making it a little competition.

So nothing unusual. Nothing out of the ordinary. The sort of typical activity he'd get up to with Orla or any other fellow Padawans while away on a mission.

And yet here he was, stuck in front of a canyon he should have been able to bound over without a moment's thought.

He wondered if something was wrong with him. But then the same thought circled around his head: Why take the risk? Surely the onus was on him not to be reckless.

Perhaps that was it. Perhaps he was learning. When he was younger, he wouldn't have thought twice before launching himself over such a jump. But maybe that was the recklessness of youth. What if this caution he was feeling was actually progress? It paid not to put oneself in unnecessary danger, after all.

He turned at the sound of running footsteps.

Orla.

She saw him standing by the edge of the canyon and aborted her run-up, skidding to a halt in a cloud of dust and sandy soil.

She fixed him with her colorless eyes, furrowing her brows. Her pale Umbaran skin was ghostlike in the glare of the beating sun.

She walked over, her hands on her hips, not even out of breath despite the exertion of her run.

"Problem?" she asked.

Cohmac shook his head. "No. No problem."

She narrowed her eyes. "You took a shortcut over the dunes."

Cohmac did his best to feign affront. "What? Me? A shortcut?"

Orla shook her head. "You're *always* taking shortcuts." She reached back and raised the hood of her robes to shield herself against the oppressive glare from above. "The competition's off."

"Hmmm," was Cohmac's only response. He knew he'd been found out.

"In fact, it's not off. You forfeited, so *I* win," she said.

Cohmac held up both hands in defeat. "All right, all right! You got me." He glanced at the canyon and then turned away. "I suppose if you've already won, we should think about turning back. There'll be chores to complete at the camp."

Orla studied him for a moment. "What's going on?"

Cohmac shrugged. "You found me out again, that's what!"

She watched him silently, her stare penetrating. Cohmac felt as if she were seeing right through him. He supposed she was, at least in the metaphorical sense. He'd known Orla almost all his life, and she knew him better than perhaps anyone, even Master Simmix.

There was no keeping anything from her.

He sighed and held up his hands again. "All right."

"Good," she said. "Tell me."

Cohmac glanced back at the yawning canyon behind him. If it were anyone else, he might have felt embarrassed—but not with Orla. "I reached the edge and just . . ." He shook his head. "I faltered. I couldn't jump."

Orla walked up to the edge of the drop and looked over. Then she walked back to his side. "Why? It's an easy enough jump if you use the Force. I've seen you clear much bigger jumps than that."

"I know," said Cohmac. "I just . . . I started thinking about what would happen if I didn't make it. And then I thought, why take the risk? And then I started questioning everything."

"You're overthinking it," said Orla. "Which is very unlike you, Cohmac."

"Very funny," said Cohmac.

"Isn't Master Simmix always telling you to stop being so cautious?"

"Well, yes . . ." agreed Cohmac.

"There you are, then." Orla started to back away from the edge of the canyon. "Shall we?"

Cohmac turned. "Okay."

Don't think about the drop. Don't think about the drop.

He took a few paces back, his boots scraping on the loose ground.

"Ready?" said Orla.

Cohmac took a deep breath. He let it out. "No. I can't. I'm sorry."

Orla nodded. She came back over to stand next to him.

"What's holding you back, Cohmac? We both know you can do this."

He looked at Orla's pale face, her searching eyes. "I don't know. All of a sudden it just seems . . . too dangerous."

"I see."

"You do?"

"Of course."

Orla could be so infuriating at times.

"Well?" he asked. "I'm open to ideas here."

"It's not the canyon you're trying to jump."

"What do you mean? Of course it is! That's what I'm doing here, isn't it? That's why I'm standing here, right in front of it."

Orla offered him another wry smile. "Let's try again tomorrow." She turned and started back in the direction she'd come from, breaking into a light jog. "Oh, and the competition still counts, by the way," she called over her shoulder. "First one back to camp . . ."

She picked up her pace, leaving a trail of dust in her wake.

TEN

The boarding ramp lowered slowly, allowing the thick musky scent of the trees to swirl in as the hatch eased open.

"Phew. It's warm out there," said Leox, running a finger under his collar.

"Warm and humid," said Affie. She smoothed the front of her coveralls and looked around for any sign of the two Jedi.

The ramp settled on the ground. Affie hurried down, glancing over at the still-smoking wreckage of the Nihil ship. A group of Oisinian soldiers—or at least she presumed they were soldiers, based on their clothing and weapons—were already swarming all over the wreck. She watched a small detachment of them clamber inside through the rents in the hull that the Jedi had opened earlier.

"I don't think it'll fly again," said someone behind her. "But then I'm surprised such a heap of junk could get off the ground in the first place."

She turned, beaming, to see Zaph standing with his arms folded across his chest. His lightsaber hilt was back in its holster at his belt, and he didn't seem in the least disheveled from his experience on the Nihil ship. There wasn't even a single smear on his pristine robes or a bead of sweat on his brow.

She peered around his shoulder to see that Eve was giving directions to some of the Oisinian soldiers as they led three Nihil prisoners out of the wreck, hands cuffed behind their backs, faces still hidden behind ugly masks.

"You're okay," she said redundantly.

Zaph shrugged. "Of course."

"You made it look so easy," said Affie.

"Nothing about it was *easy*," said Zaph. He glanced back at Eve, then looked at Affie again, this time painting on a smile that she could tell wasn't entirely genuine.

She frowned. Was something bothering the younger Jedi? He'd acted so at ease during the flight, but now some of that calm confidence seemed to have ebbed away. Not that he was behaving any different than a typically stoic Jedi. It was just the expression on his face, the way he was holding his shoulders a little stiffer than before.

She supposed it wasn't surprising, after what he'd just been through. There'd been more than three Nihil on that ship, for sure. The implication was clear. Affie raised her hand, hesitated, then reached out and squeezed his arm. "I'm glad you're okay," she said.

Zaph looked at her hand for a moment and then smiled. "Thank you."

The roar of approaching ground transportation drowned out any hopes of further conversation.

Affie turned to see a large convoy coming down the asphalt road that appeared to link the landing zone with the settlement beyond. It consisted of three hover trucks and an escort of speeder bikes. The vehicles looked old and well-used.

Someone in the forward truck raised a hand and bellowed a command, and the convoy halted about thirty meters away from where Leox had set down the *Vessel* on a landing pad. Leox himself had remained on board with Geode to begin preparations for unloading the shipment of critical supplies.

"I imagine I'm needed," said Zaph with a reluctant smile before turning and hurrying off to join his master, who was making a beeline for the head of the convoy.

Affie watched as a human female climbed down from the truck's cabin to greet them.

Others were getting down from the backs of the trucks, too. They were all dressed in gray coveralls and had the appearance of dockworkers or laborers. And even from this distance, they looked hungry. To a person, they seemed thin and tired, with drawn weary faces. These were people used to being let down.

This was the toll the Nihil were having on the innocent people of this region, even indirectly. It broke Affie's heart.

But then—when she saw the looks of relief and joy on their faces as they greeted Eve and Zaph, she felt good, too. She'd done something worthwhile here. She'd helped make this happen. She'd helped the Jedi prevent a Nihil raid and ensured these people would have food and nourishment, even if it was only a temporary fix.

That was enough.

She heard footsteps and glanced back to see Leox approaching. "You all right, Little Bit?"

She grinned at her old friend. "Yeah. I really am. We did good here, Leox. You can see it on the faces of those people."

Leox sighed and wrapped an arm around her shoulders, giving her a quick hug. "I suppose we did. Thanks to you."

"Thanks to all of us," said Affie.

※|⅏

"There," said Zaph, dusting his hands. "I think we're done."

The Zeltron's red face shone with exertion. He'd been helping the Oisinian workers unload the supplies. Close by, the *Vessel* sat on the landing pad, its cargo doors open, the hold now empty and cavernous. Leox and Geode were already preparing the ship for its return journey to Coruscant.

The vast piles of crates had been loaded into the three massive trucks, which would be taken back to the settlement for storage and distribution.

And yet, Zaph still hadn't returned to that calm easy manner he'd displayed during the journey. Nor had he seemed to relish this brand-new environment like she'd expected him to. It was as if something was on his mind. Affie supposed it was none of her business . . . but then, what sort of friend would she be if she didn't at least ask?

"You okay?" she said as casually as she was able.

Zaph looked puzzled. "Of course. Why do you ask?"

"Oh, nothing really," said Affie. "It's just—you seem a little preoccupied, that's all."

Zaph studied her for a moment, as if weighing his response. Then he gave a barely perceptible nod. "It was nothing. When I first set foot here, I had a fleeting feeling. Like a shadow passing through the Force. It was there for a moment, and then it was gone." He shrugged and exhaled, then smiled. "I was probably just picking up on the concern of the locals. They've been through a lot."

Affie studied him for a moment. "Okay . . ."

"Don't worry," he said, obviously sensing her concern. "I'll talk to Master Byre about it."

"Right," said Affie, relieved. That was how Jedi were supposed to work, so far as she could gather: Talk to their masters about what they were feeling. Trust their instincts. If Zaph had the presence of mind to be open with his master about whatever was bothering him, then it had nothing to do with Affie. "As long as you're all right. Don't forget—you're not my first Jedi."

He laughed. "I'm not?"

Affie shrugged. "What can I say?"

They both grinned.

Affie watched Eve walk over to join them. She'd been locked in deep discussions with the Oisinian representatives since their arrival but was smiling warmly.

"I think we're done," said Eve. "The Oisinians extend their thanks and admiration to the captain for their help and bravery." She clasped Affie by the shoulder. "And so do I. Thank you for what you did back there."

Affie shrugged, embarrassed. "Of course. We may not be Jedi, but we're here to help."

"And once again, you proved that today," said Eve.

"Well, I suppose we should be on our way," said Affie. "Watch out for any more Nihil." she jerked her thumb in the direction of the still smoking wreckage. "Although it looks like you have it all in hand."

"We do," said Zaph. "Thank you, Affie. I'll look forward to seeing you again for the return journey."

"Speaking of which . . ." said Affie, fishing a small comlink out of her pocket. She handed it to Eve. It fitted neatly in the palm of the Jedi's hand.

Eve looked at it quizzically. "What's this?"

"For when you're ready to leave," said Affie. "Geode has been experimenting again."

"I have a comlink," said Eve, reaching out to return the device to Affie.

"Not like this one," said Affie. "It's set to a fixed frequency.

It'll call us directly on the *Vessel*. Plus, it's fitted with a homing beacon." She lowered her voice. "Can't be too careful out here, so close to the border of the Occlusion Zone."

Eve smiled. "Thank you," she said. She slipped the device into the pocket of her robes, then turned to Zaph. "Ready, Padawan?"

"Yes, Master." Zaph turned to Affie and inclined his head. "Goodbye."

Affie gave them a little wave and then watched them walk away toward the Oisinian convoy.

With a bright smile on her face, she turned and hurried back to the *Vessel*, and home.

ELEVEN

"**P**ass me that, would you, Amadeo?"

Amadeo turned to see Reath was holding out his left hand expectantly, palm up. His shoulders were stooped, his head bowed as he peered intently at a holo-image projected by a large protonscope on the workstation before him. He motioned with his fingers for Amadeo to hurry up.

"Pass you *what*?" said Amadeo, frowning. They were standing in Reath's lab and had been for several hours, both dressed in uncomfortable protective suits.

Reath looked up, blinking at Amadeo. "The sample," he said, jabbing his finger at a clear glass dish a few meters away.

Amadeo nodded. He reached for the sample.

"*Carefully*," said Reath.

Amadeo gave him a look.

Reath seemed pained. "I'm being patronizing again, aren't I?"

"A little," said Amadeo, handing him the sample.

"Right," said Reath. "Sorry." He switched the sample on the protonscope bed and peered at the new holo-image that shimmered into view.

Amadeo folded his arms and leaned back against the wall, studying the Jedi Knight.

Reath was only a couple of years older than Amadeo, but he'd been through so much. He'd been part of the group that had been stranded on the Amaxine space station and first discovered the Drengir; he'd fought the Nihil on various fronts; he'd lost two masters—first Jora Malli, who became one with the Force during a Nihil attack, then Cohmac Vitus, who left the Order of his own volition. And now he was shouldering an incredible burden, attempting to figure out a solution to what had generally become known among the Jedi as "the Nameless problem."

While Reath was not working entirely alone—others such as Jedi Master Emerick Caphtor were out in the field, seeking answers that were helping piece together the full picture—he clearly felt the pressure to come up with results. The philosophical side of his research—the long hours spent poring over records in the Jedi Archives, cross-referencing ancient stories and mission reports—might have proved easier if Master Cohmac were still around to help. As it was, though, Reath had shouldered the burden with grace.

And despite everything, he appeared to be taking it all in his stride.

Amadeo admired Reath for that steadfast determination. It was one of the things that had led Amadeo to seek him out, to offer to help with the research—that and a burning desire to see an end to the horrors he was witnessing out on the frontier. He just wanted to help, in any way he could, and if the only thing he could really do was offer encouragement and act as a sounding board, he'd do it.

They were both young, and they'd both seen too much death and destruction for their short years. Such were the times. The Republic was immersed in conflict. The blight was appearing on apparently random worlds, consuming everything it touched. And the Nihil wanted to eradicate the Jedi and had the weapons with which to do it, too.

It was all so much.

And yet, Amadeo had never been one to sit back and leave matters to the older, more experienced Jedi. He wanted to be part of the solution—just like Reath.

Reath had seemed wary yesterday, when Amadeo had first shown up at his door, as if the last thing he wanted was a Padawan hanging around while he worked. But after they'd talked for a while, after Reath had come to understand a little of what Amadeo had seen, it felt as if something had changed between them. They'd somehow reached an unspoken mutual understanding, the sense of a shared goal. Reath appeared to have *accepted* him, not as a person or a Jedi—that went without saying—but as a fellow researcher, a colleague, a partner. From that point on, it was as though they were in it together.

Reath's entire demeanor had changed. He'd babbled theories and unformed ideas at Amadeo, and Amadeo had helped him shape those ideas by asking questions or sharing his own observations about the blight. They'd spent hours in the Jedi Archives, searching through the old legends, looking for more clues that might have been buried in the mists of time. And in doing so, they'd advanced their theory even further, about the potential relationship between the Nameless and the blight.

Now they were searching for something more concrete that could help prove their ideas—evidence that they were on the right path, that the connection between the two things was real and could lead them toward that point of common ancestry.

And so here they were, back in the lab, with a higgledy-piggledy assortment of vials, samples, canisters, cylinders, and tools spread out before them on the workbench.

Reath was running more diagnostic tests, this time taking recovered matter from the sites of several Jedi "huskings"—the locations where Jedi had been killed by the Nameless—and comparing them to the material left behind by the blight.

He lifted his eyes from the holoprojection. He seemed jittery, excited by something he'd seen on the two slides he'd been comparing.

"Take a look at that," he said, shifting out of the way so Amadeo could get a better view. "Look at the difference between the two specimens."

Amadeo faced the projection. "I'm not trained in using instruments like this. Or knowing what to look for when I do. I probably won't be able to see anything."

"Trust yourself," said Reath. "Just take a look and tell me what you see."

Amadeo placed his hands on the workbench and hunched forward, studying the two projected images. Each one appeared to be a bunch of cells.

"The top image is the sample taken from the husked remains of Pola Sheel, a Jedi Knight who died on Meridaus after an encounter with a Nihil hunter and their pack of Nameless," said Reath.

Amadeo studied the shape and form of the cells, trying not to think about the fact they'd come from a deceased Jedi. The edges of the cells had all burst.

"The bottom image is a sample taken from the stump of Cair San Tekka's blight-infected hand, showing the effect of the blight on a similar living body," continued Reath.

Amadeo peered at the other sample. It was almost a mirror image of the one above. He stepped back from the protonscope, blinking. "It's like I thought. I don't know what I'm looking for. I can't see the difference."

Reath actually hopped from foot to foot, bouncing with excitement. "No! That's exactly right. That's just it, Amadeo."

"What is?"

"There. Is. No. Difference," said Reath, practically shouting. "They're exactly the same."

"Meaning?" Amadeo thought he could see what Reath was getting at but wanted to be sure before he let himself get excited.

"Meaning you were right! About everything. About the blight treating worlds as macroorganisms rich in the Force." Reath's words were coming so quickly that he was almost tripping over himself as he spoke.

"So this is it? This is what proves the connection between the

Nameless and the blight?" said Amadeo, his voice rising in pitch as the gravity of what Reath was saying began to sink in.

Reath was laughing. "So much more than that, Amadeo! It proves that, on a molecular level, the blight is doing exactly the same as what the Nameless do when they husk their victims. It suggests the common ancestry we speculated about is real!"

Amadeo wasn't entirely sure what to do with that information. He lowered himself onto a stool. "Wow. Okay. That changes everything. Does that mean the blight is a weapon? Are the Nihil responsible for unleashing that on the galaxy, too?"

Reath pursed his lips in thought. "I don't know," he said. "Maybe. Though it seems to be affecting them as much as it's affecting the Republic and all the other independent worlds. But it would explain how Marchion Ro is able to control it. Just like he controls the Nameless."

"But there's no doubt now," said Amadeo. "The blight is related to the Nameless. It has to be. It's too much of a coincidence to be anything else. The results speak for themselves."

"Yes," agreed Reath. "Which means we're not facing two independent problems after all."

"Fix one, and we fix the other?" said Amadeo.

"Let's hope so," said Reath, hedging his bets.

"There is one thing, though," said Amadeo.

Reath looked at him warily, as if expecting him to point out a major flaw in their findings. "Go on. . . ."

"Why does the blight have all the qualities of an infection or plague, passable by contact, while the Nameless husks are all inert?" asked Amadeo.

Reath nodded. "Another good question, and one we don't have the answer to yet. But regardless, this is a major find. I feel like we're finally turning a corner." He put his hand on Amadeo's shoulder. "Thank you, Amadeo. I wouldn't have gotten there without you."

Amadeo felt his cheeks flush. "I'm just happy to help," he said. "Master Lox was certain that we'd find a solution. And with this, it feels like we're getting so much closer. Thank *you*, Reath!"

Reath grinned.

"So, what now?" asked Amadeo.

"Now I speak with Elzar Mann," said Reath. He was already heading toward the door. "He'll get us before the Jedi Council. He'll know what to do. Then we can figure out the next step."

Amadeo grinned. "Okay." He hopped off his stool. "I promised Master Lox I'd be back to practice lightsaber drills, anyway. We're working on a new maneuver. You'll let me know what Master Elzar says?"

Reath smiled. "You can count on it."

TWELVE

Beep. Beep. Beep.

Vernestra groaned.

The medical equipment was beeping again, and the sound of it was driving her to distraction. She'd even tried meditating, but the constant background rhythm was breaking her concentration, leaving her unable to rest.

"Can't you shut that off?" she asked, and was embarrassed by the pleading tone in her own voice.

"The equipment is monitoring your vital signs, Jedi Knight Vernestra Rwoh," said the tall skeletal medical droid in its ever-so-patient and yet obnoxiously patronizing tone. "It would be inadvisable to shut it off, in case it fails to alert me to an unexpected change in your condition."

Vernestra resisted the urge to tell the droid that the only unexpected change that was likely was a spike in her blood pressure if it continued to treat her like a youngling. "It's hardly a matter of life and death," she said. "I have a few bruised ribs and a cut on the back of my head."

"Precisely," said the medical droid, and Vernestra couldn't help hearing satisfaction in its tone, as if she'd simply defeated her own argument by outlining her injuries.

Perhaps she was projecting.

She laid back on the bed, trying to release some of her pent-up tension.

As if in acknowledgment of the fact she was at least *trying* to relax, the droid reached over and fiddled with some controls on the panel above her head. The volume of the beeping dropped. Still there but better.

"Thank you," she said.

"You're welcome," replied the droid haughtily as it studied her readouts.

"How's it looking?" she ventured.

"Well," said the droid, placing its hands on its mechanical hips, "I'd recommend at least two weeks of complete rest with only mild exertion, to allow the ribs to fully heal—"

"Two weeks!" exclaimed Vernestra, sitting up again.

"And if you'll allow me to finish," continued the droid waspishly, "I am very aware that I am unlikely to persuade you to follow my advice. So instead, I have initiated a process that will accelerate the healing of the damaged tissue. It will be painful, but the recovery time will be vastly reduced."

"How long?" asked Vernestra.

"You'll be able to leave here tomorrow with around ninety percent functionality," said the droid.

"Thank you. What about my head?"

The droid looked down at her as if contemplating the question. "For psychological issues and concerns, I refer you to—"

"No, no. I mean the gash on the back of my head. Was there any further damage?" said Vernestra.

"Ah," said the droid. "Just a small radial fracture around the impact point, and some necessary sutures to close up the flesh wound. I've already seen to it. You may retain a small scar."

"I'll add it to the others," said Vernestra.

The droid gave her one final judgmental look and then walked away to see to another of its patients in the next room.

Vernestra leaned her head back against the pillow, glad for the numbing effects of the pain relief.

Beep. Beep. Beep.

She sighed.

"Vernestra?"

Vernestra glanced up at the figure standing in the doorway and smiled as she recognized the tall young man hovering awkwardly like he didn't quite know what to do with himself. "Hello, Reath."

"Can I come in?"

Vernestra shrugged, trying not to let the sudden stab of searing pain in her ribs show on her face. "Be my guest."

Reath edged into the room as Vernestra pulled herself up into a sitting position. He dragged out a stool and sat beside the bed.

"I heard you were back. And that you were injured," said Reath. The concern was evident on his face. "Are you okay?"

Vernestra shrugged again and then wished she hadn't. "I'm mending up well enough," she said. "Apparently I'll be out of here tomorrow."

"What happened?" said Reath.

"Well, that's kind of a long story, but the short version? I had a fight with Marchion Ro that didn't end too well."

Reath's eyes widened almost comically. "A *fight* . . . with *Marchion Ro*?"

"Yeah."

"Well, it sounds as if it could have ended a *lot* worse."

"It was bad enough," said Vernestra. "I couldn't stop him. He just . . . walked away."

Reath shook his head. "You need to look out for yourself, Vernestra."

She smiled. "I'm here, aren't I?" She waved to encompass the array of medical equipment—most of it unnecessary—that she was presently wired up to.

"You know that's not what I meant," said Reath. "I'm just glad you made it back in one piece."

They sat in companionable silence for a moment.

"I got the hand you sent," said Reath.

Vernestra almost laughed out loud at the absurdity of the statement. "Cair's hand? I thought you might find it useful for your studies."

"I did. I mean, I *do*," said Reath. "I've been monitoring the progress of the blight while the hand remains in the suspension field. It's definitely slowed the rate of decay. But more importantly, it's allowed me to make a side-by-side comparison between the effects of the Nameless and the blight on living tissue."

Vernestra grinned. "I knew you'd figure out what to do with it."

Reath nodded.

"Go on," said Vernestra. "Ask."

"Ask what?" said Reath.

"Whatever it is you're burning to ask me," said Vernestra.

Reath looked decidedly uncomfortable.

"Look, I get it. You're the one trying to figure this all out. If I can help in any way, I will. What is it?"

Reath nodded. "You've seen the blight firsthand," he said. "And you've . . . been close to the Nameless, seen what they can do."

Vernestra shuddered at the memory. "Yeah . . ."

"Well, I've been trying to figure out whether there's a connection between the infection and the effect that the Nameless have on, well . . ."

"Jedi," said Vernestra.

"Jedi," confirmed Reath.

"This is what you were talking about," said Vernestra. "The side-by-side comparisons."

"Yes. If I can prove that connection, I might be able to trace it back to a common ancestry. And I'm close. The science adds up. The chemical composition of what's left behind by the blight is identical to what's left behind after a person is husked by a Nameless. The process is the same."

Vernestra sat forward, wincing again. "That's huge, Reath."

"The stories from the Archives seem to back it up, too. I've found fragmentary reports, ancient legends and folklore that mention creatures like the Nameless, alongside stories of plagues or infection. It seems like too much of a coincidence for them not to go hand in hand."

"Have you told the others, the Council?" asked Vernestra.

"Not yet. I was on my way to see Master Elzar when I heard you were back. I wanted to drop by and make sure you were okay."

"Well, thank you. I'm fine," said Vernestra.

Reath gave her a look.

Vernestra sighed. "Okay, I'm sore. And it's been a lot to process. But honestly, I'm all right."

Reath nodded. "Okay."

Vernestra waved her hand dismissively. "Anyway, what can *I* do? What did you want to ask?"

Reath furrowed his brow. "I don't know, really. Just—you've seen it all, out there. And I wondered if you had any observations that would help to back up my theory? Anything you've seen that would suggest I'm on the right path. But you're tired, and recovering, and I should leave you to it. . . ."

He started to get to his feet, but Vernestra grabbed his sleeve. "No. Wait," she said. "There is something."

Reath slowly lowered himself back onto the stool. "There is?"

"First, I have a question, too. If the blight and the Nameless originate from the same place, would that mean they could be controlled the same way?" asked Vernestra. Her thoughts were swimming.

"Perhaps," Reath said, in a way that suggested he'd considered it already. "There's no evidence either way. You think the blight has been weaponized by the Nihil, too?"

Vernestra rubbed her temples. "I don't know. I don't want to confuse things further. It sounds as though you're onto something."

"Whatever you've seen, I want to hear about it. Even if it means I have to rethink my theories," said Reath.

"It's about Marchion Ro."

"Go on."

Vernestra told him how she'd seen Marchion Ro walk through the blight, even scoop it up and touch it, without becoming infected himself, how he'd used it to infect a Drengir right before her eyes and then simply walked away, ignoring the blighted ground all around him.

When she'd finished, Reath slowly nodded. "Then I think it's clearer than ever. We have coincidental evidence from my studies in the Archives. We have scientific proof that the effects of the blight and the Nameless on living tissue are the same. And we have your eyewitness account of Marchion Ro, who we already know can control the Nameless, seemingly controlling the blight, too. The link is there." By the time he'd finished, he was standing again, practically shaking with excitement. The scholar in him had finally been rewarded for his months of patient painstaking research. He was on the verge of a breakthrough that could make all the difference, for the Order and for the people of the Republic and beyond.

Vernestra grinned. "So, what's next?"

"First I talk to Master Elzar like I was supposed to," said Reath. "Then I'm heading back to the Archives. If the blight and the Nameless have a common ancestry, a shared origin, then I'm going to find out where it is." He beamed at Vernestra. "Feel better. I'll see you tomorrow."

He rushed out of the room.

Vernestra lay back on the bed, laughing and clutching her painful ribs.

She doubted she'd ever again see anyone quite so excited about visiting the library.

THIRTEEN

Thirty Years Earlier

The following day, Cohmac woke feeling bright and positive. The sun was shining, the mission was going well, and he was certain that his meditation the previous evening had cleared his mind and banished any lingering doubts or concerns about the incident at the canyon.

He emerged from his berth on the ship, stretching in the morning light.

Master Soveral—Orla's master—was eating breakfast in the small camp they'd made by the stationary ship. They'd decided, so Master Simmix had explained, to refuse bunks in the settlement itself, preferring to remain more visible on the outskirts, to better make their presence known to the raiders.

It was a tactic that appeared to be working, too. Fixian Wrak's ship had been seen scouting one of the neighboring areas the previous evening and had apparently left rather hastily when the locals made it known that there were Jedi close by.

Still, Cohmac couldn't help thinking the beds might have been a little softer in town.

Master Soveral nodded her greeting. She was a tall human woman—even seated—with striking features and warm brown eyes. She looked amused. "Overslept, did you, Cohmac?"

Cohmac lumbered down the ramp. "Not as far as I'm aware. . . ." He glanced about, but there was no sign of his master. "Was Master Simmix looking for me?"

"No," said Master Soveral. "But I understood you had a race. With Orla."

"What? *Now?*" said Cohmac with a low groan.

"She left about five minutes ago. You'd better hurry up if you have any hope of catching her," said Soveral with a laugh. "Although I wouldn't bet on it."

"You might want to reconsider that bet, Master Soveral," said Cohmac with a lopsided grin. "I know a shortcut."

⚜

Cohmac ran.

He ran with everything he had, feet thudding, breath rasping. He felt the jolt of every pounding step. Sweat prickled his brow.

The sun was already high, and the air was warm and dry. His throat felt as if it were coated in a film of dust.

Yet still he ran, taking the punishing route through the dunes as he had the day before, his feet sinking into the soft sand with every plunging step.

After around thirty minutes, he saw a solitary figure hover into view on the horizon. They were dressed in white, and they shimmered in the heat haze, as if they belonged more to a vision than reality.

Orla.

She was waiting for him.

By the canyon.

Cohmac slowed his pace, dropping into a gentle jog. His chest was burning, but as he finally approached Orla, he called out to her, his voice hoarse: "I thought this was a race?"

Orla shrugged. "More of an intervention."

Cohmac staggered to a halt, slowly catching his breath. "An intervention? For what?"

"For you," replied Orla. "We're going to jump that canyon together. Right now."

Cohmac felt a prickle of . . . discomfort. He tamped it down, fighting it back. "Okay."

Orla nodded in satisfaction. "Catch your breath."

Cohmac gave her a look. *"Thanks."*

"You're welcome."

He chuckled as he fought to regain his composure, dabbing his forehead with the back of his sleeve. He leaned forward, his hands on his knees. After a moment, his thudding heart slowed and his breathing became less shallow.

"Okay. I'm ready," he said. He peered across the canyon,

looking at it for the first time since the prior day. His stomach flipped. He ignored it.

"On my mark," said Orla.

Cohmac lowered his shoulders, rocking forward onto the balls of his feet. He flexed his neck. Breathed.

"Now," said Orla.

They launched simultaneously, immediately falling into step. Beside him, Orla's boots pounded the ground. They hurtled toward the edge of the canyon.

Cohmac closed his eyes, reaching for the Force. He felt it respond.

He opened his eyes, saw the canyon looming . . . and *stopped*.

He felt suddenly overwhelmed with doubt. He jammed his heels into the dirt, skidding and sliding toward the edge of the drop, using the Force to slow his momentum.

Orla shot onward, throwing herself up and over the chasm. She lifted gracefully, soaring across the void with ease.

She landed on the other side, sending up a plume of dust. Immediately, she spun around, her eyes searching.

Across the gaping canyon, Cohmac locked eyes with her, all his embarrassment and disappointment bubbling to the surface. He looked away.

He heard Orla calling to him, but he couldn't make out her words over the roaring in his ears, and so he turned around and set out again at a run, legs pumping as fast as they could to take him back toward camp.

Feeling despondent, Cohmac decided to seek out Master Simmix as soon as he arrived back at the camp.

It was time to speak to his master about his troubles. They clearly weren't going to go away on their own.

He just felt so . . . uncertain, even about this. He knew he could talk to Master Simmix about anything, without judgment, without censure. And yet . . . what if there *was* no answer? What if Master Simmix couldn't help?

Cohmac shook his head, trying to banish the unhelpful questions.

He found Master Simmix deep in meditation in the common area of the ship.

The Fillithar's long snakelike body was a rich mottled red, fading to a pinkish gleam on his underbelly. He was coiled in a perfect circle, his wedge-shaped head resting in the center of his coils like a small creature at the heart of a nest.

As Cohmac entered the room, Master Simmix's eyes flickered open. He raised his head and looked at Cohmac, his nictitating eyelids blinking as he adjusted once more to the light.

"Master Simmix? I'm sorry to disturb your meditation."

"No matter, my Padawan. Come. Come. I sssee that sssomething isss profoundly troubling you." He spoke with a sibilant hiss.

"Is it that obvious?" said Cohmac.

"My boy, I have watched you grow. I have trained you. I have ssseen thisss look on your face many timesss before."

"And what look is that, Master?" said Cohmac.

"You are lossst and sssseek the correct path. Yet you are uncertain what path that might be." Master Simmix's head bobbed slightly in a gesture that Cohmac knew to be an understanding nod.

"Yes," said Cohmac.

"Tell me," said Master Simmix. "Help me to undersssstand how you are feeling."

Cohmac explained what had happened at the canyon the previous day, and how matters hadn't improved that morning. Master Simmix listened intently, studying Cohmac's face closely as he spoke.

After Cohmac had finished, the Fillithar slowly uncoiled his upper body, rising until his head was level with Cohmac's. His ribbonlike tongue unrolled from between his jaws, moistening his lips.

"I sssee," he said. "Mossst troubling."

"You believe I should be worried?" said Cohmac. He was wringing his hands inside the sleeves of his robes.

"I believe that worrying isss exactly the isssue," replied Master Simmix.

"It's not worry, exactly, Master. More that I am questioning the wisdom of taking an unnecessary risk," said Cohmac.

"You are ever cautiousss, Padawan," said Master Simmix. It sounded like a bad thing.

Cohmac frowned. "You think I should take the risk regardless? Make the leap, even if it leads to my death?"

Master Simmix let out a long hissing breath resembling a sigh. "Think of it thisss way: Doesss the canyon *want* you to fall into it? Of coursssse it doesss not. It hasss no sssuch wishesss, hopesss, or idealsss. It isss merely a fissure in the unthinking rock.

An open ssspace to be crosssed like any other. The ssslightessst of obstaclesss in your path. It bearsss you no ill intent."

"But what if I cannot reach the other side?" asked Cohmac.

"Have you crosssed such obsssstaclesss before?" said Master Simmix.

"You know that I have," said Cohmac.

Master Simmix inclined his head. "Sssuch obsssstaclesss, and more. Your ability isss not in quessstion."

"Then why do I feel this way? Every time I approach the edge of the canyon, I start thinking there's a chance I'm going to fall."

"And therein liesss the crux of the matter, my Padawan. You have come to put more faith in your failure than in your sssuccesss. It isss not the canyon that sssstandsss in your way, but yourssself."

"I don't understand," said Cohmac. "Surely, I'm just being pragmatic. It feels like a needless risk. A leap I do not have to take."

Master Simmix smiled. "You're right. It isss a risssk you can turn away from. Nothing untoward will happen. No one'sss life isss in danger. If you do not make that jump before we leave thisss place, then little will have changed."

"Then I'm right. Perhaps I *should* walk away. Surely I can be of more help to others if I'm still alive," said Cohmac.

"But you musssst asssk yourssself, Padawan: Isss thisss the perssson whom you wish to be? One who shiesss from a challenge? One who choosssessss not to embrace the full extent of hisss abilitiesss out of caution? One who shrinksss away from his chosssen path becaussse it looksss too *hard*?"

"But if I fall . . ."

Master Simmix let out a long hissing sigh. "Ah. I sssee that you have already made up your mind."

Cohmac furrowed his brow. "No. That's not what I'm saying, Master. I'm just trying to understand why making this particular jump is so important. Why it's worth the risk."

"The leap you face isss one of faith, Cohmac. In yourssself. In the Order. In the Jedi," said Master Simmix. "Once you under-ssstand thisss, you will know what to do."

Cohmac watched as his master turned, his long serpentine body uncurling as he slid away into the belly of the ship.

FOURTEEN

Sicarus went in under cover of night.

Moving through the shadows, swift, swift like a hunter, the scent of his prey rich in his nostrils.

His creatures—his *pack*—were with him, wild and free, charging through the wooded outskirts of the settlement, baying for the taste of the Jedi, anxious to relieve the Force users from the torment of their lives.

Sicarus didn't look like his adopted kin—no, no, not at all, not with his young pale flesh and his gangly legs and his bald head and muscular arms—but he was the same on the *inside*. The place that really mattered.

That was because of the blood. The injections. They made him one with the creatures.

Brothers.

He snickered aloud at the irony.

A brother of the Nameless.

One of Father Boolan's *Children.*

"I am Sicarus," he said between panting breaths, "and I am free."

He leapt over a fallen tree trunk, his electrostaff bouncing in its holster on his back.

Landing on Oisin had been surprisingly easy. He'd drifted in low orbit above the small world for several hours, scanning the comms traffic for any fragmentary reports from the surface. The comms channels were fizzing with talk of the attempted Nihil raid and the so-called heroic Jedi who had stopped it. Of course they were.

By piecing the chatter together, he'd been able to pinpoint, with relative accuracy, the location of the combat and the wreckage of the downed Nihil ship. He laughed at the ineptitude of the other Nihil. They were nothing. Pirates. Small-minded. Nothing like him or Father.

They had deserved to die. But they had served their purpose, too. They had led him here. They'd brought him to more Jedi, and that would please Father. It would make him so, so happy.

And because there were two—*two!*—he knew what he would do. He would choose one. A gift for Father. Another subject for his experiments. Another plaything.

And the other?

Sicarus would let the creatures feed. And he would watch,

and cry with joy, and give the Jedi such a gift of release that they could never have imagined.

Sicarus had set down his ship close to the site of the Nihil wreckage. There'd been no guards, no one trying to interfere. He guessed they were being complacent now the Jedi had arrived. Complacent or distracted. In his experience—and he'd had a *lot* of experience—small worlds such as Oisin didn't have much in the way of orbital defenses or blockades or monitoring stations. They made do. They were naive and trusting, and that's why they were weak.

And so he'd landed the ship and unshackled the creatures, and that was the only tracking he'd needed to do.

Because the Nameless knew their prey, and they knew that they were close.

Now they were hunting.

And they were *so* good at hunting.

Over more fallen trees, they ran.

Through bushes and long grass, they ran.

Through narrow streets, slick with rain, they ran.

He killed a Rodian who got in his way on the outskirts of the settlement.

And then two more, a human and a Twi'lek, battering them with his electrostaff, so cursory, so swift that he had already forgotten about them three steps later.

They were nothing. They weren't the prey.

They weren't the reason he'd been created by Father.

Why the creatures ran.

Ran, ran, ran.

On and on and on. Ever on.

Breath panting.

Muscles burning.

Hungry. So very, very hungry.

Through empty lanes and streets and squares. Unseen amid the midnight shadows. Swift and sudden.

Running. Running.

Until they found it.

The building where the Jedi were hiding. Like a present, all wrapped up and ready to be peeled open.

The fools hadn't even had time to flee.

The pack was too swift, too stealthy.

Too deadly.

As they closed in on the small building, Sicarus could already hear the Jedi inside, panicking. Whimpering. Their lightsabers humming.

Already succumbing to the closeness of the beasts.

He giggled.

Such joy. Such fun!

The street was silent and dark. Sicarus could hardly see the creatures as they prowled, looking for a way inside the squat structure.

He could give them that. Of course he could.

He raised his electrostaff, powering it on. Energy crackled like lightning at both ends, casting an eerie glow around him. An orb of flickering power.

He felt strong. He felt righteous.

He jammed the end of the staff into the control panel next to the door. It fizzed and popped and crackled.

The door slid open.

The creatures slipped inside like moving shadows.

Sicarus grinned and hurried after them.

The Jedi were in the central chamber. An adult human female with pale skin and dark hair, and a tall Zeltron male with bright red skin.

Red like the color of blood.

The Zeltron was just a boy. A little younger than Sicarus.

He showed such vigor, such promise.

"Yes, you do," said Sicarus. "Yes, yes, you do."

But the Zeltron couldn't hear him. His mind was already gone, driven to wild confusion by the proximity of the creatures.

The effect was beautiful to watch.

The Jedi could hardly stand. He watched as the Zeltron's lightsaber tumbled from his fingers. His expression was tight with fear and desperation. He took three stumbling steps to the right and then faltered, dropping to the ground, propping himself up on one knee, clinging to the wall for support.

The woman held on for a moment longer, swinging her lightsaber wildly at the empty air, trying to cut down enemies only she could see, and all the while one of his creatures, his pack, edged closer, closer, with hunger in its eyes.

She howled, dropping her lightsaber and clawing at her head, pulling out strands of hair as if trying to rip the horror from her mind.

"Shush now," said Sicarus. "It'll all be over soon."

Or would it?

He glanced between the two dying Jedi. Which one should he save for Father?

The stronger one. The woman. She had more chance of surviving the journey home on the ship.

Yes. The master, not the apprentice. She would be his gift.

Which meant the boy was food for the pack.

Yes, yes, yes.

"Food," said Sicarus. "Sustenance."

He beckoned for the other two creatures to do as they would.

The Zeltron screamed, sliding down the wall to lie on the ground, clawing and swiping at the empty air before him. The sound was so raw, so animalistic, that Sicarus took a step backward. The two Nameless fell upon the Jedi, pinning him to the ground, and he writhed and squirmed and cried as they began to feast.

"Just like a worm," said Sicarus. "Like a maggot."

He smiled as he watched his Nameless brethren. Two of them, feeding at once. Sharing in the success of their hunt. Savoring every taste as the Zeltron slowly turned to gray dust before Sicarus's wide eyes. He held them open with his fingers, refusing to blink, wanting to witness every moment of the Jedi's slow transformation, his creeping erosion into oblivion.

It was so pretty. So profound.

An unmaking.

The complete unraveling of a being.

First his arms, up to the elbows, color seeping from the flesh. Then his left leg became gray, so gray, leached of all vitality.

Sicarus watched it spread. Watched the Zeltron scream and try to thrash and bite, his head snapping frantically from side to side, seeing only phantoms dredged from the darkest annals of his mind.

A perfect harmony of fear.

"We all must become dust," said Sicarus, his voice quivering. "All just dust."

He turned to the woman.

She was on her knees, whimpering. So strong, yet so enfeebled.

Why were the Jedi so weak?

How could they let themselves be reduced to *this*?

She didn't even know what was happening to her apprentice, how he was already almost gone.

The remaining creature—the thin pale one that seemed to be sickening—lowered its head, its muscular flanks growing taut. Preparing to pounce and feed.

Sicarus withdrew the small electronic control device from his pocket and pressed the button.

An electric current shot through the creature's brain, and it buckled, lowering itself to the ground, swinging its head so the tentacles around its mouth shook and danced. It breathed heavily, emitting a frustrated mewling sound.

Sicarus smiled.

"*I* am the pack master," he said. "Not you, pale one. *Me.* I say when you feed."

Father had made this possible. He had implanted the transmitters in the creatures' heads as a way of controlling them. And he'd given Sicarus the trigger, allowing him to shoot bolts of electric current deep into the Nameless's heads. Because Father understood that pain was the best motivator.

The creature growled but pulled back. Pacing. Circling the woman but holding off from feeding, lest it receive another bolt of pain.

"Good, good," said Sicarus. "We're saving this one for Father's experiments."

The woman was beyond delirious now. She had no sense of what was happening around her. She was on her knees, flinching and rocking and turning and looking wild-eyed as the creature stalked her. She was babbling to herself, but the words themselves were unclear. She was wringing her hands so hard that he thought she might have broken bones. Tears streamed down her face.

Sicarus walked over and collected her lightsaber, sliding it into his robes.

He glanced across at the other two Nameless, who were hulking over the heap of gray dust that had once been the Zeltron Jedi.

Sated, for now.

"I'm sorry," he said to the pale one. "The next one will be yours. I promise."

He stooped and gathered up the human Jedi, tying her arms behind her back. She was barely conscious. Her lips were still moving, but her eyes were unseeing and her body was limp. He'd have to drag her back to the ship.

He sighed.

Such was life.

But Father would be pleased.

And Sicarus had so enjoyed the sight of the Zeltron being husked. Another one to add to his collection.

He called the Nameless to gather around him, grabbed the woman's arms, and hauled her out into the silent street.

"Back to the ship. Back to your new home."

He giggled again.

Yes, tonight had been a great success.

A triumph.

Next he would pick up the trail of the Force user he'd been tracking for several months. The one that kept getting away.

Quick, quick, they were. Very quick.

But soon he'd catch up with them, and they would fall to their knees before his pack, just as the Zeltron had.

They would crumble just the same.

And it would be glorious.

FIFTEEN

"**W**ell done, Reath."

Master Elzar Mann swept a hand through his hair. He looked tired.

No, more than that. He looked *exhausted*. He looked like he hadn't slept in days.

It was growing late, and Reath had just finished outlining his and Amadeo's findings on the relationship between the Nameless husks and the effects of the blight. They were standing in Elzar's chambers, which were spartan and austere, closer in appearance to Azlin's cell than Reath would have imagined. The irony wasn't lost on him. In some ways, Master Elzar was more a prisoner than the fallen Jedi who resided deep in the bowels of the Temple. The difference was that the only one holding Elzar captive was himself.

Reath wanted to say something, but he knew there was little point. Elzar had been like this for weeks, pushing himself beyond the limits of his natural endurance, and Reath knew that several Jedi Masters had spoken with him already, encouraging him to take some rest. Elzar seemed to ignore them all. It was as if he was determined to carry the weight of all their troubles on his own shoulders, as if he saw it as his job alone to fix everything that had happened.

Reath had heard the stories, of course. He knew that Elzar had made a devastating error during the final moments of Starlight Beacon, had intercepted a Nihil who was trying to help control the station's descent and, misunderstanding them for a saboteur, had killed them. He'd carried that tragedy around with him for over a year.

Reath had struggled with mistakes, too. Like the way he'd been taken in by the Nihil girl, Nan, during the events on the Amaxine station—a mistake that had put him and his fellow Jedi in danger.

Reath understood the desire to make things right, the need to make a difference, to show everyone—himself included—that he was better than his mistakes, that he was worthy of the robes he wore and his place in the Jedi Order. And he wouldn't let them down. He'd hardly slept these past two nights, troubled by Amadeo's insights into the blight and their correlation with the Nameless, and he knew he probably looked as fatigued as Elzar.

"This is great work." Elzar rolled his neck as if trying to

loosen a crick in the muscle. "It really is. It could be the break-through we've been looking for."

"It was Amadeo, really," said Reath. "Without his insights from the field I might never have figured it out."

Elzar smiled. "If there's one thing I've learned this last year, Reath, it's that we cannot do things alone, no matter how hard we try, or how much we want to. The fact you recognize that shows me what a wise Jedi you've already become."

Reath felt his cheeks flush with embarrassment. "Amadeo came to me wanting to help, and I nearly dismissed him as a distraction. I'm not as wise as you think."

"Ah," said Elzar, grinning. "That's where you're wrong. Because you *didn't* dismiss him. You chose to listen to what he had to say, despite your initial inclination. And it led to this. The first proper breakthrough we've had in months." He patted Reath on the shoulder. "*There's* your wisdom, Reath. You're learning to trust yourself."

Reath smiled politely. He knew what Elzar was trying to do—praise him for a job well done, teach him to trust himself—but in truth, Reath didn't *feel* very wise. He felt frustrated, uncertain. He felt the pressure to deliver something useful from all the research he'd spent the past year doing. He felt tired and a little fractious. "Thank you, Master Elzar. I just hope you're right and this new insight proves useful. I can't help thinking I should have seen it sooner."

Elzar put a hand on Reath's shoulder, squeezing gently. "You've seen it *now*. That's all that matters."

Reath nodded. "So, what do we do?"

"I'll arrange an audience with the Council," said Elzar. "They need to hear this. It might change their thinking on several key matters. There's been discussion about a potential mission to retrieve a live Nameless for study. This could be a factor in their decision."

"A live Nameless . . ." said Reath. "Here on Coruscant?" All he'd had of the Nameless to study so far were some corpses that were almost useless because of the speed of their degradation, and the recording from Marchion Ro's horrific broadcast of the murder of Grand Master Pra-Tre Veter.

Elzar nodded. "Chancellor Soh has agreed to house the creature in a secure RDC facility if the order is given for the mission—or *missions*—to go ahead," he said. "And to provide a team of scientists capable of working with it."

Reath nodded. "It would certainly help to shed further light."

"I'll keep you posted," said Elzar. He glanced longingly at his bunk and then sighed and gestured toward the door. "Leave it with me?"

"Of course," said Reath, stepping out into the passageway. "Hope you manage to get some rest."

Elzar looked at him curiously, as though he'd said something outlandish. "There'll be time for that later. Right now, there's work to be done." He followed Reath out into the passageway, gave him one last tired smile, and hurried off in the other direction.

✦

The Jedi Archives seemed strangely quiet after the past two days of furious activity in the laboratory.

Reath walked the aisles slowly, collating a handful of holo-books and holocrons he wanted to revisit. Many of them featured data points he'd flagged during his previous months of study, mostly in relation to ancient or half-forgotten legends and myths from long-lost cultures—echoes that had reverberated down through the years.

Reath was certain that there had to be more information bur-ied in these fragmentary tales, clues that would help him decipher the shared origin of the Nameless and the blight. Reath knew that, just like the old nursery rhymes of the *Shrii Ka Rai*, old truths were often buried in myths and legends, encoded in cautionary tales that had become corrupted and altered in the retelling but nevertheless still held on to that central truth at their core.

He'd been researching such stories since his investigation into the Nameless began, but it had been difficult to know where to start, much less to identify what might or might not be relevant. Now he had an angle, and he thought he knew where to look, or at least where to start—with the mystical tale of the Three Ancients and the plague of the Tolemites.

He carried an armful of files over to one of the reading booths. No one else was in here at this time, but the analysis droids knew him well enough—they couldn't not—and were happy to let him go about his business undisturbed.

He settled down and began skimming through the first holobook.

Reath enjoyed these quiet moments, alone with his studies, lost in the lives of people who had existed many hundreds or thousands of years before his time. And yet, these past few days he'd found himself caught up in the excitement of discovery and the enthusiasm of his younger helper.

He suppressed a grin. Amadeo was a tonic. And he was *smart*, too, and keen to learn. He'd lifted Reath's mood immensely, and Reath found himself hoping the Padawan would stick around for a while. Of course, that would depend on Amadeo's master, Mirro Lox, and whatever their next mission would be.

Nevertheless, Reath was already planning to bring Amadeo with him to the Archives the next day while he delved further into these old tales and legends collected by some of his predecessors in the study of ancient lore—such as Barnabas Vim, who had once scoured the galaxy collecting folklore and relics from the ancient times. Perhaps Amadeo would be able to help, to approach it all with a fresh pair of eyes, just like he had before. Reath hoped so.

With renewed enthusiasm for the task ahead, Reath settled down to read.

A few hours later, Reath raised his head from one of the holo-books, rocked back in his seat, and rubbed his weary eyes.

He was finally getting somewhere. He'd gathered all the fragmentary information he'd previously found on the Tolemites—everything that existed in the Jedi Archives—and had been piecing together what he could of their story.

He still couldn't identify the location of their home planet on the star maps he'd consulted and assumed this was most likely due to a succession of different names in the intervening millennia, but the data he was working from was so sparse and disjointed that it could be one of any number of planets on the Outer Rim or beyond.

Viewing their story through the lens of his scientific work with Amadeo, however, the legend of the Tolemites was finally beginning to take shape.

The culture itself had existed around twenty thousand years earlier—or so the legends claimed—and had once been a proud, thriving civilization of people who, having built a utopian society on their home planet, had ventured out to the stars to explore the wider galaxy.

They had been governed by three mystical figures, referred to in the stories as the Three Ancients, and their culture had been based on worship of an invisible power they believed existed in and flowed through all living things. Reath, of course, had equated this power to the Force, although in the story fragments it was never referred to that way.

As the tales had it, a huge expedition ventured out into the galaxy on the order of the Three Ancients, to seek knowledge and wealth for the Tolemites, and to return only when they had found treasures worthy of the greatness of their people.

And this was where it got interesting, because, although the stories became increasingly fragmentary and apparently contra-dictory, Reath believed he'd found something that everyone else had missed.

In one version of the story—the generally accepted version—the expedition had returned with gifts and treasures from a dozen worlds but in the process of seeking this treasure had inadvertently contracted a terrible plague that had corrupted the people and the land and almost led to the downfall of the Tolemite civilization.

The story claimed that the Tolemites never truly recovered from the plague, despite eventually discovering a way to overcome it.

A lesser-known fragment contradicted this accepted version of events, claiming instead that the expedition returned not with treasures but an array of fauna they had rounded up on the lush worlds they had visited—creatures and animals to delight the Three Ancients and their people.

But some of those creatures, so placid on first meeting, had eventually turned on their new masters. What was more, the creatures were described as four-legged beasts with tentacled maws that hungered for "those of the faith."

It had to be a reference to the Nameless, surely?

When Reath had first read the Tolemite legends, among so many other piecemeal stories and myths, he had done what all his predecessors had likely done: noted the inconsistencies with interest and moved on.

But now Reath saw another picture emerging. What if these accounts weren't contradictory at all? What if they were *both* true? Could it be that the Three Ancients of the Tolemites sent out two expeditions, and one had returned with the Nameless while the other brought evidence of the blight?

It didn't seem so far-fetched a proposition now that he knew the Nameless and the blight were connected on some fundamental level.

And the legends, although old and perhaps unreliable, claimed that the Tolemites had eventually found a way to defeat their "plague."

Could the answer to defeating the blight and the Nameless lie with the Tolemites?

Reath rubbed the back of his aching neck. He found himself eager to share the news with Azlin, too. He would understand Reath's excitement. He'd see the potential in what Reath had uncovered here.

Tomorrow.

Tomorrow he would figure out the next steps. He'd talk to Azlin. And Amadeo.

Now, though, he needed to sleep.

Head still buzzing with possibilities, he rose from the study table and left for his chambers.

SIXTEEN

The ruined city seemed unreal, the sort of place inhabited only in dreams—a grandiose landscape of form and function that had been forgotten and passed over so the buildings were now nothing more than strange irregular shapes that were slowly being reclaimed by the world from which their building blocks had been hewn.

Cohmac wandered through it slowly, marveling at the sight. He was walking in the footsteps of the ancients, and he felt a kind of reverence for all that had passed, all the people who had once lived their lives on these very streets. He hoped they would trust him with their secrets.

Ahead of him, the leaning tower he'd spotted earlier had churned the loam and cobbles around its foundations as it toppled, but the thick snaking roots of several nearby trees had unwittingly ensnared it during centuries of growth, effectively pinioning it in place, forever freezing the structure on the precipice of its own destruction. To Cohmac, it was another tableau derived straight from legend—the sort of thing he read about in the myths and fables of the Jedi Archives. A fragment of beautiful architecture saved from destruction by benevolent trees.

He stood in the shadows at the tower's base, gazing up at the seemingly impossible structure.

Several stories had sheared away, leaving a ragged lip of dressed stone, but the lower levels appeared surprisingly intact, despite the alarming angle at which they now stood.

The upper half of the tower hung almost entirely over the edge of the chasm, while the bottom was partially buried where it had pressed into the subsiding ground.

Another part of the original structure, a small squat chamber or hall that had previously been attached to the tower, was partially collapsed, its remaining walls standing at obtuse angles and its roof only moderately intact. Another tower, perhaps mirroring the first, had clearly stood on the far side of that hall-like structure, too, but was now entirely gone, marked only by the circular remains of its foundations and the handful of scattered stones that had once formed its walls.

A part of him wished Reath were there to witness it all with him. But that was just another echo of his old life, like the memories of Orla and Master Simmix that had been filling his thoughts these past few days.

Cohmac entered the base of the crooked tower, ducking his

head beneath the skewed lintel and through the twisted door frame.

Inside, the effect of the tower's bizarre lean was even more alarming. Cohmac found himself walking on the tilted wall, with the floor rising at a sharp angle to his right.

It had once been covered by an elaborate geometric mosaic that had shattered, spilling black, gold, and white tiles everywhere like so many discarded teeth. It smelled of damp leaves and rot. Vines had colonized the stonework, and mulch had seeped in through the gaps in the brickwork, forming a stinking layer that squelched beneath Cohmac's boots.

The tower appeared not to be divided into separate rooms, or if it once had been, the internal structure had long since collapsed. What Cohmac had first mistaken for separate stories was just a series of concentric decorative rings, and the tower inside was completely hollow, with a single flight of spiraling steps looping around the inner edge as they climbed toward the open sky.

The stones were bare and lacked decoration, although he could see where flakes of plaster still clung resolutely in forlorn patches, presumably once having covered the walls throughout. There was nothing that might constitute a record or a wall painting that could serve his purpose.

He decided to try the other building.

Cohmac climbed out the other side of the tower, clambering through the ragged hole where it had once been adjoined to the hall. Here, the undergrowth had grown thick in the gap between the two structures, and with no lightsaber to cut a path, Cohmac had to rely on his hands, parting the long grass and avoiding the thorny bushes that had made the place their home. He scrambled through it, tumbling awkwardly through the hole on the other side.

"You're getting old, Cohmac," he muttered to himself as he got to his feet, dusting himself down. He took in the interior of the old hall.

The light was thin, streaming in through the gaping holes in the ceiling in wide shafts. The walls bowed outward, huge cracks running through the stonework like a network of veins and arteries. It looked as if it might collapse in on itself at any moment, might come down on his head if he so much as breathed in the wrong direction.

He looked up and for a moment was taken aback by the stark beauty of what he saw.

"Oh, my . . ."

Where parts of the vaulted ceiling remained, he could see that it had once been brightly decorated in swirling patterns of midnight blue and lustrous gold. At first, he took it to be nothing but the remnants of some ostentatious furnishing, but after a moment of peering up at it, he realized that the broken image described a massive partial map. A star map. The faded swirls of blue and gold denoted different star systems, their names written in an indecipherable language on small plaques beside their primary stars. Some of the planets were similarly labeled, too.

It was countless millennia old, perhaps even older than the Republic itself.

Cohmac felt breathless. This was what he'd come here to find. The people who'd built the city on Thall had lived around the same time as the Tolemites, and his research suggested the two cultures had traded goods and shared ideas.

If the map could show him the way to the Tolemites' homeworld . . . well, he'd have a lot of thinking to do.

He half turned, as if sensing a presence beside him, but there was no one there. Of course there wasn't.

"Stop looking over my shoulder, Orla," he said, his voice echoing around the empty hall. He knew she wasn't really there, that there was no way she *could* be there, but it was reassuring to imagine all the same. "Now, let's take a proper look at this map."

Craning his neck, Cohmac circled the structure, searching the map for any markings or constellations he might recognize, any sign that would help him figure out how to read the ancient chart.

Much of the ceiling—and thus the map—had been destroyed by the quake that had opened the chasm outside. Hunks of stone were missing, and where the rain and damp had been able to get inside, the old paint surface had become blistered and mildewed, or had flaked away completely. Cohmac reckoned that at least half of it was gone. He only hoped that the information he was looking for was still there—assuming it ever had been.

Out of context, though, the chart simply wasn't making sense. It was like looking at a series of scattered dots with no discernible meaning. He knew it was a map, that the planets and stars depicted bore a relation to one another and the planetary bodies the Thall knew and had visited—but he could find no way of locating a starting point, not with the chart so damaged by age and dilapidation. If he could find Thall, he'd be able to work from there, but if the map had ever shown it, it didn't seem to now.

Still, there was one thing left to try.

Cohmac closed his eyes, centering himself.

He might no longer have been a Jedi, but he still knew how to use the Force. He reached out his hand, extending his index finger, calling on the Force to guide him.

He took a step. Two. Three. His finger wavered.

Cohmac opened his eyes and followed the line of his pointing finger. He peered up at the peeling map, at a small globe painted in gold. The letters carefully inscribed beside it made no sense to him. But he knew what it was, with a surety that, these days, he felt about very little else.

Tolis.

The homeworld of the Tolemites.

He'd found it.

Heart thudding, Cohmac wheeled on the spot, trying to make sense of the surrounding network of planets and stars. They were all unfamiliar.

He cursed. With access to the Jedi Archives he'd be able to cross-reference the chart against all the other ancient maps, along with the more recent navigational charts, transposing the star systems and, accounting for time and error, pinpointing the exact coordinates of Tolis. Without them, though, he was as lost as he had been before.

He chewed on his lower lip.

This was what the memories were about. Orla and Master

Simmix, urging him to make that leap of faith, to jump the canyon and face his fears.

But Cohmac wasn't ready for that just yet. How could he be? The thought of going back to the Jedi, not as one of them but as an outsider, of facing Reath . . .

It was too soon.

And yet, how could he not if he was able to help? How could he sit on information that could make a difference in the fight against the Nameless, could draw a line under what had happened to Orla and the others?

Frustrated and feeling more alone than ever, Cohmac slung his pack off his back and began searching inside it for his datapad.

He didn't have to think about the implications yet. His work here wasn't finished. He needed to make a comprehensive record of what he'd found, a copy of the chart that could be cross-referenced later. That was the priority. He'd see to that and then make camp for the night.

In the morning, he would decide what to do.

SEVENTEEN

"How many more errands are we going to run for the Jedi, Little Bit?"

Leox was sitting opposite Affie in the gleaming booth of an old-fashioned diner in CoCo Town, in one of Coruscant's industrial zones, swigging from a steaming cup of Jawa Juice.

The place was busy, with a mix of beings from any number of species lining the long bar or crammed into the overflowing booths. The rich aromas of stew and eggs and cooking meats drifted from the kitchen, causing Affie's stomach to rumble.

She looked up to try to catch the eye of one of the sparkly server droids who were scooting on wheels across the black-and-white-checkered floor, but they were both busy with other customers.

They'd left Geode back at the docks, presumably tinkering with the ship's engines. Affie was beginning to worry he'd become a little obsessed, although she knew eateries like this weren't really his thing. She hoped he'd make the most of being back on Coruscant, though, and at least check out the nightlife like he usually did. He was too young to put his partying days behind him.

"Affie? You still with me?"

Affie looked over at Leox and shrugged. "Sorry. Was thinking about my belly." She took a sip from her glass of fruit juice. "Why does it matter how many more missions we run with the Jedi? They pay, don't they?"

Leox took another swig from his drink and then leaned back, drumming his fingertips on the tabletop. "That they do."

"And we're making a real difference," said Affie. "You know how much that means to me. Because of us, people's lives are better. Maybe only in a small way, but it *matters*. I know we could be making three times as many credits profiteering off the conflict—"

"More like *ten* times," interjected Leox with a smirk.

"But we make *plenty*," continued Affie. "And we're doing what's right. We're helping people. Isn't that reward enough?"

"You know it is," said Leox. "It's just—we don't *have* to do this, you know? We keep putting ourselves in harm's way. That Nihil raider on Oisin—it could have worked out very differently."

"And Starlight Beacon could have, too," said Affie. "Or the Amaxine station. Or any number of jobs we've done since. But they haven't. Because we're a team. We get it done, together, no matter the odds."

Leox eyed her over the brim of his drink. "All I'm saying is . . . you've done enough. It's okay to let the Jedi and the Republic take it from here. You've already shown what you're capable of, and you've already made a difference to so many people. It's okay for you to sit back a bit."

"I couldn't live with myself if we stopped now, Leox," she said. "I know I'm asking you to take a risk every time we accept a new mission. And I hate to think I'm putting you and Geode in danger if you don't want to be there."

"It's *you* I'm worried about, Affie," said Leox. "Geode and I can look after ourselves. But I couldn't bear to see you hurt. Those monsters the Nihil are using against the Jedi might not be quite so dangerous to us, but the Nihil themselves are."

"Have you ever thought those 'monsters' might be just as innocent as the Nihil's other victims? Creatures pushed into service as if they were tools, or blasters, or droids," said Affie. "It's the Nihil who are the *real* monsters here. Marchion Ro and his cronies are the ones who've put us all in danger. That's why it's so important to keep fighting back."

Leox placed his cup on the table and raised both his hands in surrender. "I hear you. And for what it's worth, I agree. *Someone* has to show the Nihil that they can't keep us down. If people don't make a stand, they'll win."

"But?"

"But, like I said, it doesn't always have to be us," he said.

Affie sighed and leaned back in the booth. "If you ever want out, Leox, you only have to say."

"Whoa there, Little Bit! Since when would I abandon you? Never. That's when." He leaned forward, his hands on the table. "But what sort of a friend would I be if I didn't at least ask the difficult questions from time to time? I just want you to know that you always have a choice. Just because you've chosen to walk down this path doesn't mean you have to stay on it. Hell, if that were the case I'd never have made it beyond my twentieth year."

Affie smiled. "So, you're still with me?"

"Of *course* I'm still with you!" said Leox, with an amused shake of his head. "You'd have to do a lot more than that to shake me off. We're a team. A *family*. I just want you to remember that you can choose a different route for us at any time, and you'll always have my backing, no matter what."

"Thanks, Leox," she said.

"You've got it, Little Bit."

"And the rest of the Byne Guild? Are you hearing rumblings of discontent?" she asked, a little hesitant.

Leox shrugged. "They wouldn't be the Byne Guild if they weren't complaining, but they trust you, Affie. You're a leader now. They'll do as you say, so long as the credits keep flowing and the risk isn't too high. You've gone and got them believing in the cause, which is a feat for the ages, if you ask me."

Affie laughed. "Yeah. If you'd told me to imagine that just a couple of years ago, I'd have thought you'd lost the plot."

Leox grinned, and any tension Affie had been feeling bled away. This really was what families did, wasn't it? Poked and challenged and checked in on each other. And Leox was right to ask the question, too. The mission to Oisin could have gone badly wrong, and she was putting them in danger every time they took on a mission for the Jedi. But she stood by everything she'd said. It was a risk she was happy to take. She was just glad Leox and Geode were there to take it with her.

"So, you've heard nothing from Master Byre and her Padawan yet?" said Leox.

"Not yet. But give them time. We don't know how bad the situation on Oisin really is. It may take them a while to figure out how best to help." She drained the last of her fruit juice. "Besides, if I was the betting sort, I'd say the Jedi will have another transport job for us before too long. I let them know we're available."

Leox nodded. He finished his Jawa Juice and dropped a few credits on the table. "In that case, we'd better be checking on Geode. I think he's got half a mind to start stripping the *Vessel* down to its constituent parts looking for this mysterious fault."

Affie rolled her eyes as she slid out of the booth. "Come on, then. Last one back's a nerf herder."

EIGHTEEN

Reath hadn't slept well.

His dreams had been plagued by thoughts of distant lands and ancient people, of a glorious vibrant culture, now lost. Of the Nameless rampaging through their streets, feasting, husking, leaving nothing but a trail of dust in their wake. And of the blight, welling up like a bubbling spring to consume everyone and everything in its path—pulsing like a black heart as it spread throughout the galaxy.

He knew these images to be no vision, no echo through the Force but merely the musings of his unconscious mind, still turning over the revelations he'd come to in the Archives. A mind trying to make sense of the horror those people must have faced, and the horrors the Jedi and the Republic now faced in turn.

Reath understood that history moved in cycles, like leviathan waves washing against the shores of time. He'd learned as much from his years of study. Civilizations rose and fell in constant rhythm. Mistakes were made and remade with mind-boggling regularity. That the Nameless and the blight had been encountered before—and beaten—should have been a comfort, a reminder that all things were possible.

And yet . . . *something* was unsettling him. Something wasn't quite right. He couldn't put his finger on what it was. He just had a feeling, like a low-level buzzing in the background of his mind—the notion that he was missing something, that a threat was lurking somewhere he couldn't see.

He would meditate on it later.

Maybe he was working too hard. Or perhaps he was just spending too much time with Azlin, down in the lower levels of the Temple.

And here he was again, come to knock on the fallen Jedi's door.

Talking to Azlin about his findings and theories and research was like a pressure release, the opening of a valve. It was a way of sharing the burden he felt to solve everything. The only other person who might have understood was Emerick Caphtor, and he was still out in the field, trapped on the Nihil side of the Occlusion Zone.

And maybe Master Cohmac, too. But he'd made his choice. He'd left the Order, and Reath. And while Amadeo had shared in his excitement, had been a big part of helping Reath see things from a different angle—it was really only Azlin who would *truly* understand.

Reath wished that weren't the case. But there it was. And if it had to be a part of his process, the way he got to where he needed to be, got clarity on his findings, then so be it.

He tried to shake off the cowl of uncertainty that had settled over him. He'd had a breakthrough—two, in fact, first with Amadeo in the laboratory and then last night in the Archives. He was getting close. Now he would see if Azlin could shed any further light on the history of the Tolemites, before going to find Amadeo. From there, he would take his findings to the Council, assuming Master Elzar had managed to arrange the meeting they'd spoken of.

Reath rounded the familiar bend in the passageway. The Temple Guard stood where he always did, just to the left of Azlin's door, with the same posture—favoring one leg over the other—the same adherence to Temple Guard doctrine.

Reath nodded at the guard as he passed and received the usual curt nod in reply.

He knocked on the door to Azlin's cell and entered.

Azlin was sitting cross-legged on his bunk, looking expectantly in the direction of the door. His hands were steepled under his chin, and he had a knowing smile on his paper-thin lips. He'd already lit his lamp, and as Reath entered the room, he gestured minutely at the single chair before the old wooden desk.

"I see you're finally ready to listen, my boy" said Azlin, his voice reedy and old.

Reath frowned as he lowered himself into the chair. "What do you mean? I always listen to you. You know I do."

Azlin smiled, that same disturbing thin smile. "You hear, but you don't *listen*. But something has changed. I sense it. You have questions."

Reath's mouth was dry. Could Azlin truly read his mood so accurately? Was he sensing Reath's disquiet? He moistened his lips. "Yes."

"Excellent," said Azlin. He turned his face toward Reath, tilting it slightly to one side. His long hair fell in greasy strands around his shoulders. "Proceed."

"What do you know about the Tolemites?" said Reath.

Azlin's smile broadened, revealing sickly-looking rows of teeth, deeply discolored by age and decay. "Ah. Interesting. I have heard of the Tolemites. You believe they have a bearing on your research, do you?"

"Perhaps," said Reath, his excitement mounting and quickly dispelling his reservations. If Azlin knew more, perhaps he could help fill in some of the gaps in Reath's research. "Tell me, what stories have you heard?"

Azlin nodded. "The Tolemites lived long ago, when the galaxy was still small and the Jedi were but a fledgling order, yet to tread its first true footsteps upon the wider stage. They were peaceful beings who worshipped the Force in all its aspects and understood the deep connection between all living things. As a people, they channeled the Force to achieve great things, straying neither too far toward the light, nor too close to the dark. They understood the need for balance in all things, and they took that message out to the galaxy around them."

Azlin moved, uncurling like a feline to cross the room. He took up the kettle and set it on the heating unit. Only once he had finished did he return to his perch and continue his tale. "Yet, like all such civilizations, they grew too arrogant, too confident in their own worth, and in their hubris, they brought about their own demise."

So far, aside from some embellishment, Azlin's tale followed the widely accepted story of the Tolemites, as Reath had found in the records. "Go on."

"The stories speak of a great plague that they brought down upon themselves, a scouring that spoiled their world and brought the people to their knees." Azlin raised a single eyebrow. "Ah, I see. You're equating the great plague of the Tolemites with the blight."

Reath shrugged. "Anything else?"

Azlin grinned slyly. "Yes. The Three Ancients of the Tolemites escaped the destruction of their civilization, along with a smattering of other survivors. They found a way to end the plague that had decimated their people and founded a new kingdom on an isolated island chain elsewhere on Tolis, vowing to preserve what remained of their culture."

Reath narrowed his eyes. This was new. "And where did you learn of this?"

Azlin cackled. "The Jedi are not the only sect to maintain a library. I have spent two lifetimes scouring the galaxy for any information that could lead me to my goal. That is what I have learned of the Tolemites. And while I applaud you for your diligence, Reath, I believe it is perhaps a leap too far to associate any mention of a plague with the appearance of the blight. After all, it might have been a simple pathogen they discovered on a neighboring world that devastated their culture so badly. Something for which they had no cure."

The kettle had begun to whistle. Reath walked over, seeing to the tea. "No. There's more to it than that. The Tolemites knew of the Nameless. An expedition brought them back to Tolis, along with other captive creatures. But they turned on their new masters and fed on them." He stirred the tea. "This was around the same time that the other expedition arrived home carrying the so-called plague."

Azlin's gnarled fingers seemed to dance on his lap. He was agitated, excited even. "Yes, Reath! Yes. This is a remarkable discovery. Another piece of the puzzle that clicks into place." He turned his empty eyes on Reath. "I am proud of you."

Reath wasn't entirely sure how he felt about hearing those words from Azlin but smiled all the same. He didn't—he *couldn't*—put too much stock in Azlin's opinions of him, but nevertheless, the recognition was welcome. No one had made him feel that way since Master Cohmac, and Master Jora before him, like he'd achieved something worthwhile just through his dogged determination to *understand*.

"What will you do now, hmm?" prompted Azlin.

"Find Tolis," said Reath. "And see what else we can learn. If the Tolemites defeated the blight and the Nameless, then surely we can, too."

Azlin's cackling laughter sent a chill shiver down Reath's spine. "If only it was that simple! Don't you think I've scoured the Outer Rim, searching for the ruins of the old ones? Tolis is lost. Gone. There are dozens of worlds it could be. And in the greatest of ironies, the Tolemites' new kingdom was destroyed by a flood." Azlin laughed again.

"Gone?" said Reath.

"Swallowed by the ocean, just like your Starlight Beacon."

Reath worked his jaw but didn't rise to the jibe. He turned and handed Azlin one of his herbal brews. He felt a little crestfallen. "Then why indulge me with the story? To tease me with false hope?"

"No. To *give* you hope. I may no longer be a Jedi, Reath, but I have not yet given up on hope. That you have come to the Tolemites yourself, through no interference by me, means you may have uncovered a different path to their story, a new or unrelated version of the tale passed down through the millennia by different hands. And in that tale, there may be clues to the location of Tolis that may yet bear fruit." Azlin sipped his tea, nodding slowly in satisfaction. "I have worked alone for many years. Now you have the resources of the Jedi Order to bring to bear on this puzzle. Solve it, and we may yet survive this trial intact. If anyone can do it, Reath, it is you."

Reath eased himself back into the chair. So that was it, then. "Thank you, Azlin," he said, his voice low.

"You're welcome." Azlin paused. "But that's not the real reason you came, is it, Reath?"

Reath eyed Azlin from across the room. "What do you mean?"

"As I explained, I sense the turbulence in you."

Reath shook his head. "It's nothing. It's just . . . I sense something unsettling. A disturbance. And I'm unsure what it could be." He sighed. "I'm probably just tired. Too many old stories running around in my head."

"No, Reath. This is exactly as it should be. For the first time, you've come to understand that the galaxy isn't as small as you thought it was. The old tales have shown you that there are *possibilities* out there. Different perspectives."

Reath bristled. What was Azlin trying to do? Urge him to stray from the Jedi path? "I don't want to walk the same path as you." Reath had studied the accounts of all the Jedi who had encountered the Nameless, and while each of them had suffered great torment at the hands of the creatures, *none* of them, save for Azlin, had chosen to walk the path of the dark side.

Reath felt a certain degree of empathy for Azlin and what he had been through, back when he had come face to face with the creatures on Dalna, and for the hardship of the life he had led, well beyond the natural lifespan of any human. He could hardly fathom what it must be like to find oneself trapped inside a decaying shell, twisted by fear and bitterness, slowly consumed by obsession and loneliness.

But none of that served in any way to justify the twisted morality of the fallen Jedi, or the horrors he had committed on his quest to defeat the Nameless.

"My choices are my own," said Azlin. "As is the path I walk. As you have so ably pointed out, I am not your master. I could never be. But if I were . . ." His tone was almost regretful, as if he really did wish that he'd had the opportunity to teach Reath, to help him as his other masters had done. "If I were, I would urge you only to remain true to yourself. To walk your own path. The only thing that is important, Reath, is that you *open your mind*. If there's one thing that I've learned, in all my sorry years, it's that things that are rigid are prone to break. And the Jedi Order becomes more rigid with every passing day. I say this not to tempt you, not to convince you of anything, not to try to win you over or color your thinking. Only to encourage you to see the bigger picture." Azlin had grown more animated than Reath had ever seen him, abandoning his usual considered delivery for an intensity that Reath could never have imagined from the man.

"I thought you cared about the Jedi Order. I thought you wanted to save it, too," said Reath. He felt confused. What was Azlin trying to tell him?

"I do," countered Azlin. "I will see the Nameless defeated before I can rest. And yet, don't you see? If we save the Jedi and leave the rest of the galaxy to burn, what will we have left to protect, to guide, to share in? Nothing but ashes. The Jedi are *scared*, Reath. They've retreated here to Coruscant, and while they talk and talk about what they're going to do to save us all from the blight and the Nameless, the Path—or the Nihil, as you prefer to call them—continue to rampage and the blight continues to spread."

"No. That's not true. We're out there, helping people," said Reath.

"Doing what the Jedi always do," said Azlin. "But this isn't an enemy that can be reasoned with or frightened off with a show of lightsabers. This is something much more fundamental. Something that represents everything that we are not. A threat so existential that we cannot even conceive of how it might have arisen. And meanwhile, we're not even aware of the creeping danger in our own midst." He shifted back on his bunk, returning to the same cross-legged position he'd adopted when Reath first arrived.

"What do you mean?"

"You already sense it, Reath. Stirring in the depths." Azlin sipped his tea. "It's coming for us."

"I don't understand," said Reath, getting to his feet.

"Yes, you do," said Azlin. "You just don't want to admit it. Free your mind, Reath. Allow it to roam. You'll find your truths and certainties. And you will know what to do. I believe in you."

Reath had to get out of there. He needed to clear his head. Azlin had filled in another small piece of the Tolemites' story. But Reath couldn't stand any more of his games—not right now, when he had so much riding on this. "Goodbye, Azlin." He crossed to the door.

Azlin cocked his head, as if listening to something only he could hear. "If you cannot heed my words, Reath, heed your own feelings. Trust in yourself. You already know what to do."

NINETEEN

"Now, Amadeo!"

Huffing with exertion, Amadeo ran and then leapt. He sprang into the air, using the Force to push himself high, spinning his lightsaber around his head and shoulders in an arc as if fending off imaginary blaster shots.

His left foot landed in Master Lox's outstretched palm, and then Master Lox was shoving him up and forward and Amadeo was soaring higher still, twisting in the air before curling into a forward roll as he began his descent, his lightsaber describing a wheel on his right side.

Beneath and behind him, Master Lox was spinning his own lightsaber in a defensive arc as he covered Amadeo's blind spot.

Amadeo came down hard on the other side of the training

room and tried to maintain his balance, but the landing was just a little off and his foot slid on the mat, causing him to over-balance and drop to one knee.

He shook his head, turning off his lightsaber. He remained on the ground for a moment, trying to catch his breath.

He'd almost had it, right until that landing. But that wasn't good enough. This was a move designed to deliver him right into the midst of his opponent's troops so he could come down fighting and keep them occupied while Master Lox closed in from behind.

If he'd stumbled like that for real, surrounded by Nihil, he'd probably already be dead. He felt a spike of frustration but pushed it aside. He flexed his neck and shoulder muscles.

Master Lox bounded over, extending a hand and hauling Amadeo back up to his feet. "That was a good one!" he said, grinning so broadly Amadeo could see his gleaming white teeth. "You got *really* high."

Amadeo shrugged. "But messed up the landing. If that was for real . . ."

Master Lox made a dismissive gesture. "But it wasn't for real. And that's why we practice, isn't it?"

"Well, yes," said Amadeo. He couldn't argue with his master's logic, or his enthusiasm.

"Just remember—we'll never get it right if we don't get it wrong a few times first," said Master Lox.

"*I'll* never get it right, you mean," said Amadeo. But he was smiling, too. He straightened his robes.

"No. *We*," said Master Lox. He mirrored the motion he'd made when he'd flung Amadeo higher into the air. "I'm imparting a little too much spin on the push. It's throwing your landing off."

"Okay," said Amadeo. "Let's try again. We can get this."

"That's the spirit, Padawan!" said Lox. He clapped Amadeo on the shoulder. "We're developing quite the arsenal."

"We make a good team," said Amadeo, glowing. He knew every Jedi Master was different and approached the teaching of a Padawan learner in their own distinct way, but he was pleased Master Lox wasn't one of the staid and reserved types who seemed to assign their Padawans tasks and then stand back until they were done. Master Lox had always been one to roll up his sleeves and join in with the tasks—leading by example, and enjoying himself in the process.

He was pretty sure most masters didn't fling their Padawans around in such an acrobatic fashion, for a start. But what Amadeo loved most about the process was not that it was honing his skills or that many of the maneuvers they'd developed had already proved useful in the field, but that they were doing it *together*.

"Ready?"

"Always," said Amadeo.

"Then go!"

Amadeo ran. And he leapt.

He closed his eyes, feeling his way through the Force, allowing his body to flow through the air. His foot hit Master Lox's palm. He felt the upward pressure and went with it, eyes still closed, twisting in the air, whirling his lightsaber. He curled, falling easily into the roll.

And then he was on the ground, feet planted firmly on the mat, lightsaber held at the ready.

He opened his eyes.

Master Lox was watching him from the other side of the training room. He clapped his hands. "Yes! Best one yet! I think we've got it! Do you see how far you jumped?"

Amadeo nodded, laughing. "And no spin on the push."

"Like you said, we make a good team, Padawan." He stretched. "You want to go again? Or try something different? I think the throw we did on Cethis could use a little refinement. And it must be your turn to throw me around for a while, eh?"

Amadeo was just about to agree when he sensed movement and turned to see a familiar figure standing just inside the doorway.

"Reath!" he called. He wiped sweat from his eyes. "I didn't see you there."

Reath nodded in acknowledgment. "I didn't mean to intrude. I just came by to fill you in on some new developments and saw . . . Well, I'm not sure what to call it, exactly, but it was an impressive show." He looked genuinely taken aback.

Master Lox chuckled loudly. "Good, wasn't it! Just one of the new moves we've been working on together," he said, slipping his lightsaber hilt into its holster and crossing to where Reath was standing. He winked at Reath. "You never know when they might come in handy."

"I can imagine," said Reath. "I've heard a lot about your recent missions."

Master Lox shot Amadeo a glance. "I bet he's not telling you the full story, either. Did he tell you how he tossed me across a forest clearing to stop a massive lizard from attacking a group of villagers the other day?"

Reath looked at Amadeo, impressed. "He didn't. But to be fair to Amadeo, he's been so busy helping me with my research into the Nameless and the blight that he's barely had a chance."

Master Lox nodded. "It's good work you're doing, Reath." He grabbed a carafe of water and poured himself and Amadeo each a glass. "Both of you. Amadeo told me about your theories. I have a feeling your work is going to make a real difference."

"Thank you, Master Lox," said Reath. "And honestly, it was Amadeo's insights that helped set me on the right path."

"Alongside all the research you've spent the last year doing," said Amadeo. He grinned. "Another good team."

Reath smiled. "Well, I can see that you're busy. Perhaps we can talk when you're finished here, Amadeo?"

Amadeo glanced at Master Lox, noticing the familiar indulgent expression. "It's okay. We can take a moment to rest. What have you found? Have you spoken to the Council?"

"Not yet," said Reath. "Master Elzar has arranged for me to attend a meeting later today. But I did find something in the Archives that seems to support our theory."

Amadeo sipped his water. He lowered himself onto a bench that ran along the inside wall of the training room. "Something that connects the Nameless and the blight?"

"Oh, I want to hear this," said Master Lox. "I love a good history lesson. I heard the legends of the Nameless as a youngling. I can hardly believe the old nursery rhyme is turning out to be real."

"Well, the stories are fragmentary at best. More legend than history, really," said Reath. "But I think we might be onto something." He explained his findings about the Tolemites and his theory regarding the two expeditions.

"That's incredible!" said Amadeo when he'd finished. "It fits perfectly with what we were thinking. And it explains the evidence we found in the lab."

Reath laughed. "It does. But we have to be careful not to jump to conclusions. Just because it fits doesn't *necessarily* mean it's right. But it's the best lead we have right now. If we can learn more about how the Tolemites defeated their plague and dealt with the Nameless, it might help us figure out a plan."

"Have you told anyone else about this yet, Reath?" asked Master Lox.

"Only Azlin Rell, although I'm planning to discuss it with the Council at the meeting," said Reath.

A dark expression crossed Master Lox's face. "Azlin? The fallen one?"

Reath frowned, then nodded. "Yes. I wanted to see if he'd come across the Tolemites in his own research. Whether he could add anything useful to my understanding."

"And did he?" asked Master Lox.

Amadeo watched the exchange with interest. Master Lox seemed . . . concerned.

"A little," said Reath. "He'd heard of the Tolemites. He knew of the old legends about the plague. And he had a slightly different version of the story in which the Three Ancients who governed the Tolemites had survived the plague and set up a new kingdom on an island. But he'd never heard about the second expedition and the Nameless."

Master Lox nodded. "And he'd never thought to mention these Tolemites before?"

Reath looked at him quizzically. "He probably didn't think they were relevant. He didn't know about the connection to the Nameless."

Master Lox nodded. "Of course." He seemed to contemplate his next words carefully before he spoke them. "I hate to think what that poor man went through, the nightmares he had to endure. But, Reath—remember, he *cannot* be trusted. He's had over a century to fester in bitterness and fear. His obsession with the Nameless has chewed him up from the inside out. He is not your friend or ally, despite what help he offers or proclaims to know."

Reath bristled, as if he were about to come to Azlin's defense, but then he seemed to change his mind. He sighed. "I know. It's just—I cannot leave any stone unturned. If Azlin can help us figure out how to defeat the Nameless, then I have to listen. I have to take it into account. Nothing is more important than that. Nothing."

Master Lox nodded. "If you ever need anything, Reath—if you ever need to talk, as a friend—you can count on me."

Amadeo saw the impact this had on Reath, the softening around his eyes, the slight dip of his shoulders. Just to have someone—an older, more experienced Jedi Master—reach out to him, to offer to be there for him. It was a lot.

They all knew what he'd been through when Master Cohmac left the Order, how he'd been knighted at such a young age. Not that Amadeo doubted Reath at all. He was clearly one of the most astute and committed Jedi Amadeo knew. But to have his master walk away like that, the person who had taught him, whom he'd come to rely on most of all . . . it must have been *hard*. Amadeo didn't know what he'd do without Master Lox.

But now the master he trusted above all else was extending a hand to Reath, and seeing how even such a small gesture had affected his friend brought a broad smile to Amadeo's face.

Reath turned to Amadeo. "I'll let you know when I hear more from Master Elzar or the Council. And you can find me in the laboratory or the Archives if you find yourself with more time on your hands. I . . . well, I appreciate your help."

"Of course!" said Amadeo. "I'll come find you."

"Great. Thanks. Both of you. I'll leave you to your training." Reath smiled and then turned and left.

Amadeo placed his empty glass on the bench. "So—are we going to try that other move, Master?"

But Master Lox was still watching the door. "It's good you're spending time with Reath, Amadeo," he said, his tone bright but serious. "I think, together, we should try to be there for him when we can."

"You're worried about the influence of Azlin Rell?" asked Amadeo.

Master Lox shook his head. "I'm more worried about the pressure that young man is under. He's carrying the weight of the entire Order on his shoulders. He needs good friends around him."

Amadeo beamed. "Well, that's something we can definitely do!"

Master Lox turned, grinning. "Yes, Padawan. It certainly is." He reached for his lightsaber. "Now, where were we?"

TWENTY

It had taken Sicarus a long time to get used to killing.

The people to whom he had belonged before, the *Brotherhood of the Ninth Door*, had learned to embrace the dark side of the Force, had freed themselves from the shackles of morality—but Sicarus had always failed to take the inevitable step. He had always stayed his hand. Had shown mercy.

It was a mistake. Sicarus could see that now. Father had shown him how to fulfill his potential.

"A better path," he said in his soft, whispering tones. "A *much* better one."

He was sitting on a rocky outcrop on the planet Thall, close to where he'd set down his shuttle on the scree-covered slope of a mountain. Pondering. Thinking. Remembering.

Idly, he wondered what old Carticus, his gnarly-fingered ancient tutor, would have made of him. Surely, Carticus would be shocked at how far the young man had come. Surely, he'd be envious of Sicarus's power. Of his freedom.

The stuttering memories of his old life made Sicarus feel fuzzy and unsettled. He twitched violently from his head right down to his toes. He wasn't supposed to be thinking these things. The injections were supposed to make them go away.

"Why are you still here?" Sicarus asked aloud of the memories crowding his skull. "Why won't you be forgotten like good little children? Go, go, go away and hide. Curl up in the darkness and die, just like the old Jedi did when I finished pulling their organs out."

He hadn't thought of the old Jedi for a while. Oh, how the birdlike Fosh had wailed as he plucked and picked and poked and played.

But why, when he thought of them, did he feel so strange? Untethered and unwound, like a ribbon in the wind. Like it had all happened to someone else, in some strange bedtime story, somewhere on the other side of the galaxy.

He slapped the side of his head with the heel of his right hand.

Images of Carticus swelled in his mind, but when he examined them more closely, all he could see was Father staring back at him.

As it should be. Those beady black eyes brimming with affection.

Peace. That was what he felt when he saw that face.

"Peace. Yes!"

But it wasn't *real* peace, was it?

He would never have real peace, not in the same way others did. The lucky ones. The Jedi.

That was what no one understood. No one except him, and Father, and Father's other Children. That the only real peace in this galaxy was the sweet relief Father's creatures delivered to the Jedi. The peace of obliteration. Of nonexistence. Complete and utter oblivion. That was what Sicarus was doing. What they were all doing. They were setting the Jedi free. And it was *delicious*.

Now he had a taste for it. Yes, yes he did. It had been hard at first. Messy. But just like Father had explained, you could get good at anything with enough practice. And, oh, he'd practiced.

He'd practiced *so hard*.

He felt a warm glow at the center of his being as he recalled their faces. The ones he'd done for. The *hunted*. All nine of them.

It was a gallery of precious images. And it was *his* and his alone. It was his privilege. The honor bestowed on him for all his hard work.

To be the last person to see them alive.

It was the final look that always made it special. When the lights dimmed in their eyes and their bodies went still. When the Force seeped out of their empty shells and the essence of who or what they were was dissipated. When those same empty shells collapsed on themselves, nothing but husks of dust and ruin.

Oh, how he loved that moment.

He'd been tempted to kill the one in the pen on the ship, too. The woman. She'd mewled and cried and cowered against the bars when he'd brought the Nameless close. Just like her young friend, the Padawan, the Zeltron. Sicarus had enjoyed the look on his face, too. Had marveled at how his red flesh had turned pale and ashen as it was husked, just like all the others.

But he knew he needed the woman. She was a gift for Father. A test subject for his experiments. And there were plenty more where she had come from.

Like the one he was hunting now, on Thall. One who always seemed to slip from his grasp. But not this time. No, no, no. Not today.

Nearby, one of the Nameless growled. There were three of them, currently lounging on the slope of the mountain, restless and hungry. One of the strange creatures was young and had two extra limbs grafted to its shoulders, each ending in vicious obsidian talons. He wasn't exactly certain what donor Father had used for the new arms, but they looked vaguely human in appearance, all pink and scarred. The limbs would twitch occasionally, seemingly of their own accord, and mostly hung limp as the creature went about its business. But Sicarus had seen the creature use them once to pin a victim to the wall as it fed. It was glorious.

One of the others was bluish-white and had an elaborate metal contraption fitted to its head, bigger than the skullcaps on the other two, while the third was an older beast and had begun to manifest signs of transformation. Sicarus didn't quite understand what caused these changes to occur in the older creatures, but this one appeared to be growing more feral, more desperate, less able to eke out the sustenance of its previous meal. It looked emaciated, and its once bright flesh had started to become translucent so that Sicarus could see the dark blood rippling through its veins. The same blood that passed through his veins, too.

"Blood brothers," said Sicarus, giggling. It was why the

presence of the creatures didn't affect him, like it did the Jedi, despite his relationship to the Force. They recognized their blood. They'd accepted him as one of their own.

A Force Eater. A *Shrii Ka Rai*.

A hunter.

The youngest creature growled again. It was a sound that seemed to grate against Sicarus's very soul, calling to him on a primal level. It wanted to run free, to hunt. But it was too soon.

"Not yet, not yet."

He yanked the creature's chain sharply, and it snarled before pacing a few steps away and crouching by a large rock. It raised its head, and the nest of proboscises that formed its mouth wriggled in the air as if tasting something on the breeze.

"Impaaatient," he said, drawing out the second syllable. He laughed raucously at his own joke. It was clever because the creature had been one of Father's surgical test subjects. A patient.

Sicarus didn't stop laughing for over a minute.

Afterward, he sat for a while, waiting. He knew it would come. The moment he was waiting for. The insight. The gift.

And he was right.

His left eye blinked. The world beyond the confines of his head seemed to bloom. He could *sense* things. *Smell* things.

His pulse quickened.

It was the blood. The special blood, coursing through his veins. It made his body *sing*.

There was pain, yes. But it was exquisite pain. The sort of pain that made him feel alive. Like his whole body was lit up from within.

And being on the hunt, like he was now—there was no better

feeling. Nothing. Only the hunt could give him what he needed.

It was the anticipation. The chase. The cornering of the prey. The moment before the strike.

And then it was their death.

He threw his head back, just like the Nameless, immersing himself in his heightened senses.

This was what it must be like to truly be one of *them*. To feel the Force in a way he'd never felt it before. Like he could almost *taste* it, like its very presence was enough to sustain him, to enrich him, to make him something better and stronger.

"We'll feed soon," he said, watching the creatures closely for any sign they might have understood his words, or at least his meaning.

But the Nameless did little more than flick him a disinterested glance and then look away, turning their attention to the east.

Like a creature in their pack, Sicarus followed suit, turning toward the globe of the distant sun. It was thin and watery, like a dying giant, ready to bloat at any moment. He lowered his eyes to the slopes of another nearby mountain, about twenty kilometers away. The site of some ancient ruins.

The Force user's presence was like a white-hot pain in his mind, a cauterizing tool pushed against the inside of his skull. He grinned, his secret only-for-him grin.

"*There* he is," said Sicarus to no one in particular, but mostly for the benefit of the two creatures, just in case they were listening.

They'd found the Force user they'd come here to hunt. And soon Sicarus and his two pets were going to kill him and revel in setting him free.

TWENTY-ONE

Thirty Years Earlier

"**M**aster Simmix says it's all in my head," said Cohmac.

Orla gave him a sideways glance. "He said that?"

"Not in so many words," admitted Cohmac. "But that was the sentiment all the same. He told me I'd come to believe more in my failure than my success. That the leap over the canyon had become a leap of faith."

Orla nodded. "Like I said, it's not the canyon you're trying to jump." There was no scorn in her voice, no satisfaction that she'd been right—just simple acknowledgment and understanding, coupled with evident concern for her friend.

They were sitting on a rocky outcropping at the top of a small hill, just outside the perimeter of the camp. From up here, Cohmac could see for kilometers in all directions, from the glittering white stone buildings of the settlement to the amber glow of the desert wastes. He shielded his eyes against the glare of the sun. The canyon was like a black scar running across the landscape.

"So, the canyon is symbolic," he said. "I'm projecting my psychological issues onto a physical obstacle." He'd lain awake most of the previous night trying to make sense of it all. "But I still don't really understand what that *means*, or how to overcome it. Why didn't Master Simmix tell me what to do?"

"Are you so sure that he didn't?" said Orla.

"I . . . don't know." He hung his head. "What's the matter with me, Orla? Why now? Why all this sudden doubt? I mean, everything's going so well. My training. The missions. It's not like anything has changed."

"Yes, it has."

"What?" He was obviously missing something. "What's changed?"

"*You* have," said Orla. "You're the one who's changed. We both have. We're not younglings anymore. We've seen the galaxy for what it is. We've seen what people do to one another." Orla reached over and squeezed his arm. "But we've also seen how important our work is. How we can make a difference." She released her grip on his arm. "And it's a lot. A huge responsibility. And it affects us all in different ways."

"How did you get so wise?" said Cohmac.

Orla gave him a shrewd look. "By asking so many awkward questions," she said. "And getting answers I didn't like but had to live with regardless."

Cohmac smiled. "I see."

"You can do this, Cohmac," she said. "You know you can."

"You seem so sure of that," he replied. "But how can I be *certain*?"

"You can't. Maybe you can fix the probabilities in your favor. You can train and calculate and work out all the odds. But you can never be *certain*, Cohmac. That's just life. Even for a Jedi. All we can do is choose a path and keep on walking down it. Because it's better to have faith in *something* than *nothing*." Orla stood, stretching her back and shoulders. "Nothing in this galaxy is ever perfect. Not everything will go the way you, me, or anyone will want it to. That's what makes it so exciting."

"You're right," said Cohmac. "I know you're right."

"And you know what will happen if you don't make the jump?" said Orla.

"What?"

"I'll catch you. Because you're not in this alone. You're a *Jedi*, Cohmac. And you know what that means, more than anything?"

"I have a feeling you're going to tell me. . . ."

"It means you *never* have to be alone. None of us do. Things won't always go right. But when they *do* go wrong, at least we'll have each other. That's what you need to remember. That's why it's worth taking the risks, even when you can't be certain, when they seem like they're ranged against you. Because we're stronger together. We always are and we always will be. Together we can protect the galaxy. And each other."

Cohmac got to his feet beside her. "Thank you, Orla," he said.

He looked to the horizon, where the canyon wound like a black river. "I think I'm ready now."

He reached for the Force, and it answered as he propelled himself across the gaping canyon, arms flung out from his sides. The cool wind whipped his face, causing his robes to flutter around him like billowing wings. He felt glorious, happy, content. Beneath him, the world dropped away, but it was as nothing to him, a Jedi, at one with himself and the universe around him. Supported and encouraged. A part of something greater than himself. Stronger because he was with Orla, because he wasn't alone.

And then he was down and running without missing a beat, as simple as that. As it had always been. As if he'd never once doubted himself.

Beside him, Orla was running, too, laughing and hooting as she charged on, a huge grin on her face.

Now

Cohmac groaned as he stirred awake.

The memories of Orla and Master Simmix lingered, strikingly vivid. Episodes of another life, another time—from before everything went wrong.

He sat up, shedding his blanket, and was still for a moment, arms resting on his knees as he stared into the silent morning. He could just see a hint of a hazy dawn breaking outside, light sprinkling on the ruins beyond the door.

He sighed.

There was no escaping it.

He had to go back to Coruscant. To face the Jedi. To share what he'd discovered with his former Padawan, Reath, and with the Council.

His lack of faith in himself was getting in his way, preventing him from doing what he knew to be right. He might no longer *be* a Jedi, but that didn't mean he didn't care, that he'd be able live with himself if he didn't do something to help when he could.

That was why his subconscious was dredging up these old memories, why it was forcing him to relive the lessons of the past. Because they were lessons that were still relevant all these years later.

He needed to leap the canyon, to stop holding himself back.

He was in a position to help. He didn't need to be a Jedi to do that. He shouldn't have to be.

This was just another risk he had to take.

For Orla, and for all the others who'd died.

For Reath, and for all those still alive.

And for himself, because he knew he wouldn't be able to live with himself if he didn't act.

He stood, shaking off the last vestiges of sleep, and packed up his small camp. He'd slept in the remains of the old hall, under the canopy of the star map. Now it was looking down on him, willing him to share its secrets.

He'd retrace his steps back to the *Excavator* and set a course for Coruscant. He only hoped the Council would still be willing to listen. And Reath. He had no idea how Reath would receive him.

No, that was wrong. He was fooling himself again.

He knew that he'd hurt Reath by leaving the way he did, and that was something they were going to have to work through, if Reath was even willing to see him.

He supposed he'd know soon enough. He was done running. It didn't mean he was ready to rejoin the Order, or bury his feelings, or anything of the sort—just that he knew there were people who needed him, and he had information that might be able to help.

With a grunt, Cohmac hauled his pack up onto his shoulders and ducked out of the ruined hall. He stood on the threshold, breathing in the cool scent of the morning dew, the clean air, the . . .

He hesitated, putting a hand to his head, pinching his brow. What *was* that?

A strange disturbing sensation, welling up inside him.

He felt his heart kicking in his chest, felt prickles of sweat beading on the back of his neck.

A metallic tang flooded his mouth.

He was *shaking*.

He was . . .

Cohmac screamed.

The sound erupted from his lungs, raw in his throat, but it was born from somewhere deeper inside of him, somewhere primal and instinctive.

He turned wildly on the spot, searching his surroundings, filled with a sudden flood of . . .

Fear.

They were here. They'd found him.

The Jedi hunter.

The *Nameless.*

Cohmac clutched at his throat, willing himself to draw breath. The bone-deep terror threatened to paralyze him.

He took a staggering step backward.

He panted in wild fear.

He didn't know what to do.

Except flee.

He had to flee.

Before they got too close. Before they reached him. By then, it would be far too late.

He lurched into motion, his thoughts clouded and uncertain.

He had to get back to his ship, and he was running the wrong way, scrambling over low walls, crashing through the under-growth. But the Nameless were coming from the other direction. To try to get to his ship that way was certain death.

He moaned. He was going to die. Right here on Thall. The creatures were going to feast on him like they'd feasted on so many others.

On his friends.

On Orla.

Cohmac wailed, a sound so pitiful that he could barely acknowledge it had passed through his own lips.

He'd left it too late.

He'd failed *again*.

The Nameless were here, and they were coming for him, and now he wouldn't be able to tell the Jedi what he'd found.

But he could still try.

He could still flee.

Cohmac ran for all he was worth. He felt the effect of the creatures weaken as he ran, but it was still there, like a buzzing inside his head, an ever-present latent sense of primal fear that threatened to erupt into full-blown panic at any moment.

He'd never known fear like it.

He was struggling to make sense of his jumbled thoughts. All he knew was that he had to run, had to find a way to his ship.

He had to get his news back to Coruscant.

Cohmac's thigh muscles ached as his boots pounded the hard ground. For the first time since leaving the Order, he wished he had his lightsaber, although he knew it would do him little good against these particular foes.

These monsters from the depths of his worst nightmares.

He slowed as he entered a large open plaza. Here, the ground had ruptured as tenacious plant life had pushed its way up through the cracks between the stones, creating a maze of broken columns and unchecked shrubbery.

In the near distance, something issued a raw piercing shriek, a sound so wretched that it caused Cohmac to stagger, almost losing his footing on the loose stones. He tried to right himself, but the creature screeched again, and he dropped to his knees, his mind a jumble of confusion and spiking fear. He tried to shake it clear, but it was no use.

Can't.

Let.

Them.

Catch.

Me.

With a roar, Cohmac forced himself back to his feet, but he felt like the world was closing in around him, a strange fog of pain and confusion constricting his thoughts. Every step felt twice as heavy as it should.

He altered his trajectory, staggering toward the edge of the chasm, his every thought clouded and ponderous. He reached the edge, peering down into the gloomy depths.

The shriek-like baying of the Nameless sounded again, echoing through the ruins. They were near now, almost on top of him. Cohmac's heart thrummed so fast and hard that he thought it might burst.

He was *terrified*. He knew what those creatures could do to a Jedi.

Cohmac *knew*.

And he was *scared*.

He glanced back toward the ruins, his head swimming. He felt nauseous.

How had he come to this?

Another chasm. Another leap.

From the other side of the old plaza, one of the Nameless issued its horrifying mournful shriek. They were here. The world around Cohmac began to swim, becoming feverish, filled with dancing lights of red and white that seemed to close in around him, reducing his senses to a single point of light and pain. He could no longer trust his eyes. Only the Force. There was still the Force.

Cohmac took one more deep breath—hoping it wasn't to be his last—and then leapt into the darkness.

TWENTY-TWO

Reath shifted his weight from one foot to the other. He dabbed at the sweat beading on his brow, trying not to draw attention to himself.

Was it warm in here?

He looked around at the gathered Jedi.

No one else seemed to be uncomfortably hot.

Just me, then.

He tried to suppress his nervousness.

Think calming thoughts, Reath.

It wasn't typical for him to find himself attending a meeting of the Jedi Council. He'd done so only a handful of times before, and most of those had been alongside his former masters, Jora Malli and Cohmac Vitus. Back then, as a Padawan, he'd been expected to listen and remain silent unless addressed with a direct question, a situation that had suited him perfectly.

This time, though, as a Jedi Knight, he'd been summoned to attend a top-level meeting to discuss his recent findings; so there was little chance of fading into the background. Other Jedi were still arriving in the Council chamber—Masters Elzar Mann, Indeera Stokes, and Avar Kriss among them. Reath was glad to see her up and about, following treatment for the serious wounds she'd suffered on Vixoseph I.

Master Avar shot Reath a reassuring smile when she saw him looking. It did little to settle the butterflies that were fluttering in his stomach.

The Jedi Council was all present, with the notable exception of Master Yarael Poof, who appeared in a holo from Kwenn, and the two seats vacated by the much-lamented Stellan Gios and Pra-Tre Veter. Those empty seats spoke volumes about the recent losses the Order had suffered at the hands of the Nihil and, in Master Veter's case, their monstrous weaponized creatures, the Nameless.

Reath glanced around the sea of gathered faces. Master Ada-Li Carro, Master Keaton Murag, Master Yoda, Master Xo Lahru, Master Ry Ki-Sakka, Master Adampo, Master Oppo Rancisis, and the other Council members were sitting quietly while the rest of the invited Jedi continued to arrive.

Reath had arrived typically early.

Outside, beyond the towering windows, the weave and weft of traffic filled the skies of Coruscant as it always did, no matter the time of day or night. There was so much *life* out there, all around them, so much to keep on fighting for—even if Reath himself would be more comfortable browsing the Jedi Archives than presenting in front of the Jedi Council.

He watched an airspeeder streak by, a yellow-and-silver blur, filled with laughing people. He felt a pang of longing—not to be out there among the soaring towers but for the abandon with which those people laughed, the weightlessness they must have felt, unburdened by duty, by concern. But it was only a passing emotion, flitting away just like the airspeeder itself.

A hush had fallen over the room.

Reath turned back to see all eyes had settled expectantly on Master Yoda. The diminutive green being nodded slowly, as if to himself. His eyes were hooded, lids half-closed. He turned in his seat, slowly regarding them all.

"Welcome, you are. All of you. We are gathered today to discuss the issue of the Nameless, what we have learned of them, and what must be done next if we are to defeat them." His gaze settled on Reath. "The creatures' relationship to the blight must be considered, too, yes?"

Reath nodded. *I hope he doesn't think I have* all *the answers.*

"This is a difficult time for the Order. We are besieged on all fronts," said Master Keaton Murag, leaning forward in his chair. He was a human with brown skin and bright hazel eyes. He scratched at his once-dark beard, now streaked with gray. "Despite Marchion Ro's recent overtures to save us all from the blight . . ." He paused, eyeing the gathered Jedi, monitoring their responses. To say they appeared skeptical would have been a vast understatement. "The Nihil remain an ever-present threat and one that cannot be ignored, not for a second. The blight continues to spread throughout the galaxy, and we have yet to understand its true nature or how to stop it. Then there are the Nameless and the power their continued existence gives Marchion Ro and his followers to stand against us. Not to mention the usual duties of the Order in protecting the innocent people of the galaxy." He sighed. "We don't know which way to look first."

"Agreed," said Master Lahru, the hunched Anx, with his blade-shaped head and yellow reptilian skin. "Our focus is divided, and in remaining so, we are vulnerable and less effective."

"And yet what option do we have?" said Master Yarael Poof, his long stemlike neck and small round head flickering in the light of the projected holo. "The great wheel of the galaxy does not stop turning, even for a moment. Divided our attention might be, but with good cause."

"Yes," said Master Yoda. "Indeed. Connected, all these things are. I am certain of it. Understanding the Nameless is the key to everything."

"How?" said Master Adampo, the small Yarkoran with blond hair and a gnarled pronounced snout. "In what way are the Nameless the key?"

Yoda issued a long heartfelt sigh, as if he'd been through all this before. "Without the Nameless, just another warlord Marchion Ro is. Hmm . . . like many before. His Nihil are not so easily defeated. Yet his greatest and most powerful weapon against the Jedi? The Nameless, I think, are most deadly, most mysterious, and that is why Reath Silas and Emerick Caphtor continue their research."

All eyes swiveled to Reath. He wished that Emerick were here, too, instead of halfway across the galaxy on Eriadu, trapped inside the Occlusion Zone.

"And what has that research uncovered?" said Master Murag, not unkindly. "Reath?"

Reath swallowed. "We believe that the Nameless, also known in the old stories as *Shrii Ka Rai*, Force Eaters, or Levelers, are creatures that feed on the living Force," he said. "We've all heard the old tales, the children's songs and fairy tales of the monsters that stalk the Jedi. The only creatures that could truly scare us. Little did we know that the stories were true—not until Marchion Ro's terrible broadcast, in which we witnessed Master Pra-Tre Veter so horribly murdered. I've since discovered other accounts in the Archives, dating back centuries."

"What sorts of accounts?" asked Master Murag.

"Records of mysterious deaths. Jedi who died in strange or perplexing circumstances, but whose deaths were not attributed to the Nameless because, at the time, they were not understood for what they truly were. Jedi such as Zallah Macri and Kevmo Zink." Reath paused, catching his breath. He wasn't used to having so many eyes on him at once. "We know from the testimony of those among us who have encountered a Nameless and survived that the experience is not only harrowing but affects the cognitive functions so severely that reality, for the victim, becomes warped. No one who has encountered a Nameless is left with any clear understanding of what has happened. Therefore, their accounts do not match and we haven't been able to draw a clear picture of what the creatures are and how they operate."

"Which is?" asked Master Adampo.

"As I explained, they appear to feed on the living Force. Given that, of all the beings in the galaxy, the Force is typically most concentrated in the Jedi, it seems to make us natural targets." He cleared his throat. "And yet it seems unlikely that the Jedi were always the prey of such creatures."

"How so?" asked Master Adampo.

"I believe that the Nameless must have evolved in an ecosystem where there was an abundance of prey rich in the Force. It seems only logical. The Jedi do not fit that evolutionary niche. The Order is relatively young, in evolutionary terms. So the Nameless must come from a world where they are able to regularly feed on the Force, without disturbing the overall balance of the ecosystem that sustains it. Torn from that habitat, they feed on whatever they can. The Jedi are simply the next best thing to whatever their usual meal would be." He shrugged. "Of course, it's just a theory. . . ."

"And have you been able to identify this origin world?" asked Master Ki-Sakka, another human member of the Council.

"Not yet," said Reath. "But we're working on it. There are fragments of stories in the Jedi Archives, and in the data that Emerick has managed to find in the field. Old tales, myths, legends that hint at such a place. And what's more, I now believe that the Nameless and the blight might share a common origin."

"This is all very well," said Master Lahru, "but how does it help us to combat the things? As Master Yoda made clear, we need to be able to fight them if we're going to stop the Nihil."

"I'm not sure," said Reath. His heart was thudding. "But I'm certain we're on the right track. If we can understand them, perhaps we can figure out a way to fight them. Azlin thinks—"

"Azlin." Master Ki-Sakka frowned. "The fallen one."

Reath nodded, sensing a ripple of disapproval from the Council.

"On Dalna, young Azlin was, when the Night of Sorrow fell, all those years ago," said Master Yoda.

"The Night of Sorrow?" asked Elzar.

Master Yoda nodded. "Many years ago, when the Jedi subdued the Path of the Open Hand, the religious sect that gave rise to Marchion Ro and the Nihil. A massacre, it was. Killed, many Jedi were. A tragedy for Dalna and the Order." Master Yoda paused for a moment before continuing. "Connected to this shocking event, I believe the Nameless were. Why I sought out Azlin Rell, this is."

"Dalna. The Nameless were there," said Reath, realization dawning. "That's when Azlin encountered them." He'd heard Azlin speak of Dalna only once, in an oblique reference to the time of his initial trauma. It clearly wasn't something Azlin cared to discuss.

"And you've been interviewing him, haven't you, Reath?" asked Master Ki-Sakka.

"I have. As Master Yoda explained, Azlin represents a primary source of information about the Nameless," said Reath, a little more defensively than he'd intended. "He is not to be trusted, but when interpreted correctly, his insights have proved enlightening."

Master Ki-Sakka nodded reluctantly. "Very well." The Council could hardly argue. They'd allowed Azlin to stay, hoping that such insights might prove useful, although Reath suspected it was also partly a way of ensuring the fallen Jedi was close at hand and under observation.

"But what of the blight?" said Master Lahru. "You suggested you'd discovered a link to the Nameless."

"Indeed, Master Lahru," said Reath. "I'm sure we're all aware of the obvious similarity between the effects of the blight and what the Nameless do when they . . . they . . ."

"Husk somebody," said Elzar Mann, close by. Reath shot him a grateful look.

"Yes," said Reath. "That. We started to look at whether there was a correlation in the old legends. I discovered the story of the ancient Tolemites, a civilization that encountered a devastating plague that almost destroyed them, but they eventually discovered the means to defeat it."

"And you think this plague they refer to was the same as the blight?" asked Master Carro.

"I do," said Reath, "because I also discovered a less well-known version of the story in which an expedition brought back a pack of creatures they'd discovered on an unknown world, which turned on their new masters and began 'feeding on their life essence.' I should add that the Tolemites were a Force-worshipping culture and understood the connection between all living things, and that these events appear to happen more or less concurrently. The plague and the appearance of the creatures."

"And these people survived?" said Master Ki-Sakka.

"They defeated the plague, but their civilization has been gone for millennia," said Reath. "Nevertheless, I think if we can discover more about the history of the Tolemites, maybe even locate their homeworld, then we might be able to learn more. It could provide us with the clues we need to find the origin world of the Nameless—and, it seems, the blight."

"Your scientific research backs this up?" said Master Adampo.

Reath nodded. "It does. Samples taken from the remains of husked Jedi, when compared to the blight-infected severed hand of Cair San Tekka, show that on a molecular level, the effect of the Nameless on a Jedi is identical to the effect of the blight on organic matter." He took a breath. "At least in the small samples I've been able to obtain. Realistically, I need more data so I can dig deeper. Nothing about this is clear. The blight seems to affect everyone and everything it comes into contact with. The Nameless don't. I need time, and I need more samples."

"Capture a Nameless, we must," said Master Yoda.

A murmur rippled through the gathered Jedi.

"We've discussed this before," said Master Murag, the incredulity clear in his voice.

"The risk is incalculable," said Master Adampo.

"And yet, if we are to truly understand them," said Master Yoda, "we must face them, on our own terms."

"Reath?" said Avar Kriss. "You've studied these things."

Reath felt as if the ground were about to open up and swallow him. How could they put a decision like this on him? He was just a Jedi Knight, and a recently knighted one at that. "I . . ." he started, his voice catching. He glanced at Yoda, saw the encouragement in the old master's eyes. "I agree with Master Yoda. As dangerous as it is, having access to one of the creatures would be like a hyperspace jump in our understanding."

"We've all seen the recording of what one did to Master Veter," said Master Murag. "And the others we've lost. Do we really think it's wise? If it got loose . . ." He let the implication hang.

"Then we don't keep it here in the Temple," said Elzar. "We use the RDC. Keep it in a secure holding facility. Reath can work through the Republic technicians. We keep a layer of protection between the creature and the Jedi, a buffer. We know the Nihil can operate around the creatures, presumably because they're not strong in the Force. There's no reason the RDC won't be able to do the same."

"That could work," said Reath. "A closer look at their anatomy might help us understand how they feed." He was warming to the idea with every passing moment. The opportunity it would present was undeniable. "It might also allow us to figure out how the Nihil control them. We've all seen the rod Marchion Ro used in that recording when he unleashed the thing on Master Veter. Working out why it responds to that device might mean we can figure out how to stop them."

"How would we even begin to capture one?" asked Master Ki-Sakka.

"The answer's the same," said Elzar. "We lean on the RDC. We already know the Chancellor is on board with the idea. We speak to her and Admiral Kronara. Put together a team. Play the Nihil at their own game. Raid the site of one of their outposts where we know they're keeping one of the creatures. If we can take the Nameless from the Nihil, we can stop them from using the creatures against us."

"I remain hesitant," said Master Adampo. "Whoever accompanied the RDC on such a mission would be at great risk. What of the Guardian Protocols?"

The Guardian Protocols were a set of ancient rules the Jedi Council had enacted to protect the Order, in response to the elevated threat of the Nameless. All Jedi had been recalled to Coruscant and were allowed to leave only on specific missions, each one sanctioned by the Council. Additionally, Padawans were being put through their trials with more haste, and even younglings were training with real lightsabers—all to prepare them to face the Nameless. But Reath understood that, in truth, the threat was more existential than that. The creatures weren't just a physical enemy that could be overcome with training and might, like the Nihil who wielded them. They were a danger to everything the Jedi were—the looming darkness that could extinguish the very light of the Jedi.

The Nameless were the Jedi's worst fear made manifest.

"While we must remain mindful of the protocols we have put in place," said Master Ki-Sakka, "we must also acknowledge the importance of this research in understanding the nature of our enemy. If what both Master Yoda and Reath say is true, this could be the key to finally drawing a line under everything that's happened these last three years."

"Then vote, we must," said Yoda. "All those in favor . . ." He raised his hand.

Reath held his breath.

Five more hands went up. Masters Ki-Sakka, Carro, Lahru, Rancisis, and Poof.

"Then we are agreed," said Master Yoda. "Begin preparations, we must."

"I shall arrange a meeting with Chancellor Soh," said Elzar.

"Very well," said Master Ki-Sakka. "We will gather intelligence to begin the search for a suitable target. Once identified, we will establish a team to go after one of the creatures." He glanced at Reath. "Good work, Reath. Your efforts have not gone unnoticed. Please, continue with your research in the meantime. Find us that common ancestry you spoke of. If the ancient Tolemites can lead the way, then we shall gladly follow."

Reath felt his cheeks flush. "Thank you, Master Ki-Sakka."

The other Jedi began to file out.

Reath gave a quick bow. As he was turning to leave, however, Master Ki-Sakka beckoned him over. "A word, if you would, Reath?"

Perplexed, Reath walked over to join Master Ki-Sakka by the window. They stood for a moment, looking out over the streaming traffic lanes and the tall spires of the city as the rest of the Jedi left.

Reath's palms were sweaty. What was this about?

"Master Ki-Sakka?"

The older Jedi turned to smile at him. "We're all very proud of the work you're doing, Reath," he said. "Your insights are helping to steer the future of the Order itself. That is no small thing."

"I'm very honored," said Reath.

Master Ki-Sakka nodded. "I understand the burden you must feel. The desire not to let anyone down."

"It is a burden I am happy to shoulder, Master Ki-Sakka," said Reath.

"Indeed. And a burden shared is a burden halved."

"Working with Amadeo has been most helpful," said Reath.

"Good," said Master Ki-Sakka. "Just . . . be mindful, Reath. Not everyone who offers help has your best interests at heart. Or those of your fellow Jedi."

"You're talking about Azlin Rell," said Reath.

Master Ki-Sakka inclined his head. "I know he is a resource, Reath, but I urge you to tread carefully. That is all."

"I understand," said Reath. "I know him for what he is."

"And what is that?" said Master Ki-Sakka, his eyes still taking in the pristine landscape beyond the window.

"A very dangerous man indeed," said Reath.

TWENTY-THREE

Cohmac fell.

The wind buffeted him, cold and sharp, wrenching the breath from his lungs as he tumbled. His eyes were squeezed tightly shut. He could hear nothing above the whistling howl in his ears. His stomach fluttered and he felt empty, hollow. His mouth was so dry it was painful.

He was going to die.

The creatures hadn't even gotten that close, but the sheer *presence* of them had been devastating. He wasn't sure he could trust his own mind anymore. They'd twisted his very thoughts, turning the world around him into a place of vibrant disturbing horror, setting his own senses against him.

He'd had no choice *but* to jump.

And so he fell, his robes fluttering about him like broken wings. At least his mind seemed to be clearing now. As he tumbled, over and over, the effects of the Nameless were fading, leaving him free to panic about his uncontrolled plummet toward the bottom of the seemingly endless chasm.

Reach out, Cohmac. Use the Force.

Feel your way.

The voice sounded inside his head, calm and familiar.

Orla?

He had to be imagining it, another echo from the past.

He opened his eyes, tried to crane his neck. There was a rocky ledge below, jutting from the side of the chasm. He was about halfway down the cliff wall, and Cohmac could see the rocky bottom rushing up to meet him, growing closer with every passing second.

Cohmac closed his eyes again, reaching out, feeling his way into his environment. He felt the air rushing past, the walls of the chasm, the thunderous rush of his own blood as it raged through his veins.

He felt the dark presence above, still up in the plaza, its hunger unrelenting.

And he felt peace.

Calm.

Tranquility.

He slowed, cushioning his descent, directing his tumble.

He tucked in his hands, pressed his chin to his chest. . . .

Then he slammed into an untidy heap on the very lip of the outcropping. He caught his breath, scrabbling to his feet.

Cohmac wavered there for a moment, buffeted by the wind. He didn't dare look up. He knew they would follow, somehow. They wouldn't give in that easily.

The terrifying effects of the creatures' presence had all but disappeared, aside from an angry itching sensation at the back of his skull—a warning that he wasn't out of danger, not by far.

Cohmac realized he was still shaking.

Too close.

Much, much too close.

And now he had to find a way back to his ship.

He hurried over to a narrow aperture in the chasm wall, accessible only from the outcropping on which he was standing—a sheared stub of rock jutting from the hewn bedrock. It looked like a narrow passage leading deeper into the cliff.

He knew from his earlier surveys that the opening of the chasm had wrenched apart the entire city, not just what was aboveground but what was below it, too. Ancient catacombs perforated both sides of the chasm like animal warrens.

If he could navigate through the hidden passages, perhaps he could find his way back to the *Excavator*, which was hidden in a clearing close to the main entrance to the catacomb labyrinth above.

He didn't have time to weigh any alternative options. It was this or face the Nameless.

He ducked through the opening, squeezing himself into the narrow passageway beyond.

The catacombs were dank and thick with dust and cobwebs. Cohmac fought to find a flare in his pack, then hurriedly lit it, creating a sudden bright cascade of yellow sparks and flame. The cobwebs burned away at the passing of the flare, sizzling into nothing but leaving a cloying acrid stench that lingered in Cohmac's nostrils.

He was still trying to make sense of what had happened back at his camp. The Jedi hunter must have tracked him to Thall, using the Levelers like hunting beasts, sniffing him out among the ruins.

A shudder passed down Cohmac's spine. The strange metallic taste of fear still lingered on his tongue. Every fiber of his being was urging his body to push on, to keep going, to put as much distance as he could between himself and the beasts. His nerves were alive, and every draft, every kiss of stale air was enough to make his skin crawl.

Now he understood the real horror of the Nameless. Now he understood what it was to be truly afraid.

The passages ahead were narrow and filled with hollowed-out niches that had been carved into the bedrock to accommodate the remains of the city's dead. Cohmac had been right—the tunnels were like a lattice, a honeycomb, burrowed deep into the cliff. They linked up in unexpected ways, making them difficult to navigate. That wasn't helped by the fact that nearly every passage looked the same—row after row of dust-caked hollows, each of them filled with the bones of a long-dead inhabitant. He presumed they'd been tunneled out over many thousands of years, with successive generations digging deeper and deeper as the need for more burial space grew exponentially alongside the swelling population.

He peered into some of the hollows as he hurried past. Most of the deceased had long ago crumbled to piles of gray dust, their bones eroded by the passing of eons.

Just like they were husked.

Cohmac tried to put the thought out of mind.

Some of the niches contained small stone sarcophagi or the remains of votive offerings or weapons, long degraded. He wished he could have taken time to study them, to discover more about this near-forgotten rich culture and the people who had built and lived in the once spectacular city. What would these long-dead people say to him now? What had they known about their place in the galaxy? How delighted Reath would have been to witness it all.

Despite his scholarly fascination, however, all Cohmac could really think about was getting out of there as quickly as possible.

He had to make it. He had to survive. He needed to let the Jedi know what he'd found on Thall.

He shuddered, suddenly uncomfortable.

He was exhausted—so tired that his head was swimming. He dragged at the air, shook himself to try to bring himself around.

It had to be the air. It was so stale and thin. These tunnels hadn't been disturbed for centuries. He needed oxygen. He had to slow down, catch his breath.

But he couldn't. He couldn't stop.

He knew the Nameless and their Nihil master would not have given up—not that easily. Even down here, the creatures would sniff him out, find another way into the catacombs to come after him. He was certain of it.

Fear prickled the back of his neck.

Were they closing in even now?

He glanced behind him as he ran. There was nothing but empty darkness in his wake.

Cohmac sighed. His experiences up in the plaza had obviously shaken him more than he'd realized. He just had to keep going, one foot in front of the other.

Just then, his left foot caught on the protruding edge of a low niche. He twisted, falling, throwing his hands out to protect himself as he sprawled. His flare tumbled from his grip, clattering to the floor and rolling ahead of him into the inky gloom.

He slammed against the rough stone ground, his palms smarting. His head struck the wall, drawing beads of warm blood, and he rolled onto his side, groaning.

Dust plumed around him, choking him, clogging his throat, his nostrils, causing him to hack and gasp.

He felt hemmed in, as if the narrow walls were closing in on him, as if the darkness were pouring down his throat, flooding his lungs.

He thrashed in the confining space, scrabbling for purchase to haul himself up, his fingertips scraping against the chiseled walls.

Finally, desperately, he pulled himself up until he was resting on his knees. His breath came back in short sharp gulps. His head felt like it was vibrating, and his thoughts were sluggish, sticky, unwilling to form. The result of the blow. A concussion.

His vision was blurred, unfocused.

Ahead of him, a shape floated out of the gloom. It was coming toward him. Indistinct. A figure.

"Reath?"

The figure didn't answer.

"Reath?"

But it wasn't Reath.

It came closer.

The figure hovered a meter off the ground. It was humanoid, but its features were hazy, shifting, almost as if . . .

Cohmac scrambled backward, eyes wide in terror.

It was a Jedi. A Jedi wearing white robes, with pale skin and bright staring eyes.

"Orla?"

Tears streamed down Cohmac's cheeks. He tried to reach out to her with both hands.

"Orla!"

But the shimmering wraith, the translucent specter of his dead friend, just stared at him blankly, her familiar face contorted in a visage of pure hate.

As he watched, cowering, she raised her hand to point at him accusingly, throwing her head back in a soundless scream.

Cohmac whimpered. He couldn't move. Couldn't think. Couldn't do anything as, to his abject horror, more of the figures swam out of the underground night, crowding into that narrow space, their features similarly twisted in anger and hate.

He could feel the menace radiating off of them, the malign desire for revenge.

Reath. Jora. Stellan. Nib. Loden. So many more.

Cohmac was trembling. How could this be happening?

Ghosts weren't real. He knew that. They *couldn't* exist, not outside of bedtime stories. So how were they here now? Why had they come to torment him as he tried to flee?

The figures closed in, arms outstretched, mouths wide in silent screams. They swarmed him, close but never touching, crowding but leaving him just enough room to see their horrible hate-filled expressions, to understand their pain as they leered over him, threatening, warning.

"I'm sorry!" he cried. "I'm sorry. *Please.* Please don't do this. I just . . . I just need to get away. I just need to keep moving. . . ."

He was so *scared*.

So, so scared.

He tried to fight it, to control it like he'd always been taught. To make sense of his fear and then push it to one side. To become bigger than it.

But he couldn't, not this time. It just kept coming in vast tidal waves, washing away all sense of normalcy, of identity, all trace of his rational thoughts.

Cohmac screamed.

They were here.

They'd found him already. The Nameless were in the tunnels.

He couldn't think, could hardly move.

His vision was warping. The light of the ghosts was wavering in a horrific weaving dance, merging together at the far end of the passageway, the direction from which he'd come, as if trying to describe something impossible, a nightmare that should never have existed.

And yet it was there. It was coming for him.

Cohmac screamed again, clawing at his face. He felt warm blood erupt beneath his fingernails. Tears streamed down his cheeks.

In the tunnel, the ghost light was still morphing and twisting, but he knew that the thing it represented wore a hungry slavering maw.

He heard a voice, echoing in the distance, thin and fluted: "Now, now, now, my beloveds. We must share. We must be slow. We shall free this pretty Jedi from his torment."

A crackle of electricity.

Cohmac flinched, but it wasn't aimed at him.

Something mewled.

"There, see. There. You will do as I say."

The words seemed to make no sense.

I'm not a Jedi.

I'm not a Jedi.

Cohmac covered his ears, hunching forward, trying to drown out the sound of the horrible voice.

It was echoing around his head. He couldn't see. Everything hurt. He just wanted to get away from it. He tried to shift his weight, to get to his feet, but he could hardly move. Instead, he succeeded only in rolling onto his side.

"No!"

He felt something cold and hard, like a coffin.

He was already dead. That was it. He was . . .

Beneath him, the ground opened up.

Blackness pulled at him.

He fell into it. Plummeting. Dropping away.

Was this it? Was this dying? The last vestiges of his conscious mind ebbing away into darkness? The Nameless feasting on him, making him small, reducing him to dust?

And then he struck something hard. He rebounded, struck again, felt the wind knocked from his lungs. He threw out a hand, tried to stop himself, but it only struck something hard and uneven, smarting with sharp and sudden pain.

What was happening?

What—

He came to a stop, gasping for breath.

The fog had lifted. The pain was different. He peeled open eyes that were gummed shut with tears and blood.

He'd fallen.

He wasn't sure how. He thought perhaps he'd rolled into one of the alcoves and the ground had given way. He could hear screaming and cursing somewhere above.

The Jedi hunter.

Groaning, Cohmac staggered to his feet. He was battered and bleeding, and his left arm was useless.

Worse, his mind was still spiraling, still racked by fear and uncertainty.

But he could run. He had to keep running.

Running was all he had left.

He knew now that the ghosts had never been there. They'd

been figments, conjured by his own mind under the duress of the Nameless.

Fear manifested as primal horrors.

He leaned shakily against the wall, glancing ahead to see a shaft of natural light filtering down through the rocks. Around him were more catacombs filled with the remnants of the dead and lost.

Cohmac staggered toward the light, wincing with every step.

A roughly hewn staircase had been chiseled into the rock. At the top, the light of dawn was like a beacon. He hurried toward it, dragging himself up every step.

∗∗∗

Cohmac emerged into the hazy light a few minutes later, exiting the catacombs via an overground tomb complex on the other side of the ruins. He was shocked to realize that, in the darkness of the tunnels, he'd traversed the entire span of the ancient city—or at least the half of it that remained on this side of the chasm.

The air was chill but fresh, and Cohmac gulped at it, feeling his awareness sharpen slightly.

There wasn't much farther to go.

Desperation, latent fear, and pain drove his every step as he weaved unsteadily through the slumped buildings and tottering pillars. And then, rounding the walls of a collapsed structure that might once have been a temple, Cohmac set eyes on perhaps the most welcome sight he'd ever seen: his ship.

It was hidden in a small stand of trees just beyond the boundary of the tomb complex, and while modest—a battered cylindrical *Venture*-class cruiser that had seen much better days—it would more than serve to get him free of Thall and the monstrous creatures that hunted him there.

He hurried over, calling down the boarding ramp from the port side of the vessel and clambering aboard.

Inside, the vessel was as tired as it looked from the outside, with discolored wall paneling, exposed wiring hanging in hoops from the ceiling, and a hastily fixed coolant system, accessible through an open pit in the center of the main common area.

He rushed to the cockpit and engaged the ship's systems, trying not to wince at the dried blood on his hands and the searing pain that still racked his body—this time from the self-inflicted wounds and the battering he'd taken during the fall that had saved him.

The boarding ramp hissed as it began to rise. The ship's engines gave a choking stutter and then roared to life. Cohmac let out the breath he hadn't realized he was holding.

The *Excavator* trembled and then rose into the bright Thall sky, the hull rattling dramatically with the strain.

Drawn by an unexpected urge, Cohmac looked out of the starboard viewport, gazing down on the shrinking ruins as the *Excavator* steadily rose.

The ship banked, and down below, amid a stand of broken stone plinths, he saw a small black-clad figure emerge from the catacombs, an electrostaff fizzing in his hands, pale face upturned to watch as the ship climbed above the ruins.

The Jedi hunter.

Cohmac looked away, breathing a heartfelt sigh of relief as

the *Excavator* flew through the strata of the lower atmosphere, finally bursting free into the inky sea of stars beyond.

He'd made it. He'd survived.

Barely.

And all he wanted to do was go home.

He wasn't even sure Coruscant *was* his home anymore, but his every instinct was crying out for him to go. To flee. To be safe, as far away from the Nameless as he could possibly get.

And to share with the Jedi everything he had learned.

Cohmac punched in a course for Coruscant and then slumped back in his seat, body still trembling. He didn't dare close his eyes for the horrors he knew might still be lingering there, behind his weary eyelids.

TWENTY-FOUR

Reath was down in the tunnels again.

This time, though, something was different. His movements seemed jerky, unnatural, as if every step he took was stuttering through broken time. As if he and the world around him were operating on different planes and he didn't really belong here.

And yet . . . Reath felt oddly welcome, too.

Invited.

The light was strange and confusing. Shadows crept where there was no light. And the sounds were all wrong. His footsteps seemed muffled, as if he were deep underwater, unable to properly discern everything that was going on around him. He tried to stop walking but found he couldn't control where he was going. His body was moving of its own accord, leading him on, ever deeper, down, down into the depths of the Temple structure, leading him toward something he knew he had to see, something appalling that lay hidden in the depths.

He turned, sensing danger. But no one was there, just the flicker of a passing shadow, the trace of a ghost.

He broke into a run. Sweat beaded on his brow, and he fought against panic.

He was lost in the maze of dank tunnels. There was no light, but still he could see. He felt enveloped by darkness. Warm and comfortable, it draped itself around his shoulders, urging him on.

Down stone steps, slick and damp.

Finally, he recognized where he was: the Shrine in the Depths. The ancient Sith temple, built on a vergence in the Force. The buried secret at the heart of the Jedi Temple. The seeping well of darkness the Jedi had tried to hide, tried to nullify with their presence.

The Order had built their temple on this site millennia ago. But still this place remained, bleeding shadows, a dark reflection of the place of light above.

Reath walked toward the towering stone doors that led to the inner shrine. His heart was thudding. He felt breathless, anxious. He knew he shouldn't go inside, shouldn't open those doors. And yet he knew, too, with a horrible certainty, that he must.

His legs were still carrying him of their own accord. He wanted to stop, to turn around and run, but he could not. He sensed a presence here, close by but out of sight.

It was powerful. And it was hungry.

Azlin?

Reath tried to say the name, but while his lips formed the correct shape, no sound was forthcoming.

He reached the doors. They were ancient beyond belief, crumbling, engraved with filigree patterns and arcane symbols.

Reath knew something was beyond them, waiting, something inside the shrine, something dark and malign.

He told himself to turn and run. To flee that terrible place. To seek help.

But still he could not stop himself from reaching for the doors, pushing them open. . . .

A figure stood inside the Sith shrine, dressed in tattered white-and-gold robes. Their hair was long and lank, tumbling around their shoulders. They looked old and emaciated.

And they had no eyes, just stark staring sockets crusted with dried blood where the organs had once been.

But it was not Azlin.

It was Reath.

A twisted parody of the man he was—a dark and broken reflection from which shadows flowed like spilled ink, pooling across the flagstones, climbing the walls, reaching for him . . . and still he could not move.

Reath screamed until his throat was raw and the darkness enveloped him.

He woke with a start.

For a moment he was unsure where he was. He sat up, gasping for breath. It took a moment for his eyes to focus.

He was in his bunk, in his chambers.

He was dripping with sweat, his hair plastered to his scalp, his bedsheets damp and ruffled. It was still dark.

He ran a hand over his face.

A bad dream, inspired by the tumult of emotions he'd been dealing with of late? By his conversation with Azlin?

Perhaps.

Reath swung his legs out of bed and padded over to the table, where he kept a jug of water. He poured himself a glass and took a long cool draw.

No. As much as he wanted to dismiss the experience he'd just had, to forget about it and crawl back into his bunk, it was more than a dream. It was a warning—a *vision*.

Azlin had been right, about one thing at least: Reath knew what he had to do. He had to go down there and confront whatever was lurking in the Shrine of the Depths.

He had to face it.

But it wasn't something he could do alone. He was certain of that, too.

He took another swig of water and caught sight of himself in the small mirror on the wall. He was a mess, much like Elzar had looked earlier that day—dark bruises beneath his eyes, unshaven and unkempt, with a glossy sheen of sweat. He turned away.

There was no point going back to bed—not now. It would be dawn in a couple of hours. He'd take a shower and then go deal with the problem.

He already knew whom he was going to ask for help.

Vernestra Rwoh.

"Vernestra?"

Vernestra groaned and stretched her aching neck and shoulders, trying to ease some life back into her weary muscles.

She looked up at the hesitant upside-down face of fellow Jedi Knight Reath Silas, peering down at her from above. She yawned, smiled, and then slowly uncurled from the cross-legged position she'd been sitting in most of the night.

Dawn was breaking beyond the window of the meditation chamber. She hadn't been able to sleep, so she'd come here in the hope of finding some peace. Her ribs had more or less healed following the ministrations of the medical droid, but she was still finding it difficult to rest.

The meditation had helped a little, but her mind was just too active to switch off completely. Whenever she tried to sleep, it was like something kept prodding her awake again, an annoying itch she couldn't scratch—like something in her unconscious mind was trying to make itself known.

She hadn't yet gotten to the bottom of what it was. She supposed it would have to wait.

"Hello, Reath," she said, slowly getting to her feet.

Reath looked like he hadn't had much sleep, either. He was pale, with dark bruises beneath his eyes. "Sorry to disturb you," he said.

"You look worse than I do," said Vernestra. "And that's saying something. Is everything all right?"

Reath shook his head. "No. Definitely not."

"Don't I know it. It's past dawn and I haven't had any sleep *or* any caf."

Reath offered her an indulgent smile, but she could tell his heart wasn't in it.

"Ah. You're serious, aren't you?" she said.

Reath nodded.

She led him out of the meditation chamber and across the concourse to a balcony overlooking a wide bustling staircase. She leaned against the rail, folding her arms. "Tell me."

Reath took a deep breath, then let it out. "There's something dangerous here, on Coruscant. Down in the levels below the Temple."

"Below the Temple?" Vernestra shuddered. "You mean the ancient Sith shrine?"

"The Shrine in the Depths, yes," said Reath.

"And you know this how?" asked Vernestra. Had he been poking around down there and uncovered something? Reath did have a reputation for losing himself in his research. Had he been exploring where he shouldn't, taking things a little too far? It wouldn't be the first time someone had lost their way seeking out forbidden texts. The thought didn't sit well with Vernestra. She'd always liked Reath and considered him to be a steadying influence among the younger Knights, reliable, easy to trust.

"I . . . umm . . ." He looked vaguely embarrassed. "I had a vision."

Vernestra nodded. *Interesting.* "Okay. And what did you see?"

"I don't know," said Reath. "In the vision, I was down there, and everything was . . . well, it wasn't *right*."

"Of course it wasn't right. It's a Sith shrine."

Reath seemed a little exasperated. "No. More than that. I was being drawn toward something, in the shrine itself. Something dangerous and powerful. When I opened the doors, there was a sense of something so bleak, so malign . . ." His voice trailed off, and he bit his lip. "Look, I know it's a lot. But Azlin said—"

"Azlin?" she said, interrupting him. "You've been talking with the dark sider?" She frowned. She didn't like where this was heading.

"Yes. But the Council knows all about that. I've been questioning him about the *Shrii Ka Rai*, as part of my research. He's spent his entire life investigating them, and his insights are helping us to piece together where they came from, and how we can beat them. But that's not what this is about. Last night, he warned me that there was something stirring, a threat to the Jedi that we hadn't acknowledged. He said he could feel it and that *I* should be able to feel it, too. I almost dismissed it, but then I had the vision, and . . . well"—he shrugged—"I think he was telling the truth. I think there's something down there, Vernestra."

"And why did you come to *me* with this?"

"I figured you'd be able to help. That you were a good person to talk to about visions and stuff, and . . . I trust you." Reath glanced away, unable to meet her eye.

"Well, I'll do my best," she said. This sounded important.

The relief on Reath's face was almost heartbreaking. "Thank you. I *knew* you'd listen."

How could she not? Reath had put his faith in her. And whatever was going on with him, he genuinely believed they were in trouble and that she could help. She supposed she'd have to push through the tiredness, at least for a little while. She suspected it was all Azlin's doing—that he'd been toying with Reath for amusement, taking advantage of the young Jedi's trusting nature and his devotion to serving the Order. Still, it wouldn't hurt to check it out, even if it was only to help put his mind at rest.

Vernestra smiled, pushing herself away from the railing. "Okay then. Come on. I think we'd better take a look."

TWENTY-FIVE

Reath's hand kept straying to the hilt of his lightsaber as, a short while later, he and Vernestra crept through the darkened passageways beneath the main Jedi Temple building.

"You really do bring me to all the best places," said Vernestra, using her left hand to brush away a matted clump of spiderweb from the passage before her. She glanced at her hand in disgust as the clingy dusty stuff entangled itself around her fingers.

"Well, you've got to give a guy credit for trying," said Reath with a half-hearted laugh.

Vernestra shot him a glance over her shoulder. "Hmmm."

"Anyway, I'm sorry to ask you to do this while you're still

recovering," said Reath. He knew he'd asked a lot of Vernestra, dragging her down here so soon after her stay in the medical facility. But something had told him she was exactly who he needed by his side right now. He wasn't sure his instincts were totally on point at the moment, but he *was* sure about this. He had to trust in the Force to guide him.

"So, you've been coming down here to talk to *him*," said Vernestra, as if reading his thoughts. Judging by the emphasis she put on the last word, she was clearly unafraid to make her opinion on the subject clear.

"Not down *here*, exactly," said Reath. "I think giving a Jedi who's embraced the dark side quarters next to a Sith temple might be one step too far, don't you?"

"I think giving a Jedi who's embraced the dark side any quarters *at all* is a step too far," replied Vernestra, fighting with more cobwebs, "especially after what he's done. But nobody asked me."

Reath wasn't sure how to respond to that. In truth, he was still trying to work out how he really felt about his relationship with Azlin. He could in no way condone what the man had done, the choices he had made. And he didn't really care what Azlin thought about him, either. But then Azlin's words *had* struck a chord with Reath, despite the man's evident self-interest. Maybe Reath *was* playing everything a little too safe. Azlin had spoken about opening his mind, considering all the different routes to success in their fight against the Nameless and the blight, seeing the bigger picture and refusing to stick doggedly to the narrow views of others. What Reath didn't quite understand was exactly what that *meant*. He supposed it might mean taking more risks, putting himself out there, doing things like delving into the depths of a Sith temple on a sudden whim. . . .

It was difficult to know. Azlin was nothing if not opaque. But nevertheless, he did listen. And he did seem to genuinely want to help Reath solve the puzzle of the Nameless.

"Anyway, his cell is back there," he said, jabbing his thumb over his shoulder. "Much closer to the surface. And it's not like I'm visiting him every day. Just when I have questions he can help with."

"And does he?" said Vernestra. "Help?"

Reath considered his response as they rounded a bend, heading even deeper underground. "Sometimes. He often talks in riddles and suggestions. But they can be useful. And yesterday he shed some light on a lead I've been following that could make a real difference."

Vernestra glanced back over her shoulder again. She looked concerned for Reath, as if she was worried he was being taken in by Azlin's games. He bristled at the idea but kept his cool. "If he truly wanted to help," she said, "don't you think he'd have told us everything already? I mean—why withhold things? Why make us cajole him into giving up what he knows in dribs and drabs?"

It was a good question, one that Reath had often asked himself. "He claims it's because I'm not ready. That I have to discover some of it for myself. He argues that if he interferes too much, everything will go wrong."

"That I *can* believe," said Vernestra wryly.

Reath didn't reply. He was looking around at the chamber

they'd just entered, reacting to the sight of the fading frescoes on the walls, the dripping stalactites that encrusted the ceiling, the odd geometry of the walls. Shadows crept in his peripheral view. It was an echo of what he'd seen in his vision, like the dark itself was somehow becoming deeper, less penetrable, more oppressive.

He ignited his lightsaber, holding its green blade before him like a ward to keep the evil at bay.

"Reath?" Vernestra had hesitated by the low stone arch that led from the chamber deeper into the tunnels.

"We're here."

"What do you mean? The shrine is *that* way," she said, gesturing to the arch.

"No. This is where I was in my vision when it started." He gripped the hilt of his lightsaber a little tighter. "Just be on your guard. We don't know what we're dealing with."

Vernestra gave a curt nod. "Reath, you're worrying me."

"There's something very wrong down here," he said. "Can't you sense it?"

Vernestra looked pained. "Well, now that you mention it . . . something down here does seem off. More than usual, I mean. It's like . . . this is going to sound strange, but it's like the Force feels *sour*."

"Yes! That's it exactly," said Reath. He glanced sharply left, then right, trying to glimpse whatever it was he could sense hovering in the corner of his eye. But there was nothing there, only shadows.

"I don't think either of us should spend any more time down here than we have to," said Vernestra.

Reath followed her through the low archway, dipping his head beneath the ornate keystone.

More passageways. More shadows. More feelings of being closed in, watched, followed. Reath's discomfort grew with every step. Every passing moment felt like another fragment of his dream made real. His head was swimming, disoriented. He put one foot in front of the other, following Vernestra's lead, feeling hemmed in by the creeping shadows that seemed dispelled only by the glare of his lightsaber.

They reached a flight of stone steps, which Reath knew would lead them down to the outer vestibule of the shrine and the great carved stone doors that opened onto the shrine's inner sanctum. That was the place where dangerous artifacts were taken to be purified when they were retrieved by Jedi on missions out among the stars.

It was also the source of the aching hollow sensation that threatened to overwhelm Reath, a feeling of such loneliness and disillusionment that he could hardly bear it. And yet, he could feel its strength, too, like an endless well of emotions that could be drawn on, harnessed—the sheer raw power of the dark side calling out like a siren song, its melody filled with poisoned promise.

Vernestra remained at the top of the flight of steps as he approached. "Well, Reath. You were right about one thing," she said without turning to regard him.

"What's that?"

"Something down here is very wrong indeed." Reath studied Vernestra for a moment, watching her prepare herself to venture down the steps. She'd closed her eyes, focusing. He could see her jaw working back and forth in an anxious rhythm, a vein in her temple throbbing with the quickened beating of her heart.

Reath couldn't stand to be so close to that surging darkness. The sooner he could get away from there the better. "It's like a scream inside my skull, Vernestra. Like something is calling out through the Force. Like something is dying, and it's *angry*."

"I feel it, too," she said. "But we're not alone. We have each other." She started down the steps. "Come on. Let's find out what we're dealing with."

Slowly, Reath followed.

The outer vestibule was dimly lit by the glow of Reath's lightsaber. The shadows were long and deep, the air oppressive and warm. He could hear rodents scurrying about in the dust and filth, could smell the must of time and abandonment.

The four statues brought back from the Amaxine station were still here, standing in a line against one wall as if awaiting judgment. In the end, the statues had proved not to contain any residual dark side energy of their own. They'd just been part of the rituals used by the ancient Sith to contain the Drengir. Now their silent staring faces loomed out of the gloaming, their blank expressions locked in place for all eternity.

Ahead, the tall stone doors of the shrine's inner sanctum awaited them. The twin doors were framed by pillars of stone, each capped by an ornate lintel, the carvings on which defied easy comprehension.

Reath heard a *vwoosh* and turned to see Vernestra had ignited her lightsaber. "Okay?"

"Not in the slightest," she said, edging forward.

Reath knew exactly what she meant.

Vernestra had reached the double doors. She paused, her hand outstretched, fingertips tracing the faded engravings in the smooth stone. "I've been here before. We both have. But it's never felt like this." She withdrew her hand. "What's waiting for us in there, Reath? What did you see in your vision?"

Reath breathed in deeply, then let it out slowly. "I don't know. In the vision it was a twisted reflection of me, but I haven't had time to meditate on it or try to draw any meaning from it. All I know is that it's dangerous."

"Then we'll face it together," she said. She put her hand on the left door while Reath positioned himself to her right. He reached out his hand, pressing his palm against the cold stone. "On the count of three. One, two . . ."

They both shoved, and the doors grated open in unison.

Reath's heart thudded. He felt sweat prickle his brow. He didn't want to look. He didn't want to see what he'd seen in his vision. . . .

But there was nothing but darkness, a thick impenetrable gloom.

Reath and Vernestra stood in the doorway, lightsabers held aloft. After a moment, the shadows began to shrink away, as if reluctant to abandon their haven.

And the full extent of their problem became horribly, startlingly apparent.

The far end of the chamber was filled with the ashy residue of the blight.

It had been left to run riot over the rear wall, swelling out, consuming the very stone itself. White ash where once there had been, not life exactly but a place of faith, a place still rich in the Force, a place of vergence.

The room was filled with a dusty odor, reminiscent of decay but thinner, like even the mold and the dirt had been consumed.

Reath felt nauseous.

Vernestra took a step back. "Oh . . . Oh, no . . ." Then she took another step. She reached out, touched Reath's arm, shaking him from the reverie of his appalled shock. "Back away. Now."

He did as she said.

"We can't let it out of this shrine. If it reaches the tunnels, it'll spread exponentially. The whole temple could be overrun." Vernestra was staring at the swirling white particles disturbed by the shifting air currents.

"We can't stop it," said Reath. "There's no way to contain it. It's already attacking the walls."

The vestibule seemed suddenly very small and very dark, as if the world were closing in on them.

"What are we going to do?" said Reath.

"I'm going straight to the Council," said Vernestra.

"I'll come with you," said Reath. He started for the flight of steps.

"Whoa, no. Just hold on a minute," said Vernestra, hurrying to catch up. "You're needed elsewhere."

Reath couldn't believe what he was hearing. "What could possibly be more important than *this*?"

"Don't you see? Your research is more crucial now than ever." Vernestra put a hand on his shoulder. "Reath, what you said was right. We can't stop this. Not for long. We need answers. And we need them *soon*. Whatever you have to do to figure this out, you need to do it. I can deal with the Council. At least for now. They're going to want to speak to you, about the vision, and about Azlin. But that can wait. Right now, you're our best hope for finding out how to stop this thing."

"You're right," said Reath. "I know what I have to do."

"Good. Then get it done. Whatever it takes," said Vernestra, hurrying up the steps ahead of him. "And may the Force be with you."

TWENTY-SIX

Reath stood over his workstation in the laboratory, staring at Cair San Tekka's severed hand in its preservative canister.

It still hadn't changed, at least not appreciably. He wondered if there might be a way to hermetically seal off the chamber in the Sith shrine, to create some sort of temporary suspension field that might at least slow the advance of the blight. But he couldn't quite see how it could work. The hand was organic, and it was entirely enclosed within the suspension field. A whole room—that was a different matter entirely. Although he thought it might be worth some sort of experiment, just in case. Any long shot had to be worth considering right now, didn't it?

He stepped back from the bench, rubbing his chin in thought.

He was so lost in his musings that he didn't hear the approach of a newcomer until they rapped on the clear barrier to get his attention.

Distracted, Reath walked over to the door, still not taking his eyes from the canister on the workbench. When he reached it, he finally looked up.

A man was standing on the other side of the divider. He looked shabby, dressed in a blue-gray tunic, brown pants, and a brown robe, with healing patches affixed to both of his cheeks.

At first Reath almost didn't recognize him.

Then, as the identity of the newcomer struck him, he took a step back, as if he'd been caught unguarded by a powerful blow to the chest.

His breath had abandoned him.

His words caught in his throat. "Master Cohmac."

"Hello, Reath," said Cohmac.

Reath's heart thudded like it was trying to punch its way out through his ribs. His mouth was dry.

It couldn't be.

Could it?

He steadied his breathing.

"What are you . . . ? Why are you?" The words seemed to tumble from his lips unbidden.

"I'm here to see you, Reath," said Master Cohmac, his voice level. "Can I come in?"

Slowly, Reath gathered his senses. The shock of seeing his former master like this was almost too much to bear. "No."

Cohmac's face fell. He gave a brief nod of understanding. "All right. I'm sorry to spring it on you like this. I hope . . . perhaps we can talk later instead. I have news."

Reath shook his head. "That's not what I mean. You can't come in the laboratory without a suit. Hold on. I'll come out."

Reath fumbled with the door controls, stepped into the interior lock, and stripped off his suit. He stood for a moment as sterilizing gases hissed from jets in the walls, and then he was done.

He beckoned Master Cohmac back and exited through the other side of the lock.

They stood for a moment in the passageway outside the laboratory entrance, staring at each other.

Reath didn't know whether he wanted to hug him or yell at him.

Master Cohmac studied Reath's expression for a moment. His eyes narrowed. He looked pained. "I'm sorry, Reath. I know it's been too long. I should have reached out long before now. There's so much to say. So much that I need to tell you. Things that I should have said before. I know you felt you weren't ready, but you were and I . . . Well, I needed . . ." It came out in a sudden rush, a torrent. Reath realized these were things Cohmac had been rehearsing, maybe wanting to say for some time.

"Stop," said Reath. It all sounded too much like one of Azlin's games, all that talk of things that needed to be said, of being ready for the truth or not. He couldn't face any more of it, not now, not from Master Cohmac. He wasn't angry. He just needed to know what was going on. He just wanted the truth. "So—are you back?"

"Not really. I came to help. I have information. Something that might help with your research," said Master Cohmac.

Reath ran a hand through his hair, unconsciously feeling for where his Padawan braid used to be. "So you're *not* back?" He was so confused. Why couldn't anyone be straightforward with him?

"I know you think I ran away," said Master Cohmac. "And I suppose I'd be lying if I said that wasn't true. But I never stopped searching. I want you to know that. I've been looking for clues. Trying to figure out where the *Shrii Ka Rai* originated. How to beat them."

Reath stared at his former master, uncomprehending. "You kept on looking? This whole time?"

"Reath, I think I've found something. There was an ancient people who worshipped the Force, over ten thousand years ago. They were called the Tolemites. And they knew about the creatures."

Reath felt tears brimming at the corners of his eyes, but he brushed them away, fighting them back. He'd never quite come to terms with the fact that his master had walked away from him, from the Order, but he also knew that his role here was to try to understand, to forgive. Wasn't that the Jedi way?

That didn't mean it wasn't hard, though.

He nodded. "I know about the Tolemites. I've been research-ing them myself. They knew about the creatures *and* the blight. I think there's a connection between them, and I think the Tolemites knew what it was."

Master Cohmac nodded, encouraged. "I *knew* you'd find the answers, Reath."

Reath blanched at the praise. It was too much, hearing Master Cohmac say something like that. "I haven't found the answers. The trail has gone cold. I don't know how to find their planet."

Master Cohmac smiled. "That's just it, Reath. I do! I've found a map."

Reath shuddered as he took a deep emotion-filled breath. He was so confused about his former master's sudden return, but if Cohmac knew something that could help them find Tolis, he had to listen.

He studied Master Cohmac's dirty bruised face. "You do?"

Master Cohmac nodded. "If we can find their repository, it might provide the answers we're looking for."

"Repository?" echoed Reath.

"Yes. The Three Ancients of the Tolemites built a repository when they retreated to their island nation to die. A place to store all their knowledge of what had happened to them so that it might serve as a warning to those who came after. That's what the people of Thall believed, anyway. I think it's worth the risk of trying to find out. It might still be there."

Reath gaped. A repository. And a location. "We need to tell the Council."

"I already gave Elzar a briefing while I was getting patched up. They're calling an emergency meeting," said Master Cohmac. "I . . . I wanted to talk to you first, Reath. There are things unsaid."

"Later," said Reath. "There'll be time for that later."

When he'd had time to process the shock of it, to work out how he felt, what he wanted to say to Cohmac in return. He'd imagined this moment so many times over the course of the past year, and he'd never thought it would happen like this, with him caught unawares in a passageway outside his own laboratory.

"What happened to you, anyway? You look like you've been wrestling a rancor."

Master Cohmac's expression darkened. He looked away. "I had a run-in with a Nihil Jedi hunter and a few of his pets," he said. The inference was obvious, and Reath stared at him, appalled.

Nameless. He'd faced the Nameless and survived.

Reath felt a sudden flood of compassion for the tired, injured, lonely man standing before him—a man who had been not just a teacher to him but a friend.

Reath took a hesitant step forward, and then, unable to stop himself, he threw his arms wide and pulled Cohmac into a firm hug. "I'm sorry."

Reath fought back tears as Cohmac slowly squeezed him back. "So am I, Reath. So am I."

TWENTY-SEVEN

Despite Master Lox's reassuring smile, Amadeo felt a sudden rush of apprehension as they approached the tall doors to the Jedi Council chamber. Master Lox had explained that an emergency meeting had been called in light of Master Cohmac's unexpected return and that he and, by extension, Amadeo had been invited to attend.

Amadeo had never been to a Council meeting and had no idea what to expect, and the thought was both exciting and daunting. More than that, though, he wanted to make sure that Reath was okay, in light of Master Cohmac's return. Amadeo knew that Reath had been missing his old master terribly but also that he was probably feeling a little confused and uncertain about the surprise return. He made a mental note to check on his friend after the meeting was over.

The door slid open and they entered the chamber. A hush fell over the assembly that awaited them inside, all eyes turning to regard their small party.

The Council had gathered in its entirety, aside from Master Carro, who would soon embark on the first of the Jedi's missions to attempt to obtain a living specimen of the Nameless.

There were several other invited guests in attendance—Elzar Mann, Avar Kriss, and Reath foremost among those Amadeo recognized.

As they crossed the room, Master Lox squeezed Amadeo's shoulder in a gesture of solidarity. He shot Amadeo a broad smile. "Just keep quiet and listen," he whispered. "And enjoy your first real Council meeting."

Amadeo nodded, trying not to look too wide-eyed in front of all these important Jedi.

They took their places in the circle of assembled guests.

A ripple of understanding seemed to pass through the gathered Council members. Amadeo glanced over at Reath, who caught his eye and gave him a thin smile. He was standing beside a rather battered-looking Master Cohmac, who'd clearly been involved in some kind of skirmish, judging by the series of fierce red scars on his cheeks. He no longer looked like a Jedi, dressed as he was in a simple blue-gray tunic, brown pants, and a tattered brown robe.

"Another meeting, so soon," said Master Yoda, looking at

each of them in turn. "But meet again we must, to discuss the news that our friend Master Cohmac has risked his life to share."

Amadeo noted the use of the honorific. So was Master Cohmac back, as in part of the Order again, or was this just a friendly visit to share intelligence? He guessed the lack of Jedi robes meant the latter.

"You are most welcome, Master Cohmac. Your presence has been missed," said Master Ki-Sakka warmly.

"Yes, it is good to have you back," added Master Lahru, the Anx's finlike head bobbing slightly as he spoke. "And it seems the information you have brought to share with us was obtained at great cost."

Master Cohmac looked uncomfortable. "Yes, well . . ." He sounded grave. "A Nihil Jedi hunter has been stalking me these last few months. He found me on the planet Thall. I almost succumbed to his Nameless."

A murmur of appalled shock passed through the room.

"I'm sure I speak for all of us when I say that we are heartily relieved that you did not," said Master Agra. Her eyelids flickered across her jet-black eyes, and her Nautolan head tendrils shifted on her shoulders.

Master Cohmac nodded. "My thanks." He straightened his back, looking at each of the Council members in turn. "I should be clear. I am here to help. To share my findings and do whatever I can to address the Nameless problem. It does not mean that I have returned to the Order. But I cannot, in good conscience, keep from you the things that I have learned."

"We understand," said Master Ki-Sakka, "and we wish you to know that you are always welcome, Master Cohmac."

"Heartening, this is," said Yoda. "Your counsel shall be invaluable."

"It seems you've been rather busy while you've been away," said Master Agra.

"We all have," said Master Cohmac. "Much has changed. The Jedi Order's position in the galaxy seems more tenuous than ever before, its enemies more confident. And with just cause."

"Indeed," said Master Murag. "With the blight taking root and the Republic considering a treaty with Marchion Ro, things have never looked so bleak."

"And yet, if there's one thing that I have learned from all of this," said Cohmac, "it's that there's still hope. An old friend reminded me of that." He looked thoughtful. "The truth is, we're close to a breakthrough, thanks in no small part to the work of Reath here. He's filled me in on his work. It seems we stand on the precipice of finally understanding the truth about what we face and, I believe, learning what we must do to defeat it."

"Master Elzar has already made us aware of your recent findings," said Master Adampo. He stroked his whiskers while he spoke. "Your discovery of the star map and the location of the planet Tolis, where you believe the ancient Tolemites once resided, and where their Three Ancients established a repository that, if real, could hold the answers we so desperately seek."

"Some of them, at least," said Master Cohmac.

Amadeo glanced at Master Lox. So *that* was what was going

on. Master Cohmac had returned to Coruscant with the location of the Tolemites' homeworld. Amadeo could hardly believe it.

Like master, like Padawan.

"And what do you propose our next move should be?" asked Master Ki-Sakka.

"I propose that Reath and I carry out an urgent expedition to Tolis to attempt to recover the Tolemites' cultural archive," said Master Cohmac almost immediately.

Amadeo watched Reath ball his fists inside the sleeves of his robes. He clearly hadn't been expecting that.

Master Ki-Sakka leaned forward in his seat. He was looking directly at Reath. "What do you say to this proposition, Reath?"

Reath cleared his throat. "I agree with Master Cohmac." He had a slight tremor in his voice, and he glanced at his former master once, quickly, before looking back at Master Ki-Sakka. "There is nothing more I can do in the Archives or the laboratory until we have fresh samples or a living Nameless subject with which to confirm my theories. Our best hope, for now, is that the Tolemites might have left us a clue, or at least a direction for further study." He took a short breath. "I understand that the Tolemite legend is just that—a legend—but until recently the Nameless were just a fairy tale, too. Master Cohmac's findings prove that Tolis is real. I think we have to take the risk and make an expedition."

"And you believe that you, a young Knight, and your former master, now outside of the Order and beyond our tenets and protocols, are the best people to make this expedition," said Master Murag. Amadeo could hear the dubiousness in his tone.

Reath nodded. "I do. And please, understand that it is hard for me, Master Murag. It has been a difficult year since Master Cohmac left." Amadeo could see the strain in Reath's expression as he tread carefully around the subject of Cohmac's leaving. "But we are the two people best placed in this room to interpret and make sense of the Tolemites' repository, if it does exist." He paused for a moment before continuing. "So many of us have died at the hands of these creatures. So many have sacrificed themselves to enable us to continue the fight. And now the blight is coming for us, too, here in this very temple. I just want it all to stop."

The blight. Here on Coruscant!

Amadeo *really* needed to catch up with Reath.

"Correct you are, Reath Silas," said Master Yoda. "An end to this, we must find. And soon. A great burden this Council has placed upon the shoulders of one so young."

Several of the Council members exchanged glances.

"Now is the time to look forward, not dwell on what has already passed. Second, I do, Master Cohmac's proposal that he and Reath journey to Tolis to continue their investigation."

"All in favor?" said Master Ki-Sakka.

The show of hands was far from unanimous—with both Masters Agra and Murag abstaining—but the motion carried.

"My ship needs some repairs," said Master Cohmac.

"Um, we could travel with members of the Byne Guild," suggested Reath before anyone else had a chance to interject. "Affie Hollow and the crew of the *Vessel*. They've become great allies in recent months, running dangerous transport missions to take Jedi into territories bordering the Occlusion Zone."

"True, this is," said Master Yoda. "And you have traveled with them before. An ideal fit, I believe."

"Very well," said Master Ki-Sakka. "We shall make the necessary arrangements. A Byne Guild ship will be less conspicuous than a Jedi ship, especially with this Jedi hunter still on the prowl."

"Excellent," said Master Cohmac. "Reath?"

"Thank you," he said, addressing the Council as a whole. "We won't let you down."

"We know, Reath," said Master Murag, his tone diplomatic. "You have the well-wishes of us all. The Force guides our hand, and we must place our trust in it. And you."

Amadeo couldn't tell if the comment was intended as a backhanded compliment or a criticism, but Reath inclined his head graciously all the same.

"What, then, of our other mission?" said Master Lahru.

"Yes," said Master Rancisis. "Our plan to capture the creatures for study. Master Carro will be leaving soon aboard the *Innovator* to undertake such an endeavor, but we feel, given the risks involved, a second mission is required."

Amadeo had heard about this mission from Master Lox—an attempt to trap a Nameless. It was a bold plan but the sort of plan the Jedi needed right now.

"Indeed," said Master Ki-Sakka. "For those here who are unaware, Chancellor Soh has agreed to a series of joint missions between the Jedi and the RDC. Construction of a holding facility is almost complete, several levels down in the city. For this second mission, two Jedi will be joined by a field specialist drafted from a mercenary unit, their combat droid, and an RDC medical officer, along with a small team of RDC volunteers. They've all been vetted and show no deep connection to the Force, meaning they do not share the Jedi's vulnerability to the creatures." He glanced at Reath then, as if seeking verification. Reath nodded.

"The Jedi will lead the mission," continued Master Ki-Sakka, "but the RDC personnel will be strictly responsible for handling the creature during and after its capture. A second, smaller RDC ship is being outfitted with a triple-layered holding pen, and the creature shall remain sedated during transfer to the facility back on Coruscant. This second ship will be transported inside the hold of the main vessel at the outset of the mission but will travel back to Coruscant independently once the creature is aboard, to protect the Jedi from its malign influence."

"A well-conceived plan, this is," said Master Yoda.

"Yes," said Master Lahru, "at least in terms of the necessary precautions needed to handle such a beast. But where are we going to find one? We don't yet know where the Nameless occur in the wild, and we can't simply knock on Marchion Ro's door and ask him to donate a specimen."

"We've identified a small Nihil base on the planet Angoth, where we believe one of the creatures is being held in preparation for the so-called Jedi hunters the Nihil are using to target our teams in the field. Such as the one encountered by Cohmac on Thall," said Master Ki-Sakka. "With a targeted attack, we could strike quickly and efficiently. They won't be expecting us, so we have the element of surprise. The Jedi can keep the Nihil busy while the RDC and their military support rounds up and neutralizes the creature. Then both vessels will make a swift retreat before the Nihil can deploy reinforcements."

"You make it sound easy," said Elzar Mann. "But we all know there's a lot that could go wrong."

"It's a dangerous mission," agreed Master Yarael. "One of the most dangerous we've ever countenanced. The risks are beyond measure. How do we even begin to ask two of our number to take on this burden?"

"I'll go," said Master Lox, stepping forward from beside Amadeo.

Amadeo's heart thrummed. *Really?*

Master Lox glanced at Amadeo, and a flicker of understanding passed between them. "With Amadeo. We have more recent field experience than most, and we're ready to take on the Nihil. And their pets."

Master Rancisis looked surprised. "You understand what you're saying? What might happen if the mission goes awry?"

"I do," said Master Lox. "We both do." Amadeo knew that Master Lox felt a certain obligation to step up, having been on the other side of the galaxy when both Valo and Starlight Beacon were attacked. They both wanted to play their part.

"Amadeo?" said Master Ki-Sakka. "Like Reath, I believe you should speak for yourself in this. It is a dangerous mission, and one of the utmost importance. Do you concur with Master Lox? You should understand that it is perfectly acceptable to say no."

Amadeo felt stricken at even being addressed by a member of the Jedi Council, and he hesitated for a moment, considering the question before answering. Then he puffed out his chest, standing tall. He crossed to stand by his master's side. "Yes, Master Ki-Sakka. I do. I believe it's the right choice. We're ready. Our time on the frontier has prepared us well. We can do this." He glanced at Reath out of the corner of his eye. Reath smiled encouragingly.

Master Ki-Sakka nodded. "Very well." He looked to the other members of the Council. "Do I hear any objections from the Council?"

A brief flurry of mumblings was followed by silence.

"Then, Mirro, Amadeo—we wish you every success. You carry us all with you as you walk into the jaws of danger, for the good of the Order and the entire Republic," said Master Ki-Sakka.

A rumble of agreement passed through all those gathered.

"I declare this meeting of the Council adjourned," said Master Lahru. "And I thank you all for your courage. May the Force be with you."

Amadeo felt a flush of excitement. This was huge. He and Master Lox were being trusted with a mission of incredible importance. Dangerous, yes, but this was what they'd been training for.

Master Lox patted him on the shoulder. "You sure you're okay with this, Padawan?"

Amadeo grinned. "Of course. You were right. We're best placed to do it."

"Well, I'm proud to have you by my side, Amadeo."

"And I'm proud to *be* by your side, Master."

Master Lox guided him toward the door. "I suppose we should get started with the necessary preparations. We don't have long."

Amadeo watched as Reath walked out with Master Cohmac. The pair were deep in conversation. But then Reath broke off abruptly, hurrying in the opposite direction. For a moment Master Cohmac watched him go and then sighed and turned back to catch up with Elzar and Avar.

Master Lox had noticed him watching. "I'm pleased to see you're still keeping an eye on your friend. But give them time. Everything is going to be okay."

Amadeo beamed. "Yes, Master. I hope so."

TWENTY-EIGHT

Reath felt his breath catch in his throat as he stood outside the door to Azlin's chambers, debating whether to go in.

He knew he shouldn't have come, not after everything that had just happened in the Council chamber. He had a mission to prepare for, and time was already short. And yet he found his sense of fairness challenged by the notion of rushing off to Tolis without sharing the news of their discovery with Azlin.

Perhaps more than anyone else Reath knew, Azlin would appreciate how momentous their find was. He'd spent decades—over a century, in fact—searching for answers about the Nameless, and thanks to the final piece of information from Master Cohmac, the Jedi finally knew where to look. If the legends were right, they were close to discovering the truth of the *Shrii Ka Rai*'s origins and their link to the blight.

So Reath had hurried to give Azlin the news in person before making the final arrangements to leave.

It was the right thing to do.

And besides, he was still trying to process his feelings over his reconciliation with Cohmac. Everything was happening so fast: Cohmac's return. The mission. He hadn't had time to figure out how he felt about it all. And he still didn't really understand why Cohmac had left, and whether Reath himself had played a part in his decision. That was Reath's deepest, most uncomfortable fear—that Cohmac had only taken him on as a Padawan because he'd felt obliged after what happened on the Amaxine station and following Jora Malli's death.

Azlin wasn't a kind man, or a good mentor, but at least Reath knew where he stood with him. Most of the others wouldn't understand. They had each other, their friends, their masters or Padawans. Take Amadeo—Reath had seen the look on Lox's face when they'd walked into the chamber. It was the same look Cohmac might once have given him, back in the days before the Nihil and the Nameless and everything that had happened since.

Reath didn't have that anymore—not really. He had friends, of course, people he cared about and who he hoped cared about him. But that closeness was gone.

Which had brought him back to this door—again. But then it was healthy to talk about things. Cohmac had taught him that. Maybe discussing things with Azlin would help him gain some clarity and perspective that, in turn, would help him navigate his emotions when he spoke with Cohmac later. At least, that was what he told himself as he stepped inside.

He found Azlin sitting cross-legged on his bunk, toying with a small wooden puzzle box. He held the thing in both hands, balanced on his lap. Reath had seen their kind before, in the markets on the lower levels of the city. It was designed as a series of interlinking rods and slots that could be removed only in a particular sequence. They all had to be undone in order to access the tiny chamber at the puzzle's heart. The idea was that someone— whoever was gifting the puzzle—placed some sort of prize in that cavity, something special to the person solving the puzzle, that would serve as both a motivation and a reward.

Reath wondered where Azlin had obtained it. Master Yoda, perhaps? He knew of no one besides himself who visited the outcast in his dismal lair.

Azlin didn't turn around as Reath entered the room. His brows were creased in concentration, although it didn't yet look as though he'd attempted to remove any of the wooden rods.

"Hello, Azlin," said Reath, crossing to the small side table. As usual, he prepared the kettle and placed it on the heating unit to boil for tea. Still no response. Perhaps Azlin wasn't feeling in a communicative mood. Reath decided he'd make the tea and then leave if Azlin remained absorbed in his puzzle.

When Reath settled into his usual chair, however, Azlin's head snapped around alarmingly, as if he'd only just become aware of Reath's presence. "You're leaving."

"I am. On a mission." There was no point in protesting.

Azlin's preternatural abilities were a constant source of awe and discomfort, usually in equal measure.

Azlin's fingers danced over the surface of the puzzle box on his lap. He faced Reath, his eyeless pits seeming to draw the weak light of the emitter, as if leaching all illumination from the room. Reath found himself wishing the man were wearing his customary goggles.

"You've identified it, haven't you? The homeworld of the Tolemites." Azlin leaned forward as he spoke, his tone anxious, enthused—perhaps even nervous. Reath had never seen him quite so intense. And that was saying a lot, as Azlin was one of the most intense people he'd ever met. "I sense your eagerness, your need to tell me."

"Yes. We have. We've located Tolis. Master Cohmac found a star map in the ruins on Thall. It was partially destroyed but still readable in places. It matched up perfectly with my research."

"And?"

"We leave in the morning. If the Tolemites really did find a way to defeat the Nameless and the blight, if you're right that the Three Ancients managed to start again on an island there, we're going to find it."

Azlin exhaled slowly. He steepled his hands before his chest. "You really are exceptional, Reath. The work you are doing . . . it will save us all."

The kettle whistled shrilly. Reath rose from his seat to attend to it. "I'm just part of a team," he said. "If it wasn't for Amadeo's insights, we might never have made the connection between the Nameless and the blight. If you hadn't told your version of the Tolemites' legend, I wouldn't know about the island, and if Cohmac hadn't been following the trail to Thall, none of this would have happened. All I've done is help put the pieces together."

"No," said Azlin emphatically. "What you've done is *listen*. Not many would have given a young Padawan the opportunity to assist in their research. You sensed in Amadeo a connection and an insight you could use. And you listened to *me*. Despite the criticism of the Council and your peers. You saw the value in an old, decrepit outcast. . . ."

Reath handed him a mug of steaming tea. "I thought you deserved to know what was going on. The progress we'd made. That's all," he said.

"And for that, I thank you, my boy," said Azlin. It was the most genuine thing Reath had ever heard him say. "I am proud of the progress you have made. Now you are setting out on your own quest for truth. Just like I did so many years ago."

"It's not like that," said Reath, feeling uncomfortable at the suggestion. There was no comparison to be made between him and Azlin—none at all. "It's a sanctioned mission."

Azlin laughed, clearly amused by Reath's sudden irritation. "I understand your frustration, Reath. Your uncertainty. Your old master has returned, and you do not know what to make of it."

Reath shifted uncomfortably in his seat. "Perhaps."

"It is not yourself that you doubt. Be clear about that. That troubled feeling, that well of guilt and uncertainty inside of you—it is not yours to bear. That pain belongs to Cohmac. He was the one who walked away from you, Reath. He must carry that burden, not you. Never you."

Reath looked away, staring at the scrawl on the far wall.

"You must be strong. You must recognize the strength inside of you. Do not allow anyone to make you doubt it. Not me, not Cohmac. It is the only way you will see this through."

More cryptic words. Reath didn't know what to make of it all. Perhaps Azlin was right; perhaps it was Cohmac's guilt to bear. But that didn't mean he couldn't repair things with his old master, did it? "You say that I understand you, Azlin, but I don't," said Reath. "Whatever it is you're trying to tell me, just say it."

"Very well," said Azlin. "If I may, I would offer a piece of advice to take with you on your quest. Despite what you may think, young Reath, I would prefer for you to return from this dangerous pursuit in one piece. Will you hear me out?"

"Of course," said Reath.

"Excellent," said Azlin. "Then understand this: to survive the *Shrii Ka Rai*, there is only one recourse, a single path you might take."

"And that is?"

Azlin placed his tea on the side table. He turned his unseeing eyes on Reath. His thin lips curled, not in a smile but in a knowing sneer. "You must embrace your fear, Reath."

Reath looked away, unable to meet that terrible gaze. "What you're saying . . . You're talking about the dark side."

But Azlin merely smiled and turned his attention back to his puzzle box, indicating that their conversation was over.

TWENTY-NINE

Vernestra hung back in the gloomy stone recess at the far end of the passage and studied the figure of the Temple Guard with interest.

Just like all the other Jedi Temple Guards she'd encountered on her way down here, this one was stoic and unmoving, standing just a few meters away from the door to Azlin's cell. A slight lean to one side from what she guessed was an old injury, highly polished armor, smooth anonymous mask. The very image of dedication. It was a comfort to know he was there, keeping a watchful eye on the cell's inhabitant.

She didn't think the guard was aware of her. In fact, she was certain that he would have challenged her by now if he had been.

Nevertheless, she pressed herself deeper into the shadowy alcove, just to be sure.

Reath had been inside Azlin's cell for around twenty minutes. Vernestra wondered what the two of them were talking about. Was Reath reporting back on what they'd found in the Sith shrine below? Was he challenging Azlin as to why the fallen Jedi hadn't thought to mention his suspicions sooner?

She also wondered if she was doing the right thing even being there. She was effectively spying on people, after all, which hardly felt like the sort of thing a Jedi should be getting up to. If Reath found out, he would most likely see it as a terrible betrayal of trust. But to Vernestra's mind, it wasn't that at all—far from it. It was more that she was trying to look out for him, to protect him.

From *what* exactly, she still wasn't sure. But she hadn't yet shaken that nagging sensation that something was wrong or off-kilter. She'd hoped it would subside following their discovery of the blight—which was certainly a huge problem by any definition—but much to her dismay, the feeling had only intensified. She hadn't talked to anyone about it yet, simply because she didn't know what to say. She wanted something more solid first, to be able to properly articulate what it was that had her feeling so on edge.

So as usual, she'd trusted her gut, and her gut had brought her here.

She knew it wasn't Reath himself that was troubling her. Vernestra trusted him implicitly. He was dedicated to the Order, perhaps as much as anyone she'd ever known. More than that, though, she knew him to be a good man.

But Azlin Rell? How could anyone trust the fallen Jedi, after the way he'd manipulated Master Yoda and killed all those people on Travyx Prime? Yes, he'd been through a lot, and she knew only too well how horrendous it must have been for him to face the Nameless alone all those years ago. But while she sympathized with Azlin's plight and understood how that fear might have colored everything that came after, her compassion didn't extend to forgiving him for the casual way he had killed so many people. And she didn't trust that he wasn't trying to manipulate the rest of the Jedi Order into doing his bidding, either.

She understood that Reath had been authorized—even encouraged by some—to use Azlin as a resource, that he had a duty to find out everything Azlin knew about the Nameless. But she couldn't discount the idea that Azlin was somehow using Reath in turn.

Azlin was hardly being forthcoming, either, judging by what Reath had said. How long had he known about, or at least suspected, the blight infection in the Sith shrine? Could he have raised the alarm sooner? Had he waited to ensure the timing of the discovery suited his own unclear purpose?

Perhaps she was reading too much into things, but she intended to find out—partly to look out for her friend and partly to ensure they weren't all idling toward some kind of trap.

Vernestra heard a noise and peered around the edge of the alcove.

She watched Reath exit the cell looking flustered. The door slid shut behind him. He walked briskly down the passageway toward her.

She tucked herself into the shadows.

Reath was too preoccupied to notice her. He hurried by without a glance in her direction. She let out a long breath.

So what now?

She supposed she'd come here for nothing, really. She wasn't going to learn much skulking in shadows.

Just as she was about to leave, she heard a knocking sound coming from the direction of Azlin's cell.

Rap, rap, rap.

Like the tapping of knuckles on the wall, summoning attention.

As Vernestra watched, the Temple Guard slowly straightened, glanced down the passageway after Reath, and then turned and approached the door to Azlin's cell. The door opened and the Temple Guard slipped inside. The door slid shut behind him.

Vernestra fought the temptation to edge closer. There was every chance she'd give herself away, and then there'd not only be an awkward conversation—for which she didn't have an explanation quite prepared yet—but she'd have alerted Azlin that she was . . .

What *was* she doing?

Keeping an eye on him, she supposed.

A couple of minutes passed, and then the door opened again, and the Temple Guard stepped out. He glanced up and down the passageway and then, clearly assured that no one else was present, returned to his post a few meters down the corridor, standing attentively with his back to the wall.

Vernestra frowned. What was going on? Was the Temple Guard simply checking on his prisoner following Azlin's meeting with Reath? Was that protocol? Or was he supposed to be prohibited from interacting with the fallen Jedi? She realized she didn't know.

And she was damn well going to figure it out.

PART
TWO

THIRTY

Amadeo looked at the huge *Pacifier*-class transport ship, the *Invictus*, sitting squat and dark on the landing strip, and found himself fighting back an ominous brooding sensation that was threatening to worm its way into his mind.

He always felt like this before a mission. Didn't he?

Yes. He was certain of it. Especially since the coming of the blight. It was just his usual trepidation, the tension he always felt before heading off into the unknown. It was what gave him an edge, a form of hyperalertness to danger.

It had nothing at all to do with the fact they were going after one of the Nameless.

Amadeo drew a deep breath, held it for a moment, and then blew it out, expelling all his fear and anxiety along with it.

The mission was going to be a success.

It was.

He walked along the landing strip, buffeted by the cool crosswinds high among Coruscant's upper levels. People in RDC uniforms were milling about, loading crates and supplies into the main hold of the ship. One—a slim woman with pale skin and dusty red hair—was bent over an open crate, apparently examining the cache of equipment within.

A tall sleek silver droid was standing close by, its hands on its hips. It had a vaguely humanoid shape but was stocky and imposing, with two long forearms and a blaster mounted on a frame on its back. It had a single large eye in the center of its head that shone a stark red as it looked at him.

Amadeo had never seen anything like it. He guessed these were the mercenaries hired to assist the RDC.

"You're staring," said the woman, who Amadeo now realized was looking up from the crate to peer at him in apparent amusement.

"I'm sorry?" said Amadeo, tearing his eyes from the droid.

"No need," said the woman. She put her hand to her mouth as if sharing a secret with him. "He is a strange-looking droid, isn't he?"

"I shall ask you to refrain from referring to others in such a pejorative manner," said the droid, the deep resonating timbre of its voice seeming to vibrate through the soles of Amadeo's boots. "It is both impolite and unnecessary."

"Ummm . . ." Amadeo didn't quite know what to say.

The woman rolled her eyes. "Don't be touchy," she said with a lopsided grin. She returned her gaze to Amadeo. "You must be the younger one."

"The younger what?" said Amadeo, feeling utterly confused.

"Jedi," said the woman. "You're too short to be the master, so you must be the Padawan."

"What did I *just* say?" said the droid.

"That wasn't offensive," said the woman. She looked puzzled. "Was it?"

"You called him short. A short Jedi," countered the droid.

"I was just explaining how I figured out he was a Padawan and not a master," said the woman. "I didn't mean to cause offense." She looked genuinely confused.

"You can tell that from the hair braid," said the droid. "You didn't have to bring his stature into the conversation at all. Now he probably thinks we dislike short people and we're not going to defend his life against the Force Eaters during the mission. He probably thinks he's going to die a miserable death all because of your prejudice against him because he's not tall enough to meet your exacting standards of what a Jedi should be."

Amadeo held up a hand to try to interrupt the pair, but they both ignored him.

"Now you're just projecting, Sevens. I bet the nice young Jedi doesn't think that at all. You're just fed up with the fact you don't look as fancy as all those ridiculous protocol droids they have shuffling around this place serving drinks and mumbling in a thousand different languages. But just think—how would *they* handle themselves in a fight? What would you rather be, eh? Boring and fancy, or interesting and deadly?"

The droid seemed to consider this for longer than Amadeo would have imagined necessary. "I'll concede that point," it said after a while, "but *only* that point. The rest still stands. And besides, you know I don't *choose* to be deadly."

"Yes, of course," said the woman. "You're a peace-loving defender. You hate violence." She shot him a glance. "You just happen to be rather good at it."

"A perfect summary," said the droid, who Amadeo had gathered was called Sevens.

The two of them lapsed into silence, both turning their attention to Amadeo.

"Let's start again," said the woman after a moment. "I'm very pleased to meet you . . . ?"

"Oh, right. Yes. Jedi Padawan Amadeo Azzazzo," he mumbled. "It's, er . . . nice to meet you, too."

"See?" said the woman beneath her breath. "I was right."

"Yes, we've already established that," said Sevens.

"And you are?" ventured Amadeo.

The woman nodded to herself, as if deciding that she would provide Amadeo with her name, after all. "Ashton Vol," she said. "And this is El-Seventy-Seven. But he prefers Sevens."

"No, I don't," said L-77.

"Nice to meet you," repeated Amadeo hurriedly, in an effort to ward off any further arguments.

"Yeah," said Ashton. "It is."

Amadeo wasn't sure whether she was expressing mutual

pleasure at meeting him or simply agreeing that it was, indeed, nice to meet her.

"You're in charge of capturing the Nameless and bringing it back to the facility?" asked Amadeo.

"We are," said Ashton. "We're here to help. We have a lot of experience fighting the Nihil, helping to defend settlements on the border of the Occlusion Zone. We'll do our best to help you bring one of those creatures home."

"And no matter what she implied earlier, young Jedi, we *will* do everything in our power to protect you from the creatures when the time comes. Your height is utterly irrelevant," added L-77.

"Thank you," said Amadeo, suppressing a smile. "I'm glad to hear it."

Ashton shook her head and returned to studying the contents of the crate. "Dorian's already on the ship," she said without looking up.

"Dorian?" queried Amadeo.

"The medic," said Ashton. "Nice guy, and handy in a scrape."

"How about I go and say hello," said Amadeo.

"Very wise," said L-77. "Good to keep the medics on your side. Never know when you might need a field amputation, after all."

"Riiight." Amadeo hurried up the ramp.

Inside, the ship was spacious but poorly appointed for comfort. There was a roomy hold to the rear, accessible through a large hatchway that was currently open, revealing a hangar space occupied by another, smaller vessel. This was the *Orchid*, the secondary ship that would be used to bring the captured Nameless back to Coruscant once the mission had proved successful.

Various ground crew were carrying out tests, running fuel lines, and generally being industrious in a manner that made Amadeo feel dizzy. Everything seemed to be happening so quickly. They were leaving for Angoth in less than an hour. A few hours after that they'd be there. And then . . .

He put the thought out of mind and concentrated on his surroundings.

Here, in the central section of the ship, the space had been fitted out in a typically efficient style, with low benches running the length of both inner walls, dotted at intervals with straps and webbing so personnel could secure themselves during particularly adverse flying conditions. The cockpit was accessible through another small hatch, equipment lockers were fixed to the walls overhead, and a small field medical station was at the rear, off to one side.

Standing at the medical station was a tall thin man with a gentle jawline and a fuzz of downy beard. He was young. Amadeo guessed he was maybe the same age as Reath, so probably just a year or two older than Amadeo himself. He was wearing a loose-fitting RDC uniform and had his blond hair swept back in a neat wave. He turned and flashed Amadeo a crooked grin.

"Umm, hi," said Amadeo. "You must be Dorian."

"Dorian Innes, medical officer," he said. His voice was soft, with a husky crack like the shushing of dried leaves. "And you're Amadeo Azzazzo."

Amadeo felt an immediate pull of attraction—and then a sudden flush of embarrassment. He'd always been attracted to both men and women, and something about Dorian's warm smile seemed to draw him in.

He acknowledged the feeling and then put it aside. Now wasn't the time for such thoughts, and—despite his occasional flush of teenage hormones—he'd learned just recently not to allow himself to be overtaken by these things. Especially when he had such an important mission to focus on.

He smiled. "Yes. That's me. Amadeo."

"I'd guessed as much from the robes," said Dorian. "And the medical records I studied before the trip." He looked Amadeo up and down appraisingly. "For what it's worth, you're not short at all."

"You heard that?" said Amadeo.

Dorian laughed. "Don't take it to heart. Ashton means well. She has a good heart, and she'll do everything she can to help make the mission a success. She's had a tough time of it fighting back against the Nihil, and she wants to make a difference. She's just not great with people, that's all."

"And not much better with droids, by the look of it," said Amadeo, joining in with Dorian's laughter.

"Oh, don't let their bickering fool you. Those two are as thick as thieves. Always have been." Dorian returned to whatever he'd been doing at the medical station when Amadeo arrived. He appeared to be taking a final inventory of supplies.

"So, I hear you're an expert in field amputation," said Amadeo, walking over and taking a seat on the nearest bench.

"Oh, yeah. I love it. Can't get enough of all that blood.

Any opportunity, I'm out there with a vibrosaw." For a moment Amadeo was almost disturbed by the gleam in Dorian's eye, before the beaming smile returned. "They're just messing with you. I've never carried out an amputation in my life."

"Well, I guess that's reassuring, at least," said Amadeo.

"There's always a first time, though," said Dorian with a sly wink. "So you'd better do what the droid said and keep on the right side of me."

"Noted," said Amadeo. He was just about to ask Dorian how many missions he'd been on when another figure appeared in the open hatchway, blocking out most of the natural light.

Amadeo cupped his hand around his eyes to see, but he already sensed the familiar reassuring presence of his master.

"Padawan. Good to see you're eager." Master Lox strolled over to join them. He was dressed in his mission robes, just like Amadeo. He shot Dorian a thin smile. "You must be Dorian. I'm—"

"Master Mirro Lox," finished Dorian. "It's good to meet you."

Lox inclined his head. "I hope we won't have need of your services, Dorian, but your company is most welcome." Master Lox glanced at Amadeo, smiled, and then made for the cockpit.

Dorian caught Amadeo's eye. "Don't worry. If I do need to practice my amputations, I'm sure he'll offer to go first."

Amadeo couldn't contain his laughter.

THIRTY-ONE

"**R**eath!"

Reath hadn't been quite ready for the running, leaping embrace Affie Hollow enveloped him in the moment he walked into the bustling hangar bay, but he leaned into it happily, squeezing the young woman gently until she finally released her hold.

It was still early, but Reath had been told to meet the crew—and Master Cohmac—here at the civilian transport hub, where ground crew were already busy ushering haulage vessels in and out in quick succession, filling the air with the constant whine of engines and the commingling scents of hot oil and ozone. They'd be on their way to Tolis within the hour, and Reath was carrying a knot of anxiety wound tight in his chest.

Affie held him by the shoulders as she studied his face. "Hi. It's been a while."

Reath laughed. "It's good to see you, Affie."

Affie was dressed in her usual gray coveralls—practical for life aboard her ship, the *Vessel*—and her dark hair was tied back from her beaming tan face. Her happy demeanor lifted Reath's spirits. She was like a breath of fresh air.

"It's *great* to see you," said Affie. "I want to know everything, all right? All your news, everything that's been going on since I last saw you."

Reath tried not to bristle at the very idea. Where would he even start? Though it wasn't as if Affie had had an easy time of things, either, by all accounts. She'd been aboard Starlight Beacon as it fell, escaping at the last minute on the *Vessel*. He'd heard that she'd spent some time on Eiram, too, in the aftermath of the disaster, helping rally the relief effort and organize the refugees. And since then, she'd been working to reestablish the Byne Guild as a collective whose members were working to protect each other from the Nihil and reporting to the Republic on Nihil movements. Not to mention the fact she'd volunteered to help out with missions such as this one, ferrying Jedi from place to place when they needed to travel clandestinely or their scarce resources were otherwise engaged.

Affie was one of the good ones, a true ally and a friend.

"I gather we've both been busy," said Reath, somewhat understating the point.

"That we have," said Affie, miming weariness with an exaggerated sigh.

"All right, Little Bit, leave the poor guy alone for a minute."

The familiar voice came from over by the ship, and Reath peered around Affie to see Leox Gyasi and Geode standing by the *Vessel*'s boarding ramp.

Leox gave a little salute in greeting, touching one fingertip to his temple and then pinging it in Reath's direction with an outstretched thumb, as if mimicking a blaster. The man looked like he hadn't aged a day since Reath had seen him last in the aftermath of the Drengir attack on the Amaxine space station. His dark blond hair curled messily around his ears, and his jaw was covered in the same perpetual day-old stubble. He was grinning broadly.

Beside him, Geode, the towering Vintian, greeted Reath with his usual welcoming silence.

"Leox, Geode!" called Reath, offering them both a little wave. It really was good to see them all, a reminder that, even when things looked bleak, there were still those who persevered regardless, who didn't give up—good people doing great things.

"Ah! There he is," said Affie.

Reath turned to see Master Cohmac walking across the hangar bay. Unlike Reath, who was wearing his mission robes, Cohmac was wearing the same tunic, robe, and pants he'd worn for the Council meeting, and the scratches on his face seemed to be healing well. He looked a little hesitant but was smiling warmly. He held up his hand in greeting.

"Hello, Affie," he said.

"Just like the old days," said Affie. "Reath, Cohmac, and the crew of the *Vessel*, heading off on an adventure."

Reath couldn't help smiling. It definitely wasn't going to be quite like the old days, but perhaps it could be something new. At least, that was what he hoped. He was just going to have to take each day as it came.

Still, the only thing that *really* mattered was what they found on Tolis. This mission—he had a sense that it might be their best and last chance to make a real difference, to stop the tide of oblivion that threatened to wash over not just the Republic and the Jedi but the entire galaxy.

No pressure, then, Reath.

Being surrounded by these people was a potent reminder of everything that was at stake. He couldn't allow anyone else to be hurt—not by the Nihil, or the Nameless, or the blight. He had to protect these people he cared about, all of them. And he would do anything—*anything*—to do so.

Master Cohmac turned to regard him. "Are you ready, Reath?"

"I am," said Reath, his tone unequivocal.

"Then let's do this. Together."

Together. The word seemed to echo around the inside of Reath's head.

They followed Affie and the others up the boarding ramp to the ship.

⚜

The *Vessel* plunged through the flickering depths of hyperspace, silent and serene. The only sound was the background hum of the engines.

Reath wondered if the old adage was true and this was merely the calm before the storm—the moment of quiet inhalation before the chaos set in.

He'd spent the first hour of the journey catching up with Affie, exchanging stories of their adventures in the intervening time since they'd last seen each other. He'd told her all about his research and the reason they were heading to Tolis in the first place.

Now Affie, Leox, and Geode were all up front in the cockpit, debating the best route to get them there, while Master Cohmac and Reath sat alone in the common area, sharing a companionable silence.

They'd agreed to leave the navigating to the experts, having provided the coordinates they'd derived from the old star map on Thall. Reath gathered they'd be following a series of old hyperspace lanes that hadn't been used—at least not by any Republic or Jedi vessels—for decades.

Tolis—if it still existed—was on the edge of Wild Space, and no one had had cause to come this way for trade or exploration since the days of the old Pathfinder teams. There was nothing there.

Except, perhaps, the answer to everything, waiting for them on a world that had been long forgotten.

Reath let out a long sigh.

Master Cohmac looked over at him from his seat. "Are you okay?"

"Yes, fine," said Reath, dissembling. "I hope this isn't a wild bantha chase, is all. There's so much riding on us. It feels like we're running out of time, and we don't have any other leads."

"Maybe we don't need any other leads," said Master Cohmac. "Maybe the Force has led us to this point for a reason. I think we're exactly where we need to be."

"I admire your optimism," said Reath.

Master Cohmac gave him a wan smile. "It isn't optimism. I suppose it's a little bit of hope."

"And faith in the Force?" asked Reath, careful to weigh his words so the question didn't seem too unkind. It was a genuine query.

"Something like that," said Master Cohmac.

"All the same," said Reath. "I hope you're right."

Master Cohmac leaned forward, his hands on his knees. "Since when did you become such a cynic?"

Reath felt himself shriveling under his old master's stare. "I don't know. . . ." He pinched the bridge of his nose. Did he really want to talk about this now? He supposed he didn't have much choice. "So much has happened. So many terrible things." He met Master Cohmac's gaze. "And then you left, and the Stormwall went up, and I didn't know whether you were dead or alive."

Master Cohmac looked pained. "I'm sorry, Reath. I know you found it hard to understand, but I needed time. Everything that we'd seen, everything that was happening, the horror of the Nameless . . . The Order wasn't built to deal with a crisis on this scale. Our tenets can't help us navigate the galaxy we now find ourselves in. I found myself facing choices where the only outcomes were bad, no matter what I tried to do. Kill or be killed. And then Orla . . ."

"She died on Starlight," said Reath. "I'm sorry."

"She shouldn't have had to die. We should have been better prepared. I should have been there for her." Master Cohmac's voice was a gravelly rasp. He hung his head. "And I was selfish. I couldn't just push it aside. I couldn't get past it. I needed time to process it, to find my own way to reconcile with what had happened, and to figure out what I could do to help, on my own terms." He ran a hand down his face. "Sometimes we're just people, too. I know the Jedi are supposed to be strong, but sometimes all our training, all our discipline—it's not enough. Sometimes the only thing that gets us through is *time*, and the best thing we can do is recognize that need in ourselves. I wasn't going to be a healthy person for you to be around, not until I'd managed to get my head straight."

"And you think it was healthy to leave me alone, instead?" said Reath.

Master Cohmac hung his head. "You weren't alone, Reath. You were never alone. You have friends. The Order. People who care about you. Surely you can see that."

"But you were my master. We'd only just learned to trust each other. To work as a team." Reath swallowed. His mouth was dry. "I might have been able to help. Unless . . ." He hesitated. "Unless I was part of the problem. If the only reason you took me on was because you felt obliged after Master Jora died . . ." He looked away.

"No, Reath. Not that. It was never that. It was about *me*," said Master Cohmac. "Still is."

"Then you're not coming back? This really is just a one-off?" said Reath.

Master Cohmac shrugged. "I don't know. That's the truth, Reath. I don't know. The very fact we're on this mission goes some way to helping me think things might change. But for now . . ." He sighed. "One step, and one mission, at a time. I need to see if I can find my way again." He looked up, meeting Reath's eye. "Besides, you seem to be doing well."

"I do?" said Reath. "Sometimes it's hard to know. I'm not sure I was ready to be a Knight."

"You were ready," said Master Cohmac emphatically. "You're brilliant, Reath. The way you bring history to life. Where other people hear stories, you see people's lives. Your insight is what's gotten us here. Sure, I helped. And so did Emerick, and even Azlin Rell." Master Cohmac's face darkened at the name, as if simply speaking it left a bad taste in his mouth. "But you're the one who's put it all together. If anyone can find a way out of this, it's you."

Reath leaned back in his seat. "I hope you're right."

"I know I am." Master Cohmac looked at him again. "And I'm sorry. For everything. For leaving you. For not being in touch. For the fact you're carrying this burden. I can see what it's doing to you, Reath. But right now, I'm here, and you *can* talk to me. You can share it with me. I'm here for you, and I will help you bear it. We're in this together."

Together. That word again.

Reath looked away. "All right," he said.

They lapsed into silence again, the tension heavy in the air between them. Reath was struggling to take in everything Master Cohmac had said. His admission of weakness, his need to spend time alone, his difficulty dealing with everything they'd faced.

Maybe he was right. Maybe behind all the training they were all just *people*, trying to navigate a way through the chaos of life. Perhaps that was the thing that really scared Reath. He'd seen Master Cohmac as strong, infallible, a Jedi Master who had all the answers. He'd seen them all like that—Stellan, Avar, Ry Ki-Sakka, Yoda, and the rest. People to look up to.

And he'd hoped that one day he'd be like that, too—that all his doubts and fears and questions would be answered, that they'd bleed away until he was left with only certainty and conviction. Wasn't that what a Jedi was supposed to be?

And then Master Jora had died and left so many unanswered questions. He'd thought Master Cohmac could help him fill that void, and he had, for a while. But then he had left, too, and Reath had seen how shortsighted his belief had been, how naive. They were all like him. They were all just as uncertain, all struggling with their own mistakes. They were all trying to do the best they could in a galaxy that had been turned on its head, clinging to one another to find strength in numbers.

That was what Master Cohmac had shown him. That was his final lesson as Reath's master. He'd revealed his own vulnerability. He'd shown Reath how the galaxy really worked.

Maybe Master Cohmac had thought it would be reassuring. But to Reath, it was terrifying. Because if everyone felt just like Reath did, how were they ever going to get through this terrible mess?

Reath watched as Master Cohmac got to his feet and crossed to a large metal trunk that had been placed against the rear bulkhead.

He dropped to his knees—still wincing from the last vestiges of the injuries he'd sustained on Thall—and opened the lid with a creak of rusted hinges. He began to rifle noisily through the contents.

"What's that?" said Reath, walking over to join him.

"Just a few things I had transferred to the *Vessel* from the *Excavator*," said Master Cohmac. "There's a lightsaber in here somewhere. One that I recovered from an old temple on Deneba. Figured it might come in handy." He lifted a bundle of what looked like droid components from the chest and placed it on the ground, followed by a broken stone idol, a coil of rope, and a large disc-shaped object, about half a meter in diameter, wrapped in coarse brown fabric.

"It's in here somewhere," he muttered.

"Master Cohmac," said Reath.

"Hmmm?"

"There's no need. Here." Reath reached inside his robes and withdrew the hilt of Master Cohmac's old lightsaber from an inner pocket.

Master Cohmac turned, looking up at Reath and the lightsaber hilt in his hand. "You kept it."

"Of course I did," said Reath. "In case you needed it again."

Master Cohmac chewed his lower lip for a moment. He reached out, hesitant. His hand hovered over the hilt in Reath's grip.

"It's okay," said Reath. "It's yours. Whether you're a Jedi or not. And like you said, you might need it."

Master Cohmac nodded. His fingers curled around the lightsaber, and he hefted it in his palm. "Thank you, Reath." He looked at the weapon. "Feels good to hold it again. I could have done with this on Thall."

Reath nodded but said no more.

Master Cohmac began stacking the contents back inside the

crate. As he lifted the large disc-shaped object, the burlap wrap slipped, revealing a glimpse of a tarnished gold frame emblazoned with a central motif in the form of a flower or leaf.

"And this is for you," said Cohmac. "A gift."

"A shield?" said Reath quizzically.

Master Cohmac slid the rest of the fabric wrap from the shield and passed it to Reath. "I rescued it from a dealer on Batuu, soon after I left the Order. I recognized immediately that it was something special, an antique well over a hundred years old, with real history from the look of it. So I bought it. I never felt right carrying it, though. It's a rare, seldom-used tool of the Jedi."

Reath turned the shield over in his hands. It was made from a lightweight metal with a golden hue and shaped like a ring, with a large central bar that bore the grip on the reverse. Aside from the small ornamental insignia on the front, it was smooth and unadorned. Reath hefted it, impressed by its lightness.

"Here." Master Cohmac reached over and depressed a hidden switch beside the grip, close to where Reath had positioned his thumb. The shield hummed, and two shimmering panels of plasma flared to life, filling the open spaces between the circular bars with flickering blue light. It hummed as he swung it back and forth on the back of his left arm, testing its weight.

"I didn't know the Jedi used shields," said Reath.

"Very few did, but this is clearly of the Order," said Master Cohmac. "I put it aside for when I saw you again. I know you love a good story, and I thought you'd enjoy researching its history, figuring out where it came from and whose hands it passed through before now. Plus, it might come in useful."

"Thank you. I've never seen anything like it." Reath held out his arm, running through a series of defensive postures. It felt good, solid. He'd never even imagined a Jedi using a shield before. Typically their lightsaber would serve the same purpose, deployed for defensive as much as offensive capabilities. But the idea carried a certain appeal.

"I'm sure it's seen some things," said Master Cohmac. He watched Reath appraisingly.

Reath slid the shield off his arm, powering it down. He ran his fingers around the rim, over the tiny dents and scratches that marred its ancient surface. He wondered how many battles it had seen, how many times it had saved a life. Once they were back on Coruscant, he'd take a look in the Archives, try to discover the full story of the shield and the history of its previous owners. "Thank you," he said. He wanted to say more, but he couldn't find the words. "Thank you."

Cohmac simply nodded. He looked satisfied.

They both turned toward the door as Affie appeared in the opening. "If you two are finished bonding, I thought you'd want to know that we're almost there."

"Already?" said Reath.

Affie laughed. "Already. We're approaching Tolis's orbit now. Thought you might want to take a look."

Reath and Cohmac exchanged glances.

"We're on our way," said Reath.

THIRTY-TWO

The lower Vernestra descended, the more the temperature dropped. She pulled her robes tighter around her shoulders as she walked through the passageways and corridors beneath the Jedi Temple.

She told herself it was the cold causing her to shiver, nothing at all to do with the bleak atmosphere down in these untrodden levels, or the knowledge of what was festering in the ancient Sith shrine close by.

The blight.

Here on Coruscant.

Right in our midst.

The Jedi Council had been quick to act after she'd reported the discovery. They'd decided to keep the information about the blight's existence beneath the Temple contained, in much the same way they hoped to contain the infection itself. For now, only the Council and a select few Jedi had been told. There was no sense yet of how the blight had manifested on Coruscant, but they all knew that if news were to get out, it would create a panic of devastating proportions. The logistics involved in evacuating whole districts of the city were unimaginable. People would die. There'd be chaos in the streets.

So the Jedi had decided to keep the news to themselves for now. Better that they find a way to deal with the blight before it became a far bigger problem.

At least, that was the theory. Whether it was actually achievable was another matter entirely. Especially as the only other option was to turn to Marchion Ro for help. If Chancellor Soh or the Jedi Council was forced to resort to that . . . well, their standing on the galactic stage would be reduced forever.

Which meant it was up to Reath, Cohmac, and Emerick to figure out a solution while the rest of them did all they could to hold the infection at bay.

Master Yoda had taken it upon himself to lead the fight against the blight here on Coruscant. They'd learned from what Burryaga had tried to do back on Vixoseph I that, with a concerted effort and deep concentration, it was possible for a Jedi to effectively slow the progressive spread of a small patch of the blight, but only for a short time and only at great cost to the Jedi in question.

Because of the size and risk of the infestation on Coruscant, some of the Jedi were taking it in shifts to do just that—to sit down in the Sith shrine, giving themselves over to a kind of meditative trance, during which they attempted to use the Force to arrest the spread of the infection. It was too early to tell if it was working, but the toll it was taking was clear. Those returning from spending time down here were weary, drained, and physically spent—almost as if they were giving up a part of themselves to try to keep the blight at bay.

Vernestra only hoped they could keep it up long enough for Reath and Cohmac to return. And even then, she knew they might not have all the answers.

Still, she remained resolute. She would do whatever she could to help, whatever the cost.

Vernestra hesitated as she reached the outer lobby that led to the shrine. The lingering sense of the dark side was palpable and as discomforting now as it had been when she'd first ventured down here with Reath.

She wondered how he was faring on his mission to Tolis. Probably getting overexcited about the archeological and academic importance of the ruins he was there to explore. She grinned and felt a little better because of it. She willed the mission to be a success—for all of them. Time was not on their side.

She stepped into the shrine.

Master Yoda sat just inside the open doorway, cross-legged, his staff laid across his lap, his hands folded neatly on top of it. He might almost have looked serene, as if lost in deep meditation, save for the deep furrows in his brow and the anxious expression he wore on his face. His head was tilted slightly to one side.

Before him, the strange ashen waste of the blight looked

much as it had before, bubbling up through the stone on the far wall, turning everything it touched to dust.

Also in the room, two other Jedi sat in postures that mirrored Yoda's, one on the left of the circle of festering blight, one on the right. Vernestra recognized them both—Master Peleg Ryn, a small Noghri with gray skin and horns cresting their domed head, and Master Jenneh Ley, a human woman with tan skin and striped facial tattoos, her jet-black hair scraped back in a tight ponytail. Both were concentrating deeply and didn't look up as she approached.

Master Yoda, however, slowly opened his eyes and turned to regard her. Despite his evident weariness, he offered her a warm, if slight, smile. "Come to check on us, you have, Vernestra Rwoh."

Vernestra nodded, noting that the other two Jedi's frowns had deepened as they took on the extra strain of Master Yoda's distraction from the task. "Yes, Master Yoda. I came to see if you needed anything, or if I could offer my assistance with the vigil."

The thought of sitting in these bleak surroundings for a prolonged period, helping ward off the infection, was not at all appealing. But Vernestra knew her duty. If she could help, she would.

"Admirable, this is," said Yoda. He slowly stretched, taking up his staff and using it to pull himself to his feet. "But another purpose, you must serve. Sense it in you, I do. This is the true reason for your visit to this place. Answers, you seek."

Vernestra sighed. Master Yoda had a habit of doing this— seeing through the layers of obfuscation a person threw in their own way, the little justifications they gave to themselves, the excuses they made for their own behavior. She nodded. "As ever, Master Yoda, you see the truth that I do not always share with myself. I suppose I am here looking for answers."

Master Yoda nodded to himself, but there was no self-satisfaction in the gesture, merely acknowledgment. "To find such answers, one must first understand the nature of the question."

He beckoned toward the door, and Vernestra followed him, feeling guilty for distracting him from his task. The extra strain his absence was already causing the other meditating Jedi was abundantly clear, even more so when a third Jedi—a female Pantoran named Inith Lowera—hurried in past them to help shoulder the burden.

"I cannot keep you from your task, Master Yoda," said Vernestra. "I really did come here to offer my help."

Yoda smiled indulgently. "Please. Tell me what troubles you, my young friend." He'd reached the center of the outer lobby of the shrine and was leaning heavily on his staff. Clearly, the effects of the vigil were potent, even to a master of Yoda's experience and power.

"I don't know," said Vernestra. "I sense . . . something is wrong. I thought after Reath and I found the infection down here, the feeling would go away, but it hasn't."

"You are worried for your friend, hmmm?" said Yoda.

Vernestra guessed he meant Reath. "Yes. I suppose I am. He's taken on such responsibility."

"Trust him, do you?"

"Of course," said Vernestra, surprised by the strength of her own conviction. "He's one of the most dedicated Jedi I know. He intends to solve this crisis. And he'll do it. I'm certain of it."

"Then why do you worry?" asked Yoda with an infuriating chuckle that suggested he already knew the answer.

"I just . . ." Vernestra turned her thoughts inward. What *was* this really about? Why had she felt so on edge since returning to Coruscant? There were dozens of reasons, but only one that seemed to be gnawing away at her like an itch she couldn't scratch. "Azlin," she said. "It's Azlin I don't trust."

"Ah," said Yoda. "Now we begin to approach the truth."

Vernestra shifted her weight from one foot to the other. "I'm concerned he's manipulating Reath somehow. Using him. Just like . . . Well, like . . ." Vernestra trailed off, appalled at what she'd inadvertently implied.

"Just as he manipulated me," finished Yoda. He nodded, his expression grave. "I understand. Azlin Rell has put his faith in the dark side of the Force. Perspective, he has lost."

Vernestra stumbled over her words. "I'm sorry, Master Yoda. I didn't mean . . ."

Master Yoda waved his hand dismissively. "The truth, you speak. That is all. And none of us should ever be afraid of the truth." He sniffed. "Azlin is a dangerous ally. Important in this quest of ours, but dangerous, yes. Reath is under great pressure. Look out for him, we should."

"Then you believe that Azlin is up to something?" asked Vernestra, surprised. Master Yoda had been Azlin's most staunch defender. But she supposed that didn't mean the Jedi Master trusted his fallen ally, simply that he understood the man's worth in the coming trials.

Master Yoda shrugged. "I believe that Azlin Rell has his own agenda. Yet trust Reath, I do."

"Then what should I do?" asked Vernestra.

Master Yoda smiled. He took his staff and tapped it gently against Vernestra's chest. "Trust in *yourself*, you must." He smiled, withdrawing his staff. "Follow your instincts. You trusted them before, when you followed Reath to find this place. Do the same again, Vernestra Rwoh, and you will not go wrong."

"I understand," she said. "Thank you, Master Yoda."

"Hmmm," said the diminutive Jedi Master. "Answers you have received. Like them, you may not. Find the truth, you will."

He turned and started his shuffling walk back toward the Sith shrine.

"Shouldn't you rest for a while?" said Vernestra.

Master Yoda paused for a moment and then started walking again. "The time for rest will come, Vernestra Rwoh. Now is the time for action."

Vernestra watched as he ambled back through the doorway and resumed his vigil before the patch of blight.

Now is the time for action.

Yes.

She knew what she had to do.

THIRTY-THREE

The mood aboard the *Invictus* was somber, even among the squad of ten RDC volunteers, who mostly seemed to be taking the opportunity presented by a few hours in hyperspace to catch up on sleep. Four of them were playing a game using polished stones over a grid they'd marked out on the floor grilles, but even they seemed reluctant to celebrate their victories, which was very much unlike the sort of raucous behavior Amadeo had come to expect after so many other missions with the RDC.

Their journey had been underway for several hours, and a hush seemed to have settled on everyone through unspoken consensus. Amadeo couldn't tell if it was a response to the imminent threat of combat, due to the almost mythical status that some were attributing to the Nameless—he'd overheard a few of the soldiers discussing the creatures with a kind of reverence usually reserved for superstitions—or simply because no one aboard had much to say to one another. Whatever the case, no one seemed willing to break the silence.

Even Master Lox had given himself over to a trancelike meditation. He sat across from Amadeo now, on the opposite side of the ship, his legs crossed, his hands on his knees, his eyes closed in deep concentration. He'd explained to Amadeo that he intended to try to find a way to focus through the psychological torment caused by the Nameless, to find a singular point of concentration that would allow him to ignore the terrifying hallucinations caused by the creatures' proximity, a touchstone that might help him see through the fog of fear and illusion that usually afflicted the Jedi in the presence of a Nameless. He was searching for that touchstone now.

Amadeo supposed that anything had to be worth a try. He was just pleased that the RDC were there to help them corral the creatures—if and when they managed to locate any of them. Their intelligence of the Nihil base on Angoth was patchy at best.

He peered around for any sign of Ashton Vol and L-77 but assumed they were up front with the pilot. Dorian was still fiddling with equipment at the medical station, but when he saw Amadeo looking, he set down the tools he'd been sterilizing and headed over. He nudged Amadeo's leg with his knee, urging Amadeo to shift over on the bench, and then sat down beside him.

"You done running checks?" ventured Amadeo.

"Oh, I was done hours ago," said Dorian. He, too, was keeping his voice low, either out of respect for the silence or so their conversation wasn't overheard above the slow churning of the hyperspace drive.

"Then what were you doing?"

"Keeping myself busy to take my mind off what might be waiting for us on Angoth," said Dorian.

Amadeo furrowed his brow, confused. "But you're with the RDC. You must have gone on dozens of missions like this."

Dorian shrugged. "Doesn't make any of them easier, though, does it? I never wanted to be a peacekeeper or a fighter. I wanted to be a medic. To help people in need. I never saw myself flying halfway across the galaxy as part of a raiding party to capture a semimythical monster from a band of marauders who've taken over half the Outer Rim."

Amadeo grinned. "Well, when you put it like that, neither did I. But why are you here, if you don't really want to be?"

"Like I said, I want to help people. And right now, this is where I can be of the most help. None of us expected the Nihil to *win*. So I'm just doing what needs to be done. Playing my part, just like you are. Helping wherever and whenever I can."

"The Nihil haven't won," said Amadeo. "Not yet. They may think they have, but while there are still Jedi standing, we won't give up."

Dorian gave him a wan smile. "That's the spirit." He closed his eyes, then opened them again, letting out a long sigh.

"We can do this," said Amadeo. "It's not just talk, you know. We *will* beat them. My friend Reath is so close to figuring out how to defeat the Nameless and stop the blight. The end is in sight. We just need to hold on and keep fighting."

Dorian smiled again, and it was brighter this time. "It's good to know you, Amadeo. I have a feeling your optimism is going to carry us through whatever comes next."

"I'll try my best," said Amadeo, laughing. It felt so good to laugh, after everything that had happened lately.

"Don't you ever worry?" said Dorian.

Amadeo gave him a quizzical look. "About what?"

Dorian raised a single eyebrow, as if to suggest that it should have been obvious. "About the fact we might be heading to our deaths. I mean, the Nihil are dangerous enough on their own, but we've all seen what the Force Eaters can do to a Jedi. I'm not trying to scare you. I just . . . you seem so *together*. More confident than anyone else on this ship."

Amadeo considered this for a moment. He didn't *feel* that confident. But then, he was a Jedi, after all. Perhaps he just wasn't giving himself enough credit. "Every time I head out on a mission I could be heading to my death. It's never safe. It's what Jedi *do*."

Dorian chewed his lip. "Mmm, hmm. And now for the *real* answer."

Amadeo shrugged. "I'd be lying if I said I wasn't scared," he said at last. "But as Jedi, we're taught to understand our fear. To recognize it, control it, and put it aside while we get on with what we have to do."

"Wow," said Dorian. "Sounds a lot like ignoring the problem to me. Burying your head in the sand and hoping it goes away never really works, at least not in my experience. Aren't you just building up trauma for later?"

Amadeo shook his head. "No. I know how it might sound like that. It's hard to explain. It's not about ignoring it. It's about processing it. Knowing what it's doing to us, both mentally and physiologically, and then pushing past it."

"But doesn't it ever come back to haunt you?" pressed Dorian.

"You've seen how much we meditate, right?" Amadeo grinned. "It's all about being the best we can be *in the moment*. When we're out there, protecting people, defending others from harm—we need to be sharp, alert, ready for whatever is going to happen next. Fear just gets in the way of that. We need to be able to act unimpeded, be the very best versions of ourselves. So we're trained to understand our bodies and our emotions, to process it as information, and to compartmentalize whatever isn't useful at the time, sometimes even draw strength from it. Later, when the mission's over—that's when we work through everything we've experienced."

"Interesting," said Dorian. He got back to his feet. "I'd better get back to work."

"Doing what?" asked Amadeo.

"Keeping myself busy doing nothing," said Dorian.

Amadeo laughed.

Perhaps it was time to do some meditating, after all.

THIRTY-FOUR

Sicarus picked at the carcass of the roasted bird with his fingers, ignoring the slick shiny grease that dripped onto his legs and boots or ran in rivulets down the backs of his hands.

Drip. Drip. Drip.

He chewed on the soft pale meat, wishing he could taste it like he used to. Now it tasted like ash in his mouth. He hadn't enjoyed a meal in months. Worse, he hardly seemed to draw sustenance from his food anymore.

Another failing of his meager body. More unwillingness to adapt to his new life. As if it still clung to the torpid remnants of his old existence, digging in its heels, refusing to adapt.

Humans were so weak. And this need, this base craving for physical food . . . it made him feel somehow *lesser*.

And now he couldn't even enjoy the taste of it.

It was a side effect of the blood. The vibrant singing blood that had turned his whole world around. The blood of the creatures.

That blood craved something else.

Yes, yes, it did. It craved nourishment of a different sort. It wanted *power*.

But Sicarus was not equipped to feed it that way. He cursed his frail human body.

Flesh is flesh is flesh.

And he was bound to it. In every possible way. Confined by it.

The blood had set him free, but it had also shown him how trapped he really was. How small his mind and his frail human shell had become.

"Hate it. Hate it," he said, spitting half-chewed fragments of meat with every syllable. "Hate it."

He glowered at the ruined carcass with his good eye—the other was sleeping—and then tossed it across the room. It struck the wall with a wet thud and slid to the ground.

"Can't fly now, can you?" he said, giggling. He wiped his mouth on the back of his sleeve.

"Can't fly like that little ship. No, no. Flying away."

He'd been thinking a lot about that ship lately. And thinking was dangerous. For other people, at least.

He'd been imagining what it would be like to murder that Force user, the one who'd gotten away from him on Thall.

In his mind's eye, he could see the man cowering against

the wall as the creatures—his, Sicarus's creatures—closed in. The Force user would raise his arms and scream, thrashing at ghosts that weren't really there. His eyes would be wide in horror, so wide that they were white all the way around the edges, so unlike his own special eye.

The creatures would wait. Salivating. Ready.

And then he would give the command. The man would shrink back, trying desperately to get away but frozen to the spot in fear. Sicarus giggled at the thought. How he longed to hear them whimper and beg as they died, as first their arms, then their torsos, then their heads were bleached of all animation, all life. They would be bled dry of the living Force, transforming into nothing but ashen dust.

Just like the taste of the bird he was still prizing from between his teeth.

Ashen dust.

That was what should have happened on Thall. He'd let himself—and Father—down. But it wouldn't happen again, oh, no. No, no, no.

Next time.

And besides, there was always the woman he'd been keeping alive on his ship, of course. Throwing her tidbits to eat. Taunting her with the Nameless until she screamed. He supposed he could kill her, too. She was meant to be a prize for Father, but she was growing weaker in her cage.

Maybe. Maybe. Maybe.

He'd give the matter some thought. He didn't want to disappoint Father, after all.

Slowly, he got to his feet.

It was comfortable here at the Nihil base on Angoth. Too comfortable for one such as him. Too civilized for a man who was only half-human. He wanted to be out hunting, making Father proud.

But he'd failed on Thall. He'd been too slow. He'd wanted to toy with the Force user, to make him bleed fear. He'd tried to take his time over it, shocked the creatures with the device Father had made for him, firing electric shots into their brains. Calling them off until he was ready. And he'd underestimated the man, who'd gotten away, even when he'd almost died in the catacombs.

And now the trail was cold.

So he was here, waiting.

Waiting. Waiting.

He paced the room. His fingertips danced and fidgeted.

Out there, beyond the door, he could hear the Nihil making merry. Laughing and drinking and eating. And probably enjoying it all, too. He could kill them for that. The idea pleased him. Stop their laughing by stopping their hearts. He could do that if he tried. If he *wanted*.

The thought made him feel powerful, and he raised his head, straightening his back.

But what would Father Boolan say?

Sicarus was no Nihil. He never had been. His only loyalty was to Boolan. But Boolan liked to keep the Nihil happy, didn't he? Boolan knew just where he wanted Marchion Ro, and he wanted to keep the Evereni there. Father was clever. Brilliant. He had it all worked out.

Sicarus couldn't upset the balance. He couldn't take the Nihil and chop, chop, chop them into little pieces. He had to use them. He had to smile and bow and pretend, and use them to help him get the Jedi.

That was why Father had sent him here, after all. After what happened on Thall. Father had sent him to get more help. More Nihil, who could help him catch the Jedi, and more of the creatures, too, to help him kill them.

But now all he was doing was waiting.

Waiting. Waiting.

The door to his chamber opened with a sliding hiss. He stopped walking. He had his back to the door. He could sense someone there.

Sicarus closed his eyes, reached out with the Force. He could feel the shape of them standing in the doorway. Not their physical shape. Their mind. The shape of their emotions.

They were . . . *scared.*

Good. Good. They should be scared.

Sicarus giggled. He turned to see a Tholothian woman regarding him with wariness. She was dressed in banded leather over a gray tunic, dark blue pants tucked into tall worn boots. Her head was scaled like all her species, and she had an array of fleshy white tendrils growing from her scalp and tumbling around her shoulders like strands of hair. Her lower lip was puckered and purple where it had been torn and badly stitched after some recent disagreement. She was wearing an Eye of the Storm tattoo on the side of her neck. He seemed to remember her name was Theela, or Threeka, or something similar, but his memory wasn't as good as it used to be. Or he simply didn't care enough to remember.

"Yes?" he said. "Yes, yes, yes?" He rubbed his hands together. Maybe she was there to remove the bird carcass he'd tossed across the room.

Threeka—he decided that name would do—cleared her throat. "He's asking for you."

Sicarus wrinkled his brow. "Who is 'he'?"

"Baron Boolan," said Theela. No. He preferred Threeka. He'd stick with that.

"Threeka," he said, trying the word on for size.

"Yes?" said the woman, evidently confused.

So that *was* her name.

Maybe he'd change it back, after all. He'd sleep on it.

He met her eye, and she almost flinched. "He's here?"

"He's on a holo. In the other room." She gestured with her thumb over her shoulder.

Sicarus nodded. "I see. I see. In the *other* room. Right."

Threeka half turned in the doorway. "Are you coming or what?" Her voice was tinted with scorn.

Sicarus imagined wringing her neck. The thought made him smile. "Oh, yes, I'm coming." He took a step forward and she jerked back, her hand straying to the grip of the blaster holstered to her hip.

Sicarus giggled again. "Go on, then. Show me."

Threeka blanched and then turned and walked out, glancing over her shoulder every few steps as if she was afraid to turn her back on him for too long.

He followed, his feet scuffing the metal-plated floor.

Threeka led him down a short passageway—the base on Angoth was not big—and into another room, where an ancient holodisplay had been poorly rigged up, with masses of exposed cables still visible like writhing eels around his feet. He tried not to tread on any of them as he approached the central circular display.

A flickering blue image of Father hovered above the terminal. His hammer-shaped head was half-turned away, as if he was peering at something or someone else off camera. He was wearing his long dark robes. He turned to look at Sicarus as he approached. One of his mouths puckered in what Sicarus chose to read as a smile.

"Thank you, Threeka," said Boolan, his vocoder rendering his voice thin, mechanical, and emotionless.

"Baron," said Threeka with a nod. She turned and left the room. Sicarus watched her go. There were no other Nihil present. He was alone with Father. Sicarus felt a swell of pride. All this attention, just for him!

"Father," said Sicarus. He offered his best beatific smile. "Is everything well?"

Boolan inclined his head. "Yes, Sicarus. All is well. I have news."

Sicarus leaned forward, eager. "News of the Force user?"

"Yes, indeed. The Force user that you allowed to go free on Thall is a Jedi."

Sicarus felt the comment like a body blow. The sort that Father might have given him if he'd really been standing before him. He took a step back from the terminal, partially raising one arm as if to stave off further attack. "I didn't mean to let him go, Father. The Jedi are wily, and he tricked me. But I will find him, I promise. I'll do what needs to be done."

"I know you will, Sicarus," said Boolan. His image flickered, as if the transmission had been momentarily interrupted. "I know I can rely on you."

"Yes. Yes. Yes," said Sicarus. His eye blinked. His special one. For a moment, the world looked different, sharper, clearer. And then it passed.

"Two of the Jedi—the older one and a youth—have left Coruscant on a ship bound for Wild Space," said Boolan.

"Wild Space?" echoed Sicarus. The outer regions. The uncharted places. What were they doing out there?

"Yes. My informant tells me they're bound for a planet named Tolis. It appears on no star charts or maps that I can find, but I have someone tracking their progress. I'm sending you the coordinates." Boolan paused. "I want you to go after them."

Sicarus felt a surge of pride, and glee, and happiness. "Yes, Father. Of course. And you want them alive."

"I think not," said Boolan. "Circumstances have changed. These particular Jedi seem . . . troubling. I think it better that they're eliminated now, before they become a further threat. They're investigating the origins of both the Levelers and the blight, and we wouldn't want them finding anything, would we?"

Sicarus's heart was hammering. He felt sweat prickling his scalp. "Yes, Father. We wouldn't want that. No."

He was going to get to kill the Jedi, after all. They'd pay for what the man had done to him on Thall. Showing him up, making him look a fool.

He would watch them cower, just like he'd done in his head a hundred times already. But this time it would be real.

"And this time, leave nothing to chance. I do not want to have to explain to Marchion Ro that you failed," said Boolan.

"I won't," said Sicarus. "I will not fail. The Jedi will be destroyed."

"Very good," said Boolan. "And then you can come home. You do want to come home, don't you, Sicarus?"

"I do, Father," replied Sicarus. "Very much."

"I thought so. Well then, do this for me, and you will be welcomed back with open arms."

"And more blood?" asked Sicarus hopefully. He'd begun to feel the itch starting beneath his skin again. The inside itch that he couldn't scratch. It was mild, but it was there, and he hated it. Hated it. Hated it. He'd have to use one of his spare canisters soon.

"Of course," said Boolan. "More blood." He had already turned away, returning to whatever it was that had been distracting him when Sicarus first arrived.

Sicarus grinned. "You've made me very happy today, Father," he said. "Very happy indeed." He picked a bit of meat from between his teeth.

THIRTY-FIVE

"**T**ake us in close to that narrow landmass," said Master Cohmac, jabbing his finger at the large sliver of green floating in the swirling blue ocean that covered most of the small world of Tolis.

They'd circumnavigated the planet from low orbit, looking for the best place to set down, but as it had transpired, their options were somewhat limited. It seemed as if Tolis was now almost entirely subsumed by a single vast ocean that spanned the entirety of the globe. Presumably, this was all that remained following the epic floods.

A drowned world.

A catastrophe had fallen on these people. Twice.

Reath's hopes were dwindling. The chances of finding the ancient repository had been narrow to begin with. Now the odds seemed impossibly stacked against them. He had no idea if this narrow strip of land represented the island on which the Three Ancients had retreated to start their new kingdom or if it was all that was left of a bigger landmass. Although he supposed the Tolemites might have chosen to build their new kingdom on higher ground, so there was still hope.

"Sure thing. Hold on tight!" Leox pulled back on the flight controls, and the *Vessel* dipped, sending them plummeting through the upper atmosphere at an acute angle.

Reath squeezed the back of the copilot's chair—where Affie was currently sitting—until his fingers went white. Beside Reath, Master Cohmac chuckled, shaking his head indulgently.

Leox laughed gleefully as the ship corkscrewed in a lazy circle, buffeted by the drag of atmospheric entry, the nose shimmering red with the intense friction and heat. They drilled down like this for several minutes, as if churning a hole, or circling a drain.

Behind Leox, Geode watched impassively, but Reath could tell the Vintian was far from impressed with his friend's antics.

Leox whooped and manipulated the controls as they dropped below the wispy cloud cover, revealing a churning blue-green ocean that seemed to stretch in all directions as far as the eye could see.

The *Vessel* leveled off, stirring the choppy waters as it plowed a long furrow across the surface. Reath heaved a sigh of relief. Affie peered up at him, laughing. "Felt that, did you?"

Reath raised an eyebrow in reply.

"Too much time spent in that lab of yours, lad," said Leox. "The galaxy's a big place, and there's always time for a little fun."

"You call that fun?" said Reath, but there was laughter in his tone.

"Don't you?" said Leox, shooting him a wink. He turned back to the controls. "Ah, here we go."

The first hints of land had appeared through the forward viewport—hulking islands of a red-hued rock, hunched in an uneven row like an archipelago. Each of them climbed to a jagged point, and Reath realized with shock that they must have once been the upper reaches of a mountain range that had lined the coast, before whatever cataclysm caused the ocean to rise and swallow them.

The ship banked, dipping lower beyond the islands, following the edge of a sandy shore. Here the remains of ancient structures still stood, eroded by time and waves, running into the water like cascading dunes. Occasionally, the spur of a broken tower jutted awkwardly from the water just off the coast. There were no signs of habitation. The only life appeared to be the undulating flocks of birds that dipped and soared over the lapping water, presumably prowling for food.

"Take us along the coast for a while, if you would, Leox," said Master Cohmac. "We can always double back if there's nothing else to see."

Leox nodded, slowing their speed and keeping the ship close to the coastline. "What are we looking for?"

"We're not," said Master Cohmac. "We're *feeling* our way." He straightened, closing his eyes, steadying his breathing.

Reath was about to do the same when Master Cohmac's eyes flickered open again. He turned to Reath, his expression filled with childlike wonder. "Do you feel that?"

"Feel what?" said Reath.

Master Cohmac waved a hand, urging him to focus. Reath did as he was bid. He closed his eyes, reaching out. . . .

Suddenly, his senses erupted in swirling patterns of color and light. He felt an overwhelming sense of peace. He breathed, and it was like taking in the first breath of a new day, rich with the scents of blossom and dew.

He opened his eyes, gasping. "What is this place?" he murmured.

"There's something here. Something wonderful."

"But what?"

"I don't know, but I intend to find out," said Master Cohmac.

"What the hell is *that*?" said Leox.

They were farther up the coast now, beyond the half-submerged settlement, and the rocky tundra had been reduced to nothing more than a pale wasteland of ash and dust.

"It's awful," said Affie. "Is that—"

"The blight," said Reath. "It's here."

Leox gave a low whistle. "So the stories are true."

Reath was nearly overcome by a terrible sense of awe as Leox turned the ship, heading farther inland across the blight-ridden wastes. The area was a desert of dead things, everything leached of life, of vibrancy, of color. Even the rocks had succumbed.

No wonder Amadeo had spoken of it with such reverence.

"I thought the Tolemites had found a way to stop the blight," said Master Cohmac.

"I guess it must be back," said Reath. "Perhaps it's reemerging at the site of a previous infection. We don't really understand how it spreads."

"Destruction on a scale that's hard to believe," said Master Cohmac, "even standing here looking at it. The holos from the evacuated worlds don't do it justice. It's just so . . . desolate."

"It's worse than I'd imagined," murmured Reath.

Even Leox had lost his usual verbosity. He stared out the viewport, his expression blank, his face pale. "I can't believe it."

"You're going to find a way to stop this, right?" said Affie, twisting in her seat to look from Master Cohmac to Reath. "Right?"

"We're going to try," said Reath levelly. "It's one of the reasons we're here. Hopefully it hasn't already destroyed what we're searching for."

"It hasn't," said Master Cohmac with a conviction Reath didn't feel. "I know it. But we're going to have to move quickly."

"Where do you want us to land?" said Affie. "We can't risk bringing the *Vessel* any closer to that . . . whatever it is."

"Do you think you could find us somewhere close to the ruined settlement we saw?" said Master Cohmac.

"Sure," said Leox. He'd already started to swing the *Vessel* around, clearly anxious to put some distance between the ship and the billowing wastes of the blight.

"Hey, what's that shiny stuff?" said Affie as the ship came about. She pointed to a strange-looking structure rising out of the ruins of a half-consumed cliff. It was an almost skeletal structure, made from ribbons of something that glittered brightly in the light of Tolis's twin suns. And it was *huge*.

Leox slowed the ship.

Reath leaned forward, straining to see. Where the blight had attacked the face of the cliff, the stone was gradually being gnawed back by the infection, but whatever this material was, it appeared to have so far resisted the husking effect altogether. It formed a series of twisted strands, jutting out from the site of the disintegration. Farther afield, Reath could make out more of the strange structures, still standing while everything around them had been utterly consumed.

"Is it . . . organic?" said Cohmac.

"No," said Reath as a thought began to consolidate in his mind. He felt a sudden surge of excitement. "Look again. It's some kind of mineral or ore. Those were the seams running through the rock. But whatever it is, it's *resisting* the blight. Or at least, it's decaying at a much slower rate than the rock around it. Every-thing else has gone, but that material is still standing."

"Fascinating," said Master Cohmac.

Reath almost rolled his eyes. "Think about it! It's *resisting the blight*."

Master Cohmac slowly turned to look at him, his eyes open-ing wide as the implication struck. "You mean . . ."

"*Yes*. Precisely. I haven't seen anything like it, in all of my research. If it could be salvaged . . ." started Reath.

"Then we might be able to use it as some sort of shield," fin-ished Master Cohmac.

Reath shrugged. "Perhaps. We'll have to run tests. At the very least, we need to get a sample."

Leox shook his head. "It's too dangerous. We can't get close enough without risking the ship."

"We don't need to," said Affie. She pointed at Reath. "You think it's running through those rocks like a vein of precious metal?"

Reath nodded. "It's a guess, but that's what it looks like."

"All right. Then we land in a safe area, away from the spread of the blight. Blast some of those untouched rocks until we find a seam and take a sample," she said.

"I don't like it," growled Leox.

Affie reached over and put a hand on his arm. "We'll put a few kilometers between us and the blight. Don't worry."

"Hmmm." Leox didn't look convinced, but he didn't argue.

But Master Cohmac was shaking his head. "It'll take too long. We need to look for the Tolemite repository. We don't know how long we've got. The sample is going to have to wait."

Reath kneaded his temples. "There has to be a way. We can't lose this chance."

"There *is* a way," said Affie, pushing herself up out of her chair. "You and Cohmac go, find this temple or whatever it is you're looking for. We'll see to the sample. We don't need Jedi to blast a few rocks to smithereens, do we, Leox?"

The thought put a smile back on the grizzled pilot's face. "No, Little Bit. I don't suppose we do."

"Great," said Reath. "Thank you, Affie. Saving the day once again."

Affie laughed. "Save that thought. This isn't over yet."

"No," agreed Reath.

"All right. You'd better get ready," said Leox. "We'll drop you off by the coastal ruins. Once we're done collecting the samples we'll retreat to low orbit, just to keep the *Vessel* as far away from that damned blight as we can. You can call us when you're ready for us to come pick you up."

"Thank you, Leox," said Master Cohmac. "Thank you both."

Reath turned and patted Geode gently on the side. "And thanks to you, too, big guy."

THIRTY-SIX

"**I** suggest we go in hot. Surprise them. Hit them, take them down. Get what we need and get out."

This from Ashton Vol, who was sitting on the bench opposite Amadeo, leaning forward, watching Master Lox as if to gauge his reaction.

They were currently in high orbit around the planet Angoth, sheltering amid a ring of scattered asteroids that encircled the small world like a necklace. Here, the ship was less likely to be picked up on any sensor sweeps or spotted by any Nihil patrols. Not that there were any patrols in evidence. The outpost was small, and the Nihil were arrogant.

"What about the Jedi?" said L-77, who was standing in the doorway to the cockpit at the far end of the common area.

Disconcertedly, he was cleaning a pair of long blades that had appeared from open hatches in his slender arms.

Ashton looked confused. "Well, I don't wish to speak on Master Lox's behalf, but I'd imagine you're both keen to partici-pate in the first wave?" She looked from Master Lox to Amadeo and back.

"I think Sevens is referring to our particular . . . *vulnerability*, when it comes to the Nameless," offered Master Lox, who was sit-ting beside Amadeo on the low bench. "We need to account for the presence of the creatures."

"Ah," said Ashton, "of course." She chewed her lip for a moment. "Then perhaps it's safer if you cover our retreat? Guard the ship?"

"Guard the ship?" said L-77 with a tone that sounded dis-tinctly like he was scoffing at the very idea. "They're *Jedi*."

Ashton turned to the droid. "But—with respect—it's our job to protect them."

L-77 sighted along the length of one gleaming arm blade, then turned his attention to its opposite number. "They're our best assets. You *never* ask Jedi to guard the retreat. They need to be out there, on the offensive, doing their thing with their lightsabers."

Ashton seemed to consider this, then nodded, conceding the point. "Master Lox? Amadeo? Where should we factor you in?"

"We can serve as an early warning signal," said Master Lox. "Breach the base, help overcome the Nihil. Once we sense the Nameless are close, we'll retreat to the ship so you can do your thing."

"Very well," said Ashton. "Agreed."

Amadeo glanced up and down the gathered faces in the room. As one, the RDC personnel looked implacable, resolved. They were drawn from all walks of Republic life—three humans whose nicknames he'd gathered were Ears, Grampo, and Fires; a wide-faced Sullustan named Lort; a humanoid Kiffar named Redano, with bright facial tattoos; a green-skinned Ishi Tib with swiveling eyestalks, named Blish; and four others, a Delphidian, Pantoran, Mon Calamari, and Artiodac, all of whom had kept to themselves on the journey. They were sitting ready, affecting boredom as they waited for their orders, but Amadeo could tell they were all listening to the conversation closely as it played out. None of them were soldiers. They were peacekeepers, volunteers, used to being deployed for support or relief efforts. That was why the recruited mercenary, Ashton, was running the military side of the RDC operation. The RDC team was there to corral the Nameless—and as Ashton had already pointed out, to help keep the Nameless from getting too close to the Jedi.

The only other person in the common area was Dorian, who was loitering by the medical station, watching proceedings unfold with an uncomfortable expression on his face.

Master Lox cleared his throat. "I've been studying the plans and have a proposal."

Ashton nodded.

Master Lox reached into the sleeve of his robes and withdrew a small metal disc, which he tossed onto the floor between them. Immediately, a holoimage of the Nihil base bloomed to life, bright blue in the low light. It cast Ashton's face in a strange cool hue as she hunched forward, examining it.

Master Lox rose from his seat. "We've all studied the intel. It's patchy at best, and we can't rely on it too much on the ground. We're going to have to think on our feet. But what we *can* discern is that the Nihil are most likely holding the Nameless here," he said, indicating a small set of rooms on the far left of the complex.

"How can we be sure?" asked Ashton.

"We can't," said Master Lox. "But we know the outpost was formerly a small detention center for the processing of smugglers, before the Nihil moved in and slaughtered the civilian staff. Those are holding cells. Ready-made for keeping a dangerous creature penned up until required."

Ashton nodded, impressed. "Okay. That makes a lot of sense."

"So, what I'm proposing is that Amadeo and I go right"—he indicated the other rooms in the complex with a sweep of his arm—"while the rest of you head for those cells. We'll keep the Nihil busy while you secure the target. Get it out of there and into the holding pen on the *Orchid* as quickly as you can."

"You're going to take on *all* the Nihil," piped up Grampo among the seated volunteers. His voice was like churning gravel. He sounded older than his years, judging by his fresh-faced appearance and sandy hair. "By yourselves?"

"We can handle the Nihil," said Lox with a glance at Amadeo, who nodded his agreement. "You just focus on getting that creature back to the *Orchid* alive. And keeping it as far away from us as possible."

"Agreed," said Ashton. She looked more serious now than she had at any moment since Amadeo had met her. "Just promise me one thing."

"What's that?" asked Master Lox.

"If things don't go to plan in there, you get out on my word," she said.

Master Lox offered her a reassuring smile. "Understood. But I have faith. This is going to work. I'm sure of it."

A rumble of agreement passed through the team.

Amadeo only hoped his master's legendary positivity would once again prove true.

⚜

They moved under cover of darkness.

If the Nihil had spotted the *Invictus* and the *Orchid* coming in, they hadn't raised any alarms. Tribute, thought Amadeo, to the skill of the RDC pilots, who cut the engines as the two ships punctured the lower atmosphere, drifting them in toward their target on residual thrust alone.

They'd set down outside a large rural settlement, whose people, Amadeo assumed, were most likely suffering from their proximity to the Nihil base. No doubt the Nihil were demanding tributes from the local population and had probably burned down a few homesteads and murdered a few families just to underline their point and minimize the risk of resistance. It was the usual story, and Amadeo would be pleased if their actions that night were to drive the Nihil away from this place completely.

Amadeo and Master Lox had circled around to the right

of the old detention complex while Ashton, L-77, and the RDC team prepared to move in on the left. The plan was for Master Lox and Amadeo to go in first and draw the attention of the Nihil occupiers, allowing the others to move in afterward and—hopefully—get straight to the target.

So far, their approach had been unimpeded. The Nihil's perimeter defense seemed meager at best. Amadeo wondered if it was the result of sheer laziness or the Nihil's legendary arrogance. They couldn't comprehend that anyone would move against them on Angoth, and if they did—well, they had one of the Nameless locked up, ready to help them defend against even the Jedi.

Perhaps their arrogance was more justified than Amadeo had initially allowed.

"What do you sense?" whispered Master Lox. They were moving slowly and lightly through the undergrowth that surrounded the isolated base, using the shadows and the trunks of trees as cover. Their breath plumed in the cool air. Ahead of them, the lights of the outpost glowed stark in the gloom.

Amadeo reached out gingerly with the Force. He probed the surrounding area, sensing the timid heartbeats of wild creatures, the slow exhalation of the trees, the chaotic but wonderful web of nature that surrounded him.

He pushed his senses wider, into the Nihil base. Yes, there were people inside, forming several groups that were scattered throughout the nearest sections of the small complex. Individuals lit up like pinpricks in his mind. His insinuations slid off their surface thoughts. Laughter. Anger. Desire. He counted them. Ten . . . twelve . . . nineteen.

The base was bustling with Nihil. And that was just the areas closest to them. He extended his hand, fingers splayed, feeling his way further and further into the irregular structure—and then withdrew sharply, sucking at the cold air. His eyes flickered open. He felt as if a hot spike had been driven right through the center of his head. He took a step forward, clutching his temples in both hands, wavering for a moment . . . and then the feeling passed, leaving nothing but an echo of the terrible lancing pain.

He'd never felt that before, but he knew exactly what it was.

"Amadeo?" said Master Lox, close at his side.

"I'm all right," he said, catching his breath. "I just . . . I felt it."

"The creature?"

Amadeo nodded. "It's here, all right. And I think it knows we are, too." He turned to Master Lox, gritting his teeth. "It's hungry."

"Then we tread with caution. Did you get a sense of how many Nihil we're facing?"

"Nineteen at first count. But there'll be more, deeper inside the structure," said Amadeo. "Plus any that are guarding the creature."

Master Lox turned to him and grinned. "Nineteen? Is that all?"

Amadeo smiled, but he couldn't mirror Master Lox's confidence, not with one of those creatures in there. They were walking into a rancor's den, and he felt ill prepared for the battle to come.

Amadeo was ill at ease as they continued to edge through the undergrowth, the echo of the Nameless's touch still ringing in his mind. His instincts told him to hold back, to call off the whole operation, but he knew that wasn't an option, and besides, it was probably just his nerves. He tried to focus, following Master Lox's lead as they slipped from shadow to shadow, drawing closer to the outpost with every step.

Presently, they came upon the thick perimeter wall that separated the Nihil compound from the surrounding woods. Access in and out of the outpost was through a well-guarded gatehouse around the far side—the point where Ashton Vol and her team would sneak in once the Nihil were distracted. Amadeo and Master Lox were going over the wall.

They made eye contact and nodded, and then Amadeo leapt, calling on the Force to help propel him higher. He wheeled his arms as he fell, almost getting his trajectory wrong and coming down on the far side. Instead, he braced himself, closed his eyes in concentration, and landed square on the top of the wall, both feet scuffing clouds of dust and gravel.

He turned quickly to see Master Lox leaping up alongside him.

Master Lox grunted as he landed, and then he reached for the hilt of his lightsaber. He turned to Amadeo. "Just like Ashton said. We go in hot. Capitalize on our advantage."

"Which is?"

"They don't know we're coming," said Master Lox.

"And we're only distracting them, right? We don't kill unless they come for us first," said Amadeo.

"Right," said Master Lox. "We try to drive them out. But

be prepared. These are Nihil we're talking about. There's no way they're going to give up fighting when they have their backs to the wall."

Amadeo sighed. He'd been dreading this moment. It wasn't the Jedi's role to carry out raids like this. They weren't soldiers. They were defenders. But without the Nameless Reath and the others needed to complete their investigation, there was a very real risk there wouldn't be anyone left to defend before too long.

Still. He could never relish the taking of a life. Especially since the Nihil would be on the defensive.

Beside him, Master Lox's lightsaber blazed to life with a whoosh of blue light. His master cast him one last glance and then leapt off the wall.

Already, Amadeo could hear panicked voices calling from within as the Nihil caught sight of Master Lox's lightsaber, blazing a trail through the night. Blaster fire erupted in the small compound.

Unable to shake the feeling that something on Angoth wasn't quite right, Amadeo activated his own weapon and leapt into the fray.

THIRTY-SEVEN

The ruined settlement on Tolis was infested with swarms of strange creatures the size of astromech droids, with enormous swirled shells of enameled chitin the color of pink Panshan blossom. Within these shells, the creatures themselves appeared to be formed of a clear gelatinous flesh that rippled as they moved, leaving a trail of stinking slime in their wake. Eyestalks peered out timidly through circular holes in their shells, and they watched passively as Reath and Master Cohmac jogged through the decaying dwellings, reduced to little but the stumps of old stone walls.

The creatures seemed docile, and Reath figured they must have crawled out of the sea to search for food and would inevitably return to the churning waves before the tide fully receded.

So far, they'd seen little that looked as if it might have once housed a repository or library. The structures were so old and eroded by the waves and saltwater that there was little evidence anyone had *ever* lived here. Master Cohmac was clearly growing frustrated as he scanned the horizon searching for something— *anything*—that would serve as a clue.

Yet all Reath could think about was the odd structures they'd seen in the blighted wastes, shimmering silver and blue in the sun.

An ore that resisted the blight.

What was it about the substance that kept it from succumbing? Or was it eroding still, just at a much slower rate than everything else the blight had touched?

There was more work to be done when they got back to Coruscant—not just the analysis of the ore itself but a relative comparison of the decay rates between different blighted samples. He already had a suspicion that the blight was affecting people differently. All the data pointed to the fact that the younger a person was, the more quickly they were overcome—but he didn't know why. Perhaps this would prove to be the key that unlocked the final pieces of the puzzle, helping him truly understand how the blight worked.

If that was all they took from this mission to Tolis, it would still be something.

A few meters away, Cohmac had come to a stop standing atop a fragment of stone wall, shading his eyes with his hands.

Reath slowed to a walk, ambling over to join him while he caught his breath. He adjusted the straps at his shoulders, fiddling with the makeshift harness he'd fashioned for the shield so he could wear it on his back.

"Might take a bit of getting used to," said Cohmac, looking down at him from his vantage point.

"It'll be worth it," said Reath. "When we get back to Coruscant I'll figure out something better. For now, this'll do."

Cohmac turned on the spot, gesturing around them. "But this won't. We're getting nowhere. There's nothing here but old stones."

"And snails," said Reath, dragging his boot out of a puddle of stringy goo.

"And snails," agreed Cohmac. "Big ones."

Reath laughed.

"It's good to see you laugh," said Cohmac.

"It *feels* good to laugh," said Reath.

Cohmac hopped down from the wall. "I've been worried about you. Ever since I returned to Coruscant."

"Worried? Why?"

Cohmac gave him a knowing look. "You haven't been yourself, Reath. I think you know that."

"I've been busy," said Reath. "And maybe I have changed. You were away for a while." He regretted the stinging remark almost as soon as it left his mouth.

"It's true," said Cohmac. "But this isn't about me. You've been dragging a weight around with you like a manacle and chain."

Reath studied Cohmac for a moment, the concern in his eyes. It was a face he knew well, the face of the man who'd taught him so much in such a short space of time. He wanted to open up, to express the confusion and doubt he'd been feeling of late. But the words just wouldn't come. So much of his doubt was tied up in how Master Cohmac had left, how, despite what the other man had said back on the *Vessel*, he still wondered if he'd been a factor in Cohmac's decision to leave.

"I'm fine," he said after a moment, and he could see the disappointment on Master Cohmac's face, the slight dip of his shoulders as he realized he'd failed once again to draw his former Padawan out.

"I'm told you've been talking to Azlin Rell," said Master Cohmac.

It was a leading statement, and Reath didn't know quite how to respond. Was Master Cohmac *jealous*? Worried? Relieved?

"Sometimes," said Reath after a moment. "He's one of the few of us who understands what it's like to carry this burden, and to try to make sense of everything we're learning. His insights can be useful."

"And that's all you talk about?" asked Master Cohmac.

"Mostly," said Reath. He didn't want to have this conversation. He didn't want to justify himself to Master Cohmac. He didn't have to anymore. He was a Jedi Knight. He knew what he was doing.

And yet a part of him wanted to trust his old master again, to be fully open with him. He just wasn't ready yet. He supposed he was scared, afraid to trust him after what had happened. What if he opened up to Master Cohmac now and then he simply up and left like before? Could he afford to take that risk, when he had so much else to think about?

Reath felt a churn of guilt, deep in his guts. He thought of Azlin's words, reminding him that this was Master Cohmac's guilt to bear. That it shouldn't be about him. That he had to be strong.

Reath closed his eyes and drew a deep breath. He was so confused. He'd always believed that talking openly about his feelings was the best way to resolve them. With Cohmac gone, he had opened up to Azlin, perhaps more than he should have. Or at least, he had allowed Azlin to get into his head.

Now he didn't know what to think.

But now wasn't the time for dwelling on things. They had work to do. "We should make for the coast," he said. "Perhaps we'll find something there."

Master Cohmac inclined his head. "All right. But I want you to know that I'm here, okay?" He didn't wait for an answer but set off at a jog once again, heading for the sound of crashing waves.

✦

The coast was like none Reath had ever seen before. There was no sandbar or pebble beach, no rocky inlet or sheer cliff demarcating the edge of a landmass. The ruined city just sloped away into the ocean, disappearing beneath the blue-green tide. A little farther out, the heaving waves crashed on the smooth stumps of homes built and inhabited by the long dead, and at Reath's feet it lapped gently at the sloping flagstones of floors that hadn't been tread in millennia.

Even farther out, the spine of mountains he'd seen from the ship during their flyover emerged from the water like the tips of immense icebergs, suggestive of awe-inspiring depths. He wondered what had happened to cause such a calamitous flood. Had it been the fault of the Tolemites themselves, or a purely natural disaster? Could it have been related to the blight? He supposed he'd never know.

Master Cohmac was standing with his chin raised, his dark hair ruffled by the breeze. Reath wasn't sure whether he was soaking up the atmosphere or had seen something noteworthy on the horizon.

Overhead, birds wheeled in the clear sky, squawking in frustration at the two interlopers whose presence had driven them from their shore. Reath watched them for a moment, saddened by the thought that one day soon they would probably be gone, too, if the blight continued to slowly spread across this doomed landmass.

It was a morose thought, and Reath tried to put it out of mind. They had a job to do. No matter that the settlement was mostly gone—they couldn't give up searching for the Tolemites' repository until they were certain it was no longer here.

Reath sought out a dry spot on the ground just below a low wall, where the water lapped gently, rocking back and forth with the waves. He filled his lungs with the salty air and then lowered himself into a meditative position, crossing his legs, straightening his back. He placed his hands into the folds of his sleeves, exhaled, and closed his eyes.

"The Force is with me," he murmured. "And I am with the Force."

He opened his mind.

Color. Light. Life. Reath felt swept away in a tide not of the ocean but of vibrant life—of power. Master Cohmac had been right: there was something here, something incredibly powerful.

Reath felt closer to the living Force than he ever had before. He could feel it flowing *through* him, felt every breath as if he were breathing light instead of air. He felt giddy, more alive than he had in years.

There were others here, too. Cohmac, yes—but beyond him, out among the waves, living beings so rich in the Force that Reath sensed them like boulders in a stream, causing the light to bend and twist and spiral in new and unexpected ways.

He reached out to one of them, but its mind was so complex and alien that he could hardly comprehend what he was sensing. He felt it reach back, a vast wash of warmth and contentment of a sort he had never experienced before.

For the first time in a long time, Reath felt a moment of peace. The creature understood that he was no threat. How could he be? Its presence was so immense, so huge, that Reath felt dwarfed by it. It contained power on an immeasurable scale. What were these things? Oceangoing leviathans? It made sense that on a drowned world such as this, the main inhabitants would be bound to the water.

But then . . . that didn't feel right.

And then it came to him, and his eyes flickered open in wonder. These ancient creatures had always been here. They were old. They'd seen the rise and fall of the Tolemite civilization. They were most likely why the Tolemites had devised a religion based on worshipping the Force.

"Master Cohmac."

Master Cohmac, who'd remained standing, his head raised, turned to regard Reath, catching sight of him sitting on the ground. Reath hadn't noticed, but the tide had risen ever so slightly, and the water had swirled in around him, soaking his legs and his robes. But it hardly mattered.

"What is it?" said Master Cohmac.

Reath pointed out to sea. "Those mountain peaks, rising from the water?"

"Yes?"

"They're not mountains at all," said Reath. "They're living creatures. Hibernating offshore. They're massive living beasts!" He laughed, unable to contain his incredulity. "And they're rich in the Force. More than anyone or anything I've ever felt."

Master Cohmac was grinning, staring out at the immense shapes that still looked, to Reath's eyes, like nothing more than a sloping range of jagged rust-colored rocks. "Well, I'll be."

"This place is remarkable," said Reath. "There's so much we could learn here, regardless of the Tolemites." He heaved a heartfelt sigh. "And left unchecked, it'll all be gone. We have to find a way to stop the blight. Before it can do this to any other worlds."

"I might have some news on that front," said Master Cohmac.

Reath got slowly to his feet, ignoring the chill water that ran from his robes. "Go on."

Master Cohmac turned back toward the waves.

"It's *here*, Reath. Close. Just out there, under the water."

Reath studied the glittering waves. Whatever Master Cohmac was seeing, it wasn't visible to Reath. "What is? What's here?"

"The repository," said Master Cohmac, his voice tinged with reverence. "I can feel it. Like it's reverberating through the Force, calling to us."

"It's beneath the waves," said Reath, walking over to stand beside his former master. "It sank, like most of the city around it."

"Exactly," said Master Cohmac.

"But how are we going to reach it down there?" asked Reath. "If it's under the waves, what hope do we have of finding anything useful?"

Master Cohmac grinned. "We're not going down there, Reath," he said, his voice gravelly. He stood back, as if readying himself for something momentous. "We're going to bring the repository back up to us."

THIRTY-EIGHT

Amadeo flung himself left, rebounded off a wall, kicked to smash the blaster out of the hand of an oncoming Nihil, and then twisted, slashing his lightsaber down in a wide arc.

The fizzing green blade sliced off the end of another blaster, causing the metal to glow hot and red in its owner's hands. The green-skinned Twi'lek dropped the ruined weapon with a yelp, and Amadeo threw out his hand, shoving the Nihil back with the Force so they slammed heavily into the wall behind them and slid to the ground unconscious. He punched out with his free hand, striking a brown-skinned human across the jaw—the Nihil whose blaster he'd kicked out of his grip—and the man dropped like a sack of stones, eyes rolling back in his skull.

Amadeo flexed his fist. That one had smarted.

He whirled, sensing another attempting to charge him from behind, and reversed the thrust of his lightsaber, pushing the blade up beneath his left arm so it caught the attacker in the chest, dropping them swiftly and unceremoniously to the ground. A dagger fell from the Quarren's hand, tinkling as it struck the floor. Their pink tentacled face quivered one last time and went still.

Amadeo grimaced, mouthed his apologies to the dead Nihil, and turned to meet another volley of blaster fire coming from the far side of the room, swinging his lightsaber up and around to fend off the flurry of blasts. The deflected blasts pinged against the walls and ceiling of the large room, searing lines of soot in the old plaster. One struck the lumen strip overhead, causing it to flicker wildly so everything took on an erratic strobing appearance as Amadeo tried to make sense of what he was seeing.

Nearby, Master Lox was battling with three Nihil, two of whom appeared to be human, the other a maskless female Weequay who was hissing curses at the Jedi as she circled, a blaster clutched tightly in each fist. One of the masked humans was wielding what appeared to be a shuddering vibrosword and was trying to get in close behind Master Lox's defenses, while the other was standing farther back, swinging large metal hooks on the ends of a heavy chain, sending them soaring into the melee without any heed for their fellow combatants. As Amadeo watched, Master Lox neatly sidestepped one of the incoming hooks, only for the Weequay to inadvertently step into its path as she tried to press her advantage. It struck her in the upper thigh, piercing muscle and bone, and the Weequay fell to the ground screaming.

The other Nihil simply yanked the hook free with a vicious tug on the chain, and the Weequay grew suddenly silent, evidently passing out from the pain.

Master Lox spun, his lightsaber whipping around. The vibrosword clattered to the ground in two useless pieces. Its wielder leapt back, trying to get clear of the Jedi's next swing, but the hooks were already in motion, and one of them struck them across the side of the head with its rounded edge, sending them spinning to the floor. They didn't get up.

Master Lox moved, dancing around a flurry of new blaster shots coming from the doorway, and then lurched, thrusting his lightsaber out in a straight lunge that dropped the remaining Nihil. Their swinging hooks flew wide, punching a hole in the wall with a resounding crash and lodging in the broken panel.

Amadeo grunted, impressed by his master's combat abilities. Master Lox shot him a fleeting glance and then ran for the door, batting blaster shots back toward their attackers as he went.

Amadeo charged after him, leaping over fallen Nihil—many of them wounded in the arms and legs by their own returned shots—to follow his master into the adjacent room.

Here the sparse furnishing suggested some sort of common area where the Nihil ate and drank. And judging by the plethora of empty bottles and old pockmarks in the walls, presumably from ad hoc target practice, it was where they partied, too.

The lights seemed harsh and bright after the bizarre flickering in the previous room, and Amadeo's eyes took a moment to adjust, causing ghostlike images to stutter in his vision. But he wasn't relying on his eyes. His instincts were guiding his every movement, his senses alerting him to every threat. Every move was precise, every reaction deft and perfectly timed.

He stepped left, out of the path of a thrown knife, and then leapt forward and rolled, springing back up to his feet to slice across the chest of a green-skinned masked assailant. They fell back gurgling, and once again Amadeo felt a stab of regret.

He had no time to dwell on it, however, as more blaster fire raked the wall behind his head. He ran, pushing himself into a leap, twisting in the air, and coming back down behind two of the shooters, his elbows slamming hard into the backs of their necks.

They pitched forward, unconscious before they struck the ground.

The onslaught seemed relentless, and Amadeo realized he'd badly miscalculated. There were far more than nineteen of the Nihil within the confines of the outpost. Others were rushing in, blasters spitting, fanning out around the edges of the room as if trying to encircle the two Jedi.

Amadeo heard the hiss of escaping gas and turned to see a dirty cloud streaming into the air from several dropped canisters. A Nihil war cloud. His eyes stung as the Nihil advanced, weapons raised, their spiked helmets, daubed with the blue eye of their creed, casting sinister silhouettes amid the streaming green gas.

Master Lox backed toward Amadeo, his lightsaber still flashing in time with the repeated blaster shots coming at them from seemingly every direction.

"They've got us surrounded," called Amadeo, backing up to meet him. Master and Padawan turned on the spot, sending every blaster shot skirling away. Nihil dropped, crumpling where they stood, as still others stepped up to take their place.

"We have them exactly where we want them," replied Master Lox. He reached into his robe and pulled out his rebreather, placing it swiftly in his mouth. Amadeo did the same, sucking at the filtered air. The gas would remain an annoyance, but nothing more.

As he watched, the Nihil started to signal to one another, gesturing in some code or sign language that Amadeo didn't recognize. All the while, they kept up the pressure, a continuous barrage of blaster shots that pinned the two Jedi neatly in place.

Then, as one, the shooters all took a single step forward, narrowing the perimeter of their circle. They were planning to close in, tightening like a noose around Master Lox and Amadeo.

The marauders took another synchronized step toward them. They were coordinating their attack. The barrage was almost more than Amadeo could take, coming thick and fast. As he turned, deflecting one shot back toward its point of origin, another scored a painful hit across his shoulder, burning a streak through his robes. He winced but bit down on the pain and tried to step up his speed, wheeling faster and faster until his lightsaber blade was nothing but a smear of green light.

He wasn't sure how much longer he could keep it up. He was starting to feel dizzy as he and Master Lox twisted and turned on the spot, still back to back. The Nihil were getting closer, moving more quickly, pressing their obvious advantage. And the gas was flooding the room as the canisters continued to empty.

Master Lox turned, gesturing to him. Amadeo recognized the signal immediately. Master Lox was planning to use one of their maneuvers. He wanted Amadeo to grab his arm, spin him, and throw him using the Force, just like they'd practiced in the training room.

More turning. More blaster shots.

Master Lox threw out his arm.

Amadeo reached back, grasping his master's wrist as they swung about. He allowed the momentum to carry him, calling on the Force for strength, dragging Master Lox in his wake as he turned and . . .

Released.

Master Lox was ready. He soared like a shuttle reaching escape velocity, bringing his lightsaber around in a broad arc as he sailed, head and shoulders first, toward the nearest Nihil.

Amadeo barely registered what happened as Master Lox slammed into them, his lightsaber arcing as he barreled through, breaking the tightening circle and dropping at least five of their attackers in one fell swoop.

He tucked into a roll, immediately springing back to his feet on the other side of the fragmented circle. His lightsaber flickered in the slowly dispersing cloud of gas.

The Nihil scattered, their tactic ruined, and Amadeo took his cue, closing in on the nearest of them. His lightsaber sang as he batted away weapons, his boots shattering knees, his punches cracking jaws.

The Nihil dropped in droves.

More and more of them were spilling into the room, and

Amadeo realized he and his master were drawing the Nihil off, just as they'd planned.

The distraction is working.

We're going to do this.

He watched Master Lox drop two more Nihil with a graceful turn and sweep, coming back up out of the move to batter away another four blaster shots, all in one smooth motion.

We've got this.

Elsewhere in the compound something rumbled, causing the ground to tremble beneath Amadeo's feet. It was followed by a series of three enormous concussive bangs that sent him staggering two steps to the right, almost into the path of a wild Nihil shot. His ears rang, tinny and shrill.

And then his comlink crackled to life, spitting static.

"We're in."

It was Ashton Vol. They'd blown the main gates and were spilling into the outpost from the other direction.

While all the Nihil were here, fighting the Jedi.

Amadeo felt a surge of positivity.

He could see a path to victory opening before them. The plan was solid.

The gas had mostly cleared now, and he pulled his rebreather from his mouth, jamming it back into his belt as he turned, his lightsaber flickering.

And then the Nihil started to fall back, lowering their blasters.

Were they giving up? Surrendering? Turning to investigate the explosion at the gate?

Somehow, Amadeo didn't think so. Which meant something else was coming. . . .

He turned toward the door, sensing danger.

The air was split by a deep roar that seemed to hit Amadeo right in the gut, triggering his primal urge to run. He held his ground, catching Master Lox's eye, shocked to see his master actually *grin*.

Successive thuds. Another roar. And then a towering figure thundered through, battering Nihil out of the way as it charged into the room.

It was a hulking Dowutin—the biggest Dowutin Amadeo had ever seen. And that was saying something, as there was no such thing as a small one. They were dressed in shabby gray coveralls and towered over most of the other Nihil, being at least half again as tall as Master Lox. They had a thick scaly yellow-green hide, two massive horns protruding from their chin, and hands that ended in vicious-looking claws. They bellowed again, spittle flecking Amadeo's face even from across the room, and then charged.

Amadeo dropped low, diving, sliding through the Dowutin's legs before they had a chance to pivot their massive bulk.

The other Nihil were cheering, chanting what Amadeo took to be the Dowutin's name: "Bullgar! Bullgar! Bullgar!"

Amadeo rolled to his feet, spinning his lightsaber in his right hand. Sweat was running down the nape of his neck, and his shoulder was smarting from the blaster burn. He glanced at Master Lox, who was circling carefully, keeping his eye on the Dowutin but also wary of the surrounding mob of Nihil, who

Amadeo knew would seize any opportunity to shoot them in the back if they took their attention off them for too long.

He edged around in the opposite direction of Master Lox, steadying his breathing.

The Dowutin stooped low, sweeping up a prone human Nihil by their heels. Amadeo couldn't tell if they were dead or merely unconscious, as their arms and head lolled like a rag doll's in the Dowutin's grip.

What were they doing? The Dowutin half turned away from him, raising their arm. . . .

And then Amadeo was sprawled on the ground, his lightsaber rolling from his fingers, head ringing. He gasped for breath, flopping onto his back. He peered around to see Master Lox dancing around the Dowutin's reach, trying to nip at their legs with his lightsaber, and the Dowutin keeping him at bay with . . .

Amadeo looked on, appalled.

The Dowutin was using the other Nihil as a *club*.

He scrambled to his feet. Close by, a long-faced Pau'an Nihil had crept forward and was reaching for Amadeo's dropped lightsaber hilt. Amadeo threw up his arm, tossing the Pau'an backward onto his rump and then summoning the lightsaber into his palm.

He reignited it with a push of his thumb.

Master Lox threw him a look. "Remember the feathered lizard on Cethis?"

Amadeo nodded once.

Lox fell back, ducking another of the Dowutin's wild swings. If the human the Dowutin was using as a club wasn't dead before, there was little hope for them now.

Amadeo drew a sharp breath and then ran.

As he neared, Master Lox dropped, lowering his shoulder, and Amadeo leapt, using his master's body as a set of steps from which he propelled himself into the air, pirouetting as he soared over the confused Dowutin's head so that as he fell he was facing their back.

His lightsaber struck true at the base of the Dowutin's neck, tip pointing down, ending their life with a single stroke.

Amadeo landed lightly on his feet as the Dowutin's lifeless frame toppled forward, slamming hard on the flagstone floor. They gave a single sigh and went still.

Around the edges of the room, the remaining Nihil roared angrily, and Amadeo raised his lightsaber again, flexing his aching muscles, as the barrage of blaster fire began anew.

"There can't be many more of them," he called, climbing onto the prone Dowutin's back to gain the high ground.

"So long as we're keeping them busy, that's all that counts," replied Master Lox before charging into a small knot of Nihil, causing them to splinter and flee, scrambling for the door.

It had to be almost over. The sight of so many dead or wounded Nihil tore at Amadeo's heart. Even though they were the enemy, even though all this was necessary, it seemed *wrong*.

He roared as he pushed back another wave of blaster shots, driving them into the wall above his assailants' heads. They flinched at the narrow misses and began edging toward the door.

The Nihil were in full retreat.

On his belt, Amadeo's comlink sputtered to life. It was Ashton Vol, and she sounded furious. "Dammit! We're too late."

Master Lox thumbed his own comlink, still batting away stray blaster shots with his lightsaber in his other hand as they allowed the last of the Nihil to back through the door. "What do you mean, we're too late?"

Ashton's voice crackled, heavy with static. "There are two of them. Two Force Eaters. And the Nihil have set them loose from their cages."

Amadeo glanced at Master Lox, his eyes wide.

Two of them.

Loose.

Here.

Ashton was bellowing through the tinny comlinks. "Did you hear me? There are two Nameless loose in this outpost, and they're heading your way. Both of you—get out of there. *Now!*"

THIRTY-NINE

Reath and Cohmac stood on the shoreline, the cold waters of Tolis lapping at their feet.

What they were about to attempt felt almost elemental, like
something out of the old fables. He supposed it was, really. If they
were successful, if they actually did manage to find what they'd
come here for, it was a story that would tumble on through the
centuries to come, retold in tapbars and nurseries, homesteads
and cantinas.

*And the Jedi raised the temple out of the ocean, and venturing inside,
they learned the long-forgotten truths of the great threat that promised to
destroy them....*

Their names would be forgotten, of course, just as they
should be. That wasn't why they were here. This wasn't a story

forged from a desire for fame or remembrance but out of desperation. It was a tale written from a need to survive, a desire to protect both the Jedi and those in the galaxy who could not protect themselves.

Reath only hoped that their story would prove to have a happy ending.

Or maybe he really had just spent too much time reading the old stories in the Jedi Archives.

He watched Master Cohmac. The man was centering himself, preparing for the trial to come. Reath was under no illusion. This was going to be *hard*—maybe even impossible. For a start, they weren't even sure what they were looking for.

"How do we know this is going to work?" said Reath.

"We don't," said Master Cohmac. "We trust in the Force, and in the intentions of those who built this place. Remember, if the stories are true, they *wanted* this place to be found. They hoped it might serve as some sort of beacon to future generations, a way of transmitting their warnings down the centuries. The tale of what happened to them before they died."

"All right," said Reath. "Then we just . . . reach out?"

Master Cohmac shrugged. "Yeah. We just reach out. And if we're right, if the Force is with us, we'll find what we're looking for."

"You always have had faith," said Reath. "In the Force."

Master Cohmac sighed, glancing away. "I thought so, too. Until . . . I guess even the most faithful sometimes question their beliefs. Never my belief in you, though, Reath. *Never.*"

Now, more than ever, Reath thought he might be able to understand that. "I suppose they do," he said.

Master Cohmac snickered, as if at some shared joke. "We're quite a pair, you know. Standing on the shore of a long-dead world, hoping we're going to be able to save the galaxy by dragging an ancient library out of the ocean. It's a stretch even for us."

Reath smiled. "I suppose we'd better get on with it, then," he said, "before we realize how unlikely it is this is going to work."

"Yeah. You're right."

Reath straightened, planting his feet. His wet mission robes clung to his legs. The weight of the shield on his back was a welcome comfort.

"Are you ready?" said Master Cohmac.

"I think so," said Reath.

"Remember Master Yoda's old adage," said Cohmac with a wry smile.

"Do. Or do not. There is no try," they said in unison.

Master Cohmac cracked a grin. "He's been using that one for decades. But it holds true. Whatever happens, don't let go until that repository has risen from the waves." He glanced across at Reath. "And for what it's worth, know that I'm proud of you. And it means a lot that you're here."

"Focus, old man," said Reath.

Master Cohmac smiled but did as Reath said, turning back to the water. He raised both hands. His eyes fluttered shut.

Reath did the same.

He breathed.

In and out.

In and out.

As before, his surroundings flowered into something so much richer, so much more vibrant.

For a moment he enjoyed the deep connection to the life of this world. He sensed the beasts out in the water, like beacons themselves, rich as they were in the living Force.

He turned his attention to the waves, allowing his senses to sink below the surface, down into the swirling depths, edging through the frigid gloom. The dark water was rich with glittering life, from the smallest plankton to enormous fish that seemed to sense his presence, darting silently away as if spooked by a predator.

He could sense the lingering sadness, the ruin of so many lives, abandoned to these waters so long ago that their age was almost meaningless. The Tolemites had thought themselves safe here, but their miscalculation had been costly indeed.

And then he sensed it: the brilliant shimmering beacon of the repository. It had been built to be found, just as Master Cohmac had said.

Reath reached out to grasp it, utterly awed.

And he *lifted*.

For a moment, nothing happened. He strained, drawing on whatever strength he could find.

He felt something shift—just a little.

Something huge.

Beside him on the shoreline, Master Cohmac grunted.

Reath didn't look. He had to hold his concentration.

He staggered, sweat trickling down his face.

The weight of the thing . . .

He lifted.

And he lifted.

And he lifted.

Beside him, Master Cohmac was roaring with the strain.

Reath groaned. He took a single step forward. His hands were still jutted out before him, his eyes still closed. His heart was racing. His ears had popped from the pressure. His thigh muscles were trembling.

And still he lifted.

He could feel his jaw almost popping as he ground his teeth.

He screamed, long and deep and raw.

And still he lifted.

There is no try.

There is no try.

There is . . .

Something gave.

Reath didn't know whether it was something within him or something out *there*. He could hardly differentiate anymore.

He dropped, slumping to the ground, barely conscious.

The kiss of the cold waves was the only thing that kept him from passing out. He raised his head, breathless, exhausted, peeling open eyes that had gummed themselves shut.

Nearby, Master Cohmac was on his knees in the surf. His head was hung low, his breath coming in labored gasps.

"Master Cohmac?" Reath pulled himself up to his knees. "Master Cohmac?" He stared at the other man with bleary eyes.

Slowly, Master Cohmac turned his head. "I'm okay." He peered at Reath. "You?"

"I think so," said Reath. His own voice sounded dry and hoarse. "But . . . I couldn't hold it any longer. I'm sorry. I wasn't strong enough."

Master Cohmac raised his head, pointing a weary arm out to the ocean. "Oh, but you were, Reath. We both were."

Reath turned his head.

There, directly ahead of them, a massive stone structure jutted from the water as if it had always been there. It was squat and circular, erected from giant blocks of stone, and rose to a tapered tip, with a single entrance that led to what appeared to be a series of carved stone steps.

Saltwater ran in ribbons from the open entrance, from the cracks in the upper walls, and algae hung in slick banners from almost every visible surface. Where there had once been carved decorations, the stone was eroded to smooth featureless nubs.

Time had done its best to consume the once-glorious building, dragging it back to the soil and the waves, but it was a testament to the ingenuity of the Tolemites that it was intact, an echo from the past still ringing true in the here and now.

A stone causeway, broken and uneven, led from the edge of the water all the way up to the ominous entrance.

"Oh," said Reath. "I see."

They sat for some time in the surf, recovering their strength and staring at the ancient structure they'd pulled from the ocean bed.

It felt to Reath like a miracle. The Force had led them here, and the Tolemites, all those years ago, had considered that one day someone might come looking. They'd constructed the building to survive, and more than that, they'd built it to serve as a beacon to those who might need to find it.

The foresight involved in such an act was awe-inspiring. As was the generosity, the selflessness required to plan so far ahead for the benefit of those who came after.

This was a gift, and whatever they found inside would be remarkable. The scholar in Reath was desperate to study it, to learn from it, but the man in him was deeply touched.

Master Cohmac splashed to his feet, brushing off the loose droplets that clung to his robes. It was a pointless gesture that made Reath smile, when the rest of the man was sodden to the bone. Once he had finished, he held out a hand, offering to help Reath up.

Reath took it gladly, and Master Cohmac hauled him to his feet. "It's time."

Reath nodded. He felt ready, recovered from the exertion of the past hour. Absently, he wondered how Affie and the others were doing. Presumably they'd managed to harvest a sample of the strange ore by now and had retreated into orbit aboard the *Vessel* as planned.

Master Cohmac had already started out across the narrow stone causeway. Reath tottered after him, trying to keep himself upright as his boots slipped and skidded on the slick stones.

In this way, they slowly approached the large entrance that, now he was closer to it, looked more like the mouth of an underwater cave or grotto, encrusted as it was with the shells of tiny sea creatures.

Together, they stood in the shadow of the opening for a moment. The air was thick with the salty tang of the water and the rich pungent stink of the clinging growths. Water still streamed from the opening, splashing across their boots.

"We're the first people to visit this place in millennia," said Master Cohmac. His voice, soft and reverential, seemed to carry, echoing off the walls inside. "I don't even know where to begin."

Reath took a step over the threshold, breaking the spell. "We do exactly what you said before. We let the Force guide us."

"Yes," said Master Cohmac, stepping cautiously in to join Reath. "That's exactly what we should do."

FORTY

The Temple Guard was exactly where he'd been the last time Vernestra had visited the passageway that led to Azlin Rell's cell: standing with his back to the wall, his masked head held high and to attention, his weapon holstered, his arms folded across his chest.

Vernestra slipped quietly into the same alcove she'd inhabited before, pressing herself back into the shadows.

She didn't really know what had led her here again. Last time she'd followed Reath, trying to get a measure of his interactions with the fallen Jedi. Now Reath was half a galaxy away, trekking through ruins, searching for the answers that could save them all.

Vernestra guessed that no one else had come to visit Azlin in the intervening time, but she knew the Temple Guards would be keeping a log of all comings and goings. She would ask to inspect it later—at a more reasonable hour.

In the meantime, something down here was awry. She could feel it, that same rumbling undertone of uncertainty through the Force that had been plaguing her in recent days, that sense that something wasn't quite right.

She supposed it could be her proximity to Azlin himself that was setting her on edge, but somehow she doubted it. As unpleasant as she knew his company would be, that in itself would surely not be enough to trigger such a pervasive sense of *wrongness*.

Vernestra wished she could shake it. She still wasn't entirely convinced it wasn't just the lingering aftereffects of her encounter with Marchion Ro and her failure to take him down. A sense of guilt, perhaps, or at least a notion that, if she'd been stronger, she might have been able to end all this already. Regret for a missed opportunity.

Or perhaps she was just overthinking it.

Regardless, Master Yoda had encouraged her to trust her instincts, and so here she was doing just that—even if it was the middle of the night.

Vernestra had woken about an hour earlier, restless and unable to return to sleep, and so she'd risen from her bunk to fetch herself a drink. Instead, she had found herself slowly making her way down here.

To Azlin's cell.

A few minutes passed.

And then . . .

Rap, rap, rap.

Three knocks on the wall, just as before.

Vernestra's sense of disquiet was piqued.

The Temple Guard stirred, lowering his arms. He glanced up and down the passageway. Vernestra held her breath, her heartbeat pounding loud in her ears as the Temple Guard's gaze seemed to linger in her direction. But then he looked away, moving over to the door to Azlin's cell. She could tell it was the same guard she'd observed before, the one with the tendency to favor his left leg. The same one she'd seen go into Azlin's cell after Reath's last visit.

She waited to see if the Temple Guard would return to his post, half expecting the whole thing to be an anticlimax.

Instead, he approached the door to the cell. It slid open, and he stepped inside.

Vernestra exhaled slowly and calmly.

Was he really at Azlin's beck and call?

Cautiously, she edged out from the alcove and crept along the hallway until she was standing close to the cell door.

She studied it, wondering what—if anything—was going on behind it.

Vernestra strained to listen but could make out no sounds coming from within the room.

A minute passed.

Then another.

What could Azlin possibly want at this hour?

She decided she'd have to report it to the Jedi Council. It

seemed . . . irregular, to say the least. A Temple Guard being summoned into a prisoner's cell? Apparently at the will of the prisoner? What were they talking about?

She was about to peel herself away from her hiding place when she noticed a glint of light in the passageway ahead, just a small strip of soft illumination spilling out onto the stone floor as if from under a door.

Intrigued, Vernestra crept along the passageway toward it.

She moved beyond the door to Azlin's cell, passing three more doors on the left-hand side of the passageway, all of them standing open. Glancing inside, she saw that they were empty and thick with dust, which made sense. This part of the Temple was mostly disused, and it was only following Azlin's murderous attack on Travyx Prime that he'd been moved down here to keep him safely out of the way of any Jedi who might fall prey to his manipulations. Temple Guards had been placed at intervals, with one at the entrance to the area containing Azlin's cell, as well as the one with the injured leg, who maintained a station outside of the cell itself.

It wasn't exactly a case of out of sight, out of mind, but it was certainly an effort to manage Azlin's influence and ensure there were no opportunities for him to enact any further atrocities. It made sense, then, that the rest of the rooms down here remained empty.

Which made it even more curious that a light should be on in another supposedly disused room at the far end of the passageway.

Cautiously, Vernestra approached the door. She was fifty meters or more from the entrance to Azlin's cell, tucked away at the very end of the same passageway.

She saw immediately that she'd been right: the light was definitely on in the room beyond the door.

She ran her fingertips over the hilt of her lightsaber but didn't draw it. And then she approached the door.

It slid open.

The room beyond was small and thick with dust. It hadn't been used—officially, at least—for some years. It was devoid of furniture, save for a small table and a single chair in the far corner.

And sitting on the surface of the table was a long-range comm unit. It was powered up. She could tell from the winking lights and the low hum of the speaker, tuned to a dead channel.

Vernestra could see there were tracks in the dust on the floor leading to and from the table.

Someone had been here, using this device.

She crossed to it, examining the readout panels. Whatever connection had been made was now gone. There was no way to tell whom the user had been talking to.

Vernestra could hardly believe it. She didn't know what she'd expected to find, but it certainly hadn't been this.

She knew now why her instincts had led her down here.

They had a traitor in their midst.

Someone was using this room to make unauthorized transmissions. To whom, she wasn't sure.

But she had an idea of who was responsible.

The Temple Guards were the only ones with regular access to this place, aside from Reath, and perhaps Master Yoda and the Council. And she'd seen one of them visiting Azlin's cell twice.

It was the only thing that made sense.

The Temple Guard was up to something. He was the only one with the opportunity to use the comm equipment. And maybe Azlin was the reason. Maybe he'd been up to his old games again, manipulating the people around him into doing his bidding. Maybe that was what was happening right now in that cell, why the Temple Guard was in there.

Slowly, she backed toward the door.

There was no one else to be seen. No one hiding and nowhere for them to have gone.

The Temple Guard was the only answer.

She moved purposefully along the passageway until she was standing just a few meters from the door to Azlin's cell. Then she waited.

It was only a moment or two before the door slid open again and the Temple Guard emerged.

Vernestra's purple lightsaber ignited in her fist, casting the whole passageway in its fizzing, shimmering light.

The Temple Guard looked at her, his expression hidden behind his smooth featureless mask. Slowly, he raised his hands, making it clear he did not intend to fight.

Vernestra jutted out her chin. "We need to talk," she said.

FORTY-ONE

"**M**aster! You heard her—we have to *go!*"

Amadeo was struck by a dawning sense of dread. He didn't know if it was the effect of the Nameless drawing closer or simply his own terror manifesting, but it mattered little. All he knew was that they needed to get out of there.

"We can go out the way we came," he said. "They won't be able to get to us over the compound wall. We'll have time to get away before they figure out a way to backtrack through the blown gates."

"Yes," said Master Lox. He took a staggering step toward the door. "Yes." He looked confused, uncertain, and yet his lightsaber was held high.

Amadeo frowned, desperate. *"Master?"*

Elsewhere in the complex, the sound of blaster fire erupted, followed by bellowed commands.

Master Lox's head whipped around, and the look on his face—the vision of utter fear—felt like a body blow to Amadeo. "Amadeo! Run! You have to—"

Amadeo didn't hear the remaining words, as the world seemed to suddenly shift. He staggered, backing away, his mind reeling.

He could feel them. He could feel the fear, seizing control of his mind, spikes of lancing terror. His vision blurred.

They were close!

Too close!

It was already too late.

Amadeo bellowed, raging against the injustice, the terror, the horror. He fought for control, shaking his head, blinking. He stepped back again. And again. Fighting.

He tripped and went down, crashing to the floor. He'd bitten through his lower lip. Blood pooled in his mouth. His vision was swimming. He tried to drag himself up, but his body wasn't responding how it should.

He caught a fleeting glimpse of Master Lox raising his lightsaber, his hand wavering, trying to put himself between Amadeo and the door.

"Amadeo, *run!*"

But Amadeo couldn't breathe. He felt like something was compressing his chest. He gasped for breath, gulping at the air. He looked frantically left and then right, sensing movement.

Oh, Light! It was here! It was coming for him!

Around him, the shadows were alive, dancing and shifting, painting black flames across his vision.

He heard something bound through the door, heard Master Lox bellow in defiance. Amadeo tried to look but couldn't focus on it, couldn't hold the images in his mind. But he knew what it was: a roiling knot of hunger and fear.

A Nameless.

Amadeo tore at his hair, as if trying to pull the searing pain and horror out of his head with his fists.

Hot tears streamed down his face. He was frozen to the spot, rigid, terrified. A part of him wanted to rush to his master's side, lightsaber blazing, while the rest of him wanted to turn and run, to get as far away from this dreadful thing as he was able.

But he could do neither.

He felt as if the room were closing in on him.

Somewhere close, something screeched, and the sound was like searing talons raking his very mind.

His vision was so clouded. He couldn't *think*. He realized he was wailing, venting all his fear into a harsh guttural cry.

He was going to die.

Right here, right now.

And there was nothing he could do about it.

He clawed at his head, trying to make it all stop. His heart felt like it was squeezed so tight it might burst.

Perhaps it would be better if he let it happen. Perhaps that was the only way to make it stop. If he just . . .

Blaster fire erupted close by, loud and intrusive. A thud. A screech. A metallic clunk.

He felt something grab hold of him.

It had him!

It was happening!

He tried to squirm, to fight it off, but his body wouldn't listen, curling itself up in a tight ball.

And then he was moving, his head thudding against the ground.

Blackness engulfed him.

※

Amadeo opened his eyes.

He twisted, spitting a mouthful of blood. His heart was still hammering. And he was so scared. He flinched at movement on his left, pushing himself up against the wall, scrabbling at it.

"No, no, no, no, no . . ."

"It's all right, Amadeo. You're okay."

The voice was unfamiliar, soft.

Recoiling, Amadeo turned to look at the thing that had spoken. It was one of the RDC volunteers—the human, Ears, with dark brown skin and a warm smile.

"Amadeo? Amadeo?"

Amadeo looked at him but didn't really see him. The fear was abating, just a little. He could hear thudding sounds and blaster fire erupting on the far end of the corridor.

He sucked at the air through clenched teeth. He looked wildly from side to side, trying to make some sense out of what he was hearing.

More screeching. Blaster shots.

A metallic thud.

They were still fighting. Ashton and L-77 and the RDC had come to their aid. And Ears had dragged him to safety, down the corridor, away from the creatures. He could still feel them, like nails embedded in the back of his skull, tearing at his control, invoking fear that he'd never imagined possible.

"M . . . M . . . Master Lox?" said Amadeo, finally regaining some measure of speech. He caught his breath and tried to pull himself upright.

Ears stepped in and put a hand on his shoulder. "They've got it under control. Okay. You stay there."

Amadeo shook his head. He felt for his lightsaber, but he must have dropped it when the Nameless got too close.

Another screech. Then more firing.

Then silence.

He wavered for a moment and then rested his head back against the wall. He felt the pressure lifting. His thoughts quickened. He blinked up at Ears. "It's done."

A moment later a call echoed down the hall, sounding the all clear.

"Wait here," said Ears, hurrying off toward the others.

Shakily, Amadeo pulled himself to his feet, using the wall for support. He could taste blood and bile, and he was still woozy, although the fear and confusion seemed to have passed. Slowly, he made his way along the passage toward the sound of raised voices.

After a moment, he reached the doorway and almost fell into the room.

There were people everywhere.

L-77 was standing over the body of a dead Nameless. Amadeo peered at it, transfixed. Even though it was dead, it still horrified him beyond all measure, beyond all sanity. He forced himself to turn away, averting his eyes.

"M . . . M . . . Master?" he stammered. He reached out a hand.

Ears grabbed for it, catching him by the elbow and supporting him. "Amadeo? Just take it steady. Dorian is on his way."

Wavering, but standing, Amadeo gently pushed Ears away, peering blearily at a small huddle of people on the other side of the room. His head was still swimming. He felt nauseous.

He could see Ashton Vol, standing with her blaster pointed at something indistinct in the far corner of the room. Around her, more of the RDC personnel formed a half circle, weapons raised. The second Nameless had been stunned and sedated and was slumped on the ground unconscious.

And there, standing facing the creature with his back to Amadeo, was Master Lox.

Had it worked? Had his plan to find a point of focus actually *worked*?

Ashton edged forward, the bead of her weapon never leaving the creature. Her eyes flicked to Lox, and she almost recoiled in horror. She seemed to recover herself quickly, keeping the Nameless in her sights. "Master Lox?" she said, her voice low. "Master Lox?"

Amadeo staggered woozily. What was the matter? What was happening? Was Master Lox wounded?

"Master?" he called, blood from his wounded lip burbling as he spoke. "Master?"

He took another step forward. "Master?"

Master Lox hadn't moved, even while Ashton and the others had moved in. They were dragging the stunned creature out of the room, past the slumped bodies of the fallen Nihil.

The mission was a success.

But Amadeo knew that something was wrong.

"Master?" he said, his voice trembling.

Master Lox shifted slightly. His head twitched. He turned, but something didn't look right. Amadeo knew it had to be the residual effects of the Nameless skewing his vision, because his master's body had never moved like *that*.

And then Master Lox turned his head, and Amadeo wailed, a soul-deep cry that seemed to drown out everything around him— the barked commands of the RDC, the blaring alarms ringing out elsewhere in the Nihil complex, even his own thoughts. Everything was swallowed by that scream.

Master Lox's one remaining eye seemed to fix on him as the gray matter of his husked face began to fall away. First his jaw, then the side of his head, then his entire torso sloughing away like grains of sand.

Mirro Lox collapsed to the ground, a broken, ashen shell of the man he had once been.

A heap of dust.

Amadeo tried to run to him, screaming, but his feet betrayed him and he tumbled to the ground, and once again everything went black.

Amadeo came to with a start.

Someone was screaming. He sat up, looked around frantically, realized it was him.

He shut his mouth, tried to swallow.

He was on the *Invictus*, apparently alone.

What was he doing here? The mission! The outpost.

He swung his legs off the side of the gurney.

Where was Master Lox?

For a single blissful moment, he looked around, searching for his master, expecting him to walk in at any moment. To make sense of all this.

And then he *remembered*.

The look in that sole remaining eye. The sadness and resignation. How the man he had known and cared for almost his entire life had just . . . crumbled before his eyes.

Husked as he tried to protect his Padawan.

He'd given his life to save Amadeo.

And now he was one with the Force.

Amadeo fought back stinging tears. He just wished he could talk to him one more time. To embrace him. To tell him . . .

He wiped his eyes.

He was a Jedi. He had to be strong. There were still things to be done. Reath would need his help making sense of their findings once the Republic team had managed to run tests on the creature. Other settlements would need evacuating out on the frontier.

He would be busy. They were all so very busy.

And yet Amadeo couldn't see past the end of his nose for the brimming tears, let alone see into the future. He felt hollow—like the void left by Master Lox's passing could never be filled.

He didn't know what to do.

Sitting on the edge of the gurney, he checked himself over.

His head was still ringing, but the pain had subsided. His bottom lip had been stitched. His lightsaber was back in its holster at his hip, and he'd been lying on a medical gurney in the main hold of the ship.

It occurred to him then that there was a possible explanation for everything he'd seen.

He'd been near *two* Nameless. His brain had been scrambled. The Nameless forced you to see things, didn't they? Horrible hallucinations, manifesting your worst fears. What if that was all it had been? What if seeing Master Lox die like that had just been a sick twisted vision, conjured by his own mind under the terrible pressure of the creatures?

That could be it.

That *had* to be it.

And then Dorian walked in, and Amadeo saw his face and knew it wasn't a dream.

"You're awake," said Dorian. He approached tentatively, as if unsure how Amadeo was going to react. He stood at the end of the gurney, his arms folded across his chest. The look of utter sympathy on his face almost caused Amadeo to burst into tears again, and he looked away, unable to hold the other man's gaze.

"I'm sorry," said Dorian. His voice was soft and low.

"So am I," said Amadeo. "I just . . . I can't believe he's gone. Just like that. One minute he was there, the next . . ."

Dorian reached over and took his hand, squeezing gently. "It's always like that," he said. "Even when you're expecting it. You feel like the galaxy should just stop. That everything should pause for a while. Like the world shouldn't keep turning for something this momentous. But then the clock keeps running. Time keeps flowing. People get on with their lives. Things need to be done. And it all feels wrong because you're still standing in place, trying to figure out what happened, trying to make sense of a galaxy with that person no longer in it. And it doesn't. It doesn't make sense. And maybe it will never make sense again."

Amadeo swallowed. "You've lost someone, too."

"My father," said Dorian. "He was the only one who ever truly understood me. Who supported me through . . . everything. He was a good man, and I miss him every day. But that's a story for another time. Today we're focusing on you."

"I'm a mess," said Amadeo.

"Who isn't? Now, let's take a look at that lip." Dorian reached up, gently probing the area around the bite wound. "Does it hurt?"

"Would you be impressed if I said no?" said Amadeo.

"I'd think you were very good at lying," said Dorian.

"It doesn't hurt," said Amadeo, wincing.

"Yeah, I can see," said Dorian. He stood back, a hand on his hip, looking Amadeo up and down. "How do you feel? Beyond the obvious, I mean."

"Like I've lost a fight with Sevens," he said. "But . . . okay. I guess the effects of the Nameless are temporary."

"Hmmm," murmured Dorian dubiously.

Amadeo thought again of Master Lox, of that last, sad look.

Of his crumbling face. He knew it was an image that would haunt him for the rest of his days. He wished that were a physical effect that could be mended with bacta and stitches and a kind word.

"It's going to take time," said Dorian, evidently sensing Amadeo's thoughts.

"I don't have time," said Amadeo. "None of us do. They have to be stopped, Dorian. The Nihil have to answer for what they've done." He realized he was gripping the edge of the gurney.

"I thought you might say that." Dorian cocked his head in resignation. "Personally, I think we'd be better off taking you straight back to Coruscant. You need rest. And support."

"What do you mean? Of course we're going back to Coruscant," said Amadeo. "That was the mission. I need to tell them all what happened here."

He started to get down off the gurney.

"Whoa, there," said Dorian, stepping forward and planting a hand against his chest. The medic pushed him back with surprising strength. "You're not going anywhere just yet."

"Tell me what you meant," said Amadeo.

Dorian glanced toward the door. "Ashton? I know you're skulking out there," he called.

Boots sounded on the boarding ramp, and a moment later Ashton Vol stood framed in the hatchway. She gave Amadeo a regretful look. "I'm so sorry, Amadeo." She lifted her chin. "It wasn't meant to go that way. We were meant to protect you. Both of you."

Amadeo gave a weak smile. "It wasn't your fault. You warned us as soon as you knew. There just wasn't time. . . ."

"I know. But all the same." He could hear the sorrow in her voice.

A thought occurred to him. "Hold on—weren't you supposed to be on the *Orchid*? We have to get that *thing* back to Coruscant," he said urgently. "Otherwise, all of this has been for nothing."

Ashton held up a hand. "Slight change of plan. The *Orchid's* gone. Don't worry. We shipped that creature out of here the moment it was in the containment tank. The RDC team went with it. They have express instructions to get it straight back to the facility on Coruscant. They'll see to it."

"Then why are you still here?" said Amadeo, confused.

"We've got something to show you," she replied. "Sevens?"

More thunderous footsteps, this time from the direction of the cockpit. L-77 stalked into the room.

"Have you been there all along?" said Amadeo.

"Yes. It seemed a little awkward to interrupt your conversation."

"Anyone else hiding around here that you want to let me know about?" said Amadeo.

"No," said Ashton. "This is it."

Amadeo's headache was returning. He rubbed the back of his neck. He needed a shower. He needed time to think.

What was going on? He figured they were worried about him, and he appreciated the gesture, but surely the best thing was to get back to Coruscant as quickly as possible. "Listen, I appreciate what you're doing here, but I really think—"

"Show him, Sevens," cut in Ashton.

"You might have let him finish his sentence first," retorted the droid.

Ashton rolled her eyes. "Just get on with it."

L-77 shook his head in an exaggerated downtrodden gesture. He reached up and pressed a panel on his chest, which popped open to reveal a small cavity containing a holoprojector. Hazy blue light flickered as an image began to resolve in the space between them.

"This is a recording we recovered from the Nihil databanks in the outpost, while you were unconscious. It was the last message received by their system," said Ashton. "Obviously we only have one half of the conversation, but I think you'll find it interesting."

The holo resolved into the form of a tall Ithorian dressed in dark flowing robes, with a mechanical cradle affixed to his hammer-shaped head bearing an array of tools and instruments. A small lens over one black eye caused it to appear large and ominous.

"Baron Boolan," muttered Amadeo, recognizing the figure from recordings taken from within Marchion Ro's camp. He'd been there in the background of Grand Master Pra-Tre Veter's execution, and the Jedi knew him to be one of the senior members of the Nihil operation, dubbed their Minister of Advancement by the disgraced senator Ghirra Starros.

When Boolan spoke, his voice had the dry emotionless rasp of a vocoder.

"Two of the Jedi—the older one and a youth—have left Coruscant on a ship bound for Wild Space."

A pause while the other person spoke. And then . . .

"Yes. My informant tells me they're bound for a planet named Tolis. It appears on no star charts or maps that I can find, but I have someone

tracking their progress. I'm sending you the coordinates. I want you to go after them."

Amadeo clenched his fists unconsciously by his sides.

They were talking about Reath and Cohmac.

"I think not," continued Boolan. *"Circumstances have changed. These particular Jedi seem . . . troubling. I think it better that they're eliminated now, before they become a further threat. They're investigating the origins of both the Levelers and the blight, and we wouldn't want them finding anything, would we?"*

Another pause.

"And this time, leave nothing to chance. I do not want to have to explain to Marchion Ro that you failed."

The recording stuttered and then stopped.

Amadeo's head was spinning. The Nihil were onto them. They'd sent the Nameless after Reath and Cohmac, led by one of their grotesque Jedi hunters.

Everything was at risk. If Reath and Cohmac failed on Tolis, then all that had happened on Angoth would be for nothing. Master Lox's death would be for nothing.

On top of that, his friend was facing insurmountable danger. Amadeo didn't know how he'd be able to cope if something happened to Reath, too.

Plus, there was an informant, somewhere on Coruscant—a traitor revealing their plans to the Nihil. Which meant he didn't know whom he could trust. The thought of it was like a knife through his heart.

He knew what he should do. He should go straight back to Coruscant. He was in no fit state for anything else. He was battered, both physically and psychologically, and he was grieving.

And yet any delay could be critical. He'd already wasted too much time unconscious on the gurney.

Now was the time for action, and damn the consequences. Reath and Cohmac needed him. And maybe, if he could get there in time, if Ashton and L-77 and Dorian were prepared to help, he could still make a difference.

He glanced at Dorian, a question in his eyes, but the other man shrugged. "Your choice, Amadeo. We're with you, whatever you decide."

He felt his resolve harden. "All of you? You're willing to face more of those things? To divert from your orders and go after them?"

"We're ready to do what's *right*," said Ashton.

"And remember," said L-77, "she *does* like punching things."

Amadeo looked at each of them in turn. How could it be that these people were prepared to put their lives on the line for others they barely knew? They weren't Jedi. They didn't need to do this. And yet here they were, offering to risk everything to help him protect his friends. "Then we make for Tolis," he said. "We stop those disgusting things before they can do any more harm. And we save our own."

Ashton Vol grinned. Then she turned to L-77. "See, Sevens? I *told* you he'd want to go to Tolis," she said.

L-77 was already heading for the cockpit. "All right," he said, his tone resigned. "You get to fly. But I swear, if you screw up another landing, it'll be the last time. . . ."

Amadeo turned to Dorian. "Can you get me a comlink? I

need to contact the Jedi Council immediately. If there's an informant in our midst, they need to be found, and fast."

"You need rest," said Dorian.

Amadeo shook his head. "Afterward. I'll rest afterward. I need to speak to them *now*."

"All right," said Dorian. "Give me a minute and I'll get you set up."

Amadeo rubbed the back of his throbbing head.

He could do this.

He couldn't bring Master Lox back, but he could still save his friends.

Or at the very least, he could try.

FORTY-TWO

The atmosphere inside the Tolemite structure was thick and dank, and the stench of the glistening green slime that covered almost every surface was enough to turn Reath's stomach. It felt as if he'd entered some otherworldly grotto. It seemed more organic than intelligently fashioned, so long had it rested beneath the waves, given over to the myriad life-forms that made their home in the deep.

After crossing the threshold, they'd found themselves in a large circular lobby or hall with a domed ceiling rising high above their heads. The floor was formed from slabs of metamorphic rock that had once been highly polished but was now encrusted with the limpet-like shells of small sea creatures and thick with a carpet of spongy moss and weeds.

A single passage led deeper into the structure, sloping down. There were strange echoes resonating from that open archway, reverberating around the large room so that every drop of water, every groan of the stones as they settled seemed deeply ominous.

"Some place," said Master Cohmac, and even his voice sounded wrong, as if the structure were throwing it back at him, rejecting their presence, urging them to leave.

Reath nodded but didn't answer.

Several alcoves had been cut into the upper walls of the chamber, each of them containing the fragmentary remains of a statue. Together, Reath and Cohmac paced around the outer edges, peering up at them. There was little to be learned. The figures were humanoid, but many had lost arms or heads, some being eroded down to mere stumps of legs or broken torsos. Others were covered with so much algae that their features weren't discernible. All Reath could gather was that the people were depicted in a heavily stylized fashion, with large deep-cut eyes, long tapering noses, and prominent chins. They wore simple robes, in many ways similar to those Reath himself wore, and they seemed to be adopting peaceful poses, hands open and welcoming.

"I was expecting some sort of writing or pictographic language," said Reath, his voice barely a whisper, "but there's nothing to tell us who these people were."

"And yet you can feel the weight of history here," said Master Cohmac. "The magnitude of this place. It's a rare privilege to walk in the footsteps of these ancient ones. To look upon their faces. Just think—we're the first people to see these statues in thousands of years."

Reath nodded. He could understand Cohmac's reverence, his fascination, but to him this place felt more like a warning, a dark echo of the past. These people were extinct, lost to eternity. The Nameless and the blight had come for them, and even though this small colony had survived for a time, they had never recovered. When adversity came, they were too few to survive it. He hoped that whatever lesson this place was intended to convey would make itself clear. Because without it, there was every chance the Jedi and the Republic would end up just like them.

"Let's move on," said Master Cohmac, heading for the door. "Best we stick together."

Reath wasn't about to argue with that. He followed the other man beneath the towering archway, his boots sliding on the slick stones.

As he dipped his head beneath a hanging strand of seaweed, he reached for his lightsaber hilt, thinking to use it to shed light, but Master Cohmac reached out, catching his wrist.

"No. Just give your eyes a moment to adjust."

Reath did as he said, peering steadily into the gloom.

It took only a moment before a pale pinkish light found his eyes, and he began to make sense of where they were standing.

They were on a stone walkway in the center of a broad tunnel. As he'd sensed from the chamber above, the walkway sloped down into thinning darkness, leading to what he assumed to be another large chamber ahead. To either side of the walkway were large trenches filled with water, in which schools of dark shapes swam in concentric circles, occasionally bubbling to the surface to mouth at the air.

The light source was coming from the walls themselves, which were completely covered in a strange phosphorescent sea moss that seemed to shimmer in shades of red and pink as they passed, as if reacting to the warmth of their bodies, or perhaps the presence of oxygen in the air. It was utterly beautiful. Reath wondered whether it was a purely natural phenomenon, or whether the Tolemites had somehow engineered it to ensure safe passage into the depths. Nothing would surprise him anymore, not after this.

Cautiously, they slipped and slid their way down the incline toward the chamber at its base.

Here, Reath estimated, they had to be close to the level of the water outside, although there were only traces of it on the ground, forming shallow puddles and pools. The walls were still wet and dripping, and the air was thick and difficult to breathe.

They walked beneath another towering archway, into another circular chamber, which this time appeared to be a dead end.

It was utterly empty.

Like the passageway outside, the walls were coated in large patches of glistening moss, and the floor was completely blanketed by a few centimeters of water that hadn't yet drained away.

Once again, there was no sign of any datacron store—no friezes, pictograms, or writing. Nothing. If this had once been a repository, whatever was stored here was long gone. The only decoration in the entire chamber was a motif of three interlocking circles carved into the stone wall opposite the entrance, themselves set into another, larger circle. Just like the puzzle box Azlin had been toying with back on Coruscant.

"It's empty," said Reath redundantly. "There's nothing here. Either we're in the wrong place, or we're much too late."

Master Cohmac was staring up at the circles on the wall. "No. Wait. Think about it. The Tolemites were a culture steeped in the Force. The answer *has* to lie in that."

"But I don't see how," said Reath. "I mean, there's no instructions. Nothing to *do*. It's just an empty room."

"Nothing is as simple as it first seems. You of all people know that, Reath." Master Cohmac raised his right hand, palm splayed. He was still looking up at the carved motif on the wall.

Had he seen something Reath hadn't?

Master Cohmac closed his eyes. Reath held his breath. Time seemed to stop. Only the constant *drip-drip* of water served to punctuate the moment.

Nothing happened.

Cohmac shuddered, drawing breath. His brow creased.

Still nothing.

Reath was about to tell him to give it up when one of the stone circles *turned*.

Reath's eyes widened in surprise. The stone disc was revolving in its socket, emitting a deep gritty grinding sound.

Was it some kind of lock? A puzzle?

As he watched, the stone circle slowly reversed, returning to its original position. Master Cohmac expelled a hoarse breath. He put his hands on his knees, looking at Reath. "It's not as simple as I thought. I was hoping . . . maybe one of those discs was a lock of some sort."

Reath studied the symbols from below. He frowned. The pattern reminded him of something.

"I think you're right," he said. "But there's something more to it. A code. Those discs . . . The way they're positioned. They almost look like—"

"Planets!" said Master Cohmac, cutting him off. "It's a star map."

Reath nodded. "Of this sector. Look. It's like the map you brought back from Thall."

"Yes!" Master Cohmac sounded genuinely excited by the concept. "If the discs represent planets and they turn in their sockets, perhaps they have to rotate in the same direction as the planetary bodies they're modeled on."

"Let's try!" said Reath. Seeing Cohmac's enthusiasm was like seeing a glimpse of his old master again, his old friend. He planted his feet, raising his hand. "On your count."

Master Cohmac straightened, thumping his chest with his fist. "I'm getting old."

"Don't be ridiculous," said Reath. "Compared to Master Yoda, you're practically a youngling."

Master Cohmac laughed. "Yeah, there is that." He turned, raising his right hand again. "Okay, I'm ready."

Reath focused on the three stone discs on the left. He felt their shape, their structure, the indelible impression they made on the universe, like all things. And he turned.

Beside him, Cohmac did the same, and as they watched, all six of the stone circles turned, two of them clockwise, the other four moving in the opposite direction.

Reath felt the ground beneath him lurch.

For a moment, he thought the whole structure was sinking again, bubbling back beneath the ocean, but as he watched, the walls themselves seemed to be shifting around him. Somewhere beneath him, a mechanism was grinding, stone wheels running noisily along carved grooves, and he realized it wasn't the walls that were turning but the floor.

He steadied himself, astonished, as the entire circular floor wound like a corkscrew, driven down until the chill water rose to his calves, to his knees, to his waist.

But at the same time, something was rising out of the floor. No—not something. Some *things*.

Three tall pedestals of what looked like dirty age-stained crystal rose out of the depths like the tips of a leviathan's fingers, reaching for air.

Reath shot Master Cohmac a look. The older man was laughing gleefully, as innocent as a child with a new toy, trying to keep his balance as the mechanism continued to grind.

For a horrible moment, Reath wondered if perhaps they'd activated some sort of trap and the water was going to keep on rising until they were both completely submerged, with little hope of reaching air before they drowned. But after a moment the mechanism shuddered to a stop, and the water—which had been lapping about his chest, threatening to steal his breath with its icy chill—began to recede.

He edged over to Master Cohmac, and the pair of them locked arms, clinging to each other as the water slowly drained away.

When it was done, they stood there, sodden and dripping,

staring in wonder at the three crystal pillars that stood around two meters tall, arranged in a triangle at the center of the room.

"Well, I wasn't expecting that," said Master Cohmac.

Reath wiped droplets of water from his face. His robes felt heavy around his shoulders. He had no idea what he was looking at.

"Some sort of data storage?" he ventured. He knew certain crystalline structures could be encoded with information like the memory banks of droids, but if so, these would contain so much data that it would be almost impossible to process.

"Perhaps," said Master Cohmac dubiously. "Let's take a closer look." He crossed to the nearest pillar. Reath approached another.

The surface was pitted and scarred and caked in filth from the silt and years of submersion. But leaning closer, Reath could just make out something inside the crystal, like a shadow at its heart. He'd seen ancient insects encased in nuggets of fossilized tree sap on Batuu and wondered if this was something similar.

He raised his arm and used his wet sleeve to wipe away a patch of grime on the crystal's surface.

And he nearly fell back with a start.

There, peering out at him from inside the crystal pillar, was a stark golden face.

"Master Cohmac . . ." he said, studying what he now realized was a beaten metal mask. "I think these may be *coffins*."

The other man was running his hands over the surface of one of the pillars. "Coffins made of pure kyber," he said, his voice soft.

Reath looked again at the coffin in front of him. It couldn't possibly be. . . .

But Master Cohmac was right. The entire coffin—essentially an upright chamber—was carved from a single sheet of one of the most valuable substances in the galaxy.

Cautiously, Reath wiped away more of the grime, trying to get a better look at the occupant within.

He couldn't discern the long-dead Tolemite's gender, but the face on the beaten mask resembled those of the statues they'd seen earlier, only smaller. The mask was adorned with a bright golden disc that enshrined the head like a halo, engraved with a fan of deeply etched lines like the rays of a star. Beneath, the body of the occupant was withered and mummified, barely more than a leathery-looking sheath of ebon skin attached to dry bones.

The figure was standing upright, supported by a brace of some dark metallic substance that was reminiscent of the ore they'd seen in the blight-ridden wastes on the other side of the landmass.

"It's incredible," said Reath. "To think they've been here so long. I wonder who they were. They must have been important to deserve such a burial."

Master Cohmac had moved to the last remaining coffin and was in the process of wiping it clean with a cloth he'd torn from the bottom of his robes. Reath stood back to regard them. Each chamber contained a similarly adorned figure—three in total.

"Not just important," said Master Cohmac. "Do you remember the story? The Three Ancients of the Tolemites who built their repository to protect future generations from suffering the same fate?"

Three Ancients . . .

"It's them," said Reath. "The story was real."

"Yes," said Master Cohmac. "It was real. But it seems as though it's become corrupted over time. What we thought was a repository of information is really just a tomb." He looked utterly crestfallen. "It's a remarkable discovery. But it's not going to tell us anything about how to defeat the Nameless or the blight."

Reath studied the nearest of the mummified figures. He felt a prickle of intuition. "No," he said. "You were right, earlier, when you reminded me they were a culture steeped in the Force. Think about it. That's why there's no written records, no wall paintings or friezes. They didn't need them. They were counting on the fact their descendants would be just like them. These three dead people *are* the repository." He walked closer until he was standing just before one of the Three Ancients. "I think we're in the right place after all. I think they want to tell us their story."

He raised his hand. . . .

"Reath, we can't be certain," started Master Cohmac. "Are you sure this is a—"

Reath brushed his fingers against the kyber coffin, opening his mind to the Force.

The bolt was like a shot of electricity, jolting him back, sending him falling, tumbling through infinite darkness, flailing and crying out. . . .

And then he was somewhere else.

He looked around, surprised, trying to make sense of what he was seeing.

He was standing in a meadow, but it was unlike any meadow he'd ever seen before. Vibrant colors abounded all around him.

Huge ferns flanked the edges of a vast expanse of wildflowers. Hazy lights flickered in the sky like glittering auroras.

And there were creatures here, too.

Saurian beasts with ridged spines and flourishes of vibrant feathers in blues and golds. Squat shaggy quadrupeds with dazzling antennae and furry torsos. Lizards with towering spindly bodies and massive taloned feet. Slender humpbacked bipeds with gray shells riding their shoulders. Creatures the size of banthas with eyes on stalks like the Gran's.

And large mammalian creatures with four legs and upright heads, their flesh tinged vibrant shades of purple and blue. They frolicked among the flowers and the long grass, chasing one another, playing with their young. They were peaceful, proud, and beautiful. Just watching them made Reath smile.

Close by, a spacecraft of unfamiliar design—a kind of shining bronze cylinder with sleek fins—rested on three legs, close to a stand of immense pale trees. And there were Tolemites here, too. Living ones. Thin and willowy, with ebon skin and elongated arms, jointed twice so they had two elbows on each limb. They were carrying electrified nets, creeping forward in a line, heading for the herd of creatures.

Reath wanted to cry out, to tell them no, but he had no voice here, no control over his own movements. He looked down at his hands and saw that he, too, was holding a net. It fizzed and crackled in his hands. He was creeping forward, too, and he understood that he meant to use the net to capture one of these beautiful living things.

Reath realized he was inhabiting a memory. An ancient memory. A projection through the Force.

Understanding slowly seeped into his mind, almost as if the memory was learning to adapt, to speak to him in ways he might be able to comprehend.

This wasn't the Tolemites' home. They'd found this paradise by chance while looking for new worlds to explore. And they meant to take a piece of it home, in the form of several of the creatures.

He watched, appalled, as the nets were thrown. . . .

And then he was elsewhere.

It was dark, and he was cowering in the woods outside the settlement, drenched to the bone from the terrible storm. He was shivering, and not just from the cold.

All around him, creatures were howling. And somewhere among them, lurking in the trees, something was hunting him.

Reath could feel its presence clouding his mind, his judgment. Worse, he could feel how it closed him off from the Force, which he knew simply as the Peace. He felt isolated, alone, lost.

He could sense it drawing closer.

He pulled himself up, using the low branches for leverage. He'd twisted his ankle running. He considered trying to climb the tree but knew it wouldn't save him.

All he wanted was his matriarch. She would know what to do. If he could just make it home.

He turned and ran, stumbling blindly through the bushes, which shredded his black flesh, raising bleeding welts along the lengths of his arms, his legs, snagging his clothes, scratching his chest, his face.

He could hear the creature crashing after him, screeching as it came. It was so hungry.

So, so hungry.

But still he ran, until his lungs burned and darkness limned his vision. His entire body hurt as he stumbled into the settlement.

Not once had he looked behind him, but he knew it hadn't given up. They never gave up.

Never.

He staggered across the square, slammed his shoulder into the door to his family home, barged in, out of breath but still calling for his matriarch in a strange clicking guttural language he couldn't decipher but nevertheless understood.

Only to see nothing was left of his people but pale ashen husks heaped on the floor. All twelve of them. *Gone.*

And in their midst, a hulking wild tentacled beast that stood on four legs and had translucent skin. It was emaciated and malformed, sickly and driven to desperation by its insatiable hunger.

Reath knew this was one of the same creatures he'd seen the Tolemites rip so wantonly from their home.

It was a Nameless. A Force Eater. A *Shrii Ka Rai.* But it was twisted, corrupted, transformed by its hunger into something far worse. It had once been a peaceful creature, back in the grassy fields of its home, but now it was a predator, and nothing could stand in its way.

And the Tolemites had willingly brought the things to their home.

Reath wanted to run, to get as far away from the terrible creature as he could. But his legs wouldn't move. He screamed, fighting against the horror, the injustice, but his host simply fell to his knees, weeping, as the creature set upon him and all became dust.

Reath was standing on a mountainside in the dawn light. He peered out at the view, shading his eyes with a cupped hand.

It was peaceful here, but somber.

He stood with a small group of his people, a ragtag band of survivors who had fled both the savagery of the transmuted creatures and the spreading tide of destruction that was slowly consuming the planet.

He could see it now, out on the horizon: a plague upon their world.

A *blight*.

It was a rolling tide, a wave of utter destruction, consuming everything and everyone in its path, turning their once beautiful home to dust, just like the creatures had turned their people to husks.

It was a judgment, a curse.

His people had upset the balance of the Force, and this was the consequence: a wave of horror, spreading out through the galaxy.

Cause and effect.

He could see it so clearly.

One event leading to another.

The reason for everything that was happening.

A dying culture on a dying planet.

Sorrow was all that was left—sorrow and the need to make amends.

His people would not survive this. And neither would the

creatures. They were too far removed from their home. They'd fed on the only thing they could—on the people—and now even they were a scarce resource.

The Tolemites had died because they'd brought the creatures where they didn't belong, and now the creatures were going to die, too.

But perhaps the few people who were left could find a way to stop the spreading wave from destroying other worlds, to curtail its inexorable spread.

Perhaps.

The last enclave of the Tolemites was a sight to behold: a gathering of clans and survivors in the shell of a once great city, not so much a haven from the oncoming tide of death as a place to congregate so they might share in their fate—a mass tomb fashioned from the remnants of their old lives.

Tears streamed down Reath's cheeks, hot and wet, as he stood on the stone balcony, looking down on the last few hundred of his people. It had come to this. Some had already fled on whatever ships they could find, and he hoped they would pepper the stars, spreading word of what had happened here. They were too few to flourish, to make new lives, to raise new families on other worlds. This was the last gasp of his species, the final inhalation before their inevitable demise.

And yet, even here, at the end, there was a glimmer of hope.

He turned, walking back into the bustling workshop where six artisans labored over three wooden workbenches. They were crafting the solace of his dying people, the last hope that they could save others from the same fate that had befallen them.

Three rods, one to be wielded by each of the Three Ancients of the Tolemite people. Each would be inlaid with a precious gem, a stone that, they had learned, was imbued with the power to steer and guide the creatures—a tool to be used to shepherd them home.

They would return the creatures to the world from which they had been taken.

They could not make recompense for what they had done, but they could do this.

And they could hope that it would be enough.

Reath was back where he'd started: that bright beautiful paradise, so colorful and steeped in lush flora. The Three Ancients had used their rods to guide the creatures here, beckoning them and steering them aboard a single ship, taking them home from Tolis to this amazing world from which they originated.

The Tolemites had paid the price for their folly, with their lives but also with their legacy. Once they'd been a proud people who had looked only to a bright endless future of progress and happiness and a life among the stars. But greed and hubris had led them to this, and now their legacy would be nothing but ruination and blame. The dust of husked worlds would drift among the stars for eternity.

The Three Ancients knew they had to find a way to enshrine their story for the future, to send a warning through the millennia to come, an echo that would spread through generations, across different worlds and beings.

They had found an unblemished island amid the oceans of Tolis.

Here they would build a beacon, a repository.

A place from which to tell their story.

Here they would finally rest, safe in the knowledge that they had done all they could.

Here they would make amends.

"—good idea?"

Reath turned to look at Master Cohmac. His eyes were unfocused. He was back inside the room with the coffins, and it was spinning. Had the mechanism started up again? How long had he been . . . *elsewhere*?

"I understand now," he said, but his words sounded distant, slurred. He took a step, tottered unsteadily, and then keeled over, falling again, tumbling. Only this time he knew it was no dream.

The last thing he felt before darkness swept in was Master Cohmac's firm embrace as his old friend and master rushed forward to lower him gently to the ground.

FORTY-THREE

Sicarus cranked a lever and his shuttle dropped out of hyperspace with a sudden punch.

The black night of space filled the viewport.

"Born again," he said, sucking his teeth. His eye winked, but as usual, the eyelid didn't move. He rolled his neck, flexing his shoulder muscles. They felt tight, tense. Expectant. Ready for everything that was to come.

He scanned the horizon.

Black and black and black and black.

Reality closed in around him. The darkness of the galaxy and its oppressive plague of worlds and people and creatures. Like the massive blue planet that was swimming up beneath his ship.

"Not like the safe space," he said. "No, no. Not like that at all." He hugged himself, squeezing tight.

He always found the passage through hyperspace a soothing experience. As if by transitioning from realspace into that glowing, shimmering blue-hued dimension beyond reality—this was how he imagined it—he had somehow ascended, becoming more than just a dull sack of flesh and bones and blood. Becoming something greater.

It was like the rush he felt whenever Father pressed the plunger on the syringe, flooding his veins with the promise of greatness. Of unbridled *power*.

"Born thrice, is Sicarus. Made anew." He giggled. He was ready to make Father proud.

His blood was singing. Fizzing and popping in his veins.

He was hungry, and his prey was waiting for him on the planet below.

"Grind them to ashes," he murmured to himself. "Show them what it means to be weak and scared."

Yes, yes, yes.

He knew how that felt. And it was *awful*.

Now it was time to share that pain. To revel in his power.

To prove to everyone that he was as special as Father said he was.

Sicarus dipped the controls and started the descent toward Tolis.

Almost immediately an alarm trilled, sharp and obscene. Sicarus winced and punched a button on the control terminal.

The blaring ceased, but the proximity display continued to flash bright red.

Another ship.

He backed off the controls, allowing the ship to drift for a moment while he examined the readings.

It wasn't a Jedi ship. It was a merchant vessel. A guild ship. *Clever Jedi.*

They obviously thought they were less conspicuous traveling under the guise of guild representatives. They'd probably left a droid pilot aboard to keep the ship in orbit while they carried out their sneaky business down below.

It might have worked, too, if it hadn't been for Father's spies, wheedling out all the Republic's plans.

Sicarus knew the other ship had probably already registered his arrival, but all the same, he powered down all but the basic life-support systems and allowed the ship to drift closer to the planet on its existing trajectory.

Then, as the drifting shuttle skimmed the outer skin of the planet's atmosphere, he fired the engines for a few seconds, propelling it down at speed, punching through the resistance until the nose of the ship glowed bright red and the entire vessel trembled with the turbulence.

He allowed the ship to drop deep beneath the cloud cover, then reined in the controls, dragging the nose of the ship back up until it was on a level plane, churning a foaming path across the surface of the planet's ocean as he traced a line for the single remaining landmass.

All the while, he giggled nervously, his hands jittery on the ship's controls.

Almost there, Sicarus. Almost time.

He hoped they didn't make it *too* easy for him.

The ship approached land, and he peered down at the sea of white ash that covered the undulating landscape as far as he could see. The blight had come to Tolis, eroding, consuming, husking.

Sicarus liked the blight. He willed it on. He hoped that Father and his friends would allow it to swallow half the galaxy before they stopped it.

"Make the place a little quieter for Sicarus," he said.

But he knew there had to be more here than just the blight. The Jedi were down there, somewhere, lurking.

He kept his course, sweeping up the length of the coast.

Soon enough, the ashen wastes gave way to dark bedrock and forest, and that turned to overgrown scrub and the vague traceries of ancient ruins.

What was it about these Jedi that they loved poking around in the detritus of the long dead? First Thall, now here. Sicarus would never understand them.

He spotted an appropriate place to land and brought the ship around, circling for a moment before slowly easing it down in a clearing on the edge of what he took to be an ancient city. Now it was just the stumps of walls that had toppled years ago.

One day—soon he hoped—all the Jedi would suffer the same fate.

Not that he was sure why, exactly, he hated the Jedi so much. He'd have to ask Father about that when he returned home. Probably something to do with how smug they were, and how they wouldn't stop interfering in Father's plans.

Yes, that was it. He was sure of it.

"Interfering Jedi," he spat, wiping spittle from his chin.

He flicked a series of switches, activating the automated ship defenses, arming the laser cannons that were mounted on a swivel housing on the roof of the ship. The system was operated by the processor of an old droid Boolan had repurposed and enslaved to the targeting controls. Sicarus often wondered if the droid could still think, up there in its permanent prison. By now, it was probably insane. The notion appealed to him. It was another measure of his power. All he had to do was flick a switch, and the droid—or what was left of it—had its orders: blast any other ship out of the sky if it came within range.

That would deal with the merchant ship if the remaining crew got any ideas about attempting a rescue.

Sicarus eased himself out of the pilot's seat and walked back into the shuttle's small hold. First he collected his electrostaff from where he'd left it propped in an alcove. He hefted the weapon, enjoying its balance in his hands.

Old friend.

He'd been trained to use the electrostaff when he'd been with the Brotherhood. As a youth, he'd practiced for hours every day, enacting martial forms, improving his control, learning how to defend himself. Discovering how to use the Force to assist his efforts.

Now the thought of those days made him twitch until his left ear pressed against his shoulder and he had to bite his own tongue to regain his focus. Blood filled his mouth, bitter and metallic, but the release felt good.

No more bad memories. No more.

Time to look to the future.

The weapon would be useful, though. In the event that the Jedi proved more wily than usual, he could use it to defend against their lightsabers. And if the creatures decided to misbehave . . . Well, he could help them understand their place in the order of things.

He slung the staff into the harness on his back, settling it between his shoulders. Then he walked to the very rear of the ship, where the Jedi woman was still curled up inside her cage, wrapped in a ball as if she was trying to blot out everything around her. She was still alive, though. He could see she was trembling. The proximity of the creatures on the ship had kept her in a constant state of confusion and fear. She hadn't even tried to escape.

Sicarus smiled. He had no concerns about leaving her here while he and his Nameless went about their hunt. He'd taken her lightsaber from her. There was no way she was getting out.

"No escape," he whispered, relishing the sound of the words on his lips. "No escape."

He left her and returned to the main hatch, where he lowered the ramp, allowing the cool salty air of Tolis to rush into the ship. He drew it deep into his lungs, appreciative after the stale recycled air of his journey.

It was going to be a good day.

He was certain of it.

Close by, the three Levelers hissed and spat in their own cages, clamoring to get out. They could already sense the other Jedi, and they were famished.

Good. Good.

That was how it should be.

He would set them free, let them hunt their quarry amid the ruins. Let them roam.

They'd each been fitted with Father's ingenious gadgetry that probed the gray matter of their brains, controlling some of their more wayward instincts, forcing them to obey their master.

And today Sicarus was their master. He was the leader of their pack, and his own blood sang in time with the rhythm of their hearts.

He unlatched their crates, one at a time, standing back to allow them room.

The creatures burst forth, scrabbling for purchase on the metal floor plates.

Sicarus watched them with interest. The older one's mutation appeared to have developed even further since their time on Thall. Its flesh was almost translucent, revealing the pulsing heart, the red lungs, the map of veins and arteries threading its entire body. It looked almost withered, emaciated, its shoulders hunched. Saliva dribbled down the length of its mop of proboscises. Like the others, it wore the crown of its captivity, but its eyes were black and fierce, and Sicarus could feel the utter hatred radiating from it.

The three creatures bolted from the hatchway, pounding down the ramp toward the ruins. He hurried after them to watch.

But then something unexpected happened. The sickly translucent Nameless took a running leap at one of its kin. It crashed into the side of the blue-white one with a snarl, bowling it over into the dirt.

The two creatures rolled and snarled at each other, tearing with their claws, scrabbling in the dirt.

What was this? Some sort of fight for dominance? For control of the pack?

The third one—the one with the grafted human arms—backed away from the other two, keeping its muzzle close to the ground, emitting a low snarl.

The blue-white one roared and rose up on its rear legs, trying to push the translucent one away, but its opponent was simply too ferocious, too desperate, and it battered the blue-white one down.

Then something surprising happened.

The translucent one began to feed. On its kin.

One of them howled. It was a mournful, sorrowful lament. A sound that stirred even Sicarus's hardened soul. The wretched thing was actually crying.

He watched with mounting awe as the translucent one continued to feed.

Cannibalism.

This strange, mutated, ferocious creature was draining the living Force from its own kind.

Would the wonder of these beasts never stop?

He was tempted to watch it until the end, to allow the

creature its meal, just to see what would happen next, what the husk of a Force Eater would look like.

But he needed them alive for now. To kill the Jedi.

Regretfully, Sicarus thumbed the button on the mechanical control stick in his pocket, and the creature fell back, twitching, as an electrical charge was fired deep into its brain via Father's implant. It spasmed as it rolled on the ground, shuddering, but then, as Sicarus watched, it snarled, forcing itself back onto its feet.

Oh, aren't you determined. Aren't you beautiful.

He pressed the button again, then again, and the creature howled, screeching in pain, but held its ground, pawing at the dirt even as its muscles trembled. It turned to glower at him knowingly.

"Oh, yes," he said, his eyes wide in delight. "You're a special one."

Father would want to know about this.

He held the control stick in the air, releasing the button.

Two of the creatures turned and ran, darting off into the ruins, already catching the scent of their prey, one of them trailing behind, slower and sickly after its brief ordeal.

The third, the translucent one, raised its head, sniffed, and then shot Sicarus one final menacing look before following the others.

He watched them go with pride.

That's it, my pretty things, my blood kin.

Roam free and search them out.

Find the Jedi . . . and feast.

FORTY-FOUR

Amadeo knew he was still in shock. The truth of what had happened on Angoth hadn't hit him yet. He wondered if it ever would. How could he even begin to process such a thing?

The fact that Master Lox was gone.

One with the Force.

Dead.

Amadeo would never see him again.

On an intellectual level, he understood all this. And yet . . . everything seemed so *normal*. Just like Dorian had said. The stars kept on burning, Amadeo kept on drawing breath, and the *Invictus* kept on sailing through the arcane warrens of hyperspace, bound for Tolis.

And yet deep down inside, a part of him was still in that room, facing those creatures, screaming and crying and unable to move.

The thought made his heart thrum faster.

He realized he was wringing his hands in his lap.

Perhaps if he'd been stronger, things might have been different. He'd been so overcome by the presence of the Nameless that he'd been unable to think, let alone act.

But what if he'd been able to push through it, like Master Lox had? What if he'd been able to stand at his master's side as he faced the beast?

Would it have been enough to save Master Lox? Would he be sitting here now, alongside his Padawan, gently chiding Amadeo for overthinking everything?

It was certainly possible.

And the pain that caused was close to unbearable. Yet Amadeo couldn't stop himself from prodding it, because the alternative was to not feel anything at all, and that somehow seemed like an even worse betrayal.

He tried to focus on his Jedi training. He knew that death was not the end—that Master Lox's time here had ended but his spirit would live on in the cosmic Force, intertwined with all that had gone before and all that would come after. In time, he hoped to find peace in that. But right now everything was too raw.

He just wished he could talk to Master Lox about it. He'd always looked to his master for guidance.

He caught his breath, tried to focus on his breathing.

He closed his eyes, resting his head against the seat webbing.

He heard footsteps and then the weight of someone sitting down on the bench beside him.

Dorian.

He opened his eyes but didn't look, didn't say anything. He didn't want to look at the other man and see pity in his eyes.

"Hi," said Dorian simply.

"Hi," said Amadeo.

"You look like you could use some company."

Amadeo swallowed. "I'm not sure I'd be very good company at the moment, Dorian."

The medic nudged him with an elbow. "Exactly why you need to talk."

"What is there to say?" said Amadeo. "Master Lox is dead, and I made the decision to go chasing halfway across the galaxy to put us all in terrible danger again, in the vain hope that we're going to be able to get to Tolis in time to make a difference."

Dorian exhaled loudly. "I see."

Amadeo turned his head a fraction. "Told you I wasn't much fun to be around."

Dorian snorted. "Yeah, well. We all have our moments." He turned in his seat so he was facing Amadeo. "It's okay to be scared, you know. I know you Jedi are all about compartmentalizing everything, pretending you don't really feel emotions—"

"That's not strictly true," interrupted Amadeo, but Dorian waved him quiet.

"I know. I'm generalizing. But the point stands. You're sitting here beating yourself up because you couldn't help Master Lox, aren't you?"

Amadeo studied Dorian's face. He found only kindly eyes and concern looking back. "I suppose I am. It's just . . ." He faltered, trying to find the right words. "I keep on thinking if I'd just been stronger, perhaps I could have pushed through the fear and helped him."

"Have you considered that's not what he would have wanted?" asked Dorian.

"What do you mean?" said Amadeo.

"I mean, he was trying to protect you. Maybe he didn't want you risking yourself for his sake. If you'd tried, there was every chance you'd have ended up the same way." Dorian smiled. "He cared about you, Amadeo. That was plain for anyone to see. He'd be happy that you made it."

"But—"

"Stop now," said Dorian. "You aren't to blame. The effect those creatures have on you Jedi . . . it's not something you can fight. I mean, you were in pretty bad shape when I found you. Those things are practically *designed* to take you out. The fact you survived at all is a miracle."

"And now we're going to Tolis to face even more of them," said Amadeo.

"And at the risk of repeating myself, it's okay to be scared. To be *terrified*," said Dorian. "But stop for a moment to think about what you're doing. You're going through with it anyway, to help your friends. To save the mission. You're scared, but you're not letting it stop you from doing the right thing."

Amadeo nodded.

"It's times like these that we find out who we really are," said

Dorian. "When we have to face our fear and carry on regardless. When it seems like the whole world is against us and we still pick ourselves up and carry on."

"So, you've had to face fear in your life?" said Amadeo.

Dorian laughed. "Every. Single. Day. You see, I didn't start out like this." He gestured vaguely at his own face. "I had to figure out who I was, and then I had to make it happen."

"But you're so confident," said Amadeo.

"It might look that way," said Dorian. "But it took me a long time to find my way. You see, I wasn't . . ." He hesitated for a moment. "I wasn't born this way. I was somebody else."

"What do you mean?" said Amadeo.

Dorian gave a wistful smile. "My body didn't match the person I was inside. And for a long time, I didn't know what that meant, or what to do. I just felt wrong, and scared. It took me years to understand that I could put it right and be the person I needed to be. That I could stop hiding and show the world how I felt."

"*Oh*, okay," said Amadeo as realization dawned. Dorian hadn't always presented as a man. And now he was opening up to Amadeo, explaining what he'd been through, all to help Amadeo better understand his own emotions. It was a privilege, and one that Amadeo would not take lightly.

"I told you about my father," said Dorian. "How he was always on my side. How he helped me, and understood, and supported me. But at first, I had no idea how to explain it all to him. I was still so confused myself that I didn't know how to share how I really felt. What if he didn't understand?"

"How did you decide what to do?" Amadeo asked.

"I decided that I had to be true to myself. I had to face my fear and push through it. I *had* to tell him, because it was the only fair thing to do, for *me*. So when I was ready, I did."

"And everything was okay?" asked Amadeo gently.

"Well, it was bumpy at first, but we found our way."

"You're very brave," said Amadeo. "Thank you for sharing that with me."

Dorian nodded. "The point is, we're *all* scared, Amadeo. We all have huge challenges to face. And things don't always work out as we want them to. But it's how we face those fears that counts. You nearly died back there. You lost someone you cared for. That's crushing. *Devastating.* And you *still* made the decision to go after Reath and Cohmac, to make a stand against the creatures that did that to you. I'd be worried if you *weren't* scared. But what you can't do is feel guilty. You can't blame yourself for the behavior of others. All you can do is be true to yourself. And for what it's worth, I think you're doing okay."

Amadeo fought back brimming tears. He turned and pulled Dorian into a tight hug. "Thank you," he said. The words weren't enough. But they would have to suffice.

Dorian squeezed him back, and all Amadeo wanted to do was cling to that anchor, that still point in the storm.

But then Dorian was gently prizing him loose. "Okay. Time to get ready. Sevens says we're approaching Tolis. Things are about to get even more complicated."

Amadeo nodded.

"You can do this, Amadeo. But no heroics, okay. I want you

back in one piece. Otherwise, all that effort patching you up was for nothing." Dorian gave another wonky smile and then got to his feet. "I'm going to pack a field kit, just in case."

Amadeo watched Dorian cross to the medical station, where he busied himself packing a small shoulder bag with supplies.

Amadeo unhitched his lightsaber from its holster. Then, reconsidering, he placed it carefully on the bench and crossed to the small bundle of robes that were heaped on the opposite bench and withdrew Master Lox's recovered lightsaber instead.

He weighed it in his palm for a moment, nodded, and slipped it into his holster.

Now he was ready.

FORTY-FIVE

"**D**o you think they're going to find what they're looking for down there?" said Affie, easing herself back in her copilot's chair.

They'd finished collecting mineral samples from the surface—a process that had been easier than Affie had imagined, given that they were able to blast away at the rock face with impunity until they exposed a vein. Leox had seemed to enjoy it more than was reasonably decent, and she'd found herself laughing at his hooting joy as the large boulders had detonated under his brisk assault with the blasters.

Geode had watched it all in sullen silence and had subsequently chosen to stay behind on the *Vessel* while Affie and Leox collected the hunks of exposed ore from the surface. Affie figured he was sulking a little at just how much fun the two of them had had blowing up rocks.

Regardless, it was done now, and they'd loaded a heap of the samples into the hold to take back to Coruscant. She hoped they'd prove useful in the Jedi's efforts to stave off the blight. Reath and Cohmac had certainly seemed excited by the prospect, and she could already imagine Reath hunkering down over a protonscope the moment they got back, losing himself in his studies as he searched for another breakthrough. The thought brought a smile to her lips.

Now the *Vessel* had retreated into the upper atmosphere of Tolis, maintaining a secure orbital position while they awaited word from the two Jedi below.

Beside her, Leox shrugged. "Who knows. It didn't look like there was much left down there to find. But if anyone can work it all out, it's those two. Smartest people I know."

Affie thumped his arm. "Hey!"

Leox laughed. "Thought you'd say that," he said, teasing her. "But you know what I mean. Reath and Cohmac know about all that ancient stuff."

"Yeah, keep on digging," said Affie, chuckling. "And yeah, I do know what you mean. It's just—seeing this place, what the blight has done to it—it puts it all into perspective, doesn't it?"

"How do you mean?"

"I mean, all this fighting with the Nihil, people murdering each other . . . what's it all for, really? When the galaxy has problems like *this*?" Affie shrugged. "I know that's simplistic. Naive, too. But really, haven't we all got bigger things to worry about than territorial disputes and trying to kill each other?"

"I really wish that people worked the way you want them to, Affie," said Leox. "It would make the galaxy a better place. But there's always someone who isn't happy with their lot. Who wants *more*. Who gets their kicks out of making other people feel small and unwelcome. That's what I see when I look at Marchion Ro. A bully who just happens to punch that little bit harder than everyone else."

Affie nodded. "A boy who didn't get enough love," she said, "and now craves attention at any cost. Who has to feel he's the center of the galaxy. It's an old story."

"And it always ends the same way," said Leox.

"Which is?" prompted Affie.

"With tears," said Leox.

As if on cue, a light began to flash on the control panel, accompanied by a shrill alarm.

"Sounds like our two Jedi boys are ready for their extraction," said Leox. He reached over to silence the trilling alert, but Affie had already seen the readout on her screen and caught his wrist.

"No! Hold on! That's not Reath and Cohmac," she said.

Leox withdrew his hand, his brow creased in a frown. "It's not?"

Affie shook her head. "No. Think about it. They have their own comlinks. They'll call with a location when they're ready for a pickup. This is from someone else." She leaned over the control console, scanning the data readout for more information. "It's one of Geode's recall devices. It's been triggered."

Leox met her eye. "You left one of those with Eve and Zaph on Oisin, didn't you?"

Affie was still studying the screen. "Although they should have called, too. But it has to be them. No one else has an active device. It looks as though they've triggered the homing signal. I hope they're not in trouble."

"There's nothing we can do," said Leox. "We can swing by to collect them once we've dropped Reath and Cohmac back on Coruscant. Or we can notify the Byne Guild, see if any other ships are closer and willing to run the pickup for us?"

"Maybe . . ." said Affie, distracted. She was trying to figure out the origin of the homing signal. She tapped some keys, telling the flight computer to triangulate their position.

"What is it?" asked Leox. "What's wrong?"

"I've just got a feeling . . ." said Affie, her voice trailing off. She could see that the signal identifier was definitely the one she'd given to Eve Byre back on Oisin, but it didn't make sense.

"You're worrying me now, Little Bit," said Leox.

"It's Eve's beacon, all right," said Affie. "But it doesn't add up. It's saying she's not on Oisin anymore."

Leox shrugged. "Maybe they hitched a ride part of the way home?" he said. "Or maybe they had Jedi business elsewhere. Who knows?"

"No, you don't understand," said Affie. "The signal—it's coming from Tolis."

Leox sat forward in his chair. He got up, leaning on the console as he studied the screen. "Something must be wrong with Geode's coding," he said. "Or there's some interference giving us a false reading. It says she's down on the beach, right where we dropped the others."

"But how?" said Affie.

"Like I said, it must be a mistake," said Leox.

Affie shook her head. "I'm not so sure." She set the scanners to do a sweep of the area.

Moments later, she got a ping.

Her heart almost skipped a beat.

"There's another ship down there, Leox!"

Leox was shaking his head. "There can't be. We would have seen it."

But the results on the scanner were undeniable.

And what was more, the site of the ship precisely matched the location of the homing beacon.

"The signal is coming from inside the ship," said Affie.

"I don't like this," said Leox. "Not one bit. What if it's some sort of trap?"

Affie rocked back in her seat again. "But what if it's not? What if it really is Eve and Zaph, and they need our help? We can't ignore it, Leox."

"Look, before we do anything drastic, try raising them on the comms," said Leox. But Affie could already tell he was preparing himself for something.

"What if they can't reply?" said Affie. "That could be why they triggered the homing beacon in the first place."

"It can't hurt to try," countered Leox. He reached for the comlink. "Hello? Master Eve Byre? Padawan Zaph Mora? This is Leox Gyasi of the Byne Guild ship the *Vessel*. Do you read me?"

Silence.

The moment stretched.

And then the static broke, and for a moment there was just the sound of a single plaintive animal moan.

"Eve? Eve, is that you?" said Affie, urgency welling inside her. "Can you hear me? It's Affie."

The only reply was harsh ragged breathing before the line went dead and the pipping of the homing signal started up again.

Affie stared at Leox. "Okay, we're going down there. Now."

Leox nodded. "Agreed."

He grabbed the controls. The *Vessel* swung around slowly and then juddered violently, the engines squealing.

Alarms blared. Red warning symbols flashed on all the read-out screens.

"What the hell!" bellowed Affie, raising her voice over the screeching alarms.

Leox was shaking his head, punching buttons and flicking switches. He cursed loudly. "Something's wrong with the fuel regulator!"

"What? Now?" Affie could hardly believe their luck. What was going on?

"It looks like Geode was right. There's a problem somewhere in the system," said Leox. He looked hassled, frantically trying to make sense of the data he was seeing.

"Great," said Affie. "Perfect timing." All around her, readouts were turning red. "Can we still fly?"

"I don't know," said Leox. "Geode?"

If Geode was even considering telling them both "I told you

TEARS OF THE NAMELESS

so," he was showing remarkable restraint. Instead, he remained in the rear compartment making hurried adjustments to the flight systems. Affie watched as several dials retreated slowly back out of the red.

"He's bringing her under control," said Leox. "Just."

"Well done, Geode!" called Affie.

"We're not out of trouble yet," said Leox. "Once we're stable, we're going to have to run a full diagnostic. Pull the systems apart until we've identified the fault. It's going to take some time."

"We haven't got time!" said Affie, frustration bubbling. "You heard Eve! Something's wrong."

"I don't know *what* I heard," said Leox. "But we need to fix the ship, Little Bit."

"Just get us down there!" said Affie. "We can fix her on the ground. Once we know Eve and Zaph are okay."

Leox gave a heavy sigh. He studied his screen. "I can do it, but our maneuverability is compromised. If something comes for us . . ."

"We'll have to risk it," said Affie. "So far as we know, there are no Nihil or any other hostiles down there."

"So far as we knew," countered Leox, "there were no other Jedi, either."

"I know, Leox. I know it's a risk. But there are people down there who need us. All we have to do is get close. Then we can land and we'll have all the time we need to make the repairs. But you know as well as I do that we'll never be able to live with ourselves if we don't act and something happens."

Leox looked pained. He slid back into his seat and took hold of the controls. "Why do you *always* have to be right, Little Bit?"

"It's a burden I'm learning to live with," said Affie, grinning. She dropped back into her own chair. "Brace yourself, Geode!" she called. "We're going in!"

Geode's silence told her everything she needed to know.

FORTY-SIX

"**S**o the key to all of this lies in the Echo Stones," said Cohmac. He was pacing the round chamber as he processed everything Reath had told him, about the visions, the rods, and the paradise world that seemed to be at the center of everything. "Barnabas Vim was on the right track, all those years ago. He was the first of us to identify the Echo Stones. A Jedi explorer who became fascinated with the stones' origins, almost two centuries ago."

Reath sat against the wall, his knees drawn up before him, his hands resting in his lap. He was feeling more like himself with every passing moment. A part of him wanted to stay on Tolis and keep exploring the fascinating ruins, but he knew they needed to get back to the *Vessel* so they could transmit a message to the Jedi Council to let them know what they'd discovered. But he was still trying to make sense of it himself, and talking it through with Master Cohmac was helping.

Reath watched as Cohmac continued to pace the edges of the room, hands folded behind his back, his brow furrowed in thought. He was wearing a familiar pensive expression. It was just like old times.

"The stones seemed to have an effect on the *Shrii Ka Rai*," said Master Cohmac, looking at Reath, "and that's what the Tolemites placed into those rods. That's right, yes?"

"Yes," said Reath. "In the vision, it seemed to provide the Tolemites with a measure of control. The Nameless had stopped trying to husk them, for a start."

"Well, that's a bonus," said Master Cohmac. "So, logically, if we could find more of the stones . . . we'd have a way to control the creatures. That must be what Marchion Ro is using." He rubbed the back of his neck thoughtfully. "That rod we saw him use in the holorecordings—do you think it's one of the originals you saw in your vision?"

Reath considered this for a moment. "It has to be. How else would he have known what to do? I don't believe for a minute that the Nihil discovered a bunch of Echo Stones and decided to fashion them into rods. There's no evidence they've been here, to Tolis, and learned what we have from the Three Ancients. It would be too much of a coincidence that they somehow happened upon the exact same idea. He must have found it somewhere. Maybe on the same planet where he found the Nameless."

Master Cohmac was nodding. "Yes. You're right. Which

makes me wonder—what happened to the other two rods?" He stopped pacing for a moment. "It's clear what we need to do. We need to find one of them."

"But where do we even start? You'd think they would have been entombed with the Ancients if they'd intended for them to be found, and I've already checked. There's nothing in those kyber coffins."

"They probably didn't want to give anyone else the tools they'd need to remove the creatures from their home planet again," said Master Cohmac. "It seems they were pretty set on making sure their warning was heard and understood. The rods would be too much of a temptation for anyone unscrupulous or hungry for power."

"Right," said Reath. "So what would they have done with them? Scatter them among the stars? Bury them somewhere no one would ever think to look? They obviously didn't destroy them. Maybe they were worried they might be needed again."

"Perhaps there's more in the Archives. Barnabas Vim spent decades looking into the stones. And your friend Azlin might know more, too," said Cohmac.

Reath bristled at the casual accusation in that statement. "It's like searching for a single droplet in the Eiram ocean. We have no idea how Marchion Ro laid his hands on one, where it came from, or what happened to the others. They're lost to time. It's been thousands of years."

"Remember," said Master Cohmac. "No one had been *here* for thousands of years, either, until we found it. We did that. You and me. We're so close, Reath. We might not yet have the means to bring this nightmare to an end, but at least now we know *what* we have to do."

"So close, and yet still so far," said Reath. He was practically fizzing with the magnitude of their discoveries, the importance of what they'd found, the lessons they'd learned about a civilization that had existed over ten millennia in the past. But he was trying to be realistic, too. "As exciting as all of this new knowledge is, think about what you're saying. We don't even know if we're right. All we have are questions." He ticked them off on his fingers. "Will taking the Nameless back to their home planet stop the spread of the blight? Where in the whole of the big, wide galaxy do we find that world? Where are the rods or the Echo Stones that might help us, and where did *they* originate?" Reath sighed. "There's still so much to do. So much to figure out."

Master Cohmac had finally ceased his pacing to stand before Reath. He was utterly disheveled, his robes still soaked through, his hair mussed. But his eyes were wild with the same excitement Reath was feeling. "Yes, but we're so much closer. The answers are out there. The Nihil must have taken the Nameless from their home in order to start all of this again."

"And?" said Reath.

"That vision really must have muddled your head," said Master Cohmac, laughing. "Think about it. It means the Nihil know where that planet is."

Reath nodded, following his train of thought. "Okay. Right. But we still have to find a way to get that information out of them. And don't forget, they still have the Nameless at their beck and call, and we have no way to defend ourselves."

"Aye," said Master Cohmac. "I'll give you that. But it's a start. And here's something else—if we can find one of those rods, then we won't have to worry about the Nameless, either. We can walk right into Marchion Ro's fortress and take them from him. Without the Nameless, we can even the odds against the Nihil."

"Let's not get ahead of ourselves," said Reath. "There's a lot to do before we reach that point. And I think Marchion Ro would have something to say about your dismissiveness. You're forgetting—the attack on Valo. Starlight Beacon . . ."

"I'm not forgetting," said Master Cohmac. "I'm reminding you there's hope, that's all. Even after everything that's happened. Even for someone like me." He held out his hand, and Reath took it, allowing himself to be pulled to his feet. "Time we were leaving, I think."

"I'll tell the others to come get us." Reath reached for his comlink. He depressed the button. "Affie? Leox?"

There was nothing but the hiss and pop of static.

Reath tapped the thing against the palm of his hand, then tried again. "Hello? *Vessel*, are you there?"

Still nothing.

"Probably this place, shielding the transmission," said Master Cohmac. "Let's head back out and try again."

He started toward the door and then stopped, his hand going out to find the wall for support.

"Master Cohmac?"

Instinctively, Reath pulled the shield from his back, igniting the plasma panels. They suffused the room with a bright blue tinge.

"Is everything all right?"

He took a step forward.

And he felt a wave of frantic mortal terror wash over him. He fell back, moaning. He tried to form a word, but it came out as a shrill guttural scream.

He was fighting a tide of blind panic. Every cell in his body told him to flee. He couldn't think. Couldn't concentrate. His head felt heavy, like it was full of wet sand. Thoughts oozed like molten lava. He tried to focus on Cohmac, realized his former master was ushering him back from the doorway.

"They're here," slurred Master Cohmac. "They've found us."

Recognition took a moment to penetrate Reath's fraught, panicked mind.

The Nameless.

No.

Not this.

Not now.

"Master . . . What . . . What do we do?" Reath fought against the tide of fear. He raised his head, squinting, looking up into the adjoining chamber. A dark shape hovered at the top of the slope, barring the exit. It was indistinct, twisting and reshaping itself like some terrible demonic entity sent to torment him. One moment it wore Azlin's face, but misshapen, malformed, twisted in a wicked grin. The next it bore Amadeo's, its eyes accusing and hard.

Reath screamed again, trying to tear his eyes away.

The shape shifted, stirring.

Desperately, frantically, Reath tore the shield off his arm. He tossed it into the air before him, digging deep, calling on the Force. He *pushed* with both hands, throwing everything he had into the effort, and the shield shot forward, spinning through the air.

Just as the creature leapt.

The shield struck the beast full in the head as it jumped, with a velocity that should have broken its neck.

The shield rebounded, clanging against the walkway and tumbling over the side into the trench of water. The strange, flickering, horrifying shape fell in the opposite direction, splashing into the other trench.

It screeched in frustration, and the sound was like a lightsaber being pushed through the back of Reath's head. He lurched, bending double, a burning stream of vomit bursting from his lips.

Master Cohmac's hand was on his shoulder, dragging him back into the circular room.

Reath tried to wave him off. "No. We have to go. We have to run." He knew he was mumbling, unable to think properly. He thrashed, desperate to get away. All he could think about was running.

He had to *run*.

Why couldn't Master Cohmac see that? *Why?*

"No . . . time," said Master Cohmac through gritted teeth. He was holding his lightsaber, and the bright searing light seemed to burn Reath's eyes. "Back! Back!"

Reath could hardly breathe. The creature was getting closer, and with every step it took, he was losing control, unable to focus, barely able to remember who he was. It was as if he were already being eroded. Like just being near the creature was enough to begin pulling him apart.

Terror gripped him again.

His throat was raw from screaming.

Lights danced before his eyes.

He fell back, scrabbling blindly at the ground, pushing himself pathetically away from the thing with the heels of his hands.

It was over. After all this. After everything.

Tears streamed from his eyes.

"Master!"

He lifted his head in time to see Master Cohmac slashing out with his lightsaber. Was he trying to fight it? There was no way . . . no way. . . .

But then the front of one of the kyber coffins fell open, crashing to the floor.

Master Cohmac's saber went out.

Close by, the Nameless roared.

Reath threw his arm up. He knew what was coming. It would be over in a moment. He'd be just like all those husks he'd examined in his laboratory.

And when they find you, all you'll be is dust.

But the pain never came.

He looked around, confused, unable to process what was happening around him. Warped images danced before his eyes.

"Reath! Reath! Run, now!"

The voice seemed almost disembodied, as if calling to him in a dream.

He cowered, pressing himself against the wall.

He was so scared.

And then a hand grabbed his wrist. A face hovered near his own, distorted, *evil*. Reath tried to push himself back, but the wall was hard and cold against the back of his skull.

"Reath! Now! Run!"

The voice seemed familiar. He shook his head, trying to clear it.

So familiar . . .

Cohmac. Master Cohmac was here. Telling him to run.

He moved.

Unsteadily, he circled the wavering coffins, following his fellow Jedi.

The creature was still there, but it was bearing down on the open coffin, hungrily consuming the mummified remains inside.

"Reath! Run!"

Reath ran.

Under the archway. Up the slope. Past the water.

The farther he ran, the more clarity seemed to return. Blood was streaming from his nostrils, clogging his breath. He could see Master Cohmac now, ahead of him, stumbling for the exit.

They were in the Tolemite structure. There was another chamber at the top, and then they'd be out.

He coughed, stumbled, reached the top of the slope. Paused for a moment.

"Reath, come on!"

He turned, raising his hand, reaching. . . .

The shield shot from the water, thudding into his grip. He

slung it onto his arm and hurried after Master Cohmac, never looking back at the feasting horror in their wake.

They burst into daylight, spluttering, near broken, but alive. But Reath knew they didn't have long until it was back on their trail.

"How . . ." he said, hacking on the thick phlegm and bile that still stung his throat. "How did you know?"

"A lucky guess," said Cohmac. He looked as bad as Reath felt. His hands were trembling. "I figured they were so steeped in the Force that, even dead, one of the Three Ancients might present a more attractive target than either of us."

Reath nodded. "We should head into the ruins. Find more cover."

Master Cohmac nodded. "And try calling the *Vessel* again. Quickly."

They hurried into the ruins, both perfectly aware that whatever cover the low walls could provide would be as nothing to the Nameless when it came for them.

"Affie?" he huffed into his comlink as he ran. "Affie? Leox?"

Leox's genial voice erupted from the comm. "Go ahead, Reath. We've got you, loud and clear."

"We need to get out of here, now. The Nihil are here, and they've brought Nameless."

Reath heard the sudden shift in Leox's tone from casual interest to urgent concern. "Sit tight. We're already on our way down from orbit."

Ahead of him, Master Cohmac had stumbled to a stop

behind a heap of rubble that might once have been a wall. He was gasping for breath.

"There are more of them," he said as Reath lurched over. "They've played us. They're hunting us like a pack. They're closing in from all directions."

Reath looked wildly about. He knew instantly that Master Cohmac was right. He could feel them drawing closer, feel that now familiar spike of fear, the cold terror spreading through his limbs, the hyperawareness of danger overloading his mind, his thoughts.

He turned, scanning the horizon.

There was no sign of the creatures, not yet. But a lone figure was standing on one of the low walls, watching them with strange hypnotic eyes, a horrible vacant grin on his face.

He was dressed in a hooded black cloak, and he had pale skin and a webwork of fine scars across his thin, hairless face. He was carrying an electrostaff that flickered and spat purple light.

Just like Master Cohmac had described the Jedi hunter who had gone after him on Thall.

Reath raised the shield. Master Cohmac's lightsaber ignited in his fist.

Overhead, the roar of engines tore open the sky.

Reath glanced up to see the *Vessel*, diving straight for them like a falling stone.

Despite the fear, despite the danger, despite everything, he felt hope blossom in his breast. There was still a chance. Just.

His comlink crackled to life. It was Affie. "We're coming in hot. We'll swing around and open the rear doors. Do you think you can make the jump?"

Reath thumbed the comlink. His hands were shaking. "We'll try . . ." he said with as much conviction as he could muster.

He didn't know if he had it in him, but it was the only chance they had.

The *Vessel* swept in closer. The rear hatch began to open.

Laser fire erupted from somewhere amid the ruins. Light bloomed. The *Vessel* shuddered as the shots struck the ship's engines in quick succession, causing it to slew out of control.

"No!" Reath's bellow was raw, unchecked pain.

The barrage continued, and he realized the Nihil must have brought ground-to-air munitions for just such an occasion. They were learning what the Jedi were capable of and countering any such escape.

They'd won.

Again.

The *Vessel* spiraled wildly and then dropped, trailing smoke. It slammed into the ground somewhere out of view. The noise was a sickening, echoing crunch.

The laser barrage ceased.

Reath turned on the spot.

Two Nameless were drawing closer. The Jedi hunter had drawn his weapon. Reath was losing control, his entire body shaking, sweating, his mind unable to comprehend the sheer terror it was attempting to process.

The end was near.

FORTY-SEVEN

The door to Azlin's cell slid open before her. Vernestra hadn't bothered to knock.

She'd come directly from the interview with the Temple Guard, who'd turned out to be a human male named Borthas Mitto.

Following his apprehension, she'd escorted him back to the upper levels, where he'd been taken into custody by his fellow Temple Guards while they decided on the next steps. She'd roused several members of the Jedi Council and informed them immediately of what she'd discovered and then—finally—retired for some rest.

This morning, she'd been awoken by a message from Keaton Murag, asking her to join him in questioning the Temple Guard.

Mitto had proved completely cooperative but had denied everything. He claimed to have no notion of why the comms equipment had been set up in the small chamber at the end of the passageway near Azlin's cell, or how it had been powered on or used. He explained that he only ever entered Azlin's cell when Azlin knocked, which was a standing order he'd received from the Temple Guards to ensure the well-being of their elderly charge. He claimed that Azlin would ask for fresh food or drink, and while occasionally he did seem anxious for company, Mitto would not engage the man in any conversations that went beyond the superficial or his day-to-day needs.

He assured them that he had in no way engaged in any sub-terfuge and that if he had received any unusual requests from Azlin—which he had not—he would have escalated them directly to the Jedi Council, or at the very least, to the extended Temple Guard network.

He seemed frustratingly sincere.

And yet they had received word from Amadeo about the mission to Angoth and Master Lox's death and the holotransmission in which Baron Boolan claimed to have an informant in the Jedi Temple and used information provided by them to potentially compromise Reath and Cohmac's mission to Tolis.

To Vernestra, it seemed obvious. The Temple Guard had been manipulated by Azlin into making these transmissions. And he'd used the equipment she'd found to do it. She had no clear under-standing of why, but she felt certain Azlin had to be behind it.

The problem was, there was no evidence.

And that meant she had no way of proving anything.

In fact, Master Murag had even taken her aside after the interview with the Temple Guard had concluded. He'd reminded her she'd been through a lot recently—and that she was accusing a *Temple Guard,* of all people, on circumstantial evidence alone. While he understood that Azlin couldn't be trusted and she was worried about the man's influence on Reath and others, they could hardly censure Borthas Mitto for doing his job.

They'd removed the comm equipment for testing and would double the guards on Azlin's door as a precautionary measure. And in the meantime, they would continue to look for evidence of this potential informant.

It was all they could do.

But it wasn't all Vernestra could do. She was going to speak to Azlin, to confront him about the matter.

She stalked into the room, searching for the man who she believed had engineered all this chaos and disruption. She had never met him before, and the sheer sight of him caused her to come to a halt, appalled. He looked . . . *broken.* Like no being should ever look. He'd aged far beyond the natural lifespan of a normal human, sustained now only by his bleak obsession and the power of the dark side. Vernestra could sense its oppressive aura, radiating from this shell of a man.

He was sitting cross-legged on his bunk, his tattered robes draped around his shoulders, his gnarled fingers skittering over the surface of a small wooden puzzle box as he turned it over in his hands. His goggles were raised, sitting on his forehead beneath the thin strands of his hair, the empty, staring sockets of his eyes fixed unseeing on the puzzle in his grip.

He didn't turn in Vernestra's direction as she stopped in the middle of the small room, peering down at him.

"And *you* are?" he said, his voice dry like old reeds.

"Vernestra Rwoh," she ground out. "A friend of Reath's."

"Ah," said Azlin. "Yes." He sighed, as if reluctantly accepting the need to placate her. "And what can I do for you, *Vernestra*?" He turned his face toward her, a sickly smile on his thin lips.

Vernestra fought the urge to recoil. "I know what you've been doing," she said, her voice level.

Azlin grinned. "How nice for you."

Vernestra made a fist behind her back. "You could have gotten them both killed. You still might."

Azlin shrugged. "I'm afraid I have no notion of what you're referring to, young lady."

"You sent the Nihil after Reath. You sent them to Tolis," said Vernestra.

"I did?" said Azlin, surprised. "How remarkable. All from the confines of my cell, too."

"I know it was you," said Vernestra.

"Hmmm," said Azlin. "You *suspect* it was me. But that's very different from knowing something for certain, isn't it? Mights and maybes. Haves and have-nots. Who's to say?"

"So you don't deny it?" said Vernestra.

"Why should I deny the impossible?" said Azlin. "How could I have sent the Nihil after Reath? And more to the point, *why*? I have no reason to put the boy at risk. Can't you see? I've invested a lot of time in his growth. He's our greatest hope of defeating the Nameless. Why would I do anything to put him at risk?"

Vernestra faltered. "But why would the Temple Guard do it, unless you'd somehow manipulated him?"

"Why indeed?" said Azlin with a vile smirk.

"I know you're holding something back, Azlin. I can tell."

Azlin fixed his gaping eye sockets on her. "How astute of you, Vernestra. And yet we all have our own *path*, don't we?"

Vernestra almost took a step back in shock. That word, the emphasis he'd put on it. Did he know? Did he know about the Path that Mari San Tekka had placed inside her head? The one she'd been keeping to herself all this time?

How could he?

"Now, perhaps we should start again," said Azlin. "Can I offer you some tea?"

Vernestra glowered at him.

This was how he did it. This was how he worked on people, breaking down their defenses, insinuating that he knew their hidden truths. But it wouldn't happen here—not to her. "Despite everything, Reath has chosen to listen to you, Azlin. And all you've done is repay him with lies and manipulation." She shook her head. "He'll never listen to you again."

Azlin slowly placed the puzzle box on the bunk before him. "You underestimate your friend," he said, folding his hands in his lap. "He is stronger than he knows. He has it in him to see this through. Perhaps more than any of us. But first he must recognize that strength in himself." He waved his hand. "All is as it should be."

"Who are you to decide such things?" said Vernestra.

Azlin laughed. "It seems I am the only one who is there for the boy."

"He's no boy," countered Vernestra.

"And yet still he questions himself. Abandoned by his master, tasked with the impossible by those who proclaim to care for him . . ." Azlin sniffed, raising his chin. "To whom is he supposed to turn? He cannot show weakness to those who have charged him with becoming their savior. He is alone. And so it falls upon me to guide him toward his goal."

Vernestra shook her head. "No. You're wrong. Reath knows he has friends. People to turn to. He comes here out of pity. Because he sees what you have made of yourself and feels sorry for you."

By way of reply, Azlin turned his back on her and returned to his puzzle box. "I think that we are done here," he said.

Vernestra backed toward the door. "We're not done, Azlin. Not for a minute. When Reath is back I'm going to tell him everything. I'm going to make sure he knows the truth."

"And you believe it will make a difference?" said Azlin.

"I know it will," said Vernestra. "Because I have faith in Reath. Because he's my friend, and not just a tool to be manipulated."

Azlin smirked. "Ah, I see. Then you are a greater fool than even I imagined, Vernestra Rwoh."

Vernestra shook her head.

She backed out of the cell. The door slid shut after her.

No.

I'm not the fool here, Azlin. And neither is Reath.

She thought of her friend then, of the weight he carried on his shoulders, of the dangers he faced out there on Tolis.

And she knew he was going to be okay.

He had to be.

Because there was no way this fallen Jedi could be right.

FORTY-EIGHT

"We're too late."

Amadeo was sitting in the cockpit of the *Invictus* as they plummeted through the lower atmosphere of Tolis, watching the flare of surface-to-air laser fire as it struck the other ship. They hadn't had a chance to identify it before the explosions began, but Amadeo was pretty sure it wasn't a Nihil ship.

Which meant there was every chance it was the *Vessel*.

His heart was in his mouth.

"It's never too late," called Ashton, trying to steady the bucking controls. "It's all about making the right entrance."

"The only entrance we're going to be making if you continue the way you are is as a fireball that was once a Republic transport ship," said L-77. For someone without an expressive face, he gave a very strong impression of disdain.

Dorian was in the rear of the ship, evidently trying not to think about the speeds involved in their barely controlled descent.

Ashton took one hand off the controls to wave dismissively at L-77. "Don't be such a spoilsport. You never want me to fly."

"Can you blame me?" said L-77. He looked at Amadeo, as if pleading. "Won't you do something to stop her?"

"Just get us down alive," said Amadeo. "And quickly."

"On it," said Ashton.

"Oh, perfect," said L-77. "Now you're *encouraging* her. We're all going to die."

"Have I ever killed you before?" said Ashton, shooting him a look out of the corner of her eye.

"Evidently not," retorted L-77. "But it's not from want of trying."

Ashton laughed, wrenching back on the controls. "Hold on! We have incoming!"

Laser cannon fire raked their hull as Ashton swung the *Invictus* about. Warnings blared. The ship shuddered—but held.

"Well?" called Ashton over the clanging alarms.

"Well, what?" said L-77.

"Aren't you going to return fire?"

"Ah," said L-77. "I thought you'd never ask." His metallic hands danced over the weapons controls, buttons clicking and clacking. "Bring us about."

"Bring us about!" said Ashton. "Just fire the damn cannons!"

"Stop being difficult!" said L-77.

Ashton wrung her hands. "Just bring us about . . ." she muttered under her breath. She yanked on the flight controls and the ship juddered.

Amadeo caught hold of the back of L-77's chair to stop himself being thrown forward. "We need to get down there!"

"I *know!*" said Ashton.

Another barrage of cannon fire battered the lower hull. Amadeo heard Dorian shouting something from the hold, but he didn't have time to go back to check.

The *Invictus* groaned as it swung about. "It's not built for maneuvers like this," said Ashton, a panicked edge to her voice. "We're going to break the whole thing in two."

"Which would be better than your last *three* landings," said L-77. His finger was hovering over a red button on the instrument panel.

All Amadeo could see outside was a blurred impression of vast ruins flanked by a blue-green ocean, spinning past the viewport as if their descent was utterly out of control.   .

Ashton opened her mouth to scream her reply but was drowned out by the sudden roar of launching missiles as L-77 punched the red button.

The ship continued to come about, nose dipping. Amadeo watched, eyes wide, as four, five, six missiles converged on a hulking gray ship parked in a small clearing close to the edge of the ruins.

They struck in unison.

The Nihil ship flared as its shields took the brunt of the attack.

The missiles detonated.

The resulting explosion ripped through the air like a crack of thunder, a massive, roiling ball of flame and pressure boiling up from the site of the impact.

Just as the *Invictus*'s nose completed its swing around.

The blast caught the RDC ship from below, forcing it up and onto its side. Amadeo was thrown from his seat, skidding across the floor, slamming hard against the wall.

He rolled, head smarting, calling on the Force to slow his momentum as he tumbled through the hatchway into the main hold.

Dorian, he was relieved to see, had taken the precaution of webbing himself into one of the safety harnesses and was braced in a sitting position, chanting quietly to himself, his eyes squeezed shut as the ship *rolled*.

Amadeo caught hold of the edge of a bench to steady himself as the momentum tried to tear him free again. His fingers were white with the effort of holding on.

The ship's superstructure wailed with the sound of straining metal.

And then they were over, the engines were firing, and they were falling.

They smashed into the ground, churning soil and rubble, then rebounded, lifting again, before coming down heavily to settle into a long slide. Amadeo winced, both from the pain of bashing his hip against the metal floor plates and the screeching of the hull as it slewed across the ground, bending and breaking and rending as it went.

After a moment, they shuddered to a halt.

Amadeo was up immediately, rushing to Dorian's side. "Are you okay? Dorian?"

Dorian raised his head, sighed, and offered Amadeo his now familiar crooked smile. "I'm still breathing, if that's what you mean."

Amadeo nodded before hurrying toward the cockpit, only to find L-77 cutting Ashton loose from her safety harness, which had evidently jammed in the crash.

"Perfect landing, I'd say," muttered the droid as he worked, slicing through the straps with his arm blade.

"Don't give me that," countered Ashton. "We're still in one piece, aren't we? And so's the ship."

"Yes, and I'll be watching from the ground as you try to get it airborne again," said L-77. He severed the last strap and lifted Ashton gently out of her seat. "Are you hurt?" he said, his voice gentle now.

"No. Are you?" Her reply was equally concerned.

"No," said L-77.

They nodded to each other, and then L-77 set Ashton down on her feet. She looked at Amadeo. "Right, then. Ready?"

Amadeo pulled Master Lox's lightsaber from his holster. "Ready."

※

The main hatch was twisted and buckled shut from the crash, and it took L-77 a few moments to manually crack the dented airlock. As soon as Amadeo had dragged himself through and dropped to the ground, he felt the presence of the Nameless like a foul stench in the air. The sensation brought with it a sudden flood of emotion and spiking fear.

Not this.

Not again.

Not yet.

Amadeo recoiled against the battered hull of the ship, raising his arm to cover his face, gasping to find his breath. His vision swam. His emotions churned. He squeezed his eyes shut, but still he saw Master Lox, swimming out of the nightmare black, his face contorted as it crumbled to dust before him, accusing Amadeo of betrayal, of abandoning his master to die.

Amadeo cried out, trying to push the awful vision out of his mind.

He felt a hand on his arm and flinched away.

"It's okay, Amadeo. I'm here." The voice was gentle, kind. "It's Dorian."

Amadeo fought the rising tide of panic, forcing himself to breathe. The creatures weren't even targeting him yet, but the trauma of the past day seemed to be having an amplifying effect, making everything feel so much worse. Or perhaps it was the other way around. He couldn't be certain. Regardless, the guilt and shame and loss he was feeling seemed to come in waves that threatened to overwhelm him.

Slowly, he steadied himself, seeking his center. His vision sharpened, as if a heavy fog were clearing from before his eyes, although he could still feel the horrible, oppressive weight of the creatures' presence, pressing down on him. They were near. Just over the next rise, toward the water.

"You don't have to do this," said Dorian, beside him. "You've already done enough. Ashton and Sevens are here. They'll help your friends."

Amadeo pushed himself away from the downed ship. He kneaded his temples. "No. I *do* have to do this. There could be Nihil here, too. I can fight them. I can help."

"All right," said Dorian, his tone uncertain. "But I'm sticking with you."

Amadeo nodded. "I'll protect you." He ignited Master Lox's lightsaber. The blue blade flickered to life. The familiar hum was somehow both tragic and comforting in equal measure.

"That's not exactly what I meant," said Dorian. "But thanks all the same."

Ashton was scanning the landscape from atop the remains of an old wall. "We saw a ship go down over there," she said, pointing. "We should head in that direction."

Amadeo shook his head. "No. Head for the coast. That's where they are."

"You can tell?" said Ashton, shooting him a quizzical look.

"Jedi stuff," replied L-77 before Amadeo had a chance to answer. He was standing a few meters away, and he turned to look at Ashton, his single eye flashing. "Well? You heard the kid." He set off at a run.

Ashton leapt down from her perch, charging after him at full pelt, shouting something indiscernible.

"You sure about this?" asked Dorian one last time.

"No," said Amadeo. "But I'm going to do it anyway."

Dorian laughed. "I walked right into that one, didn't I?"

They set off after the others.

⚜

Reath could hardly think, hardly function.

His body was frozen with fear, ice-cold, overwhelming, drowning out almost every other thought.

His breathing was ragged, his heart was palpitating, and sweat ran down his brow. He knew Master Cohmac was somewhere close by, but Reath had lost track of him. He'd lost track of everything.

He didn't even have the capacity to scream.

There was nothing but the creatures, slowly, inexorably circling closer.

Their outlines shimmered and morphed as Reath's vision blurred. How could he fight something he couldn't even see? How could he push through such crippling, overwhelming fear? He was close to full-on panic. His ears were filled with a ringing sound that drowned out everything around him.

He clutched his shield, but he knew it would never be enough to save them.

He heard laughing and turned his head, shaking it to try to clear his warping vision. It was the creatures' handler. The man's silhouette was wavering, too, as if seen through a distant heat haze. One moment he looked human, striding forward on both legs, a wicked, satisfied grin on his awful face. The next he was one of the creatures, a hulking, slavering tentacled beast, hungry to feed. Reath moaned, fighting for a clarity that would not come.

Close by, Master Cohmac whimpered. His lightsaber rolled from his fingers.

They were about to die. Everything they'd done, everything they'd hoped for was going to end on this beach.

He dropped to one knee, crying out in terror.

But still he hefted the shield. Still he gripped it for all he was worth.

He would stand his ground to the last.

He would . . .

Something changed.

A sudden release. A moment of respite.

Reath staggered, blinking, groggy.

Something had distracted the creatures. Something . . . or some*one* was drawing them off.

He squinted into the light, trying to make sense of what his eyes were telling him.

A tall silver figure was charging through the coastal spume, kicking up spray as it thundered into the side of what could only be one of the Nameless, sending them both tumbling into a mass of writhing limbs and flashing blades. Blood fountained as the droid—that was the only thing it *could* be—slashed ribbons from the creature's chest and forelegs. And yet the Nameless fought on, slamming the droid hard across the side of the head, tearing a rent in the paneling of its chest.

Reath's understanding of what was happening was hazy, piecemeal. The proximity of the Nameless was affecting his perception, and he couldn't be certain that any of what he was seeing wasn't a figment of his terrified imagination.

Was this just his dying brain, reaching out for a last moment of hope?

He turned, trying to figure out what had happened to the other creature.

Another figure—a woman, he thought—was circling the other Nameless, twin blasters barking as she fired again and again and again into its flank. The creature reared up on its hind legs, screeching, lashing out with its claws as the woman danced away, bellowing obscenities.

And two more figures were cresting the rise. One tall and thin, the other . . .

Oh, no.

Amadeo?

What was he doing here? Didn't he realize the danger? Didn't he understand? Why wasn't Master Lox stopping him?

Or was it just the proximity of the Nameless conjuring figments from his mind? He couldn't be certain either way.

Reath tried to call out to him, to send the Padawan away, but his voice was nothing more than a hoarse croak, dying on his lips. As he watched, the Jedi hunter drew his electrostaff and turned to meet Amadeo and the other man.

Reath took a step toward them, but Master Cohmac caught his robes, pulling him back. Reath spun, about to yank himself free, but the look of outright terror on Cohmac's face stopped him short. He frowned, unsure what was happening.

And then it struck him.

He'd forgotten about the third Nameless. The one they'd left in the repository.

The hairs on the nape of his neck prickled.

Something stole his breath.

He couldn't move, couldn't think, couldn't see.

The world was spinning. Desperate thoughts circled his mind. He imagined his hands, his arms, his face turning to dust.

Fear locked him rigid.

He whimpered and fell to the ground.

⚔

Amadeo watched in horror as Reath emitted a shrill scream of terror and dropped to his knees.

Amadeo shuddered. He wanted to run to Reath, to help his friend, but there was no time. The strange hooded Nihil with the pale face was closing on him and Dorian, whirling his electrostaff before him like a wheel.

A Nihil Jedi hunter. It had to be.

Amadeo backed away. The Nameless were far enough away from him that their presence wasn't yet debilitating, but if he had any hope of holding his own in the fight to come, he needed to draw the man away.

He was so scared his hands were trembling.

What if the Jedi hunter was too strong?

What if Amadeo had come here just to die like his master?

He ground his teeth. He knew it was the fear talking. He kept on backing away.

Beside him, Dorian pulled a blaster from a holster on his hip and then turned and ran . . . directly toward Reath and Master Cohmac.

Good.

Still the Jedi hunter advanced, whirling his electrostaff, cackling with amusement. "It doesn't matter, little Jedi. You can try to run, but I'll find you. I always do."

He was thin and pale, with dark veins bulging at his neck and temples. One of his eyes was almost entirely red, shot through with traces of black, and he wore an expression that was equal parts snide and frenzied.

Gritting his teeth, Amadeo raised Master Lox's lightsaber as the Jedi hunter rushed him.

The blade clashed with the swinging staff, once, twice, a third time, humming and fizzing as they tested each other's defenses, pacing slowly.

"Little Jedi," spat the Jedi hunter in a thin, asinine voice. "Ready to die?"

Amadeo didn't answer, refusing to rise to the bait. He breathed, allowing his muscles to remember his forms, twisting, turning, thrusting on instinct. Every attack was met by the whirling electrostaff, every parry by a counterattack.

He staggered, parrying again, trying to shake the latent fear that continued to worry at the back of his mind, unbalancing him, causing him to misjudge and misstep.

With the three Nameless otherwise engaged on the far side of the beach, the effect of their presence had become a constant background distraction, but as he clashed again with the Jedi hunter, he felt the same disquieting sensation radiating from the man, only weaker and somehow different.

What was he? The corruption was more than just the influence of the dark side. Amadeo was certain of it. It was as if, having spent so much time with the Nameless, the man had been tainted by them somehow, adopting some of their unique flavor.

It was enough to cause Amadeo's mind to race, to shake his concentration and disrupt the timing of his defensive maneuvers.

The electrostaff slammed into his left hip, causing him to stagger and grunt in pain. He flung the lightsaber up in time to block the follow-up attack that would have caught him across the side of the head, but then the Jedi hunter kicked out, his boot catching Amadeo in the gut and sending him staggering back, off-balance.

Close by, he heard Ashton scream, a shrill, piercing shriek of abject pain. He twisted, finding his footing, glancing over to see that she'd gone down clutching her belly as the blurry form she'd been fighting seemed to hunker over her, its mouth tendrils reaching for her face.

Nearby, he saw L-77 look around, take in what was happening, and throw himself forward, burying the blade of his left arm through his own combatant so hard that it pierced the hide of its chest, spearing it to the rocky ground. He twisted, withdrew the blade, and ran to Ashton's aid. Amadeo caught only a glimpse, but he could see that the droid's blade had been shattered in the process, and several of its inner workings had been ripped loose, hanging like spilled entrails around its knees.

Elsewhere, Dorian was standing close to Reath, firing a constant stream of shots at what he knew to be the third creature.

He had only seconds to take all this in before the Jedi hunter was on him again, pressing his advantage. Amadeo fended off a battering succession of attacks, lightsaber juddering in his grip under the sheer ferocity of the assault. His muscles ached, his head swam, and he knew he was badly outmatched.

And yet the Jedi hunter was repeating the same pattern of attack, trying to wear him down. Amadeo could make use of that. He played along, falling back, blocking each strike as it came, watching.

Until he saw an opening. And then he lunged.

The Jedi hunter was ready for him and swung his electrostaff up and around, bringing the end of it slamming down hard on Amadeo's back. It had been a feint, and Amadeo had overextended his attack.

He went down hard, face-first in the dirt, the air forced from his lungs.

Master Lox's lightsaber winked out as it tumbled from his fingers.

The shadow of the Jedi hunter loomed over him.

FORTY-NINE

Affie was trying desperately not to panic.

Sparks were showering from the ceiling of the *Vessel*. Alarms were blaring incessantly, in rhythm with the pounding in her head. Leox was frantically hammering at the controls, trying to get a diagnostic report, and in the next compartment, Geode was surrounded by a webwork of cables that had spilled out of a panel in the wall.

The Nihil and their Nameless were loose on Tolis, Reath and Cohmac needed to get out of there urgently, and Eve's homing beacon was still pinging loudly, originating from somewhere inside the Nihil ship—the ship that had just been blasted by the RDC vessel that had seemed to arrive from out of nowhere.

Everything was a mess.

Leox had managed to get the *Vessel* down among the dunes, but the ship had taken a lot of impacts from the Nihil's defenses, and with their maneuverability compromised by the fault in the flight systems, they hadn't been able to get clear quickly enough to avoid serious damage.

The RDC ship had come down heavily, too, and Affie had no idea if the crew or passengers were still alive. She had to hope they were. It sounded as if Reath and Cohmac needed their help.

She stumbled to the console and shut off the alarms. The lighting continued to flash bright red, but at least she could hear herself think. She checked the comms. They were down, too.

"Are you okay?" she asked Leox. "You're not hurt?"

He shook his head. "Two different questions, Little Bit. I'm not hurt. . . ."

"But you're not okay," finished Affie. "I know. I'm sorry." She brushed loose strands of hair out of her face. "You think we can get her airborne again?"

"I think it's going to take some work. But yeah, hull integrity is holding. If Geode can figure out how to get the flight systems operational, I can get us out of here," he said.

Affie wanted to grab hold of him and bundle him into a hug, but she knew now wasn't the time. "Thanks. You're the best."

"Hmmm," he muttered by way of response.

Affie started for the door to the main cabin.

"Where are you going?" called Leox.

She paused in the opening, looking back. "We left orbit for a reason," she said.

"Affie . . . you're not seriously thinking of going out there.

Not now," said Leox. It was rare that he used her real name like that. He was worried. About her, about the ship, about himself and Geode.

Affie frowned. "I have to. I made a promise to Eve. If she's trapped on that Nihil ship . . ."

"It's too dangerous," said Leox. He took a step toward her, his expression pleading for her to understand. "It could be a trap. Leave the rescue missions to Reath and Cohmac."

"Reath and Cohmac have enough to deal with," countered Affie.

Leox straightened. "All right, Little Bit. Then I'm coming with you."

Affie shook her head. "No. We need to get the *Vessel* airworthy again. You stay here with Geode. I'll be back before you know it. We need to be ready to evacuate when the others figure out where to find us."

"I don't like it," said Leox.

"Neither do I," said Affie, "but it's the only choice."

Leox issued a heavy sigh. "Just be careful, okay?"

"Okay. You too." She turned and hurried into the rear of the ship, pausing to open a locker and retrieve a small blaster. Then she punched the controls to open the boarding ramp, wincing at the spears of bright sunlight that streamed through as it slowly lowered toward the sandy landscape below.

At the top of the ramp, she turned to shoot Geode a smile. "See you soon, big guy."

She hurtled down the ramp, not waiting for his reply.

Down among the dunes, her vision of the surrounding area

was limited. She clutched the blaster, hoping she wouldn't have cause to use it.

She couldn't hear anything over the ticking and groaning of the damaged *Vessel*, but she could just make out a plume of gray smoke spiraling lazily in the distance.

It had to be coming from either the Nihil ship, which had taken a heavy bombardment from the RDC vessel, or the RDC vessel itself. Either way, it meant that was the right direction.

Affie hurried up the side of a dune, her boots sinking into the sand with every step. She crested the top of it, skidding on the straw-like grasses. She stopped, shielding her eyes, then set off at a run, careening down the long slope of the dune in the direction of the rising column of smoke.

A few moments later, it came into view. Affie couldn't see the RDC vessel, but the Nihil ship sat in a depression in the sand about a hundred meters away. She dropped to a crouch, taking a moment to survey the scene.

There was only open ground between her and the ship, and no sign of any movement, be it people, animals, or droids. Which didn't mean they weren't lurking somewhere behind cover, of course. But it was a good start.

The ship itself was small and squat—a hodgepodge of dilapidated components all mashed into one craft, like almost every other Nihil ship she'd ever encountered. She couldn't even tell what the underlying structure had once been, because it had been patched and modified so many times, with clusters of weapon turrets affixed to its outer hull. It was emblazoned with an eye symbol on its flank, hastily rendered in swirling blue paint, and it was covered in scorch marks from the recent aerial barrage.

Several of its weapon turrets were now blackened stumps— the origin of the curling smoke she'd seen from afar—and the roof and tapered nose had been severely dented and scorched.

The ramp was still raised, but the outer airlock hatch was buckled and partially open.

Affie rose, scanning the nearby dunes with a sweep of the blaster.

Still nothing.

She edged closer, the blaster still tight in her grip.

If there were any Nihil in the vicinity, they didn't seem to be paying her any attention. She guessed they were off trying to deal with the Jedi.

She approached the ship, her nostrils filled with the rich, oily tang of the smoke.

She stood for a moment in its shadow, looking up, trying to judge whether she'd be able to pull herself into the airlock. She supposed she didn't have much choice.

With one final glance around, she tucked the blaster into her coveralls and jumped, catching hold of the lip of the exposed airlock and slowly pulling herself up. Her arms burned with the exertion, and her fingertips were cramped with pain, but with a loud groan, she managed to haul herself up, slipping under the buckled metal door and pulling herself through to the interior.

She paused for a moment to catch her breath, then withdrew the blaster again and crossed to the internal airlock controls. They were still intact. She initiated the sequencing process, and after a moment, the inner door opened with a hiss of compressed air.

Affie stepped inside, rolling her neck to try to banish the tension in her shoulders.

The lighting was dim, and a thick musty aroma, like the scent of captive livestock, was hanging in the air.

She shuddered. She knew what that had to mean.

The Nameless.

Affie steeled herself. She had no idea what horrors she might find on this ship, and she had to work to contain her imagination. She'd heard stories about the Nihil Jedi hunters, and she'd seen Marchion Ro's broadcast of his murder of Grand Master Pra-Tre Veter at the hands of a Nameless.

She knew what they could do to a Jedi.

She only hoped that wasn't what she was going to face now.

Something had obviously gone very wrong on Oisin, however. There was no other explanation. The Nihil must have retaliated after the attack on their raiders and come for Eve and Zaph, using the creatures to subdue them.

She couldn't think of any other reason why they'd be broadcasting the homing signal from inside this horrible ship. Unless, of course, Leox was right and she was walking straight into a trap.

Which remained a possibility.

It didn't *feel* like a trap, though. The ship was silent and seemed to be empty.

Or perhaps that was just her own optimism talking.

She realized she was doing the mental equivalent of babbling to herself, trying to quell her fear.

Focus, Affie.

She walked cautiously into the small common area of the ship. It was stripped back and functional. Bare walls that were only partially covered in paneling, exposed circuitry, a small medical station filled with vials and injectors. No seats. No tables. Nowhere to prepare meals. The very definition of function over aesthetics.

She edged her way into the rear compartment, ducking through a low hatchway, keeping the nose of the blaster raised.

Here the ship had been divided into two distinct areas, a forward section that had been given over to a series of heavy metal holding pens—the type designed for wild animals—and a rear section accessed through another hatch.

There were four of the large metal enclosures, all of them empty. The stink of animals was even stronger here.

Affie realized this must be how the Nihil transported their captive Nameless. She felt a momentary pang of sorrow for the creatures. Not that long ago, she'd asserted to Leox that the Nameless were likely victims of the Nihil, too, and seeing the conditions in which they had been held, she thought she had to be right. Regardless of whether they were mindless beasts or something more intelligent, the Nihil had enslaved them and weaponized them against the Jedi. The creatures were just as much in need of liberation as the other Nihil captives being held behind the Stormwall.

But that was a matter for another day. Right now, there were more pressing things to worry about.

"Eve? Zaph, are you there?" she called. Her voice echoed throughout the empty ship.

She heard a low groan from somewhere toward the rear.

Affie hurried to the remaining hatch and edged through. It was darker back here, the only illumination coming from a single emergency light mounted high on the far wall.

"Eve? Zaph?" she repeated as she moved farther into the space. It took a moment for her eyes to adjust to the gloom.

The area was much like the adjoining space but narrower, with only two smaller metal cages. One was empty.

The other contained a humanoid figure, slumped on the ground.

Affie hurried over.

She dropped to her knees, peering through the bars.

For a moment she thought she didn't recognize the person lying there before her, so caked were they in filth and grime, and wearing such a startling expression.

Affie almost recoiled.

Eve Byre was curled into a ball, her knees drawn up to her chest. Her robes were filthy and her hair had come loose and was tangled and matted on one side of her head. Her palms were encrusted with dried blood where it appeared she'd dug her own nails deep into her flesh as she'd balled her fists too tight.

Her eyes were open and wide with apparent shock, although she wasn't looking at Affie. She was seeing something else, something that wasn't really there, or if it had once been, was no longer.

On the ground just a few centimeters from her left hand was the comlink Affie had given her on Oisin.

Affie could only begin to imagine the horrors Eve must have been through, trapped on this ship so close to the Nameless. She'd heard stories about what they could do to a Jedi's mind, how they could drive a person into the very depths of despair and fear and confusion.

And now here was someone she knew—someone she'd transported, talked to as a friend—almost catatonic from prolonged exposure to the creatures.

The Nihil had a great deal to answer for.

"It's okay, Eve. It's Affie. Affie Hollow. I'm going to get you out of here."

Affie got to her feet to double-check the other cell, just in case she'd missed something, but she'd been right the first time. It was empty.

There was no trace of Zaph.

Affie tried not to take that as an ominous sign.

She returned to Eve's cage. The Jedi hadn't moved. She barely showed any indication that she even realized Affie was there.

Affie reached down and tried the front of the cage. It was locked. It required a passcode to open.

Or a blaster.

"Stay back for me, Eve," she said as she pointed the blaster at the lock mechanism and squeezed the trigger. "This might—"

The rest of her words were lost in a flash of light and a noise that, in the small space, sounded like an explosion going off.

Affie buried her face in the crook of her arm.

When she looked again a moment later, the cage door was

hanging open, the lock mechanism melted and emitting sparks and a foul odor.

Carefully, she got down on her knees again, reaching through to touch Eve on the arm.

The Jedi flinched away from her touch.

"Eve, it's Affie," she said again, trying to keep her tone level. "We need to get out of here. You're on a Nihil ship. I've come to take you home. Back to Coruscant and the Temple. There'll be people there who can help you."

This time the Jedi seemed to hear her words. She turned to look at Affie, her eyes wild. "The creatures! We've got to stop the creatures!"

"It's all right," said Affie. "They're gone. You're safe now. But we need to get you out of this ship." She reached inside the cage and took Eve's hand. "This way."

Slowly, as if unsure of both herself and her surroundings, Eve allowed herself to be led out of the cage. They sat for a moment on the ground, Affie holding the other woman gently in her arms. Then she got to her feet, offering both hands.

"Where's Zaph?" she said, carefully helping Eve to her feet. The woman could barely stand and needed Affie's support to stay upright.

Eve gave a single sharp shake of her head. "No."

The inference was clear. Affie could tell by the grim expression on Eve's face. Her heart sank. "Oh . . . oh, no."

Not Zaph. That sweet, calm, peaceful young man who'd wanted to savor every moment of his short life.

Gone.

Killed by the Nihil and their deadly pets.

Affie fought back brimming tears. Now wasn't the time. She had to get Eve out of there and back to the *Vessel* quickly. The Jedi needed urgent medical attention.

Together, they hobbled back into the main compartment.

Eve was mumbling something under her breath, but Affie didn't have time to stop and try to interpret it. She just needed to get them both as far away from that dreadful ship as possible.

She found the control panel and lowered the ramp, helping Eve stumble down into the bright suns of Tolis.

"Come on. It's not far," she said, half walking, half dragging Eve along beside her through the soft sand, one arm wrapped around the Jedi's waist, the other still holding on to the blaster as their only defense.

She could only hope that Reath and Cohmac were faring much, much better against the Nameless, somewhere out there over the dunes.

FIFTY

The young man—Reath had no idea who he was—was driving the creature back toward the water with a relentless stream of blaster fire, back across the beach toward the repository.

He shook his muddled head and looked around.

His vision was clearing. For how long, he had no idea.

He wanted to cower there on the ground and hide. His entire body shook with fear. And yet the farther the creature was driven back, the more he seemed to be able to cling to the fleeting moments of clarity between the bouts of terrible clenching fear.

In the distance, he saw Amadeo go down heavily on his front, saw the Nihil standing over him, raising his staff for the killing blow.

"No . . . No . . ." Reath murmured, staggering to his feet, willing himself to rise, to stand, to raise the shield that was still clutched firmly in his grip.

With a roar, he flung the shield, throwing out both hands, expelling everything he had left inside of him, every modicum of strength.

The shield whipped through the air, striking the Nihil hard in the chest and sweeping him off his feet like a rag doll. There was no time for him to even register his shock. The electrostaff flew from his grip, and he tumbled back wordlessly into the ruins, several meters from Amadeo. Reath heard him land with a wet thud.

Then buzzing silence, like the world was suddenly empty.

Reath collapsed back onto his knees, sucking at the air through clenched teeth.

He surveyed the scene. One of the Nameless lay dead on the shoreline, its hulking corpse buffeted by the lapping waves. Another—the one the young man had blasted with repeated fire—had fled, but Reath knew it would be back. He'd felt its hunger, its *need*.

The droid was locked in a vicious one-on-one duel with the remaining Nameless some distance away in the dunes—having drawn it away either by luck or foresight.

The tall man who'd saved him was tending the wounds of the injured woman.

Amadeo was picking himself up off the ground, warily glancing over at Reath.

And behind him, the Jedi hunter was rising from the ruins.

His hood had fallen back to reveal his pale face, smooth head, and strange mismatched eyes. The Nihil held something in his hand—a small disc-shaped device—that he depressed several times and then tossed away in disgust. Evidently, whatever it was had been damaged in the fall.

"Amadeo," said Reath, struggling back to his feet.

He set off at an uneven run, head still thick and painful. He sensed Master Cohmac staggering along in his wake.

Ahead, the Jedi hunter held his hand out to the side, and his electrostaff leapt from where it lay on the ground, thudding into his grip. The tips ignited with crackling fingers of dancing electric current.

The Force!

The Nihil was using the Force!

A Nihil!

How could that be, when the Nameless were so close?

Amadeo was turning to meet him, but his own lightsaber was still on the ground, and he was staggering woozily, evidently unable to call on the Force to retrieve it. Reath ran harder, almost tripping on the rough terrain, his lungs burning.

Reath watched, helpless, as the Jedi hunter swung his staff, clipping the side of Amadeo's head, sending him sprawling back to the ground with a groan.

And then Reath was there, slamming hard into the Nihil to push him back while Master Cohmac moved in to flank him, his lightsaber singing.

The Jedi hunter giggled maniacally, his eyes wide. Blood

trickled down the side of his face, and Reath could see he was carrying his weight on his right leg.

"*Shrii Ka Rai, Ka Rai . . .*" the Jedi hunter said in a singsong voice. "They're coming for you, Jedi. They're coming."

Reath ignited his lightsaber, raising it to block a sudden attack, pushing the electrostaff left while Master Cohmac cut in, pressing the advantage with his lightsaber. But the Jedi hunter was too fast, and he parried the blow, spinning his staff like a wheel and catching Cohmac hard in the shoulder on the counterattack.

Master Cohmac winced, falling back, flexing his fingers to try to restore feeling in that arm.

Amadeo was rising again, his lightsaber in his fist. He looked terrible, with the stain of dark bruises down the left side of his face, dried blood down the front of his robes, and a swollen lip that had clearly been stitched. Worse was the look in his eyes. He seemed haunted. Lost.

Reath felt his heart breaking. He bashed away another attack with the lightsaber, edging closer to try to protect his young friend. They were all so broken—so tired, and scared, and hollow. Reath wondered if they even had it in them to see the fight through.

The Jedi hunter laughed. "Yes, yes. A broken Jedi is just what Father needs. The freshest blood." He giggled again, spinning to jab at Cohmac, pushing him back as he tried to parry.

Reath could make no sense of what the man was saying, but the words seemed to excite the Nihil, and he came at them again, jabbing and spinning, wheeling about, bashing their weapons aside.

Reath was groggy. He knew the droid was still locked in battle with one of the creatures, but the effect seemed to be growing stronger. Fear was spiking. His visions seemed to leave trails as he turned his head. And still the Jedi hunter pressed on, thrusting and swiping.

The electrostaff struck Reath in the chest and he buckled, falling to the ground, his lightsaber rolling from his fingers.

Master Cohmac and Amadeo were groaning, too, clutching their heads.

Reath coughed blood and let it dribble from the corner of his mouth. He didn't know how much more of this he could take. The horror, the revulsion . . .

He just wanted it to end.

The pale man lowered his staff, eyeing them with satisfaction. "Time to die, Jedi."

"No . . ." Reath's entire body was shaking. His vision swam. He tried to focus on the Jedi hunter, but all he could see was a warping, shimmering shape rising up behind the man, its face a mangled nest of tentacles, its flesh translucent and sickly.

The Nameless. The one that had fled. It was back. And it was *hungry*.

Reath screamed. His throat burned in agony. The world seemed to be on fire all around him. He couldn't make sense of what he was seeing, what he was thinking.

It was coming.

It was going to feed. . . .

He heard a thud, followed by a shrill laugh that quickly transformed into a horrified, anguished wail.

Gasping, Reath raised his head.

And he screamed again.

The world was a shifting kaleidoscope of colors and twisted morphing images.

He could see the Jedi hunter lying in the dirt, scrabbling, screaming.

And sitting atop him, the demonic form of the creature hungrily consuming the living Force from its own handler.

"No! No, no! You don't understand! Not *me*! I'm like you! I'm *special*!" The voice of the dying Jedi hunter turned Reath's stomach.

But the man's legs were already turning to pale dust.

Reath tried to move, but there was nothing. He was crying and moaning and thrashing. It was coming for him next.

He knew it with terrified certainty.

Reath felt hands under his arms, pulling him away across the sand.

He went limp, allowing himself to be slowly dragged.

What did it matter now? It was too late. Too late . . .

He flashed in and out of consciousness. A woman's voice was bellowing for them to hurry. But he couldn't hurry. He couldn't. . . .

He realized his thoughts were growing sharper, clearer. Blearily, he looked up. The silver droid was dragging him by the back of his robes, taking him as far away as possible from the deadly terror that still stalked the coastline, and the rapidly disintegrating husk of the dead Jedi hunter it was feasting on.

FIFTY-ONE

Ashton and Dorian had led them back to the downed shell of the *Invictus*.

They'd taken shelter inside, sealing the airlock behind them, conscious of the remaining Nameless that still stalked them in the ruins.

They could hear it, howling mournfully as it circled the wreckage at a distance, teasing them, letting them know it was still out there and still coming for them.

And there was nowhere else for them to go.

It was only a matter of time.

Every time Amadeo heard it, his fear spiked, causing him to grip the hilt of Master Lox's lightsaber and shudder. He could see it was having a similar effect on the other two Jedi, who were at least as traumatized as he was.

He wondered if any of them would ever be the same again.

He doubted it.

Amadeo had made the necessary introductions after helping Dorian get Ashton onto the medical gurney, where he himself had lain only a few short hours ago. She was badly wounded—nearly disemboweled by a swipe from a Nameless's claws. Dorian had managed to patch her up on the shoreline and, after they'd all gotten back to the ship, had rendered her unconscious with medication while he tended her wounds. She was now wrapped in a thick layer of bacta bandages and sleeping. Dorian had assured him she was going to make it.

L-77 was in a bad way, too. One of his blade arms had shattered, and his torso had been torn open in at least three places, exposing swathes of his inner workings. The Nameless had caused extensive damage, and despite the droid's best efforts to keep himself operational, he kept blacking out with brief episodes of power shortage before suddenly springing back to life again as if nothing had happened.

Whatever the case, they were both out of commission for the time being, leaving it up to the Jedi to decide what to do.

Amadeo didn't know how to feel about any of it. He'd done what he came here to do. Reath and Cohmac were alive. But now they were trapped, with nowhere to go and no way to get off this blight-ridden planet. He felt numb. Like there was no emotion left inside him. Like he'd felt enough for an entire lifetime in the past twenty-four hours and he might never feel another thing again.

He wanted to talk to Reath about it all, but Reath seemed to be suffering as much as he was. Amadeo wasn't surprised. They'd all been through so much.

He hadn't told them yet about Master Lox. He wasn't sure why. Perhaps he was trying to protect them. The last thing they needed was more bad news. Or perhaps if he didn't mention it, he might be able to pretend for a while longer that it wasn't true, that it was all just a horrible dream.

He glanced at the others. They all sat in silence. Dorian was hovering close to the medical station. L-77 was out again, suffering another intermittent power drain. Reath sat with his knees drawn up to his chest, his eyes closed. He wasn't asleep, but he didn't look like he wanted to be interrupted.

Master Cohmac was fiddling with a small comlink, his brow furrowed. He jumped when it suddenly crackled to life in his palm, hissing static.

"Affie?" he said, sitting forward. "Are you there?"

More static.

"Affie? Leox? Geode? Can you hear me?"

A woman's distorted voice burst out of the comlink, loud and intrusive in the confined space of the *Invictus*'s hold. "Cohmac! Thank the Light! Are you okay? Is Reath with you?"

Amadeo saw Master Cohmac's shoulders drop as he let out a long, deep sigh of relief. Reath opened his eyes.

"We're both here, Affie. And we've found some friends." He

glanced at Amadeo, offering him a weak smile. "Are *you* okay? And the others?"

"We're fine," said Affie. "Well, Geode is *furious*, but thanks to Leox, we managed to make a landing. Even if it was a little rough around the edges." Amadeo heard someone making a sarcastic comment in the background. "And I've found a friend, too. She could do with some medical attention. Master Eve Byre was on the Nihil ship, being held captive. We have her with us now."

"By the Light," said Master Cohmac. "Thank you, Affie." He pinched the bridge of his nose. "I don't suppose you have any idea how we're going to get off this island?"

"We've been trying to get the *Vessel* airborne again," said Affie.

"And?" prompted Master Cohmac.

Affie sounded forlorn. "Our power relay inverter is busted. We're grounded without it."

"Then we're trapped," said Master Cohmac. He looked weary beyond measure. They all did.

"Not necessarily," said Amadeo, jumping to his feet. He looked at Dorian. "We could take the one off the *Invictus*. We're not going to be needing it again."

Dorian nodded.

"Would that work?" said Master Cohmac into the comlink.

"I don't know," said Affie. "Hang on."

A new voice came on the channel—presumably Leox, whom Amadeo had heard grumbling in the background earlier. "Hey, Cohmac. You say you have a replacement inverter?"

"Sounds like we do."

"Then there's a chance we can get this thing off the ground again. Can you get it to us?"

"We'll find a way. Stand by." Master Cohmac clicked the comlink off. He looked at Reath. "We can do this. We can find our way off this planet and back to Coruscant."

Reath turned to Amadeo. "We can. We can make it back. To Master Lox and the others."

Amadeo's heart lurched. He felt sick. He turned away, tears brimming, all sense of composure suddenly lost.

"Amadeo?" said Reath. "What did I say?"

"Master Lox is gone," said Dorian gently. "It happened on Angoth. The Force Eater . . ."

Master Cohmac and Reath were both on their feet.

"I forgot . . ." said Master Cohmac, his expression pained. "With everything going on here, I forgot about your mission. . . ." He didn't seem to know what to do with his hands. He folded them behind his back. "Oh, Amadeo. I'm so sorry."

"Amadeo?" said Reath. He stepped forward, reaching out a hand. He allowed it to hover for a moment and then clasped Amadeo on the shoulder. He seemed lost for words. And then: "You still came for us. Even after that. You still came to help."

Amadeo turned to Reath, saw the tears brimming in his eyes, too. "We found out the Jedi hunter was on your trail. I couldn't let him . . ." He gestured to Dorian. "*We* couldn't let him . . ." His voice trailed off.

"Thank you," said Reath. "Thank you, Amadeo."

Amadeo nodded. He dusted the front of his filthy robes self-consciously. "We'd better start stripping out that inverter."

"I'll give you a hand," said Dorian. "I think my patient is going to be out for a while."

Amadeo saw Reath hesitate, as if he needed to say something but didn't know how to bring it up. "What is it?"

Reath looked pained. "It's not that simple. We still have to *get* to the *Vessel*. Don't forget, there's a Nameless out there, just waiting for us to show our faces. Ashton and Sevens have already taken every bit of punishment they can handle. We're trapped."

Cohmac nodded. "You're right. The minute we open that hatch, it'll be waiting. Even if we could get the *Vessel* closer, we'd still have to risk going out in the open. We have to assume it knows exactly where we are."

As if on cue, the creature emitted another terrifying howl, and Amadeo shuddered. He tried to breathe, fighting the panic that was threatening to overtake him again. "We've got to get out of here. We're trapped, and it'll come for us. We don't have the means to fight it." Amadeo could hear the mounting fear in his own voice.

"Hey, hey, Amadeo," said Master Cohmac. "We understand. It's okay."

"It's not okay!" said Amadeo. His hands were trembling. "It's not okay."

"No," admitted Master Cohmac. "It isn't."

They lapsed into a somber silence for a moment.

"There is one option . . ." said Reath after a moment.

"Go on," prompted Master Cohmac.

"You saw what happened back there in the tomb when you split the coffin. You gave the Nameless a bigger target," said Reath.

"A target richer in the Force," corrected Master Cohmac.

"The point is," said Reath, "the Nameless chose to feed on that rather than us when it had the chance. Same as it chose to feed on the Jedi hunter. They must be drawn to the richest source of Force energy around them. The fattest available prey."

On the other side of the room, L-77 suddenly shuddered to life, powering up and resuming the repair work in his chest cavity as if he'd never been out.

Amadeo returned his attention to Reath. "So you're saying we need to give it a bigger target?"

Reath clicked his fingers, pointing at Amadeo. "Exactly. We need to make ourselves less interesting."

"But how do we do that?" said Master Cohmac. "We can't get back to the tomb, either." He shrugged. "Maybe one of us can draw them off while the others make a break for the *Vessel*."

"No," said Amadeo, surprising even himself with the strength of his rebuttal. "No one else dies."

Master Cohmac gave a nod of agreement.

"Remember the mountains," said Reath, talking directly to Cohmac now, "that turned out not to be mountains at all."

"You can't be serious," said Cohmac.

"I don't understand," said Amadeo.

"There's a range of mountains just offshore," explained Reath. "Or what we thought were mountains when we first arrived. But they're not mountains at all. They're massive hibernating creatures. And they're richer in the Force than anything I've ever felt before."

Amadeo looked at him, wide-eyed. "Creatures the size of *mountains*?" He felt dizzy at the very idea.

Reath nodded. "What if we wake one of them? Ask it for help? A single Nameless couldn't pose too much of a risk to a creature that size. Maybe, if it was willing to come ashore, it could keep the Nameless busy long enough for us to get away."

Master Cohmac whistled. "It could be very dangerous, Reath. The sort of power you're talking about . . ." His voice trailed off, his point made. "And besides, we're talking about endangering the life of another creature."

"We're talking about asking it for help," said Reath. "There's a difference. It might refuse. But we need to get off this planet. Not just because of the Nameless, or the blight, but the ore, too. And everything else we've discovered here. We need to get back to Coruscant. This could be our only chance."

Master Cohmac looked at Amadeo. "What do you think, Amadeo?"

Amadeo studied Reath. There was no doubt about it: his friend had been through a *lot* in the past few hours. But then, so had he. And they'd both come through it. Or at least, they were still standing, still trying to do the right thing, despite everything. Maybe they could get through all this together. "I say we do it," he said.

Master Cohmac nodded his consent. "Then we're all agreed."

Amadeo looked over to Dorian, who was already restocking his medical kit from the stash of ship's supplies. "Dorian, do you think you could manage to remove the inverter without me?"

Dorian grinned. "I'm a surgeon," he said with a shrug. "What's a few wires?"

Amadeo smiled. "Thank you," he said. He turned back to the others. "Okay. What do we do?"

FIFTY-TWO

Reath reached tentatively for the Force.

He was still scared—terrified, even. But he had to do this, not for his own survival but for the others. Cohmac, Amadeo, Dorian, Affie, all the rest of them, trapped on this dying world. He'd left a message with Affie in case he didn't make it, instructions for what to tell the Jedi Council about what they'd discovered on Tolis—what they had to do to stop the blight, to beat the Nihil. But Reath wanted to be a part of that solution, too.

Meanwhile, the others were standing by while Dorian finished up removing the old inverter, ready to make a run for the *Vessel* as soon as Reath gave the word.

And so Reath opened his mind and his heart to the Force, reaching out, joining with his fellow Jedi.

The warmth of its light flooded him, lifting his spirits.

All thoughts of his circling fear and doubt were banished. For the first time in days, weeks, he felt at peace.

He knew then that he had made his decision. He had refused to do what Azlin did when faced by the horror of the Nameless. He'd refused to embrace his fear, to try to turn that fear into power. And he would keep on refusing to do so, too. He'd endured the most terrifying, punishing moments of his life on Tolis, and through it all, in those bleakest moments, he'd stayed true to himself. That was all that really mattered.

All that uncertainty he'd been feeling fell away.

Reath pushed out with his senses, making his way down to the shore, out into the watery depths teeming with the brilliance of so much life.

He searched for the sleeping giants, out in the ocean, and found them. He guided the others, probing, testing, seeking out the most open of the creatures' strange bestial minds, the one that felt most ready to hear their call.

There.

He focused, channeling everything he had, calling to the creature, pleading with it to wake, to help them drive off the predator in their midst. He felt Cohmac and Amadeo join with him, bolstering him, adding to and strengthening his voice.

Please. Help us if you can.

There was no response.

Reath tried again, reaching out through the Force, repeating the message.

And again.

And *again*.

He knew the creature couldn't understand, not in the way another person might, but he hoped it would be enough, that it would somehow hear the echo of his call through the Force and respond.

He tried again, refusing to give up.

At last, he felt something stirring. A ripple through the Force. A disturbance.

And then the creature opened its eyes, and Reath was jolted back into his own breathless body, tumbling over with a shock like a blow to the chest.

※

Amadeo peered blearily at Reath and Cohmac, both picking themselves up off the floor.

"Umm . . . I think we did it," he said.

As if in response, a titanic bellow rent the air, so loud and so powerful that the entire wreck of the *Invictus* shook around them. Amadeo grabbed hold of a fistful of webbing for purchase.

The trumpeting roar was followed by the thunder of movement as the beast stirred, uncurling from its deep hibernation. Even from this vast distance, Amadeo felt its footsteps transmitted through the ground like a quake in the very bedrock.

Another roar split the air, leaving his head ringing. The sound seemed to resonate deep in his skull, making his teeth ache.

And then the Nameless emitted one of its shrill bloodcurdling howls, and Amadeo was struck with a sudden feeling of pensiveness.

"I'd say you were right," said Master Cohmac, helping Amadeo to his feet. "And I think we'd better get moving in case it comes to take a closer look at who woke it up."

Amadeo nodded. He hurried unsteadily down the length of the hold, grasping for purchase every time the ground beneath him shifted and the ship bounced, reverberating with every movement the creature made.

He was starting to wonder if this had been a good idea, after all.

He found Dorian in the empty hangar at the rear of the ship, where the *Orchid* had once been berthed. He was up to his shoulders in the wall paneling, face pressed against the sheet metal, wires spilled around his feet like the ruins of a bird's nest. "Dorian!"

The medic turned to glance at him, straining as he tried to reach even deeper into the ship's inner workings. "Almost there . . ." he called. "Bit harder than I'd anticipated."

"We need to go," said Amadeo.

"Oh, I *heard*," said Dorian. "Just . . . give . . . me . . . a . . . moment!" He yanked his hand free of the hole. He was scratched and bleeding, but he was holding the small black inverter in his grip. "Got it!"

Amadeo reached out and grabbed his other hand. "Now we run."

They stumbled back through to the main hold. Reath and Cohmac were getting ready to crack the airlock. L-77 was looming over Ashton, who still lay unconscious on the gurney. Her face looked placid and peaceful, blissfully unaware of any of the chaos that was happening around her.

TEARS OF THE NAMELESS

Amadeo stumbled as another trembling quake shook the wreck.

"What about Ashton?" said Dorian. "I'm not leaving her."

"I'll carry her," said Master Cohmac. He started back toward the gurney, but L-77 turned, stepping into his path.

The droid looked barely functional. Sparks cascaded from his shattered innards like blood from open wounds. "No, Master Jedi. *I* shall carry Mistress Vol."

"Sevens, you can barely walk . . ." protested Dorian.

"I *shall* carry her," L-77 insisted. "I will make sure she is safe."

"All right," Master Cohmac acceded. "But you need to keep up."

"I will not let her down," replied L-77.

"I don't think you ever could," said Amadeo softly.

He glanced up as Reath opened the airlock with the creak of buckling metal. He braced himself, hand straying for his lightsaber, half expecting the Nameless to attack at any moment. . . .

But the attack never came.

Reath dragged himself up and out. He looked utterly drained, as if the experience of reaching out to the creature had taken the very last of his reserves.

Another quake rocked the ship. And then Reath's voice, almost impossible to hear over the rumble of the leviathan's movement, floated back down through the opening. "It's working! Come on! Now!"

Cohmac ushered them forward. Amadeo beckoned for Dorian to go ahead and then followed, dragging himself up, his arms protesting at the effort. If he survived this, it was going to take weeks before his body recovered from everything he'd put it through—not to mention the mental strain. But there would be time for that later, if this gambit even worked.

He slid through the open hatch and dropped down beside the others. Behind him, Cohmac was helping L-77 lift the unconscious Ashton up and out.

Amadeo turned, scanning the horizon.

There was no horizon.

At least, the shoreline beyond the rise of the ruins was utterly obscured by the rising immensity of the leviathan. It stood on four massive stump-like legs, its wedge-shaped head towering so high that Amadeo had to crane his neck back to see it.

What they had taken at first to be the uppermost reaches of rocky mountains was, in fact, a fan of huge gnarled spines that ran the length of its back.

And it was *looking* at them with four giant shiny black eyes.

Amadeo felt like shrinking back into the safety of the wrecked ship, although in truth he knew even that would not protect him if this gargantuan creature chose to attack.

Beside him, Dorian peered up at the thing in absolute awe, seeming bewildered and stunned in equal measure. "It's just . . ."

"Beautiful," said Master Cohmac, coming to stand beside them.

". . . so big," finished Dorian.

Reath pointed to a distant ridge, where a hulking indistinct shape stood motionless. "It's here."

Amadeo tried to focus on it, but already he could feel the stirrings of that familiar fear creeping up his spine. He froze, gritting his teeth.

Maybe the plan was a failure, after all.

The leviathan was simply too big. The Nameless was running scared.

And then he watched as it raised its head and howled before charging down the slope toward the leviathan's feet.

Reath turned, waving his arm. "Now! Go, now! Don't stop until we reach the *Vessel*."

Amadeo *ran*.

Behind them, the leviathan roared, raising its head to the sky and bellowing in rage.

Amadeo twisted, glancing back to see the vague shape of the Nameless clawing its way up the side of the immense beast, scrabbling for purchase as the leviathan tried desperately to shake it off.

The movement caused the ground to shift beneath them, but miraculously he kept his balance, thundering forward, one foot in front of the other.

Ahead, Reath crested another rise, leaping over a low broken wall. Amadeo followed, skidding through a maze of ruined buildings, his heart thudding. Behind, L-77 was as good as his word, powering after them, Ashton cradled gently in his arms. Master Cohmac had his lightsaber ready and was following at the rear, his eyes obviously drawn to the titanic battle that was going on in their wake.

Amadeo tried to ignore the monstrous screams as the creatures tore into each other. What the leviathan lacked in speed and maneuverability, it more than made up for in brute strength. It twisted its massive neck, gnashing at the skittering Nameless on its back, driving it away, making it unable to feed as it clung on for its life.

Ahead, the *Vessel* came into view, resting in a dip between two ruined structures, lilting dramatically to one side. It was one of the most welcome sights Amadeo had ever seen, despite the black smoke and scorch marks still marring its rear end.

Two humans and a Vintian stood at the foot of the boarding ramp, staring up at the terrifying sight of the battle raging on the shoreline. As one, they turned to look at the ragtag team running out of the ruins toward them, their faces a picture of utter shock. Except the Vintian, who looked remarkably nonplussed by everything happening around him.

"What the hell?" said Affie, running forward to greet Reath, at the head of their party.

Reath, unable to speak, gestured his greeting and then stumbled, throwing his arm out to prop himself up against the side of the ship, sucking air into his lungs.

Master Cohmac staggered forward as they approached the ship, taking the inverter unit from Dorian and pressing it into Leox's hands. "Get. Us. Out. Of. Here," he huffed between breaths.

"Gladly," said Leox with a wink. He hurried up the ramp and disappeared into the ship.

Affie waved L-77 forward, and he followed Leox, carefully taking Ashton aboard.

"I'll go and get her settled," said Dorian.

Amadeo nodded. He turned, taking one last look at the mammoth creature that had saved their lives. It was wading back out to sea, the Nameless still clambering across its back.

Then, with a heavy heartfelt sigh, Amadeo joined Reath and Master Cohmac as they made their way onto the ship.

⚜

As the *Vessel* arced steadily into the pale skies of Tolis, Reath peered out of the viewport at the retreating landmass, wondering if it would be the last he ever saw of the place. Eventually it could be gone, consumed by the blight, and everything that had happened there would be eradicated.

He wondered if it worked the same way for memories, too. There was much about what had occurred down there that he would like to forget. But he knew, deep down, that ignoring it, pretending it had never happened was no real option at all.

Elsewhere, Affie was helping L-77 with his repairs while Amadeo sat talking quietly with Dorian, the medic. Ashton was stable and still unconscious, and Master Cohmac was up front in the cockpit with Leox and Geode.

Master Eve Byre was unconscious and medicated after the trauma of her experiences at the hands of the Jedi hunter, but Affie had made her comfortable in her own bunk, and as soon as they made it back to Coruscant, she'd receive the care she needed. None of them knew what had become of her Padawan, Zaph Mora, but Reath feared the worst.

Time would tell.

He leaned his head back against the padded seat.

They'd made it.

Just.

That was something to be grateful for. And now he was armed with the information he needed to go before the Council, to start the Jedi and the Republic on the path to freeing themselves from the terror of the Nameless and the inexorable spread of the blight.

It was over—for now.

He closed his eyes.

Just as he was about to drop off, he sensed movement and peeled open his eyes to see that Affie had come over to find him. She slipped into the seat beside him.

"Hey," she said. "You're quiet. You okay?"

Reath sighed. "It's been a long road to get here, hasn't it?"

Affie nodded, and it was heartfelt. "It sure has. A long one. But we're still here. Still fighting. Did you get what you needed down there?"

"I think I did," said Reath.

Affie smiled. "Got your samples, by the way," she said.

"Thanks," said Reath. "For all of it. Everything you've done. You saved our lives. Just by being there. You went after Master Byre when you didn't have to. And you don't know how much difference that ore is going to make. You might well have played a part in saving us all."

Affie rolled her eyes. "Now you're just being sentimental." She stood, waving her hand as she walked away. "Get some sleep. You clearly need it."

But Reath could see her grin spreading from ear to ear as she headed back to join the others.

Everything is going to be all right.

He closed his eyes, and for a while, the galaxy was calm.

FIFTY-THREE

Three Days Later

Vernestra hurried down the bustling halls of the Jedi Temple, ducking and weaving through the milling crowds. It had been busier than ever since the two expeditions had returned, with findings that looked set to change not just the face of the war with the Nihil but the potential future of the whole galaxy.

She had to hand it to Reath—he'd outdone himself this time. And yet she hadn't seen or heard from him since his return, and while she knew he probably needed a little time to recover from the trials he'd faced on Tolis—and she'd heard the wild stories that were going around—she figured it was time to try to pin him down.

She was bone-weary, returning from another shift at the Sith shrine, where they were mostly managing to keep the creep of the blight in check—at the expense of too many suffering Jedi. The vigil was taking its toll. She could feel it in herself, like she was a well that was slowly using itself up. Many of the Council members were taking shifts themselves, but the infection already had too much of a hold, and Master Yoda had ventured a theory that it was feeding on the vergence, growing exponentially.

So far, it remained contained to the lower level, but eventually, if a solution wasn't found, it would certainly spread and they would have to evacuate the entire Jedi Temple.

Thankfully, there were promising developments. The sample of ore that Reath and the others had brought back from Tolis was showing signs of resisting the blight in the laboratories, too.

That was why she was so eager to speak to Reath. He hadn't heard the latest reports.

She rounded a bend, passed through a set of double doors, and then walked across a small hallway to the door to Reath's laboratory.

The door slid open to admit her, and she stepped inside. Clearly, today he wasn't handling any hazardous materials that needed one of the onerous protective suits he always—rightly—insisted on.

Reath was there, along with the Padawan Amadeo Azzazzo. Her heart went out to the young man. The death of Master Lox had been a blow to everyone who'd known him, but there was nothing like the loss of their master to shake a Padawan to their core. She should know.

She hoped he was getting the support he needed. Maybe she'd

see if he wanted to join her for a bit of lightsaber practice in the coming weeks.

The two of them looked as thick as thieves, standing together at the workbench, poring over a data report. Vernestra cleared her throat.

They looked up in unison, both wearing startled expressions that were so similar she had to laugh aloud.

"Vernestra," said Reath, smiling quizzically. "What's so funny?"

"Oh, nothing," she said. She walked over to join them at the bench. "Looks fascinating."

"It is," said Amadeo. "Early test results from the RDC facility. On the Nameless that Master Lox captured on Angoth, as well as the three brought by Ram and the others."

"Ahh," said Vernestra. "That *is* interesting. And here I was thinking it was just another old story from the Archives." Her heart broke a little at Amadeo's insistence on crediting Lox for the creature's capture. The Jedi had sustained grave losses indeed in the undertaking of these missions. She'd also heard the news that Council member Ada-Li Carro had been killed during the *Innovator*'s parallel mission.

More Jedi gone. How many more would they lose before this was over?

"Have you discovered anything revolutionary?" she asked.

"Not yet," said Reath. "But we will. The tests have confirmed everything we thought we knew about the relationship between the Nameless and the blight, for a start."

Vernestra nodded. "It's good to see you. I've been hearing all sorts of wild stories about giant monsters and feats of derring-do. You doing okay?"

Amadeo looked away shyly. Reath smiled. "We're doing okay. I won't pretend it's been easy, but we're sticking together, aren't we, Amadeo?"

Amadeo nodded. "We are."

Vernestra laughed. "I can tell." She drummed her fingers on the workbench. "What of Master Cohmac? I haven't seen him since you returned, either. Has he . . ." She trailed off, hoping she hadn't put her foot in it. The rumor was that he wasn't rejoining the Order, despite everything they'd been through on Tolis.

"He's sticking around for a while," said Reath. "He's going to help us with our research. I think the thought of missing out was too much for him." Reath grinned, and Vernestra did, too. It was good to see him so happy.

"And you've been busy, too, I hear," said Reath, his expression suddenly serious.

"We're working hard to keep things under control down there, yes," said Vernestra.

"I was thinking more about your investigation. I heard what happened. How you discovered someone had been making transmissions from a chamber in the lower levels," said Reath. "That has to be linked to the informant Amadeo discovered on Angoth."

Vernestra nodded. "Yes. You need to be careful, Reath. Now more than ever. I'm still worried that Azlin was linked to it all somehow. He doesn't have your best interests at heart. Only his own."

"Thank you," said Reath, meeting her gaze. "I know. And I appreciate you reminding me. And in the meantime, let's hope the real culprit is uncovered soon. I understand that measures are being taken to tighten security throughout the Temple."

Vernestra nodded.

The real culprit.

Didn't Reath see it, too?

No doubt there would be further conversations to be had about Azlin. And she'd be keeping a watchful eye herself, on both her friend and the fallen Jedi. "You heard the news?" she said, changing the subject.

"What news?" said Reath.

"I'll take that as a no," she said. "Chancellor Soh has authorized another mission to Tolis. The early tests show that you were right about the ore. It seems to have a longer half-life than most other known ores, meaning it's more resistant to the blight, at least for a time. The RDC are making another trip to harvest as much as they can before Tolis is consumed."

Vernestra saw the disconcerted look on Reath's face. "Don't worry. They're not taking any Jedi along this time. The Council deemed it too much of a risk."

Reath let out a breath he'd been holding. "Good. But it's not just the Nameless we have to worry about. There's every chance the Nihil will come looking for their missing Jedi hunter, too."

"Perhaps," said Vernestra, "but I think you credit them with too much compassion. They don't care. None of them will care that a single dark sider was husked by his own pets."

Amadeo looked uncomfortable. "I care," he said. "Despite everything. He was a person once, and the Nihil had *done* something to him. He seemed . . . *broken*. And now he's just dust."

"You're right," said Vernestra. "Of course you are."

She looked at Reath. "So, what's next?"

"I've got a few things left to deal with," he said cryptically, "and then we're going to be burying our heads in the Archives for a while." He laughed. "You weren't wrong about the old story. Our priority now is trying to figure out what happened to the other missing rods. That's the key to all of this. Find one of those, and we can start to make a difference."

"Start?" said Vernestra, surprised. "From where I'm standing, Reath, you're making more of a difference than anyone. Don't forget that. Everything you've been through was for a reason. The Force is guiding your hand. Keep doing what you're doing. For the first time in a while, you've brought us something tangible we can hold on to. All of us."

"And what's that?" said Reath, puzzled.

Vernestra laughed. "Hope, Reath." She turned to go, leaving the two of them to their reports and old stories. "You've brought us hope."

FIFTY-FOUR

Affie stood in the doorway of the medical center in the Jedi Temple and smiled as she watched Eve fussing with her blanket.

The Jedi was sitting upright on the bed and was hooked up to an array of complicated devices, which trilled and beeped as they pumped fluids into her arms via feed lines and cannulas. Readouts on the wall above her head were monitoring her vital signs with a dizzying display of charts and numbers.

She'd regained some of the color in her cheeks, and her hair had been washed and scraped back into a neat, taut ponytail. Most noticeable of all, Eve had lost the look of wide-eyed shock that had so startled Affie when she'd first found the Jedi aboard the Nihil ship on Tolis.

Now she looked closer to the Eve whom Affie had first met on the journey to Oisin, although she'd taken on a vaguely haunted expression, as if she still wasn't entirely present in the here and now—as if she was *remembering*.

Affie thought it would be a long time before the woman healed from the psychological trauma of her experiences with the Nameless, even with all the support, training, and meditative practice that went hand in hand with being a Jedi.

How *did* someone come to terms with losing complete control of themselves, body and mind? With facing terror so profound, so unsettling, that they were unable to properly comprehend it? Affie had no idea. But if anyone could overcome such a thing, it was a Jedi. And yet Affie understood that it would never be easy, and her heart went out to Eve.

She cleared her throat, announcing her arrival.

Eve glanced up and saw her standing in the open doorway.

"Hello, Affie," she said.

Affie grinned. "It's good to see you looking so well. Can I come in?"

Eve beckoned her over. "Of course." She smiled, and a glimmer of her old sparkle was back. "You're honored, you know. Not many people from outside the Order have the run of the Jedi Temple."

Affie laughed. "Hardly. Reath was kind enough to make the arrangements. I wanted to see how you were doing."

"Much better, thanks to you," said Eve. "I owe you my thanks. And my life. What you did, coming to save me from the Nihil ship like that, alone—it was very brave."

"I suppose it was," said Affie with a cheeky grin. "But you would have done the same for any of us."

Eve inclined her head in acknowledgment.

"So, how are you *really* feeling?" said Affie.

"That's a question with a very complicated answer," replied Eve, "and if I'm honest, I'm not really sure that I know. At least not yet." She sighed. "Tired, mostly."

"Well, I'd be surprised if you weren't," said Affie. "After everything you've been through, the very least you need is a rest."

"For a little while, perhaps," said Eve. "But I also need to be busy. To get back out there. What happened—it just proves that the Nihil will never change. We need to find a way to stop them."

"From what I hear, Reath and Cohmac are closer than ever to finding a solution, to the Nameless *and* the blight. The mission to Tolis was a success," said Affie.

"So I understand," said Eve. "But that doesn't mean they don't need help."

Affie studied her, saw the determination in her eyes, the set of her jaw. "You really are going to get straight back out there, aren't you?"

Eve nodded. "If the Council will allow it." She raised a single eyebrow. "Besides, more than anyone, you understand how that feels. Don't tell me you're planning to sit back and put your feet up, either."

"Not a chance," said Affie.

"Then we're both gluttons for punishment, it seems," said Eve.

The Jedi was doing a good job of skirting the inevitable subject of her Padawan. Affie was of two minds whether to bring him up. She didn't want to cause Eve any further pain, but she knew that Jedi dealt with death differently than people like her. They had a way of explaining death as a beautiful thing, a transition back to the Force, a moment of tranquility and peace. Affie hoped it was true, that even in his moment of greatest suffering, Zaph had found solace in his acceptance back into the Force that had given him so much cause for joy in life.

"What about Zaph? Do you remember what happened?" she asked quietly.

Eve dipped her eyes. She toyed with the hem of the blanket on her lap. "Not really. They came for us on Oisin. They must have heard about the raid we stopped. But the Nameless—they warp our perceptions when they're close. Cause us to experience visions and a twisted, malformed version of reality. I was barely conscious. I wish . . ." She stumbled over her words. "I wish I'd been stronger. Able to do something to protect him. But I wasn't. If I could have saved him from that horror, if I could have changed places with him, I would have."

"But that's not how these things work, is it?" said Affie kindly. "We don't always get to choose."

"No, we don't," agreed Eve.

Affie offered her a wan smile. "Still, if there's one thing I know about Zaph, it's that he didn't waste a single moment of the time he had. He relished everything. He might only have had a short time with us, but it was a full life, brimming with experience and joy."

Eve met her gaze. "Yes, it was." She smiled. "And now you're even starting to sound like a Jedi. Maybe we're rubbing off on you."

Affie laughed. "No. Not a Jedi. Just an optimist."

"Zaph is one with the Force now," said Eve. "Which means he's still with us, in a way."

"That's a comforting thought," said Affie.

"It's the truth," said Eve. "He has found his peace."

One of the machines buzzed, and a tall, thin medical droid scuttled in to check it.

"We're going to make it, you know," said Affie.

Eve grinned. "You sound so certain."

"I *am* certain. Because the only other option is too bleak." Affie moved out of the way as the medical droid began to fuss over the collection of feed lines delivering fluid through Eve's arm. She backed toward the door. "We've got something the Nihil don't, you see."

"And what's that?" said Eve.

"We have each other."

FIFTY-FIVE

The tunnels beneath the Jedi Temple were as cold and unwelcoming as they had ever been—perhaps more so. And yet, more than ever, Reath was determined to see today's visit through. He owed it to himself, as well as to Azlin.

But that didn't mean he felt ready to face the fallen Jedi.

After everything he'd been through lately, after what had happened on Tolis, Reath felt he understood the man a little better than he had before. And with that understanding had come a measure of pity.

Now he saw that Azlin's choices had all been made out of fear. He didn't blame the man, and he knew that Azlin really did believe that everything he had done was to protect the people he cared about. His entire self-identity was built on that foundation.

It was the only way he could justify to himself what he had done.

It also remained true that Azlin had something to offer the Jedi in their quest to liberate the galaxy from the Nihil and the Nameless and to save everyone from the blight. He'd spent his entire long life obsessing over every detail he could find about the creatures' history, and Reath couldn't deny the part he had played in helping them uncover the truth of the Tolemites' legend.

For Reath, though, it had felt like a trial, a test.

And he'd learned something else, too: that it was okay to acknowledge his fear, to recognize when he was scared or angry or ashamed. A Jedi could still *feel*. Reath didn't have to pretend, to put on a brave face and hope those feelings went away. He just had to face up to them, to deal with them and not let them rule his decisions, his actions, his life.

He turned the corner in the passageway to see new Temple Guards had been posted, two on either side of the door. This way, Reath assumed, they'd be able to hold one another accountable.

He nodded to them before he approached.

The scent of Azlin's incense burners stung his nose with their sharp, bitter smell. He stood for a moment, gathering himself.

Then, drawing himself up to his full height, he approached the door and stepped inside.

As usual, Azlin was sitting cross-legged on his cot. The little wooden puzzle box sat in his lap, and his head was bowed over it while his fingers danced like ancient spiders over its surface, still seeking a way in.

Click-clack. Click-clack.

He raised his head as Reath entered the room, cocking it

slightly to one side as if sniffing the air like a predator. "Something has changed. You seem . . . *different*," he purred. He set the puzzle box down. "Tell me."

"Hello, Azlin." Reath set about his usual routine. He filled the kettle and set it on the heating unit to boil, then prepared two cups with the pungent herbal leaves that Azlin took as tea.

"We found Tolis," said Reath, sitting down in his usual seat.

Azlin's eyebrows rose above those terrible hollow sockets. "Indeed?"

"You were right about the island. We located the Tolemites' repository. It was a tomb, the resting place of their Three Ancients, mummified in coffins of kyber." Reath kept his tone matter-of-fact, neutral.

"And did the Three Ancients speak to you, Reath? Did they divulge their secrets across the eons?" Azlin was more animated than Reath had ever seen him. *Hungry.* He leaned forward, studying Reath with his unseeing eyes.

"They did. We know what we have to do. The Tolemites crafted three rods using Echo Stones, each of them able to influence or control the *Shrii Ka Rai*. We need to locate one of the missing rods and use it to guide the creatures home. And to protect ourselves against the creatures being weaponized by the Nihil."

Azlin slowly pressed his palms together before him, breathing deep. "So, he was right. Barnabas Vim was on the right track, all those years ago."

"It seems so," said Reath. The kettle began to whistle, and he rose to attend to the tea.

"There's more," said Azlin. "Much more. You're holding something back."

Reath poured the hot water into the cups and swilled it about. "The other teams were successful, too. We now have four Nameless in captivity on Coruscant."

Azlin stiffened. "A dangerous gambit," he said. "And ill advised. But I admit, I am impressed."

Reath looked at the cups, reflecting on how he'd grown accustomed to the perfumed taste of the brew over the past year. "It cost us dearly. But the results of the initial tests are already confirming what we suspected. It's physical proof of the link between the Nameless and the blight. We're hoping we might be able to understand more of their physiology soon, too. How they feed on the Force, how it sustains them."

"And still you refuse to tell me what you really think," said Azlin. There was an edge to his tone now, as if he was insinuating some sort of betrayal on Reath's part.

"I thought you'd want to know what happened," said Reath. "This is the culmination of everything you've worked for." He turned, holding out a cup of hot tea for Azlin. "Even if you set the Nameless on our trail and nearly killed us all." Reath kept his tone level.

The other man let him stand there. "Stop it. Stop dissembling. You know that I see things others do not. The intricate web we are weaving is so delicate, so taut, that a single error will set us on the wrong path."

"Silly games," said Reath. "Dangerous games, toying with

other people's lives and claiming that you know better." Reath faced the other man. "Did you do it? Vernestra has told me her suspicions. Did you manipulate that Temple Guard into giving away our position to the Nihil? Was it one of your games, Azlin?"

Azlin frowned. He shook his head. "No, Reath. Of course not. How could I have?"

"Don't pretend that it's not within your power," said Reath.

Azlin smiled. "Of course I am capable of such a thing. A trifling matter. But you misunderstand, my boy. Why would I endanger your life? Didn't I tell you that I wished for you to return in one piece?"

"You did," Reath acknowledged. "But those are just words."

"No," said Azlin, his voice firm, emphatic. "No. You still don't see it, do you, Reath? You're our greatest hope. Our only way through this. You're the key to everything. Why would I put you at risk? Why would I endanger the one person I believe can see a way through this, for all of us, hmmm?" He reached out a hand, blindly, feebly, as if trying to find Reath, to assure him. "I worry for you every day, Reath. Truthfully."

Reath grimaced. He had no real sense of whether this was merely one of Azlin's performances or whether the man really meant it. Nor did he know whether Azlin really could have been behind the informant, but he suspected not. He would have had too much to lose. "I don't need your concern," he said. "Just the information you're still withholding from us."

"All in good time," said Azlin, easing himself back into a relaxed, hunched posture once again.

"I faced them on Tolis," said Reath after a moment. "I faced the Nameless."

Azlin's eyebrows rose. "You faced the *Shrii Ka Rai*," he said, his voice a hoarse whisper. "You faced them, and you survived." Reath could sense the other man's awe.

"I did," said Reath.

"Well done, Reath!" rasped Azlin, gleaming with apparent pride. "This is the news I've been waiting for. You did what was necessary to survive. You embraced your fear. You have faced your moment of transcendence, as I did mine."

"It wasn't some *test*," said Reath, shaking his head. "It didn't temper me, like a Mandalorian tempers new armor to make it stronger. It was a living nightmare. A hell. I nearly died."

Azlin smiled wryly. "If that is what you wish to see, young Reath, so be it. Either way, you have learned an important lesson."

Reath swallowed, maintaining his calm. "Not in the way you think."

"No," said Azlin, emphatic. "It is the only path."

Reath shook his head. "You're wrong. When you said I had to embrace my fear, I thought you were talking about power. About using it as a weapon against the Nameless."

"I was," said Azlin.

"But there are other ways to embrace what frightens you," said Reath. "*Better* ways. That's what I realized. I have to face up to my doubts and fears. I have to acknowledge them and admit how I've been feeling. I need to talk about it with someone who can help. But I will also remain true to myself through it all."

Azlin's hand snapped forward, so quickly that Reath couldn't flinch out of the way. He caught hold of Reath's wrist. His grip was like ice, bony and painful. The teacup wobbled in Reath's grasp and tumbled to the ground, smashing into tiny pieces. The scalding liquid seeped across the cracked floor, encircling Reath's boots.

"You must protect yourself, Reath," said Azlin, his voice hard, insistent. "It is imperative that you see this through. You must remain strong."

Reath pulled his hand free with a jerk. "You don't understand, do you? That's what strength *is*, Azlin. Not wallowing in fear and isolation. Not proving you're able to withstand the darkness alone, or troubling over feelings of guilt or inadequacy. We find true strength when we look in the mirror and see our own imperfections, when we admit to others that we need help. None of us need to be alone. That's what the Jedi Order is. Despite all its flaws, despite all our mistakes, we go on together. We support each other. And we ask for *help*."

Azlin's mouth twisted in anger. "Have you learned nothing, boy? I've shown you the path you must tread. I've taught you what you need to know. Don't you think I *understand*? I've lived for nearly two centuries!"

Reath's voice was filled with sadness. "To live in fear is to not live at all."

"Go!" Azlin spat, turning away from Reath. "Go! Leave me!" He picked up his puzzle box, his fingers trembling. He sounded frail, old.

And *scared*.

Saddened, Reath crossed to the door. "You won't find any answers in there, Azlin. The heart of the puzzle is just a mirror, reflecting back at you. I understand that now. *You're* the answer. Don't you see that? Whatever it is you're searching for is inside of *you*."

Azlin issued a thin, dry rasp of frustration, and then the *click-clacking* of the wooden puzzle started over again.

Reath turned and left without looking back.

——

He found Master Cohmac hunched over a datapad in the Jedi Archives, skimming through more of Barnabas Vim's old field reports.

"Reath!" Cohmac shuffled over when he saw him approach, making room for Reath to sit down beside him. "I was beginning to think you'd disappeared into one of those reports." He caught the look on Reath's face. "You okay?"

Reath lowered himself onto the bench beside his old master. His breath caught in his throat. "Master?"

Cohmac's face creased in concern. "What is it?"

Reath swallowed. He took a deep breath. "There's something I need to talk about. I've been keeping it to myself, but I've been feeling so confused." He glanced away, unable to meet Cohmac's eye, but forced himself to continue, to get the words out.

To face his fear.

"I've been blaming you for leaving, and I've been putting too much trust in Azlin. But really, that doubt and uncertainty is inside of me. It's not about the Order, but about myself. Whether

I'm ready for the responsibilities I've taken on. Whether I'm doing the right thing. Whether I drove you away." He gulped. "I'm trying to work through it, but I can't do it alone." He felt the tears coming then, spilling down his cheeks, a flood of raw emotion. Everything he'd been bottling up. The release felt like the first breath of fresh air after a storm. "I need your help."

Cohmac slipped his arm around Reath's shoulders. "I know, Reath." He pulled Reath close, holding him tight. "And I'm here."

ACKNOWLEDGMENTS

This book was written during what proved to be one of the hardest times in my life.

In summer 2023, while working on the first draft of the book, I was diagnosed with a lesion in my left frontal lobe. The doctors didn't yet know if it was a deadly tumor or a benign growth, leading to a whole battery of tests over a period of several months. Meanwhile, I continued to chart Reath's and Amadeo's journeys to Tolis and the revelations they would discover there.

Naturally, though, writing was hard. Focusing was difficult. And the story was growing ever darker as I wrote, as my and Reath's journeys intertwined, with him falling more under Azlin's sway and me growing increasingly anxious as I waited for further tests.

It wasn't until I sat down to start the redrafting process much later that a lot of this became clear, and—in a better state of mind—I was able to put some separation between those two journeys and add some levity back into the book. Yet the writing had also been somewhat cathartic, too. And it helped to read it all back.

The reason I'm writing about this here is not to provoke sympathy (things are looking much more positive on the medical front now) but to draw attention to the fabulous people who supported me during this extremely tough time.

Often, when you write acknowledgments for a book, they're a lighthearted way of saying thank you to the people who helped you along the way. This time is a bit different, because these people really went out on a limb to have my back. They carried me through months of stress, confusion, and emotional turmoil and helped me to stand tall again on the other side.

First and foremost, my entire family, both immediate and extended, all rallied around with emotional support and cups of tea (we're British, after all) and lots of phone calls to make sure I always had people to talk to. It's a family that's spread far and wide across the globe, but they all came together when it counted.

Then my closest friend, Cavan Scott, listened when I needed to rant and kept me going when I wasn't sure how to keep going myself.

The entire team at Lucasfilm was amazing. Thank you so much for the time and patience and understanding. Mike Siglain sent Batman comics and made regular calls just to make sure I was doing okay and bought me the time I needed when all I managed to do most days was stare at the screen and tap a few keys. The editorial team pretended not to panic, and I know it was stressful, but they were so kind and generous, and they and the Lucasfilm Story Group nudged me toward a far superior book.

Friends such as John French, Nick Kyme, Kristin Baver, and SO many others carried me along while I tried to get my head around everything that was happening.

The rest of the *High Republic* writing team kept everything moving while I was running on empty and didn't let me miss a beat.

And finally, the doctors and nurses of the British NHS have been brilliant every step of the way.

There are so many more people—too many to list here—whose messages and support made a massive difference during an incredibly tough time, and I feel lucky and honored to count you all as friends.

Love you, guys.

And thanks.

George.